Luck of the Draw

It was like that reporter had said. The luck of the draw. Her letter had been chosen from all the millions written.

Dumb luck.

She'd wanted a million dollars for her mother's transplant and now she had an opportunity to earn that amount in only four weeks' time.

A million dollars.

A million dollars to decide how to divvy up two-hundred-million dollars.

Could she do it? To the benefactor's satisfaction?

A thought flitted through Amanda's mind, skidded to a stop, and lodged itself on a fulcrum balanced between inspiration and effrontery.

"Mr. Franklin?" she said.

"Yes?"

"If I want, may I keep all two-hundred-million dollars?"

He paused, and then blew out a breath. Shaking his head, he pursed his lips like a disappointed father. "Yes, if you can make a case that you are worthy enough, you may ask to keep the entire fortune. But remember—you have only four weeks to make your decision."

LUCK OF THE DRAW

Teryl Oswald

Highland Press Publishing
Florida

Luck of the Draw

For information, please contact
Highland Press Publishing,
PO Box 2292, High Springs, FL 32655.
www.highlandpress.org

ISBN: 978-0-9823615-3-5

PUBLISHED BY HIGHLAND PRESS PUBLISHING

Circles of Gold

Dedication

For Frances Myers–I won life's lottery when I drew you for my mother, friend, and muse. You are never far from my keyboard.

Acknowledgements

This debut novel represents many false starts and failed masterpieces. Thanks to the people who helped along the way . . .

Friends who read the most ghastly drafts and encouraged me–Ann Adams, Ann Gillentine, Bobbie Megel, Dee Gullikson, Mary Gasaway, Heather and Joe Lipsey, Sandi Howlett, and Sharon Hansen.

Family who did the same *and* brought me chocolate–Kellini, McKenna, and Allen Hager, Sue Myers, and the Oswalds: Maru, Kathy, Cyndy, Dee, Crystal, and Sandra.

My loving husband, Alden, who helped with the military information. Any errors are mine. Your twenty-one years, nine months and two days in the Air Force paid off.

The terrific writers of RWA for insightful workshops and instructive loops.

Amazing critique partner, mentor and friend, Renee Ryan.

Discerning editors, Polly McCrillis and Venetta Bell.

Special thanks to publisher/editor, Leanne Burroughs. You are my Dream Weaver.

Polly McCrillis, Associate Editor

Venetta Bell, Associate Editor

Chapter One

Amanda Cash cursed her luck. It may have been her wedding anniversary, but there'd be no sex tonight, and her new diet prohibited conciliatory chocolate. She stared into the azure eyes of her husband and sighed longingly for the intimacy they'd lost in the past decade.

"How do you like the *osso bucco*?" Erik asked, pride pulling a grin from his soft, full lips.

She returned his inviting smile, snuggling deeper into the intimate setting he'd created in the comfortable dining room. He'd even used their silver wedding flatware which likely had to be polished. She breathed in the lemon oil he'd used on her mother's antique cherry wood table and sighed again.

Passing her fingers over the satin finish, Amanda longed to feel the coolness of the wood on her cheek as she had every Sunday after a lazy dinner of fried chicken and candied yams. Sometimes the surface resonated with her daddy's laughter as he unmercifully teased her mother. If she lay her head down now, could she feel the ghostly tickle of the table's vibrations on her face?

"The *osso bucco's* perfect," Amanda said. Just like the rest of the menu, the table presentation, and Erik's appearance. The first two talents came via The Culinary Excellence School in New York City. The iridescent sheen of Erik's black hair, the strength of his clean-shaven jaw, and the toned muscles stretched over his tall frame were pure, natural, Midwestern appeal. All ingredients combined to make flawless the celebration of their fourteen-year marriage.

Amanda's contribution to the dinner was meager, an afterthought really—one basket of silk flowers which sat crowded among three candles mounted in hand-painted, ceramic holders in the middle of the ivory table runner. The arrangement wasn't even something she'd designed for the occasion. The delicate violets and daisies intertwined with thin, pink and blue satin ribbons were leftovers from her failed business. Staring at the centerpiece ordered for someone else's baby shower, a sourness churned in Amanda's stomach.

She set down her fork and blotted her lips with the napkin, careful not to smear her lip color onto the white linen. Geez, Erik had even used real napkins for the dinner. And she'd only managed to bring a second-hand decoration.

"The food critic for the *Omaha World-Herald* called today," Erik announced. "They're going to review the restaurant next month in their 'Dinner and a Movie' column."

"That's great." She smiled and tucked her hand in his. "I'm so proud of you, Erik. You've worked really hard to make the menu a success. Your investors must be very pleased."

"They are. I'm making them a fortune." A flash of a dream twinkled in his eyes. "Someday I'll have my own place instead of working for someone else, and all the profits will be mine."

"As well as all the risk."

Erik withdrew his hand and sat back.

In spite of the disappointment which erased Erik's smile, Amanda didn't regret how quickly she'd corrected him. Better he learn from her mistakes. While entrepreneurship had its excitement, bankruptcy was ugly and something she'd only narrowly escaped. It would take a long time to reestablish her financial security after losing Dream Weaver's Baskets and Gifts.

The drawn lips gave away Erik's annoyance at her abruptness, and Amanda wondered if they would have another post mortem about the business. She steeled herself for his lecture, but in an instant his demeanor changed and eyes once again sparkled.

"Hey, I got you a present." Erik jumped up from the table and retrieved an envelope from the buffet behind him. He handed it to her with the flourish he loved to use when lighting cherries jubilee. "Tickets to the symphony."

"Erik, we said no gifts."

Guilt deepened as Amanda thought of the ten thousand dollars Erik had invested in her business. It was money he'd inherited from his grandmother, money she'd lost and never could repay.

"I didn't get you anything," she said.

He waved off her confession. "No problem. Really. I know you enjoy the symphony and Tony Bennett is performing with them, so . . . It's no biggie."

Amanda twirled a strand of her straight, blonde hair before checking it for split ends. Then she quickly remembered how the nervous habit irritated her husband and tossed her hair back over her shoulder, tucking it behind the ear.

"Well. Thanks for the tickets." She eked out a smile.

Squirming in her chair, she suddenly felt the thinness of the cushion. How many times had they talked about recovering the seats?

He offered her more snow peas. It was the most nutritious side dish at the table, but she opted for another scoop of the whipped potatoes instead. Her diet had been more of a self-promise to eat better rather than an act of a pudgy woman. She still fit into the jeans she'd worn in college, more a consequence of her own poor cooking than any personal effort. Adding exercise to her lifestyle would reassure her mother that Amanda was actively forestalling the heart disease that so savagely plagued her own health.

Instead of digging into the potatoes, though, Amanda dragged the tines of her fork through them. "If I'd known you were getting me a gift . . ."

"Have you seen your mom yet today?" Erik had a knack for switching the subject as quickly as he could flip/fold an omelet without using a spatula—a feat Amanda had never mastered.

"I'm going over to Brookside after our dinner."

"Is she doing any better?"

"Her spirits remain good, but she has no energy. Some days she can't even get out of bed." A shadow draped across her vision. "I wish I hadn't put her in the nursing home."

"You had to, honey. Mom knows you did as much as you could for as long as you could. She couldn't stay at home."

Amanda shrugged and slid her fingers through her hair. She found the prickliness of the ends and promised herself a cut . . . soon.

Erik flipped the lock back behind her shoulder. "Brookside is a nice place."

"For what it is."

"She gets the care she needs," Erik stated.

"But not the heart transplant that might prolong her life."

"You've done everything you can do. Face it, Amanda, it's a risky operation at best, and the insurance company won't pay for it."

True enough. Her Uncle Ernie couldn't find any way to compel the medical company to pay and he was the best attorney in Chicago.

Quickly, she ran down a list of what she'd done to try to raise money. All the charities she'd contacted offered only living expenses, not the million dollars Clara would need for the surgery. Amanda had even taken steps to win the big lottery jackpot. Unfortunately, she'd already liquidated all her savings when she'd built and then lost her business. The only asset she had left was her eighteen-year-old car.

"How much do you think I'd get if I sold a kidney?" she asked.

Erik snapped his gaze to her. "*What?*"

"To get the money for Mom's operation. People live with one kidney, right?"

"Don't be silly." Erik pinched a crumb off his napkin and gingerly placed it on the edge of his plate.

His neatness grated on Amanda's nerves. It hadn't at first, but certainly had after *all* his personal habits turned persnickety. She tried to ignore his meticulous folding of his napkin, so precise he might have been creating origami.

Amanda closed her eyes and saw her mother's face. Clara Marshall always loved Erik, before and after his confession. Her sweet mother gave everyone the benefit of the doubt.

"If only I hadn't sunk everything I had into Dream Weaver's," Amanda said.

"It was a solid business idea with effective execution. If only—"

"Yeah, if only I hadn't lost it all."

"Because you were trying to take care of your mother."

There were ways she could have saved the business during her mother's illness. Amanda had to admit, in her efforts to handle everything by herself, she'd made some fatal errors, losing both Dream Weaver's and the battle to keep Clara at home.

Amanda rubbed the tabletop again, savoring the coolness against her wrist. It was a shame the dining set wouldn't fit into an apartment she could afford.

"The point is," she said, "I have no money to help Mom now, when she needs me most. I feel useless."

Erik's voice softened to a whisper. "When are you going to stop beating yourself up over it? Mom doesn't blame you."

"I know, I know. She never would."

He cupped her hand into his. The smoothness of it surprised Amanda and had her longing for the days when they'd first been married, spending long weekends reading, snuggling, and eating his cooking school assignments. Things seemed easier then—comfortable and normal—before insights and decisions had pulled them in different directions. How wonderful those first years had been when they were best friends, laughing through all their troubles.

Erik lovingly kissed Amanda's hand. "As bad as losing the business is, it does present an opportunity for us that might not come along again for a while. I mean, before you jump into your next venture."

How could she make him understand that she had no more desire left in her? Since losing the business and failing her mother, she'd staggered into a funk that strangled her confidence. Some days it was all she could do to decide which outfit to wear to her new job at the law firm.

"The timing is finally right, Amanda."

"For what?"

"A baby."

Her stomach flip-flopped. She'd known he wouldn't let the topic drop for long, yet thought he would at least wait until a decision had been made about her mother's long-term medical care.

"I'm doing well financially," he continued enthusiastically. "And now that you're just a bookkeeper, you don't have to work the fourteen-hour days for your business or the long hours to care for Mom. I think it's the perfect time for a baby."

Just a bookkeeper? He didn't intentionally mean to hurt her pride, did he?

"Oh, Erik, I don't know."

"We're not getting any younger. We always said we wanted two children. We could accomplish that before you hit forty."

"You want two kids in three years?"

He grinned.

She let out a long breath. "Things are different now. Those dreams were years ago. Besides, with Mom so sick, I don't know how much time I'd have to devote to a baby."

He broke eye contact with her, dragging a fingernail over the stitched hem of his folded napkin. "Time and effort have always been negotiable, Amanda. You can be as involved as you'd like to be."

Amanda glanced toward the ceiling, her focus caught by a fine strand of cobweb dangling between two crystal pendants of the chandelier. It was the tiniest of tightropes.

The door opened to a Hummer-sized man wearing green camouflage fatigues. The tautness of his shirt showed the effort the airman put into his physical training. He removed his cap. The blond stubble of his hair accentuated his ruddy, round cheeks. And Amanda could see at a glance why Shane and Erik were close. Major Shane McClain was the yin to Erik's yang.

"Am I interrupting?" Shane asked. He cocked his thumb over his shoulder at the entertainment center. "The game's on in a few minutes." Passing the coffee table, he scooped up the remote and snapped on the wall-mounted, plasma television.

He dropped a quick kiss on top of Amanda's head. "How you doing, Amanda Bear?"

"Good, Major."

Since it was her anniversary and she was in a good mood, she'd refrain from the rest of the nickname: Major Pain in the Butt.

"Happy anniversary." He massaged her shoulders a little too tightly for pleasure. Shane never realized his own strength. Before moving on, he double patted her back.

"Thanks." Amanda resisted the urge to rub her neck.

Shane glanced at the table. "Mmm. Looks good."

"Erik outdid himself." Amanda smiled at her husband.

Shane gave the back of Erik's neck a squeeze. "Did you ask her yet?"

That was Shane. Straight to the point. Must be how he got his flight crews on task each morning.

"Yes. I asked her."

Shane snitched a snow pea from Erik's plate, popped it into his mouth, and laid his hand on his lover's shoulder. "So what do you say, Amanda. Are you ready to have a baby for us?"

Chapter Two

Clara Marshall knew people made their own luck. Rabbits' feet, four-leaf clovers and lucky pennies had no more influence on good things happening than voodoo dolls, black cats, or broken mirrors had to do with tragedies. It was her smoking for forty-five years that had put her in her current situation, and all the luck and all the money in the world couldn't change that. Prayer might ease her pain, but even a heart transplant wouldn't save her life.

It was too late for her, but not too late for Amanda. Her daughter needed to regain her confidence and take back her life. Clara had spent most of the past week glancing out the window of her ten-by-fifteen-foot room at the nursing home. As she watched the mama duck splashing in the fountain, teaching her ducklings to swim, Clara had hatched a plan to help Amanda turn her life around. Only a few details remained to be ironed out.

Clara's favorite nurse flew into the room as if on roller skates. "Time for your meds."

Heather Tetley had recently graduated from nursing school and had the energy of a steam locomotive, wrapped in a petite caboose. Tonight the dynamo wore Betty Boop scrubs, and had her long black hair pulled up on top of her head in an explosion of curls. She was the brightness in the nursing home. Not that Clara would ever complain—out loud.

She was fortunate to be able to afford such a nice place. It was her long-term care insurance policy and the proceeds from selling her house that had gotten her into a room overlooking the courtyard three months ago. Still, sixty-seven years of possessions had been culled out to fit into a room the size of the living room in her previous home of forty years.

Amanda had grown up in a three-bedroom house and Clara had never thought it extravagant, but sleeping on a stiff-framed hospital bed, stuffing a year-round wardrobe into one dresser and a small closet took all the tolerance for adjustment Clara possessed.

All her books were crammed into one nightstand, and she had a choice to sit either in a recliner, or one side chair separated by a lamp table. The facility provided an adjustable bedside tray for meals eaten in the room on days when she felt too weak to go to the dining room. Altogether, the experience reminded her of the many times she and her husband, Jim, and young Amanda had camped out in a twelve-foot square tent.

Still, her room had reasonable comforts and Clara gratefully realized it was more than many people in the world had, but even with the family photos Amanda had hung on the walls her tiny room at Brookside could never be *home.*

Shaking the tiny plastic cup with the meds, Heather smiled. "Daydreaming again, Clara?"

"Might as well. I can't dance."

Daydreaming was all the amusement Clara could muster lately. Focused concentration was as slippery as the pills she tried to pinch out of the cup now. One squirted out of her grip, bounced off Heather's chin, and fell back into the cup.

Heather laughed. "You couldn't do that again on a bet."

The nurse reminded Clara of Amanda when she'd been in her early twenties. Nothing slowed Amanda down back then. She was convinced she would conquer the world and make a difference in people's lives. She had done exactly that, one client at a time, with her gift basket business. Maybe her efforts didn't cause earth-shaking change, but each customer valued Amanda's contribution to their life celebration. More importantly, Amanda had been happy.

When Amanda closed the doors on her business, Clara had felt the loss as her own. Months of neglecting her clients to take care of Clara had cost Amanda her business and her dreams. Somehow Clara planned to find a way to make it up to her daughter.

Still giggling, Heather dumped the capsules into Clara's palm. Then she spun around to the bedside tray and poured a fresh glass of water. "You're a hoot."

"Tiddlywinks champion–1947." Clara grinned.

"I don't doubt it." In a quick glance, Heather scanned Clara from head to toe as only a caregiver would do to assess the health and safety of a patient. "You should have your legs elevated." Heather flung the lever on Clara's recliner and her feet launched into the air.

Immediately the tightness in her calves eased. She'd wanted to flip the footrest for the past hour, but hadn't had enough strength to do it herself. "Thanks, dear."

Handing Clara the water, Heather smiled. "No problem. Hope you don't mind the meds are a bit early. It seems none of the residents wants to be disturbed during "Win a Fortune.""

"We have a bunch of millionaire wannabes at Brookside, do we?" Clara's shaky hand stuffed the pills into her mouth and she swallowed a gulp of water. A small, cool splash washed against her cheek.

Heather plucked a tissue from the box on the nightstand, dabbed Clara's face, and refilled the glass for the chaser. Clara was never able to get the meds down in one try. She handed the water to Clara. "I wouldn't mind a chunk of the jackpot myself. Pay off my husband's medical school loans. Then we could start a family."

Glimpsing over Heather's shoulder, Clara saw her daughter round the corner and enter her room. She swallowed quickly, and then winked at the nurse. She raised her voice. "Kids? They're overrated."

"If you're not nice, you don't get the leftover cherry cheesecake Erik made." Amanda breezed in and kissed her mother on the top of her head. "Hi, Heather. Mom giving you a tough time today?"

"Nope, she saves her feistiness for you." Heather turned to Clara and fluffed the pillow behind her back. "Need anything else?"

"Matthew McConaughey?" Clara said.

"I stand corrected, you're feisty with *everyone*!" Heather said.

Clara winked again. "Matthew is for Amanda."

Heather's brows snapped together and she turned to Amanda. "I thought you were married."

"I am," Amanda whispered. "Mom gets confused sometimes."

"I heard that. Don't talk about me like I'm not here."

As if Amanda's comment explained everything, the bewilderment evaporated from the nurse's eyes. "I'll check back on you later." Heather sped out the door.

Dropping her purse on the bed, Amanda smoothed out the comforter with her hand. "I brought you another book."

Adrenaline shot through Clara's heart. "I . . . I haven't finished the last one you borrowed from the library. Surely it's overdue by now." She hadn't done more than open the Dickens novel that sat in the drawer of her nightstand. Because of her growing weakness, she'd probably never read it now.

Teryl Oswald

Amanda tapped the spine of the latest paperback against her palm. "No problem. I don't check out the books from the library."

"You didn't pay those outrageous prices from the bookstore, did you?" Clara regretted her question the moment she'd said it. Ever since Amanda had lost her business, she was touchy about money. She hated discussing it.

"No, Mom. I buy the books from the thrift store. They're dirt cheap and you can keep them as long as you like."

Used books? Well that explained how Clara had found that particular bookmark in *Great Expectations*. Suddenly things made sense. The knot in Clara's stomach eased. "It's so hard for me to read these days. You keep the paperback, dear."

"I could read to you or get you books on tape."

"They sell those at the thrift shops, too?"

"Yes, they do."

"You don't have to be spending your money on me."

Amanda's lips tightened into a thin line. Clara had hurt her daughter again. If only Clara could keep quiet about money.

Amanda tossed the book on the bed next to her purse and crossed her arms over her chest. Her shoulders were weighted beyond her years. Clara bit her tongue to avoid commenting about Amanda's stooped posture. "How's your job?"

"Fine. Hey, I thought I saw Uncle Ernie driving out of the parking lot as I was coming in."

"You might have." Clara hadn't wanted the answer to sound mysterious, but it did to her own ears.

"I don't think he saw me though because he didn't stop. What was he doing in town?"

Half truths weren't really a lie, Clara justified to herself. "He was passing through to meet a client on the west coast and he scheduled a longer connecting flight to see me."

"There are flights from Chicago that connect in Omaha?" Amanda's brows lifted in curiosity.

Clara deliberately exaggerated the tiredness in the breath she blew out. "How should I know? Uncle Ernie wanted to stop to see his favorite sister."

"Mom, you're his *only* sister."

"See? Top of the list."

Amanda rolled her eyes at Clara's humor. Then she opened the vacuum-sealed lid of the container, and the richness of the cheesecake wafted forth. Still full from the mystery soup at dinner, the aroma turned Clara's stomach.

"Erik made a great dinner tonight. He sends his love."

Clara bit back a sarcastic retort. When Erik first confessed his homosexuality, four years after their wedding, both she and Amanda spent hours trading quips, even laughed about the situation. After the revelation sank in, Amanda's anger burned hot for months. Afterwards, she'd entered a grossly depressed stage Clara feared she'd never escape. During her mourning, ironic comments were taboo. Only after Amanda began focusing on her business did she seem to accept the inevitable. At least Erik hadn't left her for another lover. He'd met Shane a year after Amanda moved to her own apartment.

Now cynicism was accepted, but only if Amanda initiated it.

"Erik's a nice boy. Tell him I loved the cheesecake, but you eat it, dear. I've had no appetite for sweets lately." Clara picked up the television remote and pushed the power button.

"No cheesecake?" Amanda felt her mother's forehead.

Clara recoiled and slapped at her daughter's hand. "I'm fine. I'm just not hungry. Eat it. You're too thin."

Amanda shut the lid on the dessert, then gently took the remote from her mother and lowered the volume.

Clara frowned. She could barely hear the preview for "Win a Fortune." Why couldn't young people leave things the way she liked them?

Pointing to the side chair, Clara didn't take her eyes off the television. Even in a small room lip reading was difficult. "Sit down, Amanda. The program is about to start. They've been advertising all day that they have a special announcement."

Her daughter merely huffed.

Amanda must really be distracted by something. It was Amanda who insisted on watching this program together with her every week. Then again, if a person could believe the ratings, most of the nation tuned into this reality show.

"Erik made a fabulous dinner. And he got me tickets to the symphony."

"Oh?"

Clara strained to hear the opening comments of the television reporter. Imagine, an actual network anchor hosting the show as if it were really news. It wasn't unusual for a single person to win a two-hundred-million-dollar jackpot. What was amazing and caused wild attention was the winner vowing to give away the fortune–in whole or in parts to the most deserving person or persons.

Sneaking the remote off the tray, Clara increased the volume. The anchor with his dazzling white smile continued. "The benevolent winner, who wishes to remain anonymous, and is unknown even to us, will choose who will be a multi-millionaire. What criteria he or she uses is unknown. Exactly when the winner or winners will be decided is also not known. Although we expect a decision will be reached within the next six weeks since the lottery ticket itself . . . wherever it is . . . must be cashed within the next forty-three days, or it expires. Stay tuned for news of a surprising development, coming up after these commercial messages."

Could the plastic-faced reporter be any more dramatic? Still, it was all anyone could talk about at the nursing home.

The jackpot winner had announced simultaneously in the *Chicago Tribune*, *The New York Times*, *The Denver Register*, and the *Los Angeles Times* the intention of dispersing the fortune. Ever since that Sunday one month ago, people began writing their local newspapers, presenting their stories, making their cases to win the fortune.

For Clara, it was like watching one of those surgery shows on cable television. People spilled their guts exposing their deepest secrets and troubles, all in the hope of winning a portion of the jackpot. It was amazing, really, how some people could be so desperate.

When Amanda bent over, obstructing Clara's view of the television, her long blonde hair whipped Clara's cheek and she flinched. She stared into the face so like her late husband's, with cornflower blue eyes and wisps of blonde eyebrows and lashes. An angel's face. Her daughter used to have Jim's scrappy determination, too—something Clara hoped to help her win back.

"Mom, Eric gave me symphony tickets as a gift for our anniversary."

Clara nearly swallowed her tongue in the effort to not comment. Amanda looked like she had more on her mind, and Clara knew if she gave advice at this juncture, Amanda would shut up like a clam. "Yes, your anniversary. Tickets to the symphony. How nice."

Flopping onto the bed, Amanda grabbed a lock of her hair and tweezed the ends with her fingers. "I didn't get him anything. I felt terrible. Still do."

Clara no longer could contain herself. She snapped off the television. "Miss Manners says a gift isn't required when your husband is sleeping with someone else."

"Mom!"

"When are you going to give up this ruse, Amanda? What could you possibly be gaining from this marriage?"

"Health insurance."

"Surely you can get that through your new job. Isn't that one of the benefits of being the boss at that lawyer's office?"

"I'm the office manager, Mom, not the boss. And yes I do get insurance, but not for a couple more months."

"Then will you divorce Erik and move on?"

Amanda let go of her hair and wrapped her arms tightly around her stomach. A python couldn't have squeezed her daughter so tightly.

"It's not that easy, Mom."

"I don't see why not. Shane can wash Erik's boxers."

Amanda bit her lower lip. "They want me to have a baby for them."

"What?" Clara fumbled for the lever to lower her feet. She'd have flown out of the recliner to tussle with her daughter if her heart had been stronger.

Amanda grabbed the lever and slowly lowered Clara's legs. "I didn't say yes."

Clara rocked back and forth in the chair. Where was the strength in her legs? "How could you even consider having a baby?"

"You always said Erik and I would make beautiful grandchildren for you."

"That was when you'd be making them the traditional way and not with a turkey baster." Clara gave up the struggle and slid back into the cushion, letting out an exhausted breath.

"This could be my last chance to have a baby. And who knows if I'm even fertile?" Amanda said.

Clara pointed to the glass of water. Amanda handed it to her and she took a long drink. She steadied her hand holding the glass against the armrest so the remaining water wouldn't splash out. "Don't jump into this, Amanda. Think it over. It's not the consolation prize you owe Erik for his lost investment in your company."

"I don't think that."

"You don't?"

"Well, I *do* feel guilty, but—"

"That's no reason to bring a child into the world."

Amanda snatched the remote and clicked on the television. "Might as well. I can't dance."

Chapter Three

To capitalize on the public's frenzy, the television network had begun broadcasting "Win a Fortune" three times a week. Each night the program highlighted several candidates for the prize money. Amanda had classified the appeals. People asked for money either for a community project, for a social cause, for an environmental purpose, or for medical reasons. Her own letter fell into the last category.

As soon as the newspapers announced the anonymous winner planned to give away the lottery money, Amanda had written to the *Omaha World-Herald* pleading for funds for her mother's heart transplant.

It was a long shot, but if the benefactor decided to divide the jackpot, the million dollars she needed hardly made a dent in the two-hundred-million-dollar winnings. That was Amanda's logic anyway, and she was eager to argue her case with the producers to get the necessary air time to sway the lottery winner. However, several subsequent letters had failed to grab the network's attention. She hoped the benefactor had some system devised to review all serious proposals because Clara Marshall's condition grew graver every day.

"Isn't it awful how that whole town was flooded?" Clara clicked her tongue sympathetically before taking a sip of water. Her hand quivered as she put the Styrofoam cup on the bedside tray.

Amanda practiced her justification on her mother exactly as she would do on television if given the opportunity. "There are too many natural disasters to favor one over another. It's a matter of fairness. Besides, the announcer said that river has overflowed six times in the last century and the community keeps rebuilding on the same spot. Wouldn't that be a waste of the lottery money?"

"Amanda. That's heartless."

Clara looked frailer tonight than she had a few days ago. Her respiration seemed more labored, too. It took her more effort to push out her breath than it did to draw it into her lungs. That seemed backwards to Amanda.

"Mom, it would take most of the jackpot to rebuild that town, just to have the city washed away in another generation. Wouldn't it be better for everyone if the town relocated?"

Clara pursed her lips into a tight line—the same gesture she had used when Amanda came home late from a date with Erik in high school. The act had become less intimidating since Clara's illness.

"It's not so easy to leave what you've known all your life and start over."

"Hanging on to something that falls apart every few years is insane. They should move on to something more stable."

The condescension in Clara's gaze made Amanda bristle. No doubt her mother was thinking of Amanda's marriage.

Her mother didn't understand about her relationship with Erik. Nobody did. Amanda fell in love with Erik Cash in the third grade. She couldn't remember a time when he wasn't part of her life. Even through the transitional months after she moved out of their house, it was Erik who had comforted Amanda over the end of their marriage. She recognized she could no longer be the most important person to him, but she couldn't imagine her existence without him.

A baby would connect them forever.

"Talk about money well-spent," Clara said.

Money well-spent?

A notion flashed in Amanda's mind. Would Erik and Shane pay her to be a surrogate? With a large enough deposit she could get Clara's name on the transplant list.

It couldn't be immoral to have a baby to save another person's life. Besides, it's not as though the child would be unwanted or unloved. After all, he or she would have Clara as a grandmother on top of the bonus third parent. At age thirty-seven, this could be Amanda's last chance at motherhood.

"Oh, my God. Look at that child."

Clara's comment jarred Amanda from her plan. She focused her attention back on the television where a toddler with big, round eyes filled the screen. His deformed lips couldn't cover his teeth, and his eyes reflected the emotional pain of his birth defect.

Amanda recoiled at the image, counting her blessings that she didn't know how difficult the little boy's struggle had been. But he was one more person who pulled at the public's heartstrings, potentially drawing money from the jackpot, reducing Clara's chances for a transplant. The thought of Clara missing this opportunity tore Amanda's compassion in two directions.

"If only there was enough lottery money to help all the people with medical problems, but it seems to me there are celebrities that have taken up that particular cause," Amanda said, pointing to the television.

And even if "Win a Fortune" would promote Clara's case, putting toddlers side-by-side with seniors was totally unfair. Old people were the ones the healthcare industry left hanging out to dry and the public preferred to ignore.

If only Clara's insurance would pay for a new heart. She was a young sixty-seven. She could survive the surgery. Since Clara had been forced to give up smoking several months ago, she had a good chance of living another twenty years if she had the transplant. Amanda had spent many sleepless nights saddened by the thought she might lose the extra years with her mother.

"So you wouldn't give the money to the flood victims or the baby. Who *would* you give the money to?" Clara crossed her arms over her chest and stared curiously at her daughter.

"I don't know. But no *one* person needs two-hundred-million dollars."

"Amen. A fortune that big could ruin your life. Where would be the incentive to work?"

"One thing's for certain, Mom. You'd get a new heart."

A puff of air billowed from between Clara's lips and she waved her hand like she were shooing a gnat. "I didn't take care of the one God gave me."

"But you've learned your lesson and you'd do better with the next one."

"My time has passed, dear. I don't need a second chance." Clara pointed to the television screen. "Many people could use one though."

Tears burned behind Amanda's eyes. Her mother had never been a quitter. Why didn't she have more courage to fight now?

Amanda looked at the crumpled body that used to be her vibrant mother. Transparent skin sagged along her once strong jaw line. Aqua eyes that had been keen and sparkly now had tears pooled at the rims, not from sadness, but from the medications that kept Clara's heart pumping.

Taking another drink of water, Clara cleared her throat—the action stealing her breath. "I'm glad I don't have to decide who gets the money. That jackpot is too big for one person and not big enough for everyone to share."

Amanda suddenly realized Clara was simply denying a desire for the transplant because Amanda was heartbroken that the money for it was no longer available. If the gift basket business still existed and were as profitable as it had been a year ago, Amanda would find a buyer for it and get a good down payment for the medical procedure.

Could a life-saving surgery be purchased on a revolving payment plan?

One thing was certain; if the network producers showed up at her home and gave her the opportunity to plead her mother's case, Amanda would do everything in her power to convince them Clara Marshall deserved another chance.

"And now what you've all been waiting for." The camera zoomed in on television anchor, Brad Conklin.

Seated on Clara's bed, Amanda tucked a leg beneath her, eyes glued to the screen.

A second anchor had joined the other at the news desk—presumably to give credence to the gravity of the breaking report. Dressed in a stylish, layered beige sweater, Mallory Piper was an ideal Barbie doll look-a-like.

"This is what we know so far, Brad," she said facing the camera. "One hundred and thirty-nine days ago, the winning lottery ticket was purchased at the I-80 Fuel Smart in Grayson, Indiana. The amount of the prize—two-hundred-million dollars. The winner has yet to come forward." She turned to her counterpart, snapping closed her perfectly painted lips.

"The security camera in the store was unplugged and no record of the purchase exists." He shook his head at the blunder.

"The president of the I-80 Fuel Smart, Les Moore, reports the security system is fully operational now," Mallory said.

"Lottery rules state the ticket must be cashed within one-hundred and eighty days—roughly six months—leaving less than six weeks for the prize to be claimed," the male anchor said.

Well, that explained the large, digital clock behind the desk. It looked like the kind they had at the post office at Christmastime to count down remaining time available to ship packages.

The woman reporter stared, unblinking, into the camera. "You've watched right here for the past month as we've presented the stories, the cases of people pleading for part of the jackpot—their share of the American Dream."

"Mallory," said Brad, "we've just found out through sources we cannot reveal that the lottery winner has designated someone else to choose the lucky person or persons who will be awarded the money."

Will that give me more or less of a chance to get Mom's case heard, Amanda wondered.

"An interesting development, Brad. Who is the designated agent?"

"We don't have a name, but our sources continue to look into the mystery. For more information, let's turn to our correspondent in the field, lottery expert, Harvey Lawrence."

Lottery expert? Amanda nearly laughed. How does one become one of those?

"What a fantastic development," the young reporter shouted with his finger stuffed in his ear to hold the communication link in place. The road sign behind him read *Grayson, Indiana, Pop. 563.*

"The anonymous winner who we've been trying to track down for the past month—ever since the giveaway was announced in the major metropolitan newspapers—*that* winner has stepped aside and sent in a pinch hitter, of sorts. An agent to choose the recipients." He literally hopped with excitement.

The male anchor placed his elbow on the table, resting his cleft chin lightly on his crooked index finger. "Any idea why the lottery winner would make such a move, Harvey?"

One hand flailing, the other holding the microphone, the man looked like a carnival barker. "I suspect somebody was getting too close to discovering the identity of the winner, so he, *or she*, threw a lateral pass to a teammate."

"Geez," Clara griped. "Couldn't they find a field 'expert' who wasn't a sportscaster?"

Mallory's stiff hair didn't move as she whipped her head to gaze into a peripheral camera. "Do we know how the lottery winner chose the agent, Harvey?"

"We haven't confirmed that yet, but we do know many of the initial letters requesting money were shipped last week to a warehouse in Oak Brook, Illinois, a suburb of Chicago. It's possible the lottery winner was looking for a specific type of person to be his or *her* delegate."

Brad interrupted. "Is it possible a letter was simply chosen at random?"

Harvey shrugged, his shoulders drawing his elbows up in the air as well. The motion made him look like he was doing the chicken dance. "Absolutely possible, Brad. It could simply be . . ."—he paused and nodded for dramatic effect—"the luck of the draw."

Mallory tilted her head in response, the movement not jostling a single hair out of place. "What would that person be doing right now?"

"He, or she, is probably crisscrossing the nation interviewing candidates."

"What criteria might be used?"

"It's hard to say. No doubt the agent huddled with the lottery winner ahead of time and together they designed the play book."

Brad gave a quick nod. "What else do we know, Harvey?"

"I wish I could tell you what the representative looks like, but honestly, we don't know at this time." He turned to the camera, slapping concern onto his face. "I'd warn the public, though, to be on the lookout for someone who asks a lot of questions about your finances and financial needs, displaying a sincere desire to help."

"Puh-leeze," Amanda groaned.

"A cautionary note." The camera zoomed in while the anchor cocked his head, deepening his voice to add seriousness. "Do *not* give out personal information to *any* stranger—especially not your social security number."

"Duh," Clara said.

"That's right," Mallory said. "The person may not be the lottery winner's *real* delegate."

Amanda grunted. "I hope whoever was chosen is smarter than the typical news reporter."

* * * *

"Hi, Mr. Fisher. Did you watch "Win a Fortune"?" As Amanda closed her mother's door behind her, she greeted the man who lived across the hall from Clara. Perched on a red, motorized wheelchair, he held his hand over the joystick accelerator. His tall frame still looked sound. The only physical hint of disease was the small tremor of his head.

"Not a chance. You couldn't pay me to watch that yellow journalism. If that's what passes for news these days, then we might as well be getting our information from those rags at the grocery store checkout lanes."

Bud Fisher had been the editor of a small newspaper in Colorado for nearly forty years. Solid journalism is what mattered to him. He'd even installed a pouch on the side of his wheelchair—his go-buggy as he called it—to tote his favorites. Tonight the front page of *The Wall Street Journal* peeked out.

"You're absolutely right. You have more sense than to get caught up in the craziness, don't you Mr. Fisher?"

Amanda leaned against the wall next to his room and straightened the card held in the brass name plate on his door. Everything at Brookside was first class—including the residents.

Bud wore a Denver Broncos ball cap to cover his thinning, white hair. From under the bill, his cloudy gray eyes maintained a steady gaze as he spoke. Amanda found it difficult to resist brushing off bread crumbs from his perfectly trimmed, silver mustache.

"The public's going nuts over the *possibility* they could get some money," the man continued his rant. "If they spent as much effort working as they do posing for those publicity segments—that show is *not* news, you know." He jabbed a fist overhead. "The trouble with people these days is that everyone wants something for nothing."

Amanda nodded. "Have some cheesecake." She offered the container to the man, then gently smoothed her fingers above his lip to dislodge the crumbs.

He grabbed her hand and patted it, his smile of white teeth, some ringed in silver caps, growing broader. "Did you cook for me, Amanda?"

"You deserve the best, Mr. Fisher. That's why I leave the baking to Erik. He made the cheesecake."

The man opened the lid and snitched a cherry from the top of the dessert. He popped it into his mouth, his freckled hand, lined with large, blue veins, dragging some red sauce onto his mustache. Amanda reached into her pocket, took out a tissue, and dabbed his face.

"You take good care of me, Sybil," said Bud. "I'm so glad I married you."

Gently he planted a kiss on the back of Amanda's hand, the softness of his mustache surprising her. Lovingly, he pressed her hand against his cheek, which was smooth and cool. Amanda felt sad that, for Mr. Fisher, this was not a completely lucid day.

Wasn't it enough that age stole physical health from the elderly? Why did it so often also rob their minds?

Amanda squatted next to the wheelchair, cupped Bud's cheek with her other hand and directed his attention to her face. "I'm not your wife, Mr. Fisher. I'm Amanda Cash." She nodded to the door across the hall. "I'm Clara Marshall's daughter."

The blankness of his stare concerned Amanda. Her comment had yet to reach him, to pull him back to the present. "You called me Sybil, but your wife is gone. She passed away some years ago."

She brushed his cheek with the back of her fingers as she released his face and stood again.

Slowly the octogenarian shook his trembling head and smiled, wrinkles bursting from the corners of his eyes. "I guess I'm available then. Why don't you marry me, Amanda Cash?"

Amanda gently touched his arm and squeezed. "You know I'm already married, Mr. Fisher—to Erik. He's a chef."

Recall flashed in Bud's eyes. "He made the cheesecake." He put the dessert in the wire basket attached to the armrest of his go-buggy. "Well, divorce him and marry me."

Amanda laughed. "You crack me up."

"I'm as serious as incontinence at a senior comedy club. Every woman should marry once for love and once for money."

At least age hadn't pilfered his sense of humor. Amanda chuckled. "It's hard to pass up such a romantic offer . . ."

"I'll give you romance. The Greek Islands in the winter, Paris in the spring."

"You've been to those places?" The farthest Amanda had been was Chicago.

"Stick with me and we'll travel the world." He grabbed her hand and squeezed tightly as though the memory he wanted to share might slip from his consciousness, fall, and shatter on the floor. "You haven't lived until you've stood at daybreak in the rain forest of Costa Rica, the dew heavy on the tropical vines. All of a sudden a flock of butterflies takes flight, surrounding you in the joyous vibration of fluttering wings. It's like a hundred angels waltzing around you. Romance doesn't get any better than that."

Although he'd meant to captivate her, a feeling of loss swelled in her chest instead. She and Erik had always talked of traveling, but between his work and hers, they'd never taken a single trip. What had she missed by staying so securely fastened to Omaha, Nebraska—and to Erik Cash?

"One thing though . . ." Bud looked over one shoulder, then the other. "You'll have to drive our little red sports car. The bastards stripped me of my driver's license. Excuse my French."

Amanda slapped her knee, grinned, and countered. "Darn my luck. You're not looking for a wife, only a chauffeur."

Bud shrugged. "What difference does it make who drives along the Autobahn as long as we end up at the same chalet?"

The man was good company regardless of his age.

"What if we start with something local—see how compatible we are? How about I drive us to the symphony on Thursday night? My husband has to work and I have two tickets. What do you say, Mr. Fisher? Would you like to be my date?"

The old man's eyes glimmered. "I'd say if we're going out poodle-scooting, as folks said in the old days, you should call me Bud."

Chapter Four

Shane scraped food residue from the dinner plates into the country-style, white enamel sink, and then jammed a fork into the mess to stuff more garbage into the disposal.

"You're putting too much in there again. You'll clog it." Erik snapped the lid on a Tupperware bowl, which burped the aroma of vanilla from the cheesecake.

Erik hated the whine he'd added to his nagging.

Actually, he hated always having to remind Shane what to do in the kitchen. At least he'd trained Amanda to stay out of his way if she wanted to help. All around, she'd been much more agreeable than Shane, exceedingly malleable, and very easy to live with.

Guilt at the thought of comparing the two washed over him. Amanda was his forever friend, sweet, dependable, and fun to be with. Shane was fun, too, but in a different way. After eight years together, he couldn't imagine being with anyone else.

A baby would seal their commitment to one another. It was something Erik was desperate to have, even though a baby would complicate the masquerade of their relationship. Establishing a family could jeopardize Shane's career, but Erik was confident that should it come down to a choice, Shane would choose Erik and their life together.

Glancing around, he took a minute to appreciate what he and Shane had accomplished, and imagined how a baby would add to their life.

A high chair would fit nicely between the walk-in pantry and the baking center. He'd seen the one he wanted in the Pottery Barn catalog. It wasn't made of plastic and vinyl like most were. This one had wood trim on it to match the cherry cabinetry he'd chosen for their gourmet kitchen, a combination of stainless steel, glass, and ceramic tile, softened with a soft yellow pattern on the walls. Shiny copper-colored squares mounted on the ceiling reflected the sun streaming through the skylight. At nighttime, the lights ricocheted off the embossed metal onto the quartz counters lending a heartwarming glow, something that would bedazzle an infant.

He'd designed and built the commercial-style kitchen himself. Shane had insisted on footing the bill, although Erik could have managed with the inheritance from his grandmother.

Watching as Shane flipped the switch and the disposal whirred—not as fast as it would have if it hadn't been overloaded—Erik prayed the blades wouldn't freeze. He was in no mood to crawl under the sink and tear apart pipes.

Soon the water flowed freely and Erik exhaled.

Shane tossed the cutlery into the basket. Erik bit his lip, swallowing the comment that the forks and spoons were pointing wrong end up.

"It was a waste of time," Shane growled.

"What was?"

"Making the dinner. She's not going to do it."

Shane poured the detergent into the dispenser, excess crystals spilling onto the Italian tile floor. Then he slammed shut the dishwasher drawer, rattling the silverware. The machine whirred as he pushed the start button.

The hum of the motor and whoosh of the water jets usually calmed Erik, putting him in the relaxed state of domesticity. But not tonight. Shane had put so much hope into Amanda's acceptance of their proposal. Her hesitation created doubt in Shane's mind and his disappointment broke Erik's heart.

He would wait until Shane settled to watch television before sweeping up the detergent, rearranging the cutlery, and scrubbing the sink.

"Dinner wasn't the only reason to have her over. It was a celebration." Erik didn't know how to sound cheerier.

"Yeah, right." The crack of a wet towel made Erik jump. On the exhale of a ragged breath, Shane tossed it on the rack to dry.

Erik added re-hanging the towels to his to-do list.

He felt bad for Amanda, too. Shane had walked in right as they'd been discussing the baby. Amanda only tolerated Shane, not that he could blame her. Wouldn't any woman resent her husband's male lover?

With no time to go into the details of the arrangement, it was no wonder Amanda had balked, yet Erik felt certain once they offered fifty-thousand dollars for her involvement, she wouldn't refuse. Erik was pleased to be able to provide his oldest friend a way to recover financially from the loss of her business. If she wanted, she could save the money for her mother's surgery, although that seemed foolish since he'd heard from Clara's own lips that she didn't want the transplant.

Once Amanda had a chance to weigh all the benefits against the nominal risks, he was sure she'd jump at the chance to help him. After all, she'd always been there for him. He'd never lost when he put his faith in Amanda.

They had a symbiotic relationship. She'd willingly been his cover all these years so Shane could remain in the closet and in the Air Force. It took very little of her time. She only attended an occasional party or restaurant opening with him in exchange for the health insurance Erik provided.

She'd said that without the security of the insurance, she never would have had the confidence to start the business. With premiums being so expensive, it had been worth it to her to remain on his policy even when her business began to succeed. After her mother's heart attack and then the loss of her business, Amanda had clutched even tighter to their arrangement.

Some women relished holding their husbands responsible for all their misfortunes; thank goodness Amanda had never blamed him for her bad luck.

"You just don't understand women," Erik said.

"Who does?"

The sarcasm in Shane's voice was predictable. He liked Amanda well enough, given the whole ex-lover-aversion-thing. To wash down his apparent frustration with the topic, he snatched a Heineken from the Sub-Zero, popped the cap with the bottle opener and launched it at the trash can, missing it by mere inches. Shane guzzled half the beer before taking a breath.

Something else to add to the list. Pick up the cap and empty the trash.

Erik unwound a handful of paper towels, grabbed the bottle of disinfecting cleaner, and strolled around the kitchen, spraying and wiping the quartz counters.

Shane had wanted granite, but in the end, Erik's choice of cream-colored quartz with flecks of copper and rose had prevailed. Quartz didn't require sealant every year and it resisted the permeation of bacteria better than natural stone. Shane couldn't be expected to know a countertop's qualities any more than he was expected to know Amanda's nature.

"We have to give her time to let the idea sink in," Erik said. "Amanda doesn't do anything without thinking it over a million times. She's not spontaneous. She's steady and—"

"Did you tell her about Michelle?"

Erik gasped and spun toward the major. "God, no. You don't see *osso bucco* on the wall, do you?"

"You *have* to tell her. She can't make an informed decision without all the information."

"How do I spring *that* detail on her?" Erik squeezed the cleaner's trigger along the stove's perimeter, choking out an abundance of liquid over a puddle of sauce scorched onto a burner.

"The longer you wait, the longer we give her to think it over a million times before making a decision. We need to know now so we can go to Plan B if she refuses."

Shane's Plan B was hugely different from Erik's. The major's idea was to hire a professional surrogate to have their baby. Erik's fallback was to adopt, like any other couple that couldn't conceive.

Of course, Shane would never agree to Erik's plan because that would mean he'd have to come out of the closet and marry Erik in a state permitting their lifestyle. None of that could happen while Shane remained in the Air Force.

They'd argued incessantly about the advantages of going civilian. Erik had even offered money to Shane for the start of a private, time-share jet service. It would be exactly what Shane did now, shuttling VIPs all over the world. But these VIPs would pay him for his services and he wouldn't have to salute.

The major had flatly refused. He liked giving orders, both at work and at home.

The circles Erik made on the counter with the paper towels grew smaller and tighter. "I know. I know. I'll talk to her and give her the details."

"When?"

Flipping the soggy towels over, Erik dried the knobs of his five-burner, commercial-grade Thermador. "As soon as my schedule allows."

Shane set down his finished beer and reached inside the cherry cabinet door behind him. Yanking the calendar off the nail, he slapped it down next to Erik's hand. "When?"

Erik picked up the beer bottle, stuffing it and the mushy towels into the trash can by his feet. "Tomorrow," he barked. Under his breath he whispered, "Bully."

Chapter Five

The smell of the hazelnut coffee did nothing to squelch the growing headache that awakened Amanda two hours ago. All night she'd been chasing hearts in her dreams. They weren't the cute, Valentine-type, edged in white lace, but human organs that bounced around on severed arteries, leaving slick trails of blood to slip and fall in as she tried to capture one for her mother. She'd failed–utterly.

She took another swig from her cup and poured the rest of the coffee into the porcelain sink in the galley kitchen, used the sprayer to rinse out the mess and loaded her cup into the dishwasher. The law firm of Megel, Jeppesen, and Harris spared no expense in providing comforts for its employees. Amanda had suggested the company could cut costs by using paper cups for the employees and save the bone china and crystal for clients. Roberta Megel, the senior partner, had strongly pointed out that paper *anything* wasn't in keeping with their image.

Rubbing her neck muscles to ease their tightness, Amanda wondered if the headache was from lack of rest or tension. Or both.

Amanda had been hired to run the law office, cut expenses, and fatten the bottom line. She'd soon discovered the partners were more interested in her debt collecting skills. They were right about her expertise in that area; she'd fielded enough such phone calls when her business was going down the tubes.

Uncle Ernie had recommended Megel, Jeppesen and Harris to help Amanda avoid bankruptcy. They'd been so impressed by the accuracy of her books and attention to business operations, they'd offered her a job.

During the first two months of her employment, Amanda feared she was working at the firm on a Pity Pass with everyone aware of her financial problems. However, she'd earned her salary many times over with the successful collection of countless delinquent accounts. So much so that when she'd demanded a raise, Roberta Megel hadn't refused. That difference went straight into Clara's heart fund. Amanda didn't like her job, but debt collection was necessary in any business and her salary was the best she could find in Omaha.

She leaned over the counter, scratching ideas into her *Clara* spiral notebook. So far she'd eliminated the plan of earning money by brokering her future salary to the highest bidder. The proposal fell along the lines of indentured servitude—with health insurance benefits.

Scribbling out 'selling a kidney,' she replaced the entry with the potential money-maker, 'surrogate mother,' and considered how to approach Erik with her financial needs.

"Good morning, Amanda," a male voice boomed, startling her into kicking the dishwasher with her knee. The dishes inside rattled. She hoped she wouldn't be ordering more china as a result.

She turned, clunking into a barrel of a man who, regardless of the meager space in the galley, stood a little too close. She let out a calming breath. "Good morning, Ben."

His smile broadened to reveal large, slightly crowded front teeth. Spiky, short blond hair made him look more like an athlete than an attorney, if one overlooked the meticulously pressed pinstripe, navy suit. He'd nicked himself shaving this morning judging by a tiny scab dotting his robust cheek.

He reached around her to collect a coffee cup and saucer from the cupboard. Spicy aftershave swirled about Amanda as he squeezed by her to get the carafe. "How was your evening?"

"Terrific. After a quiet anniversary dinner with my husband, I visited my mother."

Reminding him of her married status was deliberate. Not that it deterred his friendliness, but then Ben was friendly to everyone. Wasn't he?

"How *is* your mother?" He stirred powdered creamer into his cup and then tapped the silver spoon against the rim. The noise pinched nerve-endings at the base of her skull.

"She's holding her own." Amanda hesitated, not only because of qualms about revealing personal matters, but also because of the distraction of the clanging spoon. Didn't he realize how obnoxious that tapping was?

"I'd like to meet her some day," Ben said.

Tap. Tap. Tap.

Amanda shook her head, the action causing her more distress. "Why?"

If she were single, would Ben be her type? He was the opposite of Erik who was slender, tall, and dark. Not much taller than her own five-foot, six-inch frame, Ben was built like a brick mailbox.

"To see how far the nut fell from the tree." He raised his eyebrow into an arch.

Was that supposed to be funny? Cute? Alluring?

She took the spoon from Ben in mid-strike and dropped it into the dishwasher. Picking up her notebook, she smiled and slapped some cheer into her voice. "I have to go make some phone calls now. Have a great day."

"What are you working on?" He tried to snatch her notebook, but she twisted out of his reach.

God, he was pushy.

"Ideas for fund raising," she said.

"The firm is raising money? For what cause?"

"It's not for the firm. It's for my mother's transplant." She unclipped the pen from the notebook cover and flipped to a blank page. "But you gave me an idea. What do you think of businesses sponsoring people? Sort of like offering college scholarships, only different."

"Huh?"

"Businesses could donate money to support elderly people who need medical assistance."

"Hmm. Interesting."

"Hey, it worked for schools and highways. I'd call it Adopt-a-Senior."

He nodded, pulling his lips into his mouth to squelch a smile. "You have the most vividly creative mind, Amanda Cash."

She didn't like to be teased about such serious matters. To her, if you weren't offering solutions, you were part of the problem. She turned to leave, brushing elbows with the massive man. He must work out; he was all muscle.

"Wait." Ben grabbed her arm.

The firmness of his grip surprised Amanda, as did the comforting warmth it provided. Would a neck massage by Ben Harris cure her headache?

"I was supposed to tell you that Roberta wants to see you in the conference room in five minutes."

"She wants to see *me*?"

"Yes. It's a special meeting." His face broke into a wide smile, crinkling the corners of his eyes. "I'll be there."

It was while staring into his eyes, the color of the frosted ivy that had hung in baskets on Clara's screened-in back porch, that Amanda decided Ben Harris could be mildly attractive if he weren't so . . . so eager.

* * * *

The news plunged Amanda into a mental gorge filled with dense fog. The lushness of the mahogany conference table and pecan-paneled walls blurred in the background, noises became muffled. She grew vaguely aware of Ben's warm hand on her arm.

"Amanda, do you understand what Mr. Franklin is saying to you?" The tone of Roberta Megel's voice was softer than usual, still authoritative, but more maternal.

Funny, Amanda had never thought of Roberta as motherly, although she had four children. Roberta was power suits, sound decisions, and professionalism. She'd be a judge some day, Amanda was sure of it.

"Amanda?"

The hand lying on her arm shook her a little.

She looked sideways. "Ben?"

"Do you want some time to think about Mr. Franklin's offer?" he asked.

Struggling to force the numbness from her mind, Amanda dug her fingers through her hair and pushed her palms against her temples. "Tell me again what he said."

The gentleman at the head of the table clasped his hands in front of him atop a modest stack of papers—the contract, Amanda assumed. "No problem, Ms. Cash. I'd be happy to review the terms."

He didn't work for Megel, Jeppesen, and Harris, but he looked legal enough, with his red tie and charcoal gray suit. His watch even looked expensive, although Amanda knew nothing of name-brand men's jewelry. Erik always wore Timex.

"The lottery winner, who wishes to remain anonymous, would like *you* to decide who should get the two-hundred-million-dollar jackpot. You may give the money to one person, or many people. You have four weeks to make your decision, leaving two weeks for the winner's attorneys to work out any legal details before the ticket expires six weeks from now. As long as the benefactor agrees your decision is a sound one—that the recipients are deserving of the money—you will be given a million-dollar 'finder's fee.'"

Deliberately and slowly, Amanda sucked in a breath. She looked around the conference table, wondering if she had fallen asleep. Surely this was a dream and there would be a beating heart bouncing through the room at any moment. Her own heart thumped wildly in her chest.

"But how will I decide who gets the money?"

"That's up to you. And only you," Mr. Franklin said.

Pressure built in Amanda's chest. What an inconvenient time to have a heart attack, she thought, pressing a fist against her breastbone.

Ben poured some water from the crystal pitcher and passed the glass to her. Trembling, she reached to take the drink. Oddly, she imagined herself aged, with blue veins protruding on the back of her hand.

Leafing through the papers in front of him, Mr. Franklin continued. "An account for your expenses has been established."

Amanda paused while sipping the water, not certain that she'd heard him right. "Expenses?"

"You may choose to travel to interview candidates."

"But I have to work and . . . and I have no vacation time."

"The firm has agreed to grant you a leave of absence," Mr. Franklin said.

Panic grabbed Amanda's throat. No, not again! She had no savings account to fall back on this time. Taking time off for this project would throw her into bankruptcy—right when she was about to inch back into the black with her creditors. "No. I need this job. I have bills to pay."

"This will be a *paid* LOA, and the job will be waiting for you," Roberta clarified, "if and when you return."

"If?"

Ben nudged her with his shoulder. "You may not want to come back if you're a millionaire."

Did Ben know how inappropriate his actions and comments were? All this unprofessional behavior in front of his boss, no less.

Why did Amanda care what Ben did with his career?

A million dollars?

So many thoughts skittered through her mind it was difficult to focus. Questions—she must have some pertinent questions.

"This is an overwhelming responsibility," Amanda said.

"Yes, it is." Mr. Franklin's voice sounded stern, fatherly.

Clasping her hands together on the table in front of her, Amanda held tight to stop them from shaking. "I need help. There must be thousands of letters."

Mr. Franklin scoffed. "Millions."

Of course there were millions. Already Amanda couldn't think straight. How would she ever make a sound decision?

"According to the contract, you are allowed assistance," Mr. Franklin said. "A partner from the firm could accompany you on your trips: in fact, we encourage travel in tandem. It draws less attention if you can say you're traveling on business, or what have you."

"Attention?" Amanda asked.

Ben grasped her wrist tightly. "Amanda, it's not a good idea to tell people you've been designated as the decision maker for the benefactor. The media would trounce on you. It was announced last night on television that your position exists. Reporters from all over will be looking for you."

Amanda gazed suspiciously at Ben. What was his part in this scheme? Was he excited for her or cautious from a legal standpoint?

Wait. The media.

Bud Fisher's words popped into her mind. "*The show "'Win a Fortune"—it's sensationalism at best. It's not news.*"

"Oh, of course. The media are malaria-infected mosquitoes." Amanda echoed the opinion she'd heard Bud say a million times. And he should know. He'd been one of them.

Mr. Franklin's brows crowded together. "Well, I wouldn't condemn the reporters. They've done some culling out of the candidates for you already, if you choose to review their files."

"I can do that?"

Leaning back in his chair, Mr. Franklin appeared relaxed for the first time since the meeting began, yet still managed to look like a mannequin at Neiman Marcus. "We can make that happen."

"Anonymously?" asked Amanda.

Roberta scowled. Amanda immediately felt somewhat guilty for questioning her boss' colleague.

Mr. Franklin didn't seem to notice the slight. He continued, "That's where an associate from the firm can help. He or she can be the go-between—your liaison with the newspapers, magazines, "Win a Fortune," what have you."

Why couldn't he say 'whatever', like everyone else?

Amanda pointed to Roberta and Ben. "But what about their work?"

"The firm is being compensated for our time," Roberta explained.

Of course she'd have insisted on that.

This couldn't be happening to her. Why her, anyway?

"Mr. Franklin, do you know who the lottery winner is?"

"No. I've met only an attorney who outlined the terms of the agreement. I suspect there are several layers insulating the winner."

"How will I ever decide who should get the money?"

"The method you use is entirely up to you. You can put the letters, unopened, on a cork board and throw a dart if you'd like. Just remember, the final decision is really up to the lottery winner. If he or she agrees with your choices, you will be awarded one million dollars."

Amanda's heart clattered in her chest, making her breathing shallow. She swallowed another sip of water. Still, her throat felt sandpaper dry. "What if the winner doesn't agree with my decision?"

"He or she will do something else with the money, and you won't get the finder's fee."

Looking down at her hands, Amanda rocked her head side to side. Would her neck muscles ever loosen up again?

"What if I don't want to do this?"

Mr. Franklin gathered up the contract and bounced the edge of the papers on the table to straighten them. "It's strictly your decision. But a million dollars is quite a lot of money for a month's work, wouldn't you agree, Ms. Cash?"

Amanda drew in a long breath. The next entry in her *Clara* notebook could read 'million-dollar-finder's fee.' Her mother could get a new heart in a few weeks if Amanda could complete the assignment and please the lottery winner. Given her recent tendency toward failure, that was an enormous *if.*

"How did I get chosen for this horrible assignment?"

"Horrible?" Roberta echoed. "Amanda, it's an *amazing* opportunity."

Amanda whipped her head toward Roberta. "For you. You can make multi-million-dollar decisions at the drop of a hat. *I* lose businesses and other people's money."

Roberta noticeably recoiled. Amanda cringed. Had she really just shouted at her boss?

Mr. Franklin cleared his throat. "You ask how it is that you were chosen?" He reached into his leather briefcase. "You wrote a letter requesting money for an operation for your sick mother."

Boy, it sounded so unoriginal when said aloud.

"Yes, she needs a heart transplant."

"I wasn't part of the selection process, but I suspect your letter was chosen at random. I was told the benefactor read your plea and for whatever reason, it impressed the winner and you were selected."

It was like that reporter had said. The luck of the draw. Her letter had been chosen from all the millions written.

Dumb luck.

She'd wanted a million dollars for her mother's transplant and now she had an opportunity to earn that amount in only four weeks' time.

A million dollars.

A million dollars to decide how to divvy up two-hundred-million dollars.

Could she do it? To the benefactor's satisfaction?

A thought flitted through Amanda's mind, skidded to a stop, and lodged itself on a fulcrum balanced between inspiration and effrontery.

"Mr. Franklin?" she said.

"Yes?"

"If I want, may I keep all two-hundred-million dollars?"

He paused, and then blew out a breath. Shaking his head, he pursed his lips like a disappointed father. "Yes, if you can make a case that you are worthy enough, you may ask to keep the entire fortune. But remember—you have only four weeks to make your decision."

Chapter Six

"Tell me I'm doing the right thing." Clara looked at her brother, his brown eyes glistening.

Ernie Hamilton wasn't the sentimental type, so Clara surmised the tearing up was due to spring allergies exacerbated by the blooming weigela in the courtyard. He shifted his chair to face the sun. To Ernie, sun block and market umbrellas were nuisances.

The hotshot Chicago attorney shucked his three-piece suits for visits with his younger sister, opting instead for what was commonly called business casual. Today that meant an Irish-green knit shirt and cheesy plaid pants. His golf shoes had to be in the trunk of his rental car next to his standard checked luggage—his custom clubs.

When he patted Clara's hand, she noted his manicure. Honest to God, the man paid someone else to trim his cuticles. People with money sure knew how to spend it on the silliest things.

He gathered the papers she'd signed and leafed through them, checking for omissions.

"You're doing the right thing, Clara."

"You'd say that even if I was about to bungee jump off the top of the Empire State Building."

Shaking his bald head, his eyes twinkled behind his glasses, the lenses magically darkened in the strong sunlight. "That's illegal."

She grimaced.

"Really, a guy was arrested for attempting to parachute off the observation deck."

Her grimace turned into a scowl.

"Clara, everyone needs a will."

"Lawyers. They're all so damned literal."

Ernie tucked the legal documents into a manila folder lying on the pebbled glass table. "You're doing what you have to do to protect your daughter."

Her weak knees trembled, shaking the footrest of her wheelchair. Amanda had tried to get her to buy one of those motorized jobs like Bud Fisher had, but Clara couldn't see wasting her funds. She'd be gone too soon to get her money's worth from such a purchase. Still, it frustrated her to depend on the nurses for every little thing–a drink of water, help to the bathroom, transportation to the dining room. Hell, if she wanted a sniff of the coral rosebud on the neatly trimmed bush by her window, she'd have to ask someone to pick it for her.

The loss of her independence drove her crazy.

It was easier to ask for help from her brother, but that didn't do much to ease her anger over her body's flagrant mutiny. Now she was having trouble breathing and desperately wanted to lie down, but not before everything was in order. She never knew when she might pass in her sleep.

"There'd better not be any loopholes. Amanda doesn't need to be bothered with that kind of trouble."

She wasn't accustomed to bossing her older brother, but had slipped into that pattern the past few weeks. He'd taken all her grumpiness. But then, what else could he do? They were the only two left from their original family. Despite his orneriness and occasional condescension, she loved Ernie dearly.

"There aren't any loopholes. I've had all my top people look at the paperwork."

"Costing me more money."

His dirty look put a chink in her crustiness, connected with her remorse.

She set a quivering hand on his arm. "Sorry, Ernie. I do appreciate all the time you've put in to help me out. I just get so scared sometimes."

"Of dying?"

She paused for a moment to consider the five ducklings waddling behind their mother toward the gurgling fountain, the centerpiece of the courtyard. They wobbled through the Japanese lilac bushes, bridal wreath spirea, and the last gasps of some sunny daffodils. She hoped to live long enough to see the stargazer lilies bloom this summer.

"I'm not afraid of dying exactly. But I worry. My work with Amanda isn't done yet."

Ernie jerked back his head. "She's thirty-seven. What's left to do?"

"She's naïve. Very trusting of all people. Gullible almost. I didn't teach her any street smarts."

He laughed. "This is Omaha, Clara, not Hell's Kitchen."

She gave him a small slap, mostly hitting air. "She hasn't moved on from her dead marriage. Hasn't picked herself up from her business fiasco, which was all my fault."

"Not true. Amanda chose to take care of you by herself. She could have considered your wishes much sooner and found you a nursing home."

She arched her eyebrows with indignation. "You want me to penalize her for being a good daughter?"

"I'm not saying she didn't do what she thought was necessary. I'm simply saying you can't accept responsibility for the choices she's made."

Clara huffed. "Is the lecture done, Dr. Phil?"

"You always were overprotective."

Lips pursed firmly, her gaze wandered back to the ducklings that now splashed playfully in the churning water of the fountain. Their mother, nearby, preened her feathers.

"Besides . . ."—he tapped the folder—"this will go a long way to healing those financial wounds."

Wistfully, she wished Ernie also had divorce papers for Amanda, but no, the time wasn't yet right. Forcing out a breath stubbornly stuck in her lungs, Clara whimpered. "But will she ever find love?"

He slipped the folder into his soft-sided briefcase, releasing the fragrance of leather. "Many people don't, Clara. You were blessed with Jim, and I with Denise. But lots of folks aren't so lucky."

She pointed to the Coach emblem on the side of the case. "That might intimidate some of them."

He tilted his head and hummed concurrence. "Possibly."

The mother duck's beak raised in alert as one of her babies climbed on the back of another, making the distressed one peep frantically.

Clara jerked upright and muttered at the birds to help the youngster, disregarding the futility of her efforts.

The mother duck slowly shuffled to the pair and gently nudged the upper-duckling off the other. A fluttering of wings followed as the 'bully' gained his balance.

Regaining her breath, Clara shook her head, hating the way her life had become so manipulated. Meals, tablemates, even her entertainment wasn't her own choice.

"Maybe I should be more concerned that my entire estate will end up going to doctors or this *damned* nursing home."

Ernie tapped his briefcase. "Brookside and the hospital have copies of your Health Directives, Clara. They won't keep you alive by artificial means."

Damn literal attorneys.

"They better not," Clara grumbled.

She grabbed her brother's hand and squeezed it. "I just wish I could watch over her a little longer, Ernie. But I can't even walk ten feet without getting winded. Damn heart. Damn lungs."

"You're doing an awful lot of cursing today."

"I'm entitled. *I'm old.*"

"Not even sixty-eight yet. Why, when I was your age I played all six courses in three days at St. Andrews Links in Scotland."

She rolled her eyes. "And you walked, carrying your own clubs."

Clara could see in his eyes that he regretted his haughtiness the minute the words left his mouth. Only two years her senior, Ernie's body was at least a decade younger than hers. Or was her body a decade *older* than his?

"When the time comes, Clara, Amanda will be covered."

"She better be. I'm not paying astronomical fees to leave her out there dangling as bait for some unscrupulous, greedy SOB."

He threw up his hands, exasperated. "It's covered, Clara, trust me. I'm watching out for her."

Her panting accelerated and she gripped the arms of her wheelchair. "You better be . . . or . . . or . . ."

Ernie crossed his arms over his tiny paunch. "Or what?"

"Or I'll come back and haunt you."

The corners of his mouth drew down, his squint affirming his skepticism.

"Every time you're on the tee," she hissed, "driver in hand, pin targeted, head down, backswing flowing, I'll be there." She gulped in a breath. "Bumping your elbow, shouting in your ear. Cursing the day you were born."

"You weren't there the day I was born."

"Doesn't matter. You'll never shoot below your handicap. Never. So don't screw me over."

Silent glares clashed.

"Damn little sisters."

Chapter Seven

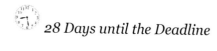 *28 Days until the Deadline*

Amanda intended to honor her date with Bud Fisher, but wondered if they wouldn't be safer driving his go-buggy to the concert. Since this morning's news that she'd been chosen to select the recipients of the two-hundred-million-dollar jackpot, she'd not been able to think clearly.

Thank goodness Roberta had the good sense to send Amanda home immediately after the meeting with Mr. Franklin. Unfortunately, she'd accomplished little all day except to set her recorder to capture tonight's episode of "Win a Fortune." At least she'd be able to see who the network thought deserved the money.

Ben seemed to recognize how shaken Amanda was and had offered to drive her home from the office. He'd even volunteered to help her plan the search, but Amanda had declined. He'd been a little too eager to help. He hadn't mentioned a commission for his time—certainly wasn't allowed to ethically—but that wouldn't stop him from expecting a gratuity if he performed his duties well in the next month. All in all, Amanda did not trust Ben Harris.

He was, however, correct about one thing; the media would pounce on her like a dog after a squirrel if they found out about her. She mainly regretted not being able to share the news or her dilemma with her most prized confidante—her mother.

A mindless evening listening to music with an old man was exactly what Amanda needed.

She opened the nursing home's front door, admiring, as always, the lead crystal window. Strolling through the lobby, she hesitated a moment at the marble-topped sideboard, considering a complimentary glass of lemonade, but the heavy fragrance of a nearby bouquet distracted her. The peach-colored lilies enhanced a matching hue in the paisley wallpaper behind the piano. An attached card advertised a local florist—a shameless marketing ploy, in her opinion. The Andrews Sisters' tune flowing from the piano must have been a comfort to some people, but Amanda thought the motion of the abandoned keys eerie, and a shiver crawled up her back. Arthritic hands aside, she much preferred seeing a resident playing the beautiful baby grand.

Rounding the corner to Bud Fisher's hallway, still distracted by the flowers, music, and events of the day, Amanda smacked into the bumper of his go-buggy.

"Whoa, girl," Bud laughed. "I know you're hot to go out with me, but you don't have to run me over."

Rubbing the area of her shin that had connected with the wheelchair, Amanda assessed her escort. "Better hurry and get dressed for the symphony, Bud. We don't want to miss the overture."

"Can't go. I'm on medical restriction." Bud pointed to his head. From under the bill of his Broncos hat peeked a gauze bandage. "I hit a ramp going thirty today and flipped the buggy."

"Oh, my God." Amanda pulled back his hat to examine the injury. On his forehead, a purple bruise brightened the knot that surrounded the edges of the dressing.

Bud tugged the cap back over his forehead, wincing when it scraped the wound. "Just bumped my noggin. No big deal."

Apparently Bud was the typical man—bearing his pain well in front of strangers. And he was the typical senior—bruising excessively—or maybe it was more noticeable through the thinning skin of the octogenarian. Either way, Amanda suspected the injury wasn't as bad as it looked.

Amanda was relieved for more than one reason. Bud seemed to be fine and now she could go home, don her pajamas and crawl into bed where she'd watch "Win a Fortune" and begin her search for worthy recipients. "I'm glad it's nothing serious."

Indignation flashed in Bud's eyes. "Not serious. Of *course* it's serious. We had a date and I couldn't sleep last night for thinking about it."

Amanda rubbed his shoulder and patted his back. "I was looking forward to it, too. There will be other concerts."

The promise eased Bud's pursed lips, shrunk thin by years.

His mood lifted and eyes lightened. "Hey, I found a stand-in date for you. Follow me." He swiveled the wheelchair around, one-hundred-eighty degrees in place, and zipped down the corridor.

It seemed to Amanda the nursing home would want to protect its residents and staff by finding a way to ratchet down the power of that chair. Bud must have been a hellion on the roads.

Quickening her steps, Amanda tried to keep up with the aged daredevil. Bud whooshed around the corner into his room and whizzed over the threshold.

"Damn it, Gramps," yelped someone from inside the room. "Watch out. Do you want to kill me?"

The voice was deep, its bass timbre resonating to Amanda's core in an oddly arousing way.

"Well, you were in my way," Bud shouted.

"Don't move. You'll get cut. I'll get a towel to clean up the mess." The pitch of the low voice held firmness tempered with kindness, annoyance mixed with concern. Amanda knew the melody well as she'd sung the same tune when she'd cared for her mother before Clara was admitted to Brookside.

Amanda entered the room as a tall man disappeared into the bathroom and closed the door. A puddle of water pooled on the floor in front of Bud's wheelchair. Shards of thin, lavender-colored glass mixed with the stems of sunny daffodils and white tulips edged in crimson.

Bud turned to Amanda and shrugged. "There's no brake on this thing. Stay here. I'll be right back."

Stretching forward, Bud twisted the handle of the bathroom door. Gently he nudged his wheelchair into the lavatory. There wasn't enough room to close the door behind him.

"Hurry up. She's here," Bud whispered as quietly as a hard-of-hearing man dared.

"*Who's* here?"

Amanda glimpsed the stranger in the vanity mirror. His hair was dark. She couldn't see his face because he was bent over using a towel to pat the front of his pants.

"Amanda Cash. The girl I told you about. The one I was supposed to go to the concert with. *Your date.*"

"Gramps, I told you I'm not interested in taking out one of your nurses."

"She's not a nurse. She's the daughter of one of the residents."

"Even worse."

Amanda felt the heat of embarrassment rise in her cheeks. This was a conversation she wasn't meant to hear—didn't want to hear.

"You'll like her, Ryan. She's very nice."

"Right. And she has a great personality." He didn't hide the sarcasm.

Amanda looked down at her khaki cotton slacks and pink sweater, dismay knotting her stomach. She could look alluring when she wanted, but tonight she'd dressed for an eighty-something man, not the tall hunk she saw turn toward the mirror. The shoulders were broad and as he bent sideways to reach another towel on the far rack, Amanda admired the way his slacks stretched over his long legs and compact butt. A familiar, but unexpected, tingle punched through her.

"Listen, I don't have time. I have work to do this evening. I lost the whole day in the emergency room with you."

Well, maybe she didn't want to go out with him either. Still, there was something in his voice. If he was as sexy as that voice . . . She didn't know what to do. She turned, glancing around Bud's room. Should she leave?

She grabbed the trash can. Squatting, she gingerly picked up the broken glass and laid it on top of a wad of bloody tissues. Bud's head wound must have been an awful mess.

"I promised I'd go to the symphony with her. It wouldn't be right to send her alone." Distress raised the pitch of Bud's voice.

This was the kind of stress that often threw Bud into confusion and increased his head tremors. She didn't want Bud getting upset about the situation or working so hard to get her a date. As badly as she wanted to run, she couldn't simply disappear, confusing Bud even more.

Plucking tissues from the box, she wiped the puddle off the floor, dropping the soggy lump into the can. It hit with a thump.

"I have to catch the red-eye back to Denver tomorrow, Gramps. Another time, maybe."

Good. She'd get to watch "Win a Fortune" after all. That was what she wanted, right?

"Now back up so I can get out of this bathroom." Impatience tinged his words.

The wheelchair inched backwards, jerkily starting and stopping. Amanda scooped up the flowers from the floor and hopped back to give Bud a wide thoroughfare. The stems were wet and she flicked one hand then another to dry her fingers. Surely the young man would at least take the time to shake her hand. She resisted the urge to wipe her palm on her drab pants, wishing she'd have worn a skirt instead. Your legs are one of your best features, Erik had told her. He'd always liked her legs—as much as a gay man could appreciate them.

The man appeared in the doorway, eyes still focused on his damp pants. Both the white shirt under his navy jacket and his gray slacks were soaked in the front. He dropped a towel, and without looking up, stepped on it to mop the floor.

"Please excuse Ryan's manners. He's really a good boy, even though Sybil spoils him rotten."

Ryan looked up.

Eyes the color of chestnuts hooked her attention with a jolt. His skin was surprisingly bronzed for so early in May. A wisp of black hair crowded his eyebrow and a quick smile broke the solemnity of his face.

"Hi, I'm Amanda Cash. Bud's friend." Amanda held out her hand. In her other hand she gripped the flowers in a fist.

Ryan's eyes crinkled beguilingly when he smiled. He had the poise of a model, straight, even teeth so dazzling they had to be the result of daily brightening strips. He reached for her hand, not even flinching when her wet palm found his dry one.

"I see you got my flowers," he said.

"What?"

"Bud asked me to pick up some flowers for his date. Since I'll be going in his place, I guess they're really from me."

"Oh, you don't have to take me." Amanda pointed beyond Ryan to the bathroom as though pinpointing the exact spot where he'd rejected her. "I understand you have an early flight and lots of work to do."

"My grandfather can be very persuasive. I'm Ryan Fisher."

He had yet to let go of her hand, or her gaze. When he clasped his other hand over their entwined fingers, Amanda hoped she wouldn't melt and add to the puddle already wetting the floor.

"Don't believe a word he tells you." Bud twisted in his chair with agitation. "Sybil caters to his every whim and has spoiled him."

"May I put those in some water for you?" Ryan reached for the bouquet, laying his fingers lightly on the back of her hand. Her stomach jumped at his touch, sending tiny explosive charges through her abdomen.

Did he feel it, too?

When she handed the flowers to him, she noticed the wet spot on her sweater. Great, now she looked dumpy, mussed *and* damp.

Ryan chuckled, motioning to his own clothes. "We match. I'll ask an aide for something to put these in."

Fragrances of floral and citrus followed in his wake and he lightly touched her arm as he passed—a gesture as natural as though they'd known each other for eternity.

She watched him walk down the hall, confidence apparent in every long stride. When she turned to Bud she was startled to see him looking fatigued.

"Are you okay?" She squatted next to him, rubbing his arm.

"When is dinner going to be ready?" Bud's gaze darted around the room before landing square on Amanda. "Is Sybil making pot roast? Tell her I want mashed potatoes and gravy."

Sympathy coated Amanda's hushed tone. "Bud, your wife passed away a few years ago. I'm Amanda, your friend. Ryan, your grandson, will be back in a moment. Does your head hurt?" She gently raised his ball cap and smoothed down hair over the bandage on his forehead. A shudder ran through him and then his tremors abated. "Would you like me to call for a nurse?"

He squinted in thought. Was he struggling to remember the past or to find his place in the present? He opened his mouth to say something only to close it abruptly. He leaned back into his chair and sighed in complete resignation. "I've lost my mind."

Amanda reached for the call button to summon the nurse.

"Tomorrow I'll borrow a book from my mom and come read to you." Amanda spun and pointed through the door and across the hall. "Clara, my mom, lives over there. How does Dickens sound?"

Light glimmered in Bud's eyes. "No one could write like Dickens. Then or now." His brows snapped together. "Whatever you do, don't ask Ryan about his job. It's top secret. He won't tell you anyway. I'm trying to convince him to move here to take care of my investments. I've come into quite a bit of money."

She tipped her head, not sure how to respond, but he didn't give her a chance.

"My favorite Dickens' story is the one with Pip. Do you have that one?"

Ryan entered the room carrying the flowers arranged in a clear, glass vase. A wide, pink ribbon adorned the vase's neck, its tails flowing in satiny curls.

Amanda stood to accept the bouquet, her smile mirroring his. "Yes, I have *Great Expectations*."

Ryan cocked his brow at her. "Me, too."

Chapter Eight

Slinking into a booth, Amanda tried to disappear into the leather cushion. She'd suggested a dozen other restaurants for a late supper after the symphony, but Ryan had insisted on Truffaut's.

Ordinarily she would have been eager to take a visitor to Omaha's newest restaurant in the Old Market. Its brick walls, creaky maple floors, and unfinished ceiling held the antique charm tourists liked. Amanda suspected Ryan's taste leaned toward a sophisticated wine accompanying an elegant meal drenched in candlelight. All that could be found at Truffaut's—Erik's restaurant.

She'd seen Major Shane McClain at the bar when she'd walked in, but fortunately, he hadn't seen her. Now if they could get a waitress who didn't know her, Amanda might be able to escape social disaster. What had she been thinking when she'd slipped her wedding ring into her purse at Brookside?

"I'm really not that hungry. Maybe we could take a walk instead." Amanda pointed toward the door, already poised to exit.

"Plenty of time for that afterwards. I'm starving. Listening to good music with a gorgeous woman always does that to me." Ryan scanned her face, his gaze lingering on her lips, before returning to the menu.

Amanda couldn't remember the last time she'd felt like a gorgeous *anything*. It had been fun pretending to be on a date, even if their discussions at the symphony had mostly been small talk. But pretending was all it was—all she dared to let it be. She was married and considering having a baby—albeit a baby through artificial insemination for her gay husband and his partner. That situation alone should disqualify her from thinking about a new relationship or anything beyond getting safely out of the restaurant before Erik saw her.

She peeked over her shoulder to locate Shane. He rolled a straw between his fingers as he chatted with the bartender, Doug. It was lucky Doug was mixing drinks tonight. He was known for talking the ears off the regulars—and the major was a regular customer when Erik was in the kitchen, which is where Amanda hoped he'd stay.

"What a variety." Ryan fanned the corner of the menu pages with his thumb. "Well, if you're not too hungry maybe we should only have dessert. Say Bananas Foster?"

Too risky. That was prepared tableside and if Eric wasn't busy enough, he'd likely be tempted to make it himself.

"Too sweet. I'm trying to choose healthier foods. Besides the last time I had that here, the bananas were bruised." She wrinkled up her nose.

"How about splitting a Caesar salad then?"

That could be prepared at the table as well.

"Oh, no, I hear they make an awful Caesar. In fact, a lawyer at the firm had one last week and had to have her stomach pumped. Must have been salmonella in the raw eggs."

"No," Ryan gasped with a shake of his head.

The man at the booth next to them whipped his head around, chin tipped up to anchor his reading glasses on the end of his nose and stared at her. He looked similar to someone at the office, but it wasn't him.

Amanda raised her hand and said firmly, "I swear."

Their neighbor's lips twisted into a frown before he swiveled back to his companion and whispered into her ear.

Whoever he was, it served him right for eavesdropping.

"Well," Ryan asked, "what do you recommend then?"

"Going someplace else, where the food's not so dicey."

A smile tugged at the corner of Ryan's mouth.

Maybe she was being too dramatic to be convincing.

The server approached their table, and Amanda realized she'd caught another break. The petite, freckle-faced redhead was new and probably had no idea of the connection between Amanda and Erik.

"Hi, I'm Kristin. Welcome to Truffaut's. Is it your first time in?"

"Yes." Ryan tapped the wine list. "You have an excellent cellar."

"We do. I can suggest many fine vineyards based on your menu selection."

"And what do you recommend for an entrée?"

Entrée? This supper was going to last *forever*. Anxiety clenched at her stomach as she glimpsed again at the bar. Shane gnawed at the end of the straw now, still listening to Doug. So far, her luck was holding.

"Tonight the chef is making seafood-stuffed filet mignon. It's prepared tableside with a Béarnaise sauce. All the customers are raving about it."

"I had that for lunch," Amanda blurt out.

Ryan looked at her askance. "Really?"

She set a palm on her stomach, brow furrowed. "Too heavy."

"Our chef would be happy to make you a fresh salmon salad with asparagus vinaigrette. That's also prepared tableside."

"What, he can't find the kitchen?" Amanda huffed. "Just bring me some green tea."

"You win." Ryan snapped the menu shut, his comment ringing with annoyance. "I'll have an espresso and the tiramisu. Two forks . . ."—he tipped his head at Amanda—"if you wouldn't object to *one* bite."

Amanda raised her eyebrows. "Yum."

"Espresso, tiramisu, and green tea. Very well." Kristin picked up the menus, covertly slipping Amanda a dirty look to show displeasure over the tip she wouldn't be receiving.

One more glance at the bar told Amanda that Shane and Doug were still caught up in conversation. If she could gulp the tea she might avoid being discovered.

Ryan looked in the same direction of Amanda's gaze. "See someone you know?" His voice held a hint of irritation.

Jerking her head around, she looked Ryan in the eye. He had a remarkably handsome face with lips so full she had to grip the edge of the table to stop herself from touching them. "No one."

She thrummed the table with her fingers searching for a topic to change Ryan's focus from Shane and *her* focus from Ryan's incredibly luscious mouth. "You're very good with your grandfather. Bud's a special man."

"He used to be. I don't mean that like it sounds, but he seems to be slipping away more each time I see him."

"Are you actually considering moving to Omaha?"

"He'd like that. I'm the only family close to him. He and my grandmother practically raised me. I'd like to do more for Bud, but my job's in Denver."

Disappointment twanged at Amanda's heart. Calm down, she ordered herself. It wasn't like her to read more into a man's actions than he'd meant, yet hadn't she been doing just that all night— imagining life with someone she'd just met? She hadn't realized how lonely she was until Ryan placed his hand on the small of her back when he'd opened the door and followed her into Truffaut's. That simple act of intimacy had her dreaming about all kinds of possibilities.

She *had* to stop fantasizing about Ryan Fisher. "What do you do?" Too late, A flashback of Bud's warning about such a question flew through Amanda's mind and pricked some concern.

"A little of this, a little of that." He snapped open the linen napkin and placed it in his lap.

Bud had said Ryan wouldn't tell her about his occupation. What could it be? All evening she had imagined many careers including government spy and Mafioso.

"Your grandfather said your job is top secret, but sometimes I don't know when he's kidding or . . ."

". . . or if it's the dementia?"

The sadness that swept over her mirrored the sorrow on his face. At least her mother still had all her mental faculties. Amanda didn't know what she'd do if one day Clara failed to recognize her. Bud's memory loss must be very difficult for Ryan, who still hadn't answered the question about his job.

She decided to let it pass. What difference did it make what he did for a living? After tonight, she'd probably never see Ryan Fisher again.

"Gramps says you're a basket weaver."

"You must have an incredible memory for details."

"When I'm motivated."

She hadn't been anyone's motivation in a long while. The prospect sparked a remotely familiar pleasure.

"No, not a weaver. I used to have a business making gift baskets."

"Used to have?"

The thought of her failure threatened her confidence. "I . . . lost . . . it. I chose to close the business when my mother got so sick. I work in a law office now."

Amanda mentally flinched at the statement. It wasn't entirely true. Technically, she was on a leave-of-absence. If he were IRS or FBI, could he catch her in a lie? And what would he do if he did?

Amanda shook her head to dislodge the ridiculous career scenarios playing out in her mind. She looked into Ryan's eyes and wished, for a moment, he would reach for her hand. Would she let Ryan kiss her good night? What if he asked to see her again? It was a long-shot, but plausible, when he visited Bud. For one crazy moment she caught herself wondering if this evening could blossom into a real relationship–with potential.

"I like you, Amanda. I've enjoyed our evening."

"I have, too." Her cheeks felt hot and she worried she was blushing. How precious would that be?

He edged closer to her in the booth and grasped her hand. "Now that I know you somewhat, next time I'll bring you something different."

"Huh?"

"The daffodils and tulips were nice." His thumb smoothed the back of her hand.

The warmth felt comforting and familiar. Given a moment, those feelings could easily escalate. Amanda didn't know how far she should push her luck. "Oh yes, they were. Thank you again for bringing them."

"Nice, but too common for someone as special as you are."

Now she knew she was blushing. There had been no one in her life since . . . since ever. It had always been Erik. Throughout high school. Throughout college. Only Erik.

Amanda didn't know what to say, so she simply smiled. Her upper lip quivered as it always did when she was nervous and tried too hard.

"Next time I'll get you anthuriums," he said.

She tilted her head. "What are those?"

"Heart-shaped, tropical flowers."

Now he was really flirting. Is this what dating would be like? It seemed he had Bud's romantic charm.

He reached for her other hand, angling his shoulders until he faced her. "Pink anthuriums. They would suit you perfectly because they are beautiful and a bit sassy."

"Sassy?"

"The flower looks like its sticking out its tongue. By the way you ordered dinner, I see you're a woman who knows what she wants and doesn't mind doing exactly what it takes to get it. I like your confidence."

He leaned over and gently dropped a kiss on her neck, lingering until his hot breath dissolved years of her self-imposed abstinence. Amanda searched her memory. God, she'd loved love.

She had no idea how to react. Dating was as foreign to her as all the places Bud had mentioned to woo her. It'd been an eternity since she'd been out with any man but Erik–Erik or Shane.

"Hey, Amanda Bear. I didn't see you come in."

The major's voice jerked Amanda from her fantasy of rolling on a sandy towel with Ryan in the Grand Caymans. She spun around, the back of her head bonking Ryan's chin, and stared into Shane's clenched face.

"Major Pain."

Heart skittering, she fumbled to create some distance from Ryan. It was foolish to get so caught up in the moment she hadn't kept track of Shane. Alone–where was Erik?–beer in hand, he had the menacing look of a jealous lover.

What was with his attitude?

His blue eyes flashed harsh, military intensity as his gaze bounced between her and Ryan. "So, Amanda, have you been thinking over the proposal?"

Chapter Nine

Tapping the message into his PDA, Ryan notified his secretary he'd be out of the office for a couple of days. Then he scrolled through his list of contacts. His resources in Omaha, Nebraska were extensive, but did he know someone who could get him through the gate at Offutt Air Force Base?

He'd bought none of Amanda's explanations. Major Shane McClain wasn't merely a friend of the family, or Ryan wasn't the best investigative reporter *The Denver Register* had ever employed. She'd hustled them both out of Truffaut's much too quickly for him to accept that the major was simply someone who had proposed a business alliance with her.

Then there was her jitteriness at the restaurant. She kept rubbing the third finger of her left hand as though there were supposed to be something there–something familiar–like an engagement ring.

It was more than curiosity that had Ryan delaying his flight back to Colorado. It was instinct. When a person took pains to conceal something, it typically led to a story.

Whether or not Amanda Cash was engaged held no critical relevance or media importance, but why she'd lied all evening might lead in an interesting direction. Besides, he was between assignments anyway. In a few hours he'd find out who Shane was and how he was connected to Amanda. The story might not have Pulitzer-potential, but his gut told him it would be worth his time.

* * * *

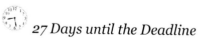 *27 Days until the Deadline*

Sitting in the lobby of the *Omaha World-Herald*, Amanda was a little disappointed. The newspaper operation was modern, and she hadn't expected frazzled reporters smoking cigars, but the lobby could have been in any number of corporate headquarters. The two-story entry was vast. Three men in suits manned the crescent-shaped security desk. Off to one side of its polished granite counter a bank of desks housed half a dozen receptionists.

She gazed at a tower display similar to those in airport terminals that announce arrivals, but in this case oversized monitors flashed full-color pages of the morning's edition, one page dissolving into the next. A different section of the paper scrolled on each of the four sides of the pillar.

Across the lobby, Ben Harris shook hands with the man who would be their guide. Amanda wondered what lies the attorney told to gain access to the letters written by people desperately wanting to be awarded part of the jackpot. Until yesterday, she'd been one of those, hoping for a million dollars to fund her mother's operation.

Clara was right. She'd always said things could change in a heartbeat. They certainly had in Amanda's case. In one month, her financial circumstances had the potential to catapult via the one-million-dollar finder's fee.

Then there were her social prospects which could also improve via a certain mystery man from Denver. She touched her lips which still buzzed from the good-night kiss she'd shared with Ryan. He said he'd be in touch, and she hoped that meant more than a phone call.

Half-skipping, Ben crossed the tumbled-stone floor and slid into a chair next to Amanda. His aftershave wafted in behind him. She'd never seen him in business casual dress. The polo shirt draped nicely on his broad shoulders, the royal blue color a complement to his green eyes which flickered like a child's at Christmas. "Okay, we're in." He jumped out of the seat like it was on fire.

Sucking in a breath, Amanda stood, hands outstretched to steady herself. "I don't even want to know the stories you had to tell to get us into the mail room."

Ben drew his head back and his mouth turned down into a frown. "Duplicity isn't always necessary to gain what you want, Ms. Cash."

"Oh?"

"But in this case . . ." He grinned slyly and leaned close to her ear. "We're reporters from *The Hoosier Gazette*. Roberta has a contact in Indiana to back us up. Let's go."

The whisper tickled Amanda. A shiver followed, skittering through her and ending above her lip. She rubbed her index finger back and forth under her nose.

Clara's adage rang in her head. *Itchy nose–you're going to kiss a fool.*

Ben set his hand in the middle of her back to steer her along. Amanda flinched, pulling away to create space between them. Did he never observe common social boundaries? It was one thing to crowd her in the galley kitchen at work, but the lobby was one-quarter the size of a football field.

The attorney seemed not to notice her distancing. Instead he swung his arms exuberantly and whistled as they walked. She giggled at his musical selection, trying not to hum along to the "Mission Impossible" theme.

His duty as her assistant was probably the most excitement he'd ever had as a corporate attorney. His energy transferred to Amanda and she caught herself trailing a step behind him in the catacombs of the newspaper building.

Their escort, a slender man, who looked no older than Amanda's car, shoved through the metal door of a storeroom. He pointed to the center of the cavern where two mail bins sat on a six-foot long table. "There they are."

"Thanks. We really appreciate it." Ben shook the kid's hand engulfing the skinny fingers in pure muscle.

For a shorter man, Ben's bearing and actions made him seem massive, which suited Amanda. If the media discovered her role in the jackpot giveaway, she suspected he'd make a formidable bodyguard–one of several she might need.

Amanda set her purse on the table and peered into one box. Even accounting for the initial letters that had been shipped to the warehouse in Illinois, she was surprised.

"Wow, I thought there'd be a lot more."

"Oh, there were," the young man said. "The first two weeks we forwarded mountains of stuff to the network for "Win a Fortune.""

Ben crowded next to Amanda, peeking over her shoulder. Shifting to the opposite end of the table, she slid the bin between them, a subtle hint that she disliked his hovering.

"Then the network issued a moratorium on the letters and we began storing them." The kid settled his hips onto the table, forcing Amanda either to move closer to Ben or insult him by relocating to the other side of the table. She chose to inch nearer to the attorney.

Ben wasn't a bad guy. He didn't have disgusting breath and didn't spit when he talked. He was simply pushy. Yes, that was it. He was stout and intrusive and didn't understand the rules of personal space. She felt a little guilty at her intolerance of his social ineptness because in fact, when Ben wasn't encroaching, he could be quite pleasant. Still Amanda needed no distractions now. She had a deadline.

For the next excursion she would request Roberta or another attorney at the firm to help her. Today, she'd have to make the best of an irritating situation.

Amanda dug into the mail bin, pushing aside envelopes of various sizes and colors. To enhance their chances, some contestants had sprayed their letters with perfume. She caught a whiff of White Linen, and thought of Clara getting dressed for church. No one looked sweeter than her mother when she slipped on a felt hat with netting over the eyes. Wearing hats was a hold-over from the Jackie Kennedy era. Clara especially loved the pillbox style and wore them for years longer than they were fashionable. Her mother always said she didn't feel completely devout unless she covered her head in church.

"And these are all the letters you got in the last two weeks?" Ben asked, plucking Amanda's thoughts from a pew in the first row.

She blinked, staring at the young man as he hopped off the table. He was a full head taller than Ben and looked thin as a chopstick.

"No, that's what came in overnight." He swept his arm to encompass the room. "These are the letters for the last two weeks."

Deep bins on wheels lined one wall. With those full, white storage boxes stacked on top of each other mounted to the ceiling. Columns in front of columns added depth to the mass.

Ben's mouth dropped open as he spun to gaze at the four corners. "Chicken a la king."

Amanda smiled at the unusual curse. His respect was cute in an innocent sort of way, but she had no time to dwell on his good points.

"Did anyone try to organize the letters?" she asked.

"I tried at first. I'm an intern and we get all the shit jobs." His face didn't even redden at the word. He was already cynical. Just like Bud. He'd make a great newspaperman some day.

"I sorted the letters into categories by request."

It was a technique Amanda first thought useful when she saw "Win a Fortune."

"Categories?" Ben asked.

And he was going to be the one to help Amanda formulate a plan of action? She hoped he wouldn't slow her down. She had a huge job to do and a strict deadline. If he couldn't keep up, she'd have to do this on her own. Her wrist moved in a circular motion as she clarified, "Like social causes, community projects, health issues." Impatience tinged her explanation.

The recoil of Ben's stance told Amanda she'd hurt his feelings and she regretted her harsh tone almost as much as she was frustrated by her distraction over his presence. She didn't want to think of Ben as more than a colleague and now she was wasting energy worrying about his feelings.

"I broke them down even further," the young man said.

Focus Amanda. "How so?"

The kid pointed to a board on the wall. Neat columns crammed with rows of hash marks trailed down the white enamel. "Well, you have your personal medical letters—those people who want money for specific medical procedures—'my kid's blind and needs new corneas.' Then there's medical research, like a cure for cancer and funding for epidemics, like AIDS in third world countries. There are requests for money to build hospitals and clinics. Get the picture?"

"Wow, and *you* did all that sorting?" Ben asked.

"I did until my bosses pulled me off the project. There wasn't enough readership appeal in the letters. I don't think the editors got one interesting story out of my week of scouring the mail." He sighed, his disappointment echoing off the walls.

Is that how Amanda would decide—whose story grabbed her attention? She couldn't let it all hinge on drama or hype. There had to be a fairer way to decide who deserved the money.

"Did you have a short stack of letters for the editors to consider?" Amanda asked.

The kid nodded. "In my cube."

"I'd like to look at them, please," she said.

His eyes narrowed in suspicion. "I have to ask my boss."

"Why? You already said your editors weren't interested in the stories. *The Hoosier Gazette* isn't in competition with the *World-Herald*." Ben's voice boomed in the storeroom filling it with authority. No wonder he'd made partner by age thirty.

"Okay. I'll get the letters."

Amanda flashed her most ingratiating smile. "Thanks, I appreciate your help. You must be learning so much in your internship."

He rolled his eyes. "I learned only one thing on this project." The slender man folded his arms over his chest, his fingers nearly reaching his back.

"What's that?" Ben asked.

"There are a lot of pathetic people out there."

And she had been one of them.

* * * *

The morning had been a waste of time. After shuffling through piles of mail, Amanda was no closer to deciding who should get the jackpot. She needed a concrete plan of action and the dart board Mr. Franklin had mentioned was looking pretty darn good. At least she'd talked the intern out of the hefty stack of letters the editors were considering printing.

"I know a place that makes a great Reuben. Aren't you starving?" Ben's eyes sparkled as he held the door open for her to exit the lobby of the newspaper office.

As if on cue, Amanda's stomach growled. "I could eat."

"Terrific. It'll be our first date."

Before Amanda could snap her gaping mouth shut, Ben whisked off.

"I'll get the car and meet you at the curb," he called into the wind above his head as he bumped into a man five inches taller than he was.

Ryan Fisher skimmed past Ben, steadying the attorney with his large hands. A hint of annoyance pinched Ryan's eyes and Amanda wasn't sure if it was because of the collision or some other distraction. Intensity creased his handsome face and she wondered what had put it there. Watching him approach, she considered not disrupting his thoughts, but then she recalled their kiss last night. And he looked so appealing in his faded jeans, gold oxford shirt, and tan corduroy blazer. The breeze danced in his ebony curls spilling over his collar.

What could it hurt just to say hi?

She jerked the rubber band from her hair, fluffed it with her fingers, and with no second thought, transferred her wedding band to her right hand.

"Ryan Fisher. I thought you'd be back in the Rockies by now." Amanda tossed her head, flinging her long hair to cascade down her back.

He pulled up short, glimpsing over her head at the logo of the *Omaha World-Herald*. His eyes widened. "Amanda. What are you doing here?"

Standing in front of the private circle drive, she couldn't deny where she'd been, but no one, not even Ryan, could know of her mission today.

"I accompanied a colleague to a meeting." She gave him a wide smile, hoping her nervousness wouldn't trigger a quiver in her upper lip. "Can't tear yourself away from our city?"

He jammed his hands into his pockets and scanned her from head to toe. A slight upward curve of his mouth hinted he liked what he saw. Amanda's heartbeat picked up speed.

"I've been putting off some business I thought I'd take care of before I head back." Moving closer, he gaped at the bundle cradled in her arms.

The letters were wrapped in clear plastic making them easy to identify which would undoubtedly stir his natural curiosity. But maybe that trait was tied to his business—whatever *that* was.

Glancing up and down the block she wondered where he was headed. The non-stop traffic poured one-way down Douglas Street, in the hub of downtown Omaha. A below-street-level park was directly across from them, lofty office buildings surrounding them.

Regardless of what Ryan did for a living, Amanda liked the feelings she had when she was with him.

"How about lunch?" Where had that invitation come from?

He looked as surprised as she felt and stammered out, "Uh, I'd love to, but I have a meeting. It'll take no more than forty-five minutes, if you can wait."

"Should we say an hour then?" She swept a strand of hair that had blown into the corner of her mouth behind her shoulder.

Ryan's gaze followed her movement, and then clicked back to her eyes. The intensity in his face had been replaced with an easy smile.

He caught a tendril of her hair before it could blow into her eyes. Holding it loosely, he rubbed it between his fingers. "In an hour then, but you pick the place. Seems I do an awful job choosing restaurants in your city." He tucked the hair behind her back, letting his touch linger on the nape of her neck.

He was flirting with her. And it felt wonderful.

After she quickly gave directions to Mario's Cafe, Ryan spun around, dodging traffic as he jaywalked across Douglas Street, lost again in his intensity, which worked for Amanda since at that moment, Ben Harris pulled up in his red BMW.

Chapter Ten

Ben bounced out of his car and hustled to Amanda, yanking open the passenger door before she could stop him.

"Listen, Ben, I've changed my mind about lunch. I think I'll run to the library to read the letters and do more research."

"We could do that before we eat. I'll help." A playful pup couldn't have looked more excited.

"No. You've done enough for today." The wind whipped her loose hair into her eyes and she angled her head using the breeze to push it out of her line of sight. What had been sexy with Ryan was plain aggravating now.

"But our date . . ." Disappointment shrouded his voice.

The weight of the letters pulled Amanda's shoulders down. "You *know* we can't date." She purposely avoided eye contact. "I'm married." Shifting the parcel, she tried to shield her hands. Now would *not* be the time for Ben to notice that she'd switched her wedding ring location.

Ben glanced across the street at Ryan's back as he disappeared down the steps into the park. "Right," he said, his lips hardening into a thin line.

For the first time, the marital status excuse truly felt like a lie. She couldn't *wait* to leave this embarrassing situation.

He exaggerated a chuckle. "I knew it wasn't really a *date* in the true sense of the word. You're married and—"

"Well, good, that's cleared up. Um . . ." Amanda glanced in the direction of Mario's Café. She had much to do before her lunch with Ryan and none of it involved Ben Harris.

"How will you get home?" he asked.

"My husband's working at Truffaut's today. I'll catch a ride with him." Amanda had become too adept at lying, a skill that gave her no pride. One look at Ben's face, the hurt and dejection obvious, made guilt bubble in her stomach.

Ben eased the package from her arms and nodded toward the front seat. "Well, get in. At least I can drop you at the library."

* * * *

It was fortunate Ryan had bumped into Amanda *before* he'd walked into the newspaper offices to meet with his colleague. In his experience, when a person learned he was a reporter, all interesting conversation wound up in the deep freeze. Not everyone was a publicity hound or political candidate who sought fifteen minutes of fame. In fact, people worth interviewing were usually the ones who *didn't* want to talk. Ryan's best stories came from individuals who buttoned up–people with something to hide. Those stories sold newspapers and captured awards for the journalist.

Amanda seemed to be that kind of person.

His luck doubled when Ryan discovered his friend had recently written an article on a new flight program at the base–one in which Major McClain was involved. The rest was basic research–Journalism 101. It took less than an hour for Ryan to discover Amanda's marriage was a ruse. The major had shared a house with Erik Cash for eight years now, but under the military's 'don't ask, don't tell' policy everyone at Offutt Air Force Base ignored the living arrangements, looking the other way.

Journalistically, Ryan wouldn't gain anything by 'outing' the major and something in his gut told him that wasn't where the story lay anyway. He did, however, hope to get answers to his list of questions when he met with Amanda for lunch. Why had she stayed married to a gay man for fourteen years? Was it simply a cover for the major or was it something more? Why was Shane so territorial when he'd seen Ryan with Amanda at the restaurant last night? And what was Amanda hiding in that bunch of letters she'd clutched outside the newspaper office?

Ryan was used to skirting suspicion from prey while hunting a story, and he chalked up his skillful recovery this morning to extensive experience. He certainly wasn't above insinuating himself into a subject's life to sniff out a scoop. And the itching in his gut told him this story would be of considerable consequence.

* * * *

Amanda nudged the shopping bag with her toe, pleased that she'd come up with a way to conceal the letters at the bottom of the bag. The new sweater would make a nice addition to her wardrobe. Now she could enjoy lunch without worrying about the letters being revealed. No one must know of her new assignment to choose the recipients of the lottery winnings, especially not someone who deflected questions about his career as Ryan did.

"So what do you like about your job at the law firm?"

Amanda's mind inexplicably flashed to Ben's face. Poor man. He'd looked so hurt look when she canceled their lunch 'date.'

"Actually, the job isn't much of a challenge," she admitted.

The waitress refilled their iced tea glasses. Mario's Café was a quaint place, a cliché of sorts, with red-checkered tablecloths and a melted candle propped in a wine bottle to serve as the centerpiece. The meals were fantastic, if Amanda could serve as food critic.

Ryan sipped his tea. "I don't blame you. I wouldn't like to work with lawyers."

Instantly, she wanted to defend Ben—and Roberta of course. They were fine people, good colleagues. She started to say so, but when she looked at him, everything but how handsome he looked fled her mind.

Ryan had removed his jacket, hanging it over the back of an empty chair next to him. His oxford shirt, an unusual shade of gold, exaggerated his tan and Amanda wondered if he was a skier. For a moment she imagined them cuddled in a condo in Aspen, drinking wine while the crystal goblets reflected the glow of the fireplace before them.

"What would you like to do instead?" Ryan asked.

Make love?

Swallowing, Amanda searched for the conversation's loose thread. "Huh?"

"If you had your dream job, what would it be?"

She sighed. "I used to have my own business. It wasn't huge. As I told you before, I made gift baskets. But I really enjoyed it."

"Yes, I remember now. You're an entrepreneur." He leaned forward, clearly interested.

His attention boosted Amanda's poise, urging a smile.

"Once, I had an account to make four thousand baskets for a company's national meeting. I hired extra help and everything."

"*Very* impressive."

She searched his face for a hint of teasing, but found none. Hard to believe someone like Ryan would be impressed by her modest local business.

"Four thousand baskets. Wow." He grasped her hand lightly as he glued his gaze to her mouth. "Tell me more."

Feeling self-conscious, she licked her lips before continuing. "Well, the meeting attendees loved the theme—items made in Nebraska. I had Baker's chocolates, Vic's popcorn, and Mannheim Steamroller CDs."

"What a shame you had to give it up." Sympathy dragged his mouth into a frown. "But I understand how family comes first. I wish I could spend more time with Bud."

Ryan had such capacity for empathic listening. Could he be a therapist or a minister? That was silly. Why would he want to hide those careers?

"I admire your spirit," he said.

"You do?"

"It takes guts to start your own business."

Well, yes it did.

It was nice of him to acknowledge that.

"Entrepreneurs are a special breed," he said. "Modern-day pioneers. Most people think it would be easier not having a boss hanging over their heads. But it takes courage and confidence to build a business on your own, putting in incredibly long hours with no guarantee of a paycheck. And I don't underestimate the power of a colleague's pat on the back. Were you the sole owner?"

"Yes."

"Amazing." He shook his head as if he couldn't be prouder if she'd designed, built and flew a shuttle to the moon and back. "You must be very disciplined."

"I can be." Her face grew warm under his intense praise. She couldn't remember the last time someone had given her so much credit.

He raised his iced tea glass. "I congratulate your fortitude, Amanda Cash."

Clinking glasses with him, she soaked in the warmth that she vaguely recalled came with compliments. He really seemed to appreciate what she'd accomplished. His admiration sparked lightness in her which long ago had been buried.

"So, do you have any desire to jump back into business ownership?"

Oddly, she did. She wouldn't have said that last week, but she seemed to have more energy now. Maybe if there was any money left-over from her mother's transplant, she could start some small enterprise.

"It's possible. Some day." She took a long swallow of her tea.

"Will Major McClain be your business partner?"

"Shane?" she choked out, pressing her napkin to her mouth to keep the tea from dribbling.

"His proposal—you said it was of a business nature."

How could she have thought she was good at lying? The only excuse she could come up with for the 'proposal' he'd mentioned was a business venture. She couldn't tell him Shane wanted her to conceive a child with his gay lover–her husband.

"I'm not sure he's going in the direction I'm interested in right now." She patted splatters of tea from the vinyl tablecloth and searched for another subject. "What about Bud? You said he raised you."

"I spent most of my formative years with him and my grandma. He was at work most of the time."

"For a former editor, he doesn't think much of the profession as it has evolved," Amanda said.

A look Amanda couldn't read cast over Ryan's face.

"No, he doesn't," he agreed. "In his day, they didn't look at publishing as a competitive business. Now with newspapers rivaling twenty-four-hour news networks and the internet, you have to slant stories specifically to attract readership. Bud doesn't understand that. He thinks truth piques public interest. Unfortunately, the facts are usually too dry to get the job done."

Amanda recalled what the intern had said–none of the letters in her bag had enough readership appeal.

She nodded. "The more titillating the better?"

"Absolutely."

"You seem to know a lot about the newspaper business," she said.

He ruffled the edges of his napkin. "What can I say? I was raised at my grandpa's knee."

Before she could again ask what he did for a living, the check came and he grabbed it, barely looking at it before placing a platinum American Express card in the leather book.

Whatever he did, he must be very successful. Amanda made a mental note to Google Ryan Fisher when she got home.

"Are things really so tough in Omaha that you have to troll nursing homes for dates?" He smiled, teasingly.

If she ever intended to come clean about her marriage, now was the time. She could let honesty win out. But what *was* the truth? She *was* married, but in name only. She could date Ryan, Ben, or anyone she wanted. Erik couldn't protest. No one could.

"I like Bud. He's a hoot. I thought it would be a kind thing to do, taking him out."

"An act of charity then?"

"Well . . ." Her imagination wouldn't spit out any more lies.

"He's quite taken with you, you know?"

"He's sweet."

"Don't let him fool you. He's a letch." He reached out and squeezed her arm." And don't ride with him in that go-buggy."

He was flirting again and it made her thoughts reel.

Maybe her mother was right. Maybe she should get a divorce. Certainly with a million dollars, she could afford the transplant and her own health insurance. But there was the question of the baby. How did she really feel about having a child with Erik? She'd thought she was looking at her only opportunity at motherhood, but in one day she'd had two men interested in her. What did that say for her chances at a 'normal' life?

"I have to head back to Denver this evening. May I call you? I get back to Omaha frequently–Bud insists."

"Yeah, he wants you to move back so you can handle his financial affairs."

Ryan reached inside his jacket, withdrew a PDA. "His financial affairs are about as rich as his romantic affairs. I know. I pay his bills. But I guess to a man who lived through the Depression, he's wealthy."

"My mother's the same way. Pinches every penny."

Stylus poised over his planner he said, "Your number?"

Now was her chance at a normal life. What this meant to Erik or Ben or anyone else, she couldn't say. She couldn't think about that now. The opportunity was simply too promising.

She gave him her cell number. Coincidentally, her phone rang at that moment.

Her mother had been rushed to the hospital.

Chapter Eleven

The confidence of Ben's usual stride faltered as he pulled open the heavy glass door at the Morning Star Lutheran Church. A 4.0 GPA at Notre Dame, editor of the *Harvard Law Review*, acing the bar exam, landing a partnership two years ahead of schedule—and still he had no idea how to prepare for a meeting of Gamblers Anonymous.

Two dozen strangers crowded four rows of metal folding chairs filling the fellowship hall. Their body heat, increased by anxiety, sent the thermometer several degrees higher than the evening's spring temperature of seventy-three degrees Fahrenheit.

Ben pretended to scour the brochure he'd picked up outside a casino in Council Bluffs, Iowa. At the time, he'd cursed—using real oaths—at the amazing stupidity of the public to vote for unlimited gambling in the city across the river from Omaha. His irritation had swelled at the nerve of the casino's management to hide the anti-gambling literature next to the exit. He could still smell the cigarette butts half buried in the dirty sand topping the colossal urns. He'd had to maneuver around the giant ashtrays to take the pamphlet from its stand.

With his gaze buried, flipping through pages of the leaflet, only the scent of thick, institutional coffee warned him of the refreshment table in his path. He skirted it just in time.

He thanked God for his lightning agility.

Several people had their heads bent, either checking their calendars, cell phones, or the same stupid brochure he had. He glanced at the faces as best he could without craning his neck into spasms.

Hockey pucks!

He'd hoped Colleen would have been among them.

He'd only agreed to come if she accompanied him, and now she had reneged. Just like her, really, to make promises she had no intention of keeping.

Fanning himself with the pamphlet, he slid into a chair in the back row. Ever the optimist, he kept glancing at the door as a humongous man stepped to the podium.

Gambling did not appear to be the man's only addiction.

The golden cross plastered on the front of the dais sent a symbolic glimmer of reflected light over the crowd, shaking a branch of shame in Ben. Surely, he could shelve his judgment for this one evening.

A bead of sweat trickled down his spine and he pinched the front of his polo shirt, fluttering it to create a breeze that might cool his steaming body.

Very quickly he lost patience with his nervousness. He'd spoken in front of the Nebraska Supreme Court and yet had no idea how he'd find words to address this audience, if asked. And he prayed now he wouldn't be asked.

Could God refuse a prayer initiated in His own house?

The only thing stopping Ben from bolting was the memory of Colleen's sweet laugh. Not the laugh that she'd used when he'd suggested this meeting. It was harsh from cigarette smoke and years of nights worth regretting. Instead he remembered the laugh she'd used from the sidelines, cheering him as he'd blasted through the offensive line to sack the quarterback at his high school football games.

Colleen smiled easily and often then at the dozens of boys who'd followed her home and lined up on the lawn to watch her and her squad practice cheers.

Everyone loved Colleen Harris. What wasn't to love?

Unlike Ben, she had beauty and height, reaching five feet ten inches by the time she was out of middle school. She was a cheerleading cliché–blonde, blue-eyed, leggy, but not skinny. Colleen had a body that would have caught his notice if she hadn't been his sister, younger by one year.

It was her laugh Ben loved. How it trickled over him like cool water swirling around smooth pebbles in a brook. Now it sounded more like dice clicking together at the end of a craps table.

Gambling was the reason Ben was here.

And probably the reason Colleen was not.

The large man at the podium introduced himself. "Hi, I'm Chuck. I'm a compulsive gambler."

The crowd greeted him. "Hi, Chuck."

Ben pinched the bridge of his nose. It was going to be a long night. He instantly remembered what he could be doing instead.

His work with Amanda was effortless. She was charming—a lot like Colleen had been a couple decades ago.

He glanced at the door again, hoping to see his sister's face. No such luck.

He'd been slow to realize that Amanda and Colleen had similar features. Colleen was taller of course, thank God, because that made Amanda shorter than him. But both women had the same honey-colored hair and sky-blue eyes. Sometimes he could see a summer's afternoon in Amanda's smile, when her eyes crinkled with laughter.

He'd been a goner the first time she'd teased him about the coffee.

What had she said?

Chuckling to himself he remembered the scene. She'd been dressed in that chocolate skirt he liked that showed her legs. The pink blouse would have been more attractive with the top button undone, but she had her hair down and that alone sent an itch over him.

He'd reached for the coffee, but she'd stolen the carafe away from him, and had poured the rest into her own cup.

"You don't need the caffeine," she'd said. "Your signature is already illegible." Then she'd giggled. Not the full-blown laugh he'd grown to love—the one he tried at every opportunity to evoke from her. That day she'd only snickered.

He wasn't sure what the comment had meant, but the gesture that went with it had kept him awake nights. Her hand had simply brushed against his forearm.

Just like that, he was in love.

Ben's second chuckle broke the silence of the church room. Returning his attention to the meeting, he squirmed as two dozen pairs of eyes scorched a hole through him.

He darted his gaze among the crowd, but the answer wasn't printed on their faces. He threw up his hands.

"What?" he protested.

"We were doing introductions," Chuck said from the dais. "Would you like to join us?"

Red chili peppers.

Heat rode over his body, strangling his words. He shouldn't be here. Not without Colleen. Gambling wasn't *his* problem.

Sweat beaded on his forehead, threatening to drip into his eyes. The crowd stared at him, demanding his 'story.'

Well, he didn't have one to give them. It was Colleen that had ruined her marriage through endless hours at the casinos. It was Colleen who'd lost custody of her children when their father sued for divorce and won all his conditions. She was the unfit parent, chucking all their savings into slot machines.

Ben had to agree with the judge. Colleen was a mess.

The man next to him coughed, the noise shattering what was left of Ben's poise. He opened his mouth to explain he'd tried to get the gambler to the meeting, but had failed. With a snap, he closed his mouth.

Maybe he'd always failed his sister.

But he was trying to make up for his mistakes now. He'd run interference with her employer when he wanted to fire her last week over excessive absences. Without a job, Colleen would lose visitation with her kids. At least Ben had been successful at saving her job.

"First names are fine." Chuck's smile wavered.

Ben glared at the glass door, willing Colleen to appear. If only he could use a subpoena to compel her attendance.

He locked gazes with the man twisted around in the chair in front of him. Crumbs from the cookies offered at the refreshment table sat trapped in his scraggly beard. Ben wondered what his game of choice might be. Cards? Roulette?

Colleen preferred slots, but she couldn't lose her money fast enough there. As a backup, she played craps.

Ben twitched. He wanted to shout out that Colleen was the one with the awful addiction. She was the big loser, not him.

He was only the sucker brother who was trying to help her.

The woman to his left touched his arm. It felt like a white-hot poker fresh from the fireplace. "Would you like to introduce yourself?"

For the first time in his life, Ivy League Ben bolted.

Chapter Twelve

Too many tables at Truffaut's were empty. The elegantly folded linen napkins, stiff from abundant starch, begged shoppers passing by in the Old Market to release them from their loose knots, but the *World-Herald* had published its review of the restaurant today.

It was unfavorable, as indicated by the extensive reservation cancellations.

Anger heated Erik like a microwave oven—from the inside out. He huddled with Shane by the walk-in cooler. "Did you read what that bastard wrote?"

"Yeah, I don't understand it. I thought the food was good that night."

"It was *exceptional*," Erik ground out. "The duck was succulent, vegetables fresh, sauces were perfect."

Shane leaned against the wall, arms across his chest. Erik's frown reflected in the major's aviator sunglasses he usually considered sexy. A ridiculous look just now, considering the sun had set two hours ago.

"Tough break," Shane said. "But people don't go by what critics say. They check things out for themselves."

Kristen, one of the waitresses, entered from the empty dining room.

A hesitant waiter approached, skittered past Shane to punch his time card and then quickly slinked away.

"Well," Erik said, his voice tight, "investors pay attention and they want to pull back on what I can spend for fresh ingredients."

Shane shrugged slightly. "So you'll wow the customers with frozen peas. You can make vending snacks taste good."

Erik gaped at him. That was the best support he could offer?

Slowly, Shane removed his glasses, hooked them onto the collar of his shirt. "We have to talk."

"Okay." Erik gave him his full attention

The major jerked his head toward the door. "Privately."

"Let's go out back."

A lone street light in the deserted alley illuminated the dumpsters, which usually reeked this time of the evening after a few busy hours. Not tonight.

The wait staff had requested a light on the stoop, but Erik thought it would lengthen their cigarette breaks and had denied the request. He regretted that decision now because he wanted to see the look in Shane's eyes.

"I got called in by the commander today." Shane sniffed.

Always a bad sign. Erik braced for either bad news or a lie. "Yeah?"

"I'm number seven in the line list for Lieutenant Colonel."

Erik's heart fell into the pit of his stomach, but he tried to put some excitement into his voice. "You knew you did well on the exam." His dry throat made the next word hard to say. "Congratulations."

"Thanks. It didn't hurt that I volunteered for extra flights shuttling the brass coast to coast."

"Yeah." Erik's voice sounded flat and suddenly he didn't regret his 'no lights in the alley' decision. Shane couldn't see the disappointment on his face in the dark.

A promotion cemented Shane to the Air Force and the military didn't approve of Erik or his relationship with Shane. Accepting the promotion meant Shane might even stay longer than the twenty-year minimum for retirement with a pension.

A cold shudder passed through Erik. Where did that leave him?

Shane sniffed again. "Here's the deal. With the promotion comes more responsibility."

"And more pay." No sense looking only on the dreary side.

"The Air Force made me squadron commander."

"All right." Erik offered a high five, which Shane didn't except.

"In Wiesbaden, Germany."

Erik felt the blood leave his head and he leaned against the brick building so he wouldn't crumple to the ground.

Germany? Impossible. They *barely* knew how to fly under the radar here. How would they ever be able to replicate the deception in Germany? Amanda wouldn't be there to be Shane's cover, the best friend's wife. The community would be smaller. In his position, Lieutenant Colonel Shane McClain would be watched more carefully.

This was a nosedive out of control.

Shane puffed up his chest, sucking in his stomach, tucking in his shirt. All nervous habits Erik so easily recognized. "Hey, I'm thrilled," Shane said. "I've been stuck here for eight years. Nothing can happen for me in Omaha."

Erik's stomach convulsed and he swallowed to keep from vomiting. "Except for me."

And the baby.

"What, they don't eat in Germany? Isn't cooking in Europe like every chef's dream?"

Erik swallowed again. "We had a different dream."

"Huh?"

"A family."

Shane squared his shoulders, his position for addressing the troops. "You haven't held up your end. It's been ten days and you haven't spoken to Amanda yet."

Tears burned Erik's eyes, but he forced them back. He had to remain calm. Shane hated it when he broke down and cried. "I know. I've tried calling, but her mom's in the hospital."

Shane slapped his back. He seemed almost relieved Erik had failed his mission. "The baby thing could still happen someday."

The baby 'thing?' Someday?

For an instant, Erik wondered if Shane might be trying to back out, despite his remarks about needing an heir. The prospect of parenthood had always excited Erik more than Shane.

"I thought you wanted a family as much as I do," Erik said.

"I did. I do." Shane sniffed. "I'm just not willing to give up my career, everything I've worked so hard for."

"You're saying it can't work out? In Europe?" A tear slid down Erik's cheek. He couldn't hold it back and didn't care if Shane saw him go to pieces.

"Maybe. If you get Amanda on board. Quick. And you have to tell her about Michelle."

The door opened, right into Shane's back. He moved aside and Kristen stepped out. "Oops, sorry, chef. It's kind of slow so I thought I'd have a quick smoke."

Shane put his glasses back on, caught the door before it closed, and slipped into the kitchen.

Erik dried his cheek and winced when onion residue burned his eyes. "No problem." He turned away from the dim street light. The cool evening air felt like a serrated knife pulled across his skin.

Shane didn't want to give up everything he'd worked for? What about Erik's oldest friendship? He'd kill it when he told Amanda about Michelle.

It had been Shane's idea and Erik had to admit it looked good on paper. But how could he ever tell Amanda about Shane's sister who attended Northwestern University?

Michelle was a lovely kid, with two years of college left, a fiancé, and tons of potential as an actress. To make their baby a perfect genetic representation of the couple, Shane wanted to use Michelle's egg fertilized by Erik's sperm.

Although she was the perfect egg donor, Michelle's hectic schedule, young age, and commitment to her fiancé prevented her from being an ideal surrogate mother. Shane and Erik wanted Amanda to carry and deliver the baby.

If loyalty wouldn't do it, surely fifty-thousand dollars would convince Amanda.

Chapter Thirteen

The dings, jingles, and tinkling of the machines at the indoor fun center put Ben on edge. He'd suggested the zoo for their Friday afternoon outing with the kids, but Colleen had insisted Lindsay wanted to eat pizza and play video games. Since it was an early celebration for her fourth birthday, he would grant her wish.

"Uncle Benji," Lindsay said, "would you ride the merry-go-round with me? Please?"

It was impossible to say no to his niece—a replica of Colleen at that age. Her honey-colored hair was pulled back in two pigtails spiked at forty-five-degree angles from the top of her head, pink ribbons trailing from both. Bless him, Don had tried, but he hadn't gotten the hang of managing his daughter's baby-fine hair. Her eyes were the color of cornflowers, glowing in the summer sun. But it was her giggle that melted Ben.

"I'll hold on to you while you ride." He picked her up off the chair, tickling her ribs to hear her laugh. She kicked her legs and a shower of crumbs fell from the folds of her lavender skirt.

He squeezed her into a tight hug and whispered into her ear. "Which horse would you like to ride?"

Bringing her finger to her lips, she answered in a hushed voice. "Purple."

"Purple it is." He flipped her upside down, then quickly turned her upright to hear her laugh again.

She wrapped her spindly arms around his neck and he carried her to the carousel. When he stepped onto the platform it tipped slightly under his weight. He plopped her on the back of the fastest, purple steed in the pack.

The chime of the music was annoying rather than festive today. If only he'd had more time to prepare, but Colleen had called him late last night, crying. She wanted to see the kids and could only do that if another adult, suitable to the court, accompanied them. He'd finally agreed. It had taken all his debating skills to persuade Don to let ten-year-old Jack skip his afternoon classes.

Lindsay sang along with the electric pipe organ. It didn't play a popular tune, and there were no lyrics, but it didn't matter to her. Instead, the child wailed her delight in a series of ta-da-da-ta-da-da-das.

"We're winning, Uncle Benji, we're winning!" Lindsay jiggled the short reins of her mighty stallion. Ben held tight around her waist as she wiggled in the saddle, her smile brighter than the flashing lights on the canopy above them.

She was an amazing child. Precocious, but still too young to understand why her mother didn't live with them. He was happy to give her the afternoon with Colleen.

The music slowed, as did the merry-go-round. Optimistically, the little girl shook, hoping her horse would speed up. She groaned at the end of the ride, but ever resilient, a smile bounced back onto her flawless, pink face.

"You're the best uncle ever." Lindsay kissed his cheek as he helped her dismount. She skipped back to her mother at their lunch table where Jack finished his third slice of pepperoni pizza.

Lindsay tugged on her brother's arm. "I want to drive the bumper cars. Take me, please?"

Jack wiped his mouth with the back of his sleeve. "Okay with you, Mom?" he mumbled through a mouthful.

"Yes."

For once Colleen had dressed conservatively. The jeans were broken-in, yet not too tight or stylishly slashed. The turquoise shirt tucked neatly into her waistband fashioned one long line from boots to chunky necklace, creating the tall-model image that used to drive the boys crazy in high school. Thankfully, all the body parts a mom should hide were covered. However, the best Ben could say about her make-up was that it was less dramatic than usual. Her soft, blonde hair was cut in a style that made her look like a pixie. That innocence was juxtaposed by the large gold earrings with blue and gold dangly beads which hung nearly to her shoulders.

Jack jerked his head back when Colleen tried to swipe a napkin across his cheek. "Mom," he whined.

Ben dug in his jeans pocket, passed Jack a handful of tokens and the children scampered away.

"Tell me again why we couldn't have gone to the new place that uses scanners with plastic cards instead of tokens." He jostled his bulging pockets, the rattle mixing with the noise from the video games.

Colleen swept her arms wide. "Look around. This is pure ambience."

Most of the equipment at Carter's Funplex was ancient by electronic standards. Video games popular in the 1980s–Pac Man, Caterpillar, and Star Galaxy dotted the worn carpeting. Some pinball machines lived in one dark, musty corner. The politically incorrect, barely-clad women beckoned players with their flashing lights and obnoxious sirens and bells.

He eased into a chair whose vinyl covering was split and squeezed his sister's arm, glancing at the wallpaper curled down from the cork ceiling, poked with holes from years of birthday banners. "Wanting to relive old times?" he asked.

"I only look forward." Her gaze caught Lindsay's, who stood in a short line of teenagers and parents with preschoolers.

What a lie. If Colleen focused on the future, she would actively take charge of her recovery from gambling. He'd reined in his anger in front of the children, but now that they were out of earshot, he planned to share his disappointment with her.

"Where were you the other night when I was at the Gambler's Anonymous meeting and you weren't?"

Her brows furrowed. With anyone else, he'd assume she was trying to remember specific times and places. But he knew Colleen searched for a plausible excuse.

"When were we supposed to meet?" she asked, a poor attempt at stalling.

"Wednesday night." Ben pitched the used paper plates into the trash can behind the table. If only her deceit could be tossed away as easily.

"Oh, yeah. Wednesday. Bob asked me to work late. I had to get out some invoices."

A flat out lie.

He'd understand if she told the truth–that she'd been scared witless to go and face her problem. The meeting had unnerved him and he didn't even have to be there.

Taking her hand, his gaze held hers. "You can't beat your gambling problem if you don't take steps to manage your addiction."

Tears welled in her eyes. She sighed, shoulders trembled. "I know. But it's so hard. I know I need help, but discussing my life with a bunch of strangers seems impossible."

"The people were nice. It's easier than you think."

Now *he* was lying.

She pulled the brochure he'd given her from her purse. "I have the schedule. I've circled the meetings close to my apartment. I'm going tomorrow."

He wanted to believe her, but remembered he was talking to a practiced liar, one who would say anything to deflect shame and blame.

"I hope you go. It's the way back into your children's lives."

Colleen blotted a napkin smeared with pizza sauce under her eyes. "I know. I'm trying. I really am."

He patted her hand. The pain of watching her suffer knotted his neck muscles. "By the way, how did you get off work on a Friday afternoon?"

Her gaze shot to the children. "Since I worked late on Wednesday night, Bob gave me the afternoon off. He doesn't want to pay overtime."

Taking a sip of his watery cola, he prayed she wasn't lying again. Her job hung by a thread as it was.

It was as though he had become the dad she'd always needed and the burden of that role was heavy. She'd never reconciled with their father, and maybe that was for the best since Tom Harris would take pleasure in beating her down over the way she'd messed up her life. It was up to Ben and only Ben to help her. And she required more guidance than most women her age. He blamed himself because when she'd needed him most he'd been away at college.

Tom Harris had kicked Colleen out of the house in her senior year of high school. She only broke curfew once, but it was all her father needed to justify expelling her.

The family of another cheerleader took Colleen into their home, but she ran away. For months no one knew where she'd gone. He discovered she'd left to escape the sexual advances of her friend's father.

Not that he could have done much for Colleen while away, but he was willing to do all he could to improve her life now. That involved protecting his niece and nephew until Colleen got help and stopped gambling so she could care for them properly herself.

"Jack wasn't happy you pulled him out of class," Ben said. "He told me he's missing a math test."

"So he'll ace it on Monday instead of today. No biggie." She scavenged in her purse, taking out a pack of cigarettes.

He hated that Colleen took her son's academic accomplishments for granted. Jack worked so hard to get Colleen to notice him and she, maybe unwittingly, made that more difficult.

"What kind of message are you sending him about the importance of school?" Ben said.

"He's in fourth grade, for God's sake. Top of his class and yet he worries he won't be *perfect*." She rolled her eyes as a teenager might. "He's so much like you at that age."

Being an honor student and a football star had been the only way Ben had known to avoid his father's bullying. For a fleeting instant at his college graduation, Ben had even felt his father's love.

Colleen tapped the package of ultra lights sharply against her palm. "Jack needs to learn how to loosen up. Maybe you do, too." Coolness coated the look she tossed him. "I'm going outside for a quick smoke." Unfolding herself from the circular, plastic table with attached benches, she sauntered out the door.

Ben looked at the parking lot of bumper cars waiting for the next load of passengers to fill them. Lindsay tugged Jack to a purple car which was old and the paint chipped.

The fun center had been around when Ben was Jack's age, but their father had never taken them there. In fact, there were never any family outings in the Harris household. Their father believed paying to entertain children was a waste of money.

Once, Ben had been to this amusement center when he was a teenager, using a huge chunk of his own paycheck to impress a girl on a first date. Gloria Ray had dumped him at the end of the evening.

Although he'd been a star football player and class valedictorian, high school had produced a series of miserable dating experiences. He never quite got the hang of talking with girls. His father hadn't been much of a role model, always cursing at their mother. With the influence of Archie Bunker, Tom Harris had taken to calling his wife 'Dingbat.' Ben never understood why she answered to the slur or why she didn't walk out on him.

He thought of Amanda. She was everything he wanted in a woman and he couldn't think of enough ways to show her he cherished his time with her.

Ever since he'd learned Amanda's marriage was a ruse, he'd set his intention to make his relationship with her work. He'd even taken to reading self-help books so he could get things 'right.'

Popular advice encouraged self-disclosure–something as alien and uncomfortable to Ben as wearing thong underwear. Surely, if she knew about his crazy, dysfunctional family she'd run in the opposite direction. Clara seemed so normal and Amanda had adored her father, so he must have been sane as well. Ben wondered how he could ever appeal to someone so well-adjusted. She was innocent and genuine, except for that little matter of her long-term marriage to a gay man. He shook his head at the paradox.

The bumper cars emptied except for Jack and Lindsay, who stayed firmly in place for another ride.

Gliding into the chair next to him, the smoke stench followed Colleen. Her eyes were clear, and face less blotchy since her crying spell. She applied another layer of lipstick to her already painted mouth.

"I'm going out of town tomorrow for a few days," he said.

"Vacation?"

"Business trip."

"With Roberta?"

"No, Amanda."

Ben's cheeks heated the same way they had the day Amanda casually brushed her hand against his forearm. The moment he'd fallen in love with her.

Colleen's attention sparked. "Who's Amanda?"

Maybe it was time to practice the self-disclosure he'd been reading about. "She's the office manager. I like her."

"Oh, *really*." Colleen stared at him as though she were a prosecuting attorney and he an accused bank robber who'd just confessed.

Now the heat spread down his neck and swept to his back. Sweat beaded on his brow. "So?"

"So. . ."—she smiled as she mocked him—"go sew your underwear."

The juvenile taunt brought back memories. He liked the child-like version of Colleen and wished she could come out to play more often.

"What's she like?"

"Nice. Normal." *Except for the gay husband.*

Her teasing expression tickled him.

"Does she like you?"

He glanced toward the award counter, recalling how Gloria Ray had broken up with him. At the end of the evening they'd cashed in their game tickets for a prize—a giant Panda with a red bowtie, which she'd squeezed tightly. Ben had ached for her to hug him instead. When he'd asked for a second date, her answer was polite and sounded rehearsed. "I don't think we have the right chemistry, but thank you for the bear."

Did Amanda feel any chemistry for him?

"Earth to Ben." Colleen waved her hand in front of him.

"What?"

"Does Amanda like you?"

"I don't know. I think so."

"Well she'd be crazy not to snatch you up like a loose diamond on the sidewalk. You're quite a catch."

"Thanks."

He hoped Amanda would think so at the end of their assignment when his covert involvement was exposed. It brought little comfort to know every lie he told her was for her own good. He had to shove Roberta aside so he could accompany Amanda on her trips to meet candidates. It was imperative he jockey himself into her schedule as much as possible. The lies and clandestine meetings were all for her protection. He had to stay close to Amanda, because clearly she was in over her head. He couldn't trust anyone else to block the probing media and protect her from unscrupulous vultures eager to feed on her vulnerability.

Now he had two women to protect: his sister and Amanda.

Colleen tugged his arm. "Uh, about the Gambler's Anonymous meeting . . ."

"Yes?"

"I want to go tomorrow, but I don't have gas money. You know how much it costs to fill a tank these days?"

"How is it you don't have money? I paid your rent in advance. Rent includes utilities."

"I gave Don some child support."

Ben sighed, not overlooking her good intentions. "But you have to mail that money into the state or it doesn't count."

She shrugged. "I gave it to Don. He took it. Ask him. He'll tell you."

Ben *would* ask. First chance he got.

"Well, you still have to mail the money to the state so it can be recorded. Otherwise you hit a list that says you're delinquent. And interest is charged."

She nodded like an obedient child, her clinking earrings spoiling the innocence.

He dug into his wallet and pulled out two twenties. "For gas," he said gruffly.

"Absolutely."

He handed the bills to her.

"Thanks, Benji. You're the best brother. Can I have some tokens so I can win a toy for Lindsay?"

He emptied his pocket.

As Ben watched Colleen drop token after token into the game whose stuffed animals always slipped through the claw of the hand-cranked crane, a sad realization struck him. His sister would never satisfy her hunger for feeding coins into slot machines.

Chapter Fourteen

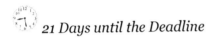 *21 Days until the Deadline*

The humidifier attached to the machine supplying Clara's oxygen gurgled. When Amanda had entered the hospital room and found Clara asleep, she didn't turn on a light. Now the pinks and corals of the sunset streaked across the walls, warming the sterile environment. Snake-like cords connected to digital monitors, blip-filled regulators, and IV bags ended their winding path by sinking their needle teeth into her mother.

Dropping into the recliner, she shuddered against the cold vinyl upholstery. Late-spring weather in Nebraska was as erratic as her mother's breathing. Yesterday's sunshine scorched the ground, but today the hospital air conditioning was too much. Amanda cinched the sweater tighter about her waist.

She fought to refrain from adjusting the nasal tubing sitting askew on Clara's face. Best to let her sleep as long as possible. Lately her nights had been restless, as had Amanda's, even more so now that she knew what she must do.

With a snort, Clara jerked awake. Taking a moment to focus, her puffy eyes registered no emotion. She blinked twice. "There's a face I know. Hey, Buttercup." Her lips stuck together making the last word sound more like "Buddercut."

"How are you feeling today, Mama?"

Forcing air into her lungs, her mother croaked. "I wish I could breathe."

When Clara had been admitted a week ago, the diagnosis had been emphysema. Seems her heart was no longer the sole organ affected by her decades of smoking. Now would she need a new heart *and* lungs?

"Remember, inhale like you smell a rose and exhale like you're blowing out birthday candles."

Amanda's heart jolted at a horrid thought. Would Clara make it to her sixty-eighth birthday in four months?

Memories of her own birthdays flooded her. Clara had always made the events special. For a moment Amanda could smell the sugary aroma of a spice cake warm from the oven. As a child she always licked the dribble from the neck of the Amaretto bottle after Clara poured a teaspoonful in the butter cream frosting. Then she'd pretend to be inebriated, whirling around the kitchen bumping into the chairs until she finally *was* tipsy and would fall to the floor giggling next to Clara's feet.

Then Clara would call to her father, "Jim, your daughter's drunk again. Guess we can take back her gifts." The fake threat was Amanda's cue to jump up and latch onto sobriety, snitching finger licks of icing from the bowl, but only when Clara pretended not to look.

"Don't you have anything better to do with your time?" Clara crooked the pulse monitor clipped to her index finger, indicating her need for a sip of water.

As Clara's swollen tongue chased the straw in a circle, Amanda trapped it between two fingers, holding it steady for her mother. Amanda sucked a phantom straw, hoping the gesture would add strength to the patient.

"As a matter of fact . . ."—Amanda now swallowed back regret— "I'm leaving tomorrow on a business trip."

Apparently wanting to conserve energy, Clara merely raised her eyebrows for more information.

"I'm going to Arizona."

Clara grunted for an explanation—one Amanda wasn't prepared to give. She'd held on tightly to security all week and had yet to tell anyone of her connection to the lottery winner. It'd been especially difficult to keep the secret from her mother—her primary confidante.

"Roberta needs me to accompany her on a deposition."

It was only half a lie. There was a deposition involved—of sorts. Only it was Amanda who hoped to get authentication of a candidate's request for the jackpot money.

The letter had been mailed to the "Win a Fortune" television show. A woman on the outskirts of Phoenix operated a ranch for disabled kids. By teaching them to ride horses, the children developed their coordination, strengthened their muscles, and most importantly, increased their confidence. The ranch had helped hundreds of children for two decades, but had recently run into funding difficulties. The photos and stories of the former 'wranglers' had touched a sympathetic chord in Amanda's heart.

It was to be her first in-depth research into a contender's request. Roberta would accompany her, but Amanda took little comfort in that fact as it was the only other honest part of the story she now told her mother.

"About time you stopped hanging around hospitals." Clara pushed away the straw inadvertently competing with the tubing for space up her nose. "Is Ben going with you?"

To make room for the glass on the bedside tray, Amanda nudged aside the bud vase of three yellow carnations with baby's breath Ben had given Clara.

It was Ben who'd helped Amanda most this week, sorting hundreds of requests into the categories Amanda wanted. He'd done everything she'd asked of him and more, including trying to fix her car when the transmission had failed. He was a terrible mechanic, but an attentive chauffeur as he seemed to show up at Clara's bedside at the close of visiting hours every evening. She had yet to decide if she should simply be thankful for the support or be cautious of his eagerness to please.

"Only Roberta and I are going."

"Too bad. Well, maybe I'll have a chat with Ben while you're gone."

Before Amanda could protest the remark, a fit of coughing took hold of Clara, racking her shoulders and jarring the oxygen tubing from her nose.

Alarmed, Amanda reached for the call button. Clara slapped away her hand and pointed to the tissue box. Collecting a handful, Amanda offered them to her. Clara promptly spat into it. With all the equipment, tubes, bags, and noise, there was no space left for dignity in the room. Clara handed the wad filled with thick mucus to her to throw away.

"Please go, Amanda. I'm so tired and you have better things to do than watch me choke to death."

Clara often joked about dying, but this time tears pricked the back of Amanda's eyes. She didn't want to leave town until her mother was discharged, but only three weeks remained for her to find the most deserving recipients of the jackpot. The lottery deadline aside, if she didn't work fast, the million-dollar finder's fee would come too late to help her mother.

"Mama, I don't want to go, but I have to."

"Have some fun for a change. Dance naked in the desert. Eat some chipotle chicken."

"Mom, it's business, not a vacation."

"You've got to eat." The chuckle that followed launched another round of coughing, and Amanda held her mother's frail body until her breathing settled.

Icy heat rose up Amanda's arms and filled her head as a torturous thought crushed her chest.

What if Clara died while she was gone?

Her throat closing, Amanda forced the notion from her mind and took a deep breath. "I'll see you in three days." She gathered her purse and turned to go as if a quick exit would speed her return.

"Amanda?" Clara's voice was barely audible over the equipment.

"Yes?" Amanda leaned over, tilting her face closer.

Shaking, Clara laid her hand on Amanda's arm. Her fingers felt bony and cold, making Amanda wish she could wrap her mother in a cocoon-like, wool carry-on bag. Then she could lay her in the Arizona sun, the warmth reviving her.

"Promise me something," Clara said.

To stroke Clara's thinning white hair reminded Amanda of the cashmere yarn her mother used to knit school sweaters years ago. "Anything."

"When I die, you'll have me cremated and—"

"Mom, don't talk like that."

Clara squeezed Amanda's arm, the grip no stronger than that of a child's—a sick one at that. Amanda winced at the effused bruising on the back of her mother's hand. She'd been tortured all week with pokes to restart IVs and blood draws for endless tests—all of which had left trails of angry violet up to her elbows on both arms.

If only Amanda could transfer some of her own strength. She could bear all the needles. The resiliency of her skin wouldn't even register the marks. She'd gladly absorb all her mother's pain and then some.

"Don't leave me sitting on your mantel," Clara ordered as loud as she could.

"What?"

"You hold on to things too long. I don't want to be something you dust around on Saturday mornings. Promise me you'll dump my ashes somewhere beautiful."

Now Amanda couldn't hold back the tears. She used the cuff of her sweater to wipe her cheeks. "Where?"

"Somewhere *you'd* like to go."

Amanda couldn't listen to any more. She kissed her mother's forehead, wondering how it was possible to feel mortality through the rose petal thinness of aged skin.

Chapter Fifteen

 20 Days until the Deadline

Slowly, Amanda pulled closed the zipper of the garment bag. Having never owned a proper suitcase, she'd bought one. She didn't trust the lottery winner would consider the purchase a legitimate expense, so she'd stretched her own credit card to the limit once again. Above all, she must be judged as completely ethical in this assignment. Her mother's life depended on it.

Besides, she justified, she'd use the bags again sometime in the future—maybe on a trip to Colorado. She pushed the button on her answering machine to repeat Ryan's message from last night.

"Hello, beautiful. Just making my connection in Chicago. Been thinking about you."

Not more than I've been thinking about you.

"My loss. I really wanted to hear your sweet voice."

Your sexy voice does something to me every time.

"Hope your mom's doing better."

So considerate of you to ask.

"I won't call when I get to New York. It'll be late and I don't want to wake you."

I was up anyway. Wish he had called.

"Take care and I'll talk to you tomorrow night."

The machine clicked off as the message ended. She'd have to call him tonight instead. Caution prevented her from telling even Ryan about her trip to Phoenix.

She glanced at her watch. Just enough time to do a Google search on Ryan Fisher. As she brought the computer to life, the doorbell sounded its sickly clang. Letting out a frustrated breath, she cursed her boss' early arrival and her building supervisor's neglect of the defective chimes.

Embarrassment had flooded Amanda when she'd called Roberta yesterday to beg a ride to the airport. She had no funds to fix her car's transmission. Ben had suggested a rental charged to the lottery expense account, but she couldn't buy into the ethics of that decision either. If she could have figured out a way to drive to the airport without putting the car in reverse, she would have made it.

She stacked her garment bag on top of the rolling case filled with more letters. Passing by the hall coat rack, she jerked a windbreaker off the hook and opened the front door.

Erik's furrowed brow said it all. He'd called twice this week, she'd assumed to discuss Shane seeing her with Ryan. If she'd tried harder to connect with him, she could've avoided this visit, but with the stress of Clara's hospitalization and the work she'd done on the lottery contest, she'd only had the energy to leave a message on his cell.

"Hey, Amanda Bear." Shane slapped her back as he brushed past her without waiting for an invitation.

"Hi, Amanda." Erik followed Shane, his long legs barely bending at the knee to step over the bags.

What, no courteous hug?

She nudged them into her tiny living room and closed the door.

"How's Clara?" Erik asked, concern lacking in his voice. Amanda slipped on her jacket. Clara? When had he moved beyond calling her 'mom?'

Irritation washed over Amanda. Even if they hadn't spoken personally this week, she'd left the name of the hospital on Erik's cell phone, yet he hadn't called or even sent a get-well card to her mother.

Clara was doing much better, but that didn't excuse Erik's neglect. "She's hanging on. She could be out of the hospital in a couple of days."

Amanda bit her tongue to refrain from scolding him about his absence. There was a time when nothing would have prevented him from sitting with her at the bedside vigil. And that was even after Shane. Wasn't it?

Straight-shouldered and regimented, Shane eased into Clara's threadbare wingback chair. The frame creaked under his compact, muscular body. He was dressed in civvies today as he always did when he was out with Erik. Still, there was no mistaking he was thoroughly military.

Glimpsing her luggage, Erik asked. "Where you going?"

Not even a question about specifics of Clara's condition. Fine. She could be cold, too.

"Out of town. On business."

"With your mom in the hospital?" Erik said.

"*You* could check on her if you're worried."

He bowed his head. Due to shame, she hoped.

"I meant to stop by."

This was too big a faux pas to forgive easily. The iciness in her voice remained. "No problem. I guess it's really not your duty anymore." Her gaze landed on Shane.

"I've been so busy," Erik said.

And she'd been out getting pedicures? Annoyance at his lame excuse gnawed at Amanda's civility, and she struggled to keep quiet.

Erik flopped into the green leather recliner—the only one of his favorite items she had insisted on taking with her when she'd left. They had divided the furniture during her angry phase.

"Things have been crazy at the restaurant. You probably saw the review."

She was cross-eyed from reading anything she could get her hands on in the last week—mostly the contestants' requests, but she'd managed the daily *Omaha World-Herald*, as well.

"I don't know how the critic could have given you such a scathing review." She dragged a stool the two feet from the kitchen and sat facing both men.

"Apparently, he went by other customers' remarks and never bothered to verify the rumor about the salmonella poisoning."

Like a smack on the head, Amanda recalled her conversation with Ryan. She'd insulted the menu and food quality the night they'd been at Truffaut's. Now she remembered where she'd seen the bald-headed man at the booth next to theirs. The food critic really needed to update his column photo.

Oddly, she felt not the slightest remorse.

"His review didn't mention salmonella," she said.

"He couldn't because it never happened. But someone at the restaurant knows someone at the newspaper, and they found out the rumor colored his judgment."

"Well, a review *is* personal opinion," Amanda said.

One corner of Erik's lip hitched into a snarl. "It doesn't matter. It's time to move on anyway."

"Surely, the investors aren't firing you over one bad review." She searched for a hint of guilt in her body, but it just wasn't there.

Apparently, there would always be a bit of the angry phase in her, especially now that Erik was distancing himself more from her.

"No. They're not." Erik glanced at Shane.

"I have a PCS to Wiesbaden, Germany," Shane said.

She huffed in frustration. "Acronyms, Major Pain."

"Permanent Change of Station. At least three years in Germany."

"Shane's getting promoted to Lieutenant Colonel."

"I guess we'll have to think of a taunt that goes with Colonel. Congratulations." She extended her hand which he shook rigidly. "When do you leave?"

Erik cleared his throat, gaining Amanda's attention. His eyebrows twisted into a funny half-arch. She'd only seen him do that one other time—the day he'd confessed his sexual preference to her. "*We're* leaving in a month."

We?

Erik was moving? She hadn't considered that a possibility. Her gaze whipped back and forth between the men. "You're moving? How could that be?"

"He's in the military, Amanda. It was bound to happen."

"To Germany?"

Amanda had never lived anywhere but Omaha. Even when Erik attended culinary school in New York, she'd stayed behind to finish her business degree at the University of Nebraska at Omaha. When he returned, he'd said the big city life wasn't for him and he'd be happy if he never left the Midwest again. Now he was moving to the other side of the world? She couldn't believe it. Omaha without Chef Cash? Amanda without Erik?

"The reassignment comes at a good time, though, because someone has been investigating me," Shane said.

"What?"

Erik leaned forward, concern deepening the lines around his mouth. "Where he lives. How he spends his time. His connection to me."

"And my connection to *you*." Shane pointed directly at Amanda's chest.

"No way." Her stomach fluttered.

Was this somehow connected to the lottery winner and her assignment? If it was, she couldn't let Erik and Shane know.

The men exchanged glances. Did they suspect she was the reason for the investigation?

"Time's running out," Erik said. "We need an answer."

"How should I know who's been investigating Shane?"

Erik huffed. "Not about that. Geez. Stay focused, Amanda."

She grabbed a strand of hair and bounced the ends over her cheek. Erik had certainly lost his patience with her since he'd gotten together with Shane.

The major now assumed a stiff, military posture—hands clasped together with elbows propped on his knees. "We'll pay for an apartment for you in Germany for the term of the pregnancy. Of course, we'll pay all pre-natal and delivery expenses. And add fifty-thousand dollars for your trouble."

A Power Point presentation would have been less formal than this.

"And there's one more thing Erik neglected to tell you. We want to use my sister's egg."

Amanda's jaw fell open. As exhausted as she was, she must have been mistaken about what she'd just heard. She rattled her head. "What?"

Erik jumped in. "Using Michelle's egg—you met Michelle at Thanksgiving last year—using her egg gives the child the exact genetic make-up of Shane and me. I'd donate my sperm. Artificially inseminated, of course."

All Amanda's muscles froze. Good thing her heart and lungs functioned involuntarily.

"Isn't that cool?" Erik said.

Erik couldn't have grinned any wider if it had been voluntary, which it wasn't. Amanda was sure Shane had put him up to this.

Spinning toward the major, she did something she was sure he'd understand. Attack. "Then why do you need me?"

Shane's voice filled every corner of the room. "My sister is only twenty and in college. A pregnancy at this point would disrupt her life. She's only donating the egg. You would carry the baby."

"I told Shane, given your mother's condition, you probably would want to stay in Omaha. For a while. I'd be willing to stay with you until the baby is born."

Was Erik serious?

He held her hand, the one still wearing the wedding ring. He'd removed his band long ago, saying it was for hygiene reasons at work, but Amanda knew differently. His voice was soft, but the tone impersonal. "Amanda, we need to know about the baby. We need your decision sooner than later."

Amanda gawked at Erik. When had he become so mercenary? What had happened to the man who used to pack her lunches, exchange cars for the day so he could wash hers—the man who'd let her warm her chilled hands on his toasty neck? This opportunist had the nerve to ask her about the baby, when he hadn't even found five minutes to visit her mother—that baby's grandmother—whom the child would probably never know even if Clara got the transplant and lived another couple of years.

Clara's grandbaby would be living in Germany?

Wait. Clara's grandbaby wouldn't even be Clara's grandbaby. And not Amanda's child either.

Erik was insane to believe she'd ever agree to such a crazy scheme. Staring at the two men exchanging looks of anxiety, she suddenly got it, *finally* understood. The baby was never going to belong to Erik and *her* even if her egg was used. The lovers had no interest in whether or not she was a part of the baby's life. This arrangement was all about meeting their needs. Not hers. Not Michelle's. And certainly not the child's.

Anger swelled inside her. The walls of the tiny living room closed in on her. Her cheeks grew hot and tears threatened to spill. She'd never imagined Erik would treat her this way—like a piece of meat to be purchased. Suddenly, she couldn't breathe.

She jumped up from the stool. "Listen, I've got to go. You've got to go, too. I can't talk about this now."

Erik and Shane stood in unison. A united front. Two against one.

"You can't keep putting us off," Erik said. "What's going on with you? You don't return my calls. Shane sees you out with a strange man. Where's the responsible Amanda I married?"

Indignation trumped anger and Amanda squeezed her hands into fists to keep from slapping Erik. "You want to pretend you still care about me? My mother is dying, but do you take two minutes to call her to offer support? I lost my business and don't even have cab fare to the airport, let alone the hundreds of dollars to fix my dead car. Did you know any of that?"

"We're offering you a way to get out of debt, Amanda." Shane's words sounded so matter-of-fact.

The pathetic truth was that a week ago she'd considered proposing a similar offer to get a down payment for Clara's surgery. But in her scenario, she would have been the baby's mother—ready to love and nurture the child—not just a convenient incubator. Shame bonded to her resentment, building her anger. She should have divorced Erik years ago.

She spun on the major. "You. Shut up."

Then she swiveled to face Erik again, stretching herself to her full height but still a head shorter than he. "And if I choose to date ... Borat ... you have no right to complain."

"We deserve an answer, Amanda," Erik said tightly.

"You want an answer? My answer is *no*. Why don't you write the jackpot winner for money to buy a baby or to impregnate everyone in Wiesbaden, or Romania, or wherever? I will *not* be your incubator."

The clang of the doorbell harmonized with the sour tone in the room. Marching to the door, she yanked it open to see Ben Harris standing in the hallway.

Heat from the confrontation still clung tight around her, and Amanda couldn't control her rage. "*What do you want?*"

Ben's eyes sprung wide and he took a wary step back. "Roberta has a sick child and I'm taking her place at the business meeting."

With a sweep, Amanda threw her hair over her shoulder and grabbed the handle on her rolling cart, jerking it out into the hallway. Erik and Shane shuttled behind the luggage, Erik pulling and locking the door behind them.

Amanda stopped, took a deep breath and blew it out. Her nerves vibrated while Adrenaline raced through her yet she held her voice steady as she made introductions. "Ben Harris. This is Erik Cash and his bowling buddy, Shane. Erik is my soon-to-be *ex*-husband."

Chapter Sixteen

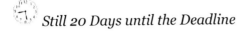 *Still 20 Days until the Deadline*

The dust kicking up as Ben drove along the winding gravel road wasn't the only thing clouding Amanda's vision. It was becoming more and more difficult to tell lies. Not only did the stories bend her ethics, but the details were hard to remember. Too bad her laptop had expired with her business or she'd have produced a spreadsheet tracking all the information.

"What are our names again?" she asked.

"Touhey. I'm Tom and you're Petula. I call you Pet for short."

"And our son is . . ."

"Jason. He's twelve. He has mild autism and suffers from asthma. We left him with my mother at our home in Pennsylvania. We didn't want him to become too excited at the prospect of attending summer camp at the ranch."

Amanda shook her head at the minutiae as she jotted the details in the spiral notebook labeled *Cases*. "How did you come up with the names?"

"Tom's my middle name. My mother used to have lots of albums of that British singer, Petula Clark. I had a thing for her." Ben shrugged as though that particular infatuation couldn't be helped by any man.

Letting the facts congeal in her mind, Amanda leaned back in the seat, loosely holding the roll bar above her. Even with her hair tied back, the ponytail threaded through the hole in the back of her baseball cap, tendrils whipped her face in the open-air Jeep. The sun on her arms felt wonderful.

It was a shame her mother couldn't enjoy the desert today. If the transplant didn't use up all the money, she'd insist they travel together in the future.

Amanda dug in her backpack for the rental car agreement. She tucked it behind the envelope clipped to the inside cover of another spiral notebook labeled *Financial*. It was where the detailed expense lists and receipts lived.

When she ran across the *Clara* fundraising notebook, she wondered how much longer she'd need to keep it with her. Then she took out her custom, computer-generated calendar and crossed off another day, leaving only nineteen full ones. A knot twisted in her stomach. If only she could buy more time.

She glanced at the cell phone display for messages. None. Her mother had been doing better this morning when she'd checked with the charge nurse. Still, Clara would be in the hospital a few more days while the doctors regulated the steroids keeping her airways open.

She clipped the phone to her jeans' pocket to remind herself time was running out—for the lottery deadline and for her mother. Her only hope was to focus on each request and make sound decisions the benefactor would respect. To that end, she reread the details of their current case.

Amanda jerked upright. "Hey, that makes me Pet Touhey."

A wide grin spread across Ben's face. "So it does. Would you check to see how much farther to the turn, please?"

She gave him a dirty look before opening the mission packet. Honest-to-God, Ben had written MISSION PACKET on the envelope. Not only had he navigated and plotted their course in three different-colored highlighters, but he'd also printed all online information about the ranch and its owner, Terri Miller.

It was research she would have done if she hadn't spent the last week next to Clara's hospital bed. Still, the color coding went beyond expectations.

Ben was exceedingly precise, as Erik had always been. No one could organize Christmas card and gift lists better than Erik did, right down to the checkbox to note when the thank you cards were sent.

Was Ben as persnickety as her future ex-husband?

As she'd located their position on the map, Ben turned into the drive for the Triple T Ranch. They passed beneath a split rail gate with the ranch brand dangling above them in wrought iron. Saguaro and barrel cacti lined the narrow drive through the desert which Amanda found fascinating. Never had she seen so many shades of brown and muted green.

She straightened in her seat and reviewed the data again. Terri Miller had written "Win a Fortune" asking for money to continue her ranch for disabled children. Although she'd founded the operation over twenty years ago, Miller had recently run into financial difficulty.

Three dogs greeted them as they pulled into the small asphalt parking lot. All tails wagged and none of the dogs barked or jumped on her as she climbed from the Jeep.

One point for Terri Miller for good dog training.

Behind Amanda loomed an empty arena. The barn lay straight ahead tucked between two small hills mounded with hay bales. Echoing clangs came from the stable.

Ben slapped the thighs of his stiff blue jeans to knock off non-existent dirt and repositioned his cowboy hat. The band may have fit his forehead, but the brim was way too wide for his squatty body. He looked like a toadstool or a cowboy Weeble.

"You buy that as a souvenir at a Tim McGraw concert?" Amanda pointed to his head, and managed to refrain from giggling.

"With my coloring, SPF 45 isn't enough."

It was the kind of comment with the same whine Erik would use. Lights flashed on Amanda's gay-dar. Ben liked an aging pop singer, dressed in costumes, and showed her way more deference than needed. Granted, Petula Clark didn't have the reputation Cher had, but she must be on the gays' top ten list somewhere.

It all made sense now. Ben *had* to be gay.

Amanda was relieved. At least that explanation for his kindness was more tolerable than greed.

Ben nodded toward the barn. "Come on, Pet."

Amanda's finger shot into the air as a warning, but secretly she appreciated his playfulness. This had been the most stressful week in her life, yet several times Ben had made her laugh.

One point for Ben Harris.

* * * *

Amanda watched in awe as Terri Miller bent at the waist, lifted the horse's leg backward, and trapped the hoof between her knees. With her left hand, she adeptly used a hand-pick to scrape dirt from the hoof. Before moving to another leg, she transferred the pick to a miniature hand that sat at the end of what would have been her right arm, but instead was a flipper.

"We'll teach your son all about ranch life," Terri said. "He'll be totally responsible for the horse and tack. It only takes most kids a few days to get the hang of things."

Terri straightened to a height matching Amanda's. Rays streaming through a skylight brightened her chocolate brown eyes and made the sun-streaked, short hair poking from under her ball cap shine. She tapped the tool against her worn chaps. Residue bounced off the tattered hem of her jeans and sprinkled onto her cracked leather boot.

After tossing the pick into a bucket filled with brushes and spray bottles, she grabbed a broom with her normal hand. Dodging the horse's legs, she swept the mess into a pile. Then switching the broom to her flipper hand, she loaded the dirt into a dust pan, flinging it into a large tub in the corner.

She looked at Ben. "You want to saddle Boo?"

Ben stared at the gray gelding whose shoulders reached his hat brim. He puckered his lips. "No, ma'am. I really don't know much about horses."

"Okay." Terri wiped sweat from her nose using the back of the hand on her deformed arm. The fingers were perfectly formed, but no longer than a toddler's.

She threw a pad on the horse's back, following it with the saddle. Her strength with one arm was impressive, but what she could do with the flipper was amazing.

When she cinched the girth, the horse shifted and Ben jumped back.

"You *really* want to ride?" Amanda asked.

Ben's Adam's apple bobbed as he swallowed. "Sure. I have to see what Jason will be doing. It's my job as his fa . . ."

Terri shoved her shoulder into the horse to shift his weight and his hoof clopped to within an inch of Ben's polished boot. He skittered backward again, this time bumping into the grooming bucket, tipping it over. Ben's back slammed into the wooden stall pole and he crashed to his butt.

The horse didn't move a muscle at the commotion.

Another point for Ms. Miller.

Terri offered her hand to Ben, easily hoisting him off the ground. "If you'd like, you both can wait for me outside. Kevin, my barn manager, should be around to answer your questions."

Amanda grinned at Ben and grabbed his elbow. "Come on, sweetie, before you give the pony a heart attack with your Touhey-Tom-foolery."

* * * *

They settled onto a bench beside the arena. A golden tabby cat laced around Amanda's legs and she bent over to rub its back.

"Terri Miller's mother took thalidomide during pregnancy," Ben said.

"What?"

"In the 1950s women took thalidomide to ease morning-sickness. It caused severe abnormalities of the extremities–the shrunken arm."

"How do you know?"

"Law school case files." Ben wiped the inside of his hat band with a handkerchief. He took great care in refolding the starched, white cloth before returning it to his back pocket.

Another telltale sign of his sexual preference.

Just when she'd started to like Ben Harris.

While Amanda was comfortable being friends with a gay man–after all she'd spent her entire youth with Erik–she cursed her luck. Would she never become involved with an available man? Even Ryan didn't fit that bill, with his secretive nature standing between them.

The tabby leapt into Amanda's lap. She smoothed her hand over his head, the soft fur caressing her fingers. The cat's purring harmonized with the hum of a small tractor at the far end of the arena. A straw hat dipped as the man drove in concentric circles, leveling the sand. He waved at Amanda and Ben.

They waved back. The cat nestled into Amanda and fell asleep. She continued scratching behind his ears, more for her benefit than his. Life seemed slower at the ranch.

It would be lovely to escape here for a while. She snapped the phone from her pocket and stared at the time. Even lacking the secondhand of a stopwatch, Amanda could hear the moments ticking by. She didn't have the luxury of relaxing.

"Must be Kevin," she said, slanting her head toward the tractor approaching them. "I'll pick his brain for information while you're working with Terri on the horse."

The corners of Ben's mouth pulled down. Arching his back, he placed his hand on his stomach. Color drained from his face.

"You really don't have to do this," Amanda said.

Ben exhaled. "I'll ride. It'll give you the opportunity to find out about the ranch. You need to know why they asked for the lottery money and how it will be spent."

"Okay, but don't sue me if you fall and break your neck."

Ben's gaze whipped to Amanda. "Is that an attempt at attorney humor?"

She shrugged.

He groaned.

The man in the straw hat parked along the rail beyond the gate. Planting two steel forearm crutches into the sand, he swung down from the tractor seat. Braces on both legs started at mid-thigh and hooked under his boots. The stiffness of the brackets caused him to waddle rather than walk.

"Hi, I'm Kevin Spencer." He loosened his grip on the crutch and pumped Ben's hand, a smile stretching over his face.

"Tom Touhey and this is my wife, Petula."

Amanda shook his hand, calloused and strong from work.

Kevin looked to be in his thirties, but with his weathered face and diminutive body, it was hard to judge his age. "Welcome to the Triple T," he said.

At that moment, Terri emerged from the barn followed by a very calm, but steady Boo.

Ben wiped his palms on his jeans. "Guess I'm up."

Terri stopped at the mounting block. On one side two steps rose to a broad platform. A ramp sloped from the other side.

Hesitantly, Ben scaled the stairs and climbed onto the horse, flinching when the saddle moved slightly sideways under his weight. "Whoa, boy. Nice Boo." His voice quavered.

He couldn't have held the saddle horn any tighter if it had been the handlebar of a giant rollercoaster. His back rounded, terror filled his eyes, but he'd plastered a smile on his face.

After Terri adjusted the stirrup length, she guided the horse along the inside perimeter of the arena, talking about posture and leg position. Repeatedly, she offered the reins to Ben who rocked back and forth matching Boo's gait, never once loosening his grip on the saddle horn or losing his fake grin.

Kevin plopped down next to Amanda to watch the lesson, his brace clunking against the wooden bench. Reaching down, he flipped the levers to unlock the brackets and his knees bent. "How'd you hear about us?"

Clearing her throat, Amanda dredged up the lies she'd rehearsed. "Tom has a friend who knows somebody who works at "Win a Fortune" and he read Terri's letter asking for money."

Kevin's face brightened with excitement. "Does his friend have any pull with the producers? We'd love a chance to show what we do here."

Guilt weighted her down. "Afraid not. Actually it's a friend of a friend. You know how that goes."

She stifled a groan at how unconvincing she sounded. Surely he could see through her lies.

"Anyway, unlike his father, Jason is crazy about horses, so we thought we'd check out the Triple T."

Kevin looked disappointed and Amanda recalled the comment made by the intern at the *World-Herald* about desperate people wanting the lottery money. He'd said they were pathetic.

This ranch hand didn't seem pathetic, but did appear distressed.

If only she could help.

"This is such a wonderful operation–specially made saddles, well-trained horses–many accommodations for safety, like the asphalt pathways. One thing concerns us, though," Amanda said.

A frown furrowed Kevin's brow. "What?"

"The letter mentioned financial difficulties and we're afraid to get Jason's hopes up if the ranch might close soon."

Stress lines tightened around Kevin's mouth. Apparently, he shared that concern.

"Fifteen years ago I came here as a twelve-year-old boy. I had no friends. I was totally introverted. Scared. But after a summer here, things turned around for me. There's something about learning to control a thirteen-hundred-pound animal that builds confidence."

"I would think so."

"I came back every summer, working as a ranch hand for my room and board. I moved here after high school to help Terri. She didn't want me to skip college, but she needed all the help she could get."

Amanda nodded. "Her one trusted friend."

Kevin's eyes narrowed and lips pursed. "No, I mean she needed *all* the help she could get. The ranch was exploding then. We'd gotten a contract with a national charity, and kids were coming from all over the country. We had to expand the dorms and buy more ponies."

"Sounds prosperous."

"We had more business than we could handle."

"What went wrong?"

Kevin gazed out into the field. He dug the tip of his crutch into the sand. His loyalty to Terri Miller ran deep. "Three summers ago a kid died here."

"Fell off a horse?"

"Out of his wheelchair. He'd been fooling around with some other boys in the dorm, having a great time playing cards when his excitement bounced him from his chair. He hit his head on the floor."

Amanda gasped and the cat sprang from her lap, jabbing his claws into her leg as he jumped.

"We called his parents, had the local doctor check him out. He didn't even have to stay overnight in the hospital."

"Then . . .?"

"A few hours later he died in his sleep from a blood clot in his brain."

Amanda's mouth dropped open. Ben passed before them still rocking back and forth. His muscles hadn't loosened an inch. She waved him on to indicate she needed more time.

Ben's smile dissolved.

"What happened wasn't the Triple T's fault," she said softly.

Now Kevin stabbed the crutch point into the ground. "No offense, but parents of challenged kids can get over-protective. Mine were." Kevin huffed. "The accident had nothing to do with riding. What happened to that kid could have happened in his own living room, but it didn't matter. We lost our contract with the charity and the referrals dried up. We've had fewer kids coming every summer since."

"So what would the lottery money do for you?"

"Terri said the money isn't quite as important as publicity. If we could get some time on the show, I know we'd get more students."

"But with money, you could advertise nationally."

Kevin pulled off his hat, dragging his sleeve over his forehead. "I don't know much about business, Mrs. Touhey. All I know is we need more paying kids or this summer will be our last."

Chapter Seventeen

Ryan's editor was wrong. He could still do his job with the same effectiveness as always. It was true that after the Danny Coomb's exposé, Ryan had become a celebrity of sorts. His face was plastered all over the news, but the public's recognition didn't extend outside of Denver—or at least not too far beyond Colorado.

That was why he'd taken a place in Phoenix. He did the majority of his writing where he couldn't be interrupted. With wireless Internet and his laptop, he could write from anywhere—any coffee shop, any restaurant, and any hotel—except those in Colorado.

Sitting down at his laptop, he Googled Ben Harris. In no time he read the highlights of the attorney's successful law career, including an overview of a couple of his noteworthy cases. However, Ryan Fisher knew there was much more to a person than his public façade, and he was more interested in the lawyer's private life. Most people had one or two secrets stuffed in a shoe box in the back of a closet.

For instance, Ryan had taken to using his grandfather's last name. No one blinked when he introduced himself as Ryan Fisher. He saved his Ryan Grogan persona for visits with the governor.

All these steps Ryan had executed to preserve his livelihood. He couldn't take the chance his target, the person he was investigating, would use the Internet against him and find out he was an undercover reporter. But he wasn't just any reporter. He was the one who'd exposed graft in the mining unions in central Colorado, and the one who'd broken the story about the State Senator taking bribes from an oil company. Soon, he would add Pulitzer Prize winner to his résumé. It was only a matter of time before the big story—the one to define his career—would land in his lap.

He knew it.

His editor was right about one thing, though. Ryan couldn't sneak up on anyone if they knew who he was, but he wasn't going to be forced to take an editing position at *The Register*.

Publishing had been fine for Bud. Not that his grandfather hadn't had his successes. He was a Pulitzer man himself. But Ryan couldn't breathe at the possibility of being cooped up in an office instead of out there dogging the stories. That was the only way he'd earn a spot on a national television news program—his ultimate dream.

Ryan Grogan could still do his job—*his* way.

For now, that meant insinuating himself into Amanda's life. His gut told him something was going on with her. She was too secretive and too innocent-acting to be on the level.

Good thing spending time with her wasn't a hardship. Her sense of humor was a little provincial, but amusing. Not hard to look at either. As long as he had to be in Omaha anyway for Bud, he might as well pursue her, and her story, whatever that might be.

He picked up his Blackberry and cigarettes. Stepping onto the balcony, he lit one up, taking a long draw. A dry breeze picked up some desert sand, swirling it into eddies below him. Blowing out the smoke, he took out the stylus and typed a list of questions:

Who is the tall stranger following Amanda?

What are Amanda and Ben Harris doing together?

Why Phoenix?

* * * *

"I want to help Terri Miller." Amanda tossed her backpack and card key on the dresser while Ben hung up her garment bag.

"Because . . .?" he asked.

"Because I hate to see anyone lose their dreams."

Ben placed the rolling case full of letters on the luggage rack. "Come on, Amanda. You can do better than that. Hitler had a dream."

Amanda pulled off her hat and with it came the band holding her ponytail. She scratched the lump of hair at her nape. "Terri Miller offers kids a safe haven from a sometimes cruel world. While helping people to help themselves, she offers them hope and encouragement. She teaches them skills."

"All good reasons to give her some lottery money."

Good. If Ben thought it was a solid decision, surely the lottery winner would, too. Pulling the *Cases* notebook from her backpack, she jotted her comments underlining the words *safe haven*.

Amanda was closer to her million-dollar finder's fee and Clara's new heart. Even with the enormous amount of work still to do, that prospect alone lifted her mood.

Ben sat on the Chippendale chair by the round table. He groaned.

"How *is* your butt?" Amanda stifled a giggle.

"You know, I think it hurts more from the fall in the barn than the actual ride."

She sighed in sympathy. "You're brave. Thank you for sacrificing your . . . self for the project."

A grin tugged at the corners of his mouth. "You can pay me back by having dinner with me."

"I can't." Amanda tugged the cell phone from her waistband to check the time, then clipped it back on her jeans. "I have too many letters to read. I have to figure out what to do with the other one-hundred-ninety-nine and a half million dollars."

"Let's order in room service then." He pointed outside. "We can eat there."

Amanda took in the features of the room. A tasteful, brocade spread covered the king-sized bed. Half the television peeked out from the large armoire in the corner by the sliding doors. An awning shaded an iron bistro table and two chairs on the balcony. "How much is this room costing?"

"Not more than the winner can afford," Ben said.

Her arms stiffened at her sides. "I don't want to do anything unethical."

"You don't want to get mugged in a dive either. This is standard, business-class accommodations."

"I wouldn't know. I've never traveled before."

Ben's eyes flew open in surprise, but before Amanda could explain, her cell phone rang. *The hospital?* She jerked the phone from her jeans and answered, her heart pounding in her throat. "Hello?"

"Hi, beautiful. Hope you're not getting too soggy in Omaha. I hear it's raining like hell."

Her heartbeat picked up speed at the sound of Ryan's chuckle. "Hold on a second, would you?"

"Sure."

Amanda pressed the phone to her chest and turned to Ben. "I have to take this call."

"Okay." His gaze shifted around the room. "I'll run and take a shower, then pick up something for us downstairs for dinner. Meet back here in an hour?"

How dangerous could a dinner with a gay man be, even in a hotel room? "Sure, that'd be great."

As soon as the door clicked shut after Ben, she returned to Ryan. "So is the weather better where you are?"

"Sunny and eighty-six."

"In Denver?"

"Phoenix."

Phoenix? Amanda shrank away from the window, good sense telling her that odds were slim that he'd chosen this hotel to stay in, but even so. Standard, business-class accommodations, Ben said. For all she knew, Ryan could be in the room next to hers, talking to her from his balcony.

Good thing she and Ben weren't going out this evening. She couldn't risk running into Ryan Fisher.

"Want to do something next weekend? I have to be in Omaha," he said.

She sank to the floor, pulling the curtains closed. "Is Bud okay?"

"Yes, but he's having a fit. He needs some investment advice and doesn't want to talk over the phone." His voice grew hushed. "Someone might hear."

"Must be a large sum."

"Millions, I'm sure." Sarcasm shrouded his tone.

"Be nice."

"I don't know the amount, Amanda. He's always so secretive. Seems this is a stash he's been hiding from me. Hell, for all I know, he could have won the lottery."

Amanda slapped a hand over her mouth, smothering a gasp. His remark hit too close to home. Slowly, she lowered her trembling hand and opened her eyes. She swallowed to wet her throat. "I'm free Friday night."

"Good. We'll fly to Paris on Gramps' fortune."

Ryan laughed before hanging up.

Amanda crawled onto the bed, the conversation roiling in her mind.

Bud has a large cache of money. He needs investment advice. He doesn't want to risk anyone overhearing their discussion.

Could Bud Fisher be *the* lottery winner?

The ramifications made her dizzy. She flipped onto her side and went through the facts again.

It couldn't be Bud. There were too many contradictions. If Bud were the benefactor, why would he hire an agent to distribute the money? Certainly he would use Ryan for that job. But maybe because of the large sum, there was more than one person researching potential recipients. After all, she'd been at it for ten days and had only found one person to give half a million dollars.

Bud Fisher, the multi-million-dollar winner?

She turned her head and stared at the textured ceiling. The stark whiteness of twists and contorted lines matched the thoughts pouring through her mind.

Surely she was crazy to believe an octogenarian with moderate dementia could mastermind this scheme—offering her exactly what she needed when she needed it.

Still, Bud liked her.

Amanda untangled the details. Mr. Franklin had said the letter was drawn *randomly*. If that were true, it would be a coincidence that she'd been chosen by Bud.

Farther fetched than that prospect was another she proposed. It was possible the lottery winner didn't ask to know the name of his agent which would mean Bud didn't even know she was his delegate.

Rolling onto her other side, she nervously ran her fingers through her hair. She couldn't shake the suspicion that Bud had chosen her specifically. That begged another question. Could someone search for and find her letter among the stacks of requests, thus giving her an opportunity to 'earn' the money needed for Clara's surgery?

For a moment, she felt like Pip in *Great Expectations*.

Chapter Eighteen

The beer tasted especially bitter tonight. Ben reasoned it was due to the back-stabbing he was about to inflict on Amanda.

People were scarce in the hotel lounge and Ben had picked the darkest end of the mahogany bar. He twisted so his back was to the wall and he could see everyone coming and going.

He had no stomach for deceit. Certainly, when she found out about his role in this set-up, Amanda would be furious, and that would end their friendship. And they *were* becoming friends. He could see that.

Smiling, he recalled her face this morning when she realized his joke in giving her the pseudonym. It had been a mixture of innocence, courage, and spirit. She was just too good, but true—a combination of integrity and freckles.

To avoid ending up broken and miserable he'd have to keep his emotional distance from Amanda Cash. Right. It was too late for that. He'd already fallen hopelessly in love with her. Breathing a sigh of longing, he prayed for a turn of luck.

"Mr. Harris." The man slid onto the stool next to Ben. He had to spread his long legs extra wide not to bump his knees on the bar.

His voice and his presence made Ben's blood run cold. He had no reason to dislike the rangy stranger, other than the fact he'd dragged Ben into spying on Amanda.

Catching the bartender's gaze, the stranger pointed to Ben's glass and held up two fingers. He pulled out a pack of cigarettes, their menace reflected in the polished countertop. "I don't like how you ditched me today." He kept his voice low.

Ben shook off a shudder. "Like she wouldn't have seen you tailing us to the ranch. It was open desert, for God's sakes."

"Your job is to keep me nearby."

"Wasn't possible today." Ben took a sip of the beer and forced a swallow. Now he had a definite reason to dislike the man. He was damned annoying and rude.

The jerk smelled of cigarette smoke and something sweet. With his dark tan, it couldn't be sun block.

Setting the beers in front of them, the bartender growled. "No smoking in here, buddy."

The stranger's eyes flashed aggravation. "Yeah, it's the same all over. People's rights flushing right down the toilet."

He had the nerve to complain when he'd clearly trounced on Amanda's private life.

And Ben had helped.

Suddenly, Ben felt despicable.

"My boss won't be happy that I lost contact with Amanda."

"Yeah, well. Like I said, unless you have a cloaking device, she would've seen you." He passed a folded piece of paper to the man. "That's what we got today."

Without glancing at the notes, he stuffed it into the chest pocket of his blue oxford shirt. It was tailored and Ben surmised the loser must do all right in his line of work.

"I'll let you know when I've booked our next trip," Ben said.

"Good. I'll be waiting." The man picked up his cigarettes and stood, tapping the package on the bar top.

"And you can have the night off. We're staying in tonight," Ben said.

The man stretched to his full height, towering over Ben. Then he sneered. "So you're following up on that information I gave you about her gay husband."

Acid roiled in Ben's gut. He wished now he'd refused that piece of reconnaissance. "We're reviewing candidates."

"Whatever you say."

"You're a sand rattler."

The snake leaned over Ben. "Like you're any better?"

Ben popped off the stool, grabbed the man's arm, and squeezed. He was used to tall men thinking they had the advantage. The jerk might've looked fit, but Ben could crush him like a beetle.

Glaring, the stranger didn't back down. "So tell me, Mr. Righteous, what are you getting out of this situation—besides money?"

Ben shoved the reptile hard against the bar, spilling both glasses of beer. Over his shoulder, he saw the bartender approaching and he released his grip. He growled. "I'll do my best to keep you closer, but you have to do something for me."

The worm raised his palm to acknowledge the bartender, who stopped a few feet from the feuding men. "I don't answer to you."

Stepping closer to the tall man, Ben spat his order. "You *will* warn me before the story breaks so I can be with Amanda."

Raising an eyebrow, the man grunted. "Why?"

"She'll need me."

"Want my prediction?" The snake rattled his head, giving a hiss. "When the story breaks, you're the *last* person she will want acting as comfort. She'll *loathe* you."

Chapter Nineteen

Granted, their work was serious, but Ben was taking it too far this evening. He'd hardly spoken and then only about business, in a polite, professional way. He'd even refused the beer he'd brought with dinner.

Amanda moved the empty pizza box to stand upended next to the trash can in the corner. They'd discussed contestants all through dinner—inside the room, not on the balcony. She couldn't risk being seen by Ryan, on the off-chance he was a guest in their hotel.

She returned to the Chippendale chair placed at right angles to Ben's at the small, round table. He finished trapping the last crumb into a paper napkin. Slowly, he walked the five steps to throw it away.

Yesterday, he would have shot the napkin like a basketball into a hoop. Tonight, he was moody.

Her mind swirled with a clutter of thoughts—none of them on the task at hand.

Was there no man in her life with whom she wasn't having difficulties?

Ryan was as secretive as ever. She'd been surprised when he'd told her he was in Phoenix. If he were CIA, the strongest truth serum couldn't loosen his tongue.

And it was a lovely tongue. And mouth. And lips. But more than the admiration she had for his physical attributes, she liked how respected she felt when with him. Maybe it was because they shared similar situations with having incapacitated family members in the nursing home. In addition, he seemed to understand and appreciate the struggles she'd had with her business. Not even her mother understood her complex emotions associated with that loss.

In frustration, Amanda unclipped the cell phone from her waistband and glanced at the time.

It would be best to forget about Ryan, at least as a romantic prospect. He clearly was unavailable. Anyone who wouldn't speak in generalities about his work surely wouldn't share deep emotions. Now, the only reason to see Ryan was to find out if Bud was the lottery winner. Their relationship had to change to strictly business. She'd use their time together this weekend to pick his brain. She snorted. *Right.* Better bring dynamite if she expected to extract any facts from that handsome man.

Strike handsome. He was only a source for information—a secretive, tight-lipped, emotionally unavailable source at that.

She sighed. Were there any men worth the time? She'd invested most of her life with Erik Cash, the user. She'd never realized how manipulative he was. It tore her heart apart to think he only cared about her uterus. That and Shane.

What did it say about her ability to judge people that she'd stayed married to Erik for so long and didn't recognize his true intentions?

No time to hike down that dead-end road again.

Now Ben Harris was acting strange. She looked at him, trying to figure him out as he riffled through another stack of letters he'd piled onto the table before them.

His shirt was crisp, which was an anomaly because it was knit. The collar clearly stood at attention. It was the mildest shade of periwinkle, complementing his complexion beautifully. He had awesome fashion sense—like Erik. Too bad he was probably like Erik in more ways than one.

She jerked in surprise. Where had that regret come from? She'd never considered Ben in that way.

To regain focus, she studied the digital clock in her hand, too aware of how time was slipping away while the deadline raced closer. She couldn't waste one more second in activities not directly related to her quest. It was her duty to her mother.

She skimmed a letter with a jelly thumbprint in the corner. "How about the sextuplets?"

Ben huffed, stealing the letter. "Well, it's up to you. The sextuplets are getting tons of press and with that comes free diapers, formula, furniture, baby clothes, and equipment. It's just a matter of time before a car company gives the family a van and some reality television celebrity builds them a house. Their college education is probably the only thing that won't be paid by Oprah or whoever would get publicity from financing it."

He was in a snit about something. Troubles with a man? Likely so.

Maybe he was having gay mood swings. Those used to strike Erik often. First, he'd get quiet and distance himself from her, more than usual. Then he'd get grumpy and pick a fight. When he'd had enough of verbally battering her, he'd apologize. The drama ended with lots of music and dancing. She'd called it his PMS—Pre-Madonna-Syndrome.

Ben tossed the letter back on top of the pile. "All this because they took fertility drugs. The husband already had a three-year-old from a previous relationship. They could have adopted one of hundreds of needy children."

She'd never heard him speak so harshly before. Is that how she'd sounded to Clara when they used to watch "Win a Fortune" together—eager to push the responsibility of helping people on to some other charity? The bluntness of his judgment was ugly. Shame crawled over her, leaving heat in its wake.

The possibility of disappointing her mother clutched her heart.

Her parents had sacrificed plenty for her and she couldn't think of one instance where either of them had disappointed her.

Both Clara and Jim earned their living packing cereal into boxes at the Kellogg's plant. Jim worked first shift and Clara worked swing, from three to eleven. Although matching schedules would have meant evening family time together and a more traditional life, Clara insisted on being available to her daughter during the day.

The staggered hours allowed Clara to volunteer in Amanda's classroom and kept her out of daycare, because her dad took over at three. Summers, they'd go to the zoo and visit nature museums. This unusual schedule also allowed Clara to supervise Amanda's first business.

Her mother had suggested a red-checkered, plastic tablecloth for the lemonade stand. Amanda had insisted on sewing multi-colored sequins into flower patterns on white linen. On the practical side, Amanda added a clear plastic sheet over the cloth, careful it didn't drape beyond the tabletop and inadvertently cover the twinkling spangles.

In the end, Clara had said the tablecloth had *stunning* curb appeal. But the presentation wasn't the only thing setting apart Amanda's lemonade stand.

To complement the clichéd drink, she offered free, homemade brownies cut into one-bite squares. The combination refreshment was a loss leader since she only charged a dime.

Where she'd made her money was selling the silver, blue, and red pinwheels. To showcase the merchandise, she'd run an extension cord from the house and plugged in a small fan aimed at the display. No one could resist the whirling fun on a stick, or rather, a straw. Amanda had crafted the toy for a mere investment of her time and seventeen-cents in materials and sold the item for a dollar.

Everyone who stopped for lemonade bought at least one pinwheel. Many people stopped just to see the toy, but once they'd played with it, they bought it. It was irresistible.

Only seven years old and Amanda had found her niche, netting three-hundred dollars that summer. None of her success would have been possible if not for her parents' sacrifices.

Now, she couldn't risk Clara's disappointment by missing the deadline and losing the million dollars. She leafed through the letters she'd marked as 'possible.'

"There are the hurricane victims from last year," she said.

"Insurance will take care of the bulk of that."

"If that's true, why are there so many letters begging for help?"

Ben pursed his lips. "Assumed entitlement."

"I don't understand."

"It's a socialist concept I see practiced all the time. People believe in capitalism, self-sufficiency until something goes wrong. Then even the strongest of independents cry to the government, lawyers, and in this case the lottery winner. 'I don't have enough. You have more than you need. *You owe me.*'"

His explanation shocked her. Was he that cynical?

She recalled how callous she'd sounded to Clara when she'd made a similar comment about the flood victims and decided to give Ben the benefit of the doubt. Maybe there was more than just man troubles on his mind. An important issue could be stressing him, suppressing the good-natured disposition she'd come to expect.

She forgave him. "Well, then who would *you* help?"

"Looking at it from a practical perspective, to meet the deadline, you'll have to go big. Give all the money to one group."

Amanda laid the letters on the table. "You mean like a medical research project?"

"Possibly."

"For a particular type of cancer—or Alzheimer's disease—something like that?"

He rubbed his forehead with his palm and groaned. "Probably not a good idea."

"Why not?" she asked.

"At some point the pharmaceutical industry would get involved. The most aggressive drug company would get the patent on the cure and then they'd jack up the prices of the medicine, exploiting the very people you meant to help—the patients."

"Are you sure? Does that happen?"

He shrugged.

Amanda shook her head, frustrated. He was absolutely no help this evening. What had happened from the time he'd left her room to shower and pick up their pizza?

He did smell good, though. It wasn't the hotel soap, but something exotically spicy, with a hint of citrus.

The trilling of the cell phone jolted Amanda from her distraction and bounced Ben out of his chair. He pinched the bridge of his nose. "Must we have an alarm at the top of every hour?"

Amanda canceled the signal, glad the reminder realigned her focus. "Do you have your laptop with you?"

He stepped to the bed and dug more letters from the rolling case. "Across the hall in my room."

"May I borrow it please to do some research on the web about medical trusts?"

"No."

"What?"

He stood over Amanda, placing a new batch of letters onto the table. "You know the firm has a strict policy prohibiting partners from sharing their computers. We have to maintain the confidentiality of our clients."

"Wait." Amanda jumped up, tipping the chair sideways. Ben caught it before the back hit the floor.

She held up her hand, palm toward him. "You spend all day lying to some very nice people about who you are and what you're doing at their ranch and *now* you have ethics?"

His face flushed. Setting the chair legs firmly on the floor, he slapped his palms on his thighs. "You're questioning my values?"

Here was the argument. Just like Erik. Ben wanted to pick a fight over a triviality. As office manager she had access to confidential information all the time. Well, she could get around this kind of stubbornness. She'd had years of practice.

"This isn't coming out right. You truly are the sweetest, most principled man I've ever met. I promise I'm not going to hack into any client files. I only want to look up some information on the internet."

Like anything I can find about Ryan Fisher.

He studied the ceiling while considering her explanation and then returned his gaze to her. A flame flickered in his eyes, startling her.

"You can't play me, Amanda."

"What?"

He inched closer. "You think if you can't get what you want through bullying, then cajoling will work."

They stood toe to toe now and Amanda didn't understand the feelings washing over her. She wasn't intimidated by Ben, but her nerves danced like they were exposed live wires. "I don't know what you're talking about."

He dropped his hands to his sides, nudged a little closer until Amanda could see flecks of gold mixed in his green eyes.

"Nobody's as innocent and ethical as you pretend to be," he said.

Her hand flew to her heart. "I pretend?"

"You seem to lie with ease when you're playing a role."

"Pet Touhey?"

"Erik Cash's wife."

The façade she'd spent years protecting crumbled around her, the crash deafening. Her breath quickened, sweat dampened the back of her neck, heartbeat echoed in her ears.

He ran his hands gently up and down her arms. "I know you've been pretending to be happily married when, for years, that hasn't been the case."

She stood dumbstruck. And here she'd thought her performance had been flawlessly presented. But not being miserable wasn't the same as being happy, and obviously her secret had leaked through her veneer.

Muscles tense, a lump grew in her throat. She forced the tears back with one labored swallow and a hard blink.

The look in Ben's eyes told her he knew Erik was gay. How stupid of her to believe Ben wouldn't notice Erik's nature when they'd met at her apartment. One gay could always recognize another.

"I can only imagine your emotional turmoil," he said.

How had he seen through her, right to her pain?

She tried containing her heartbreak, but tears trickled down her cheeks, sizzling against her hot skin.

Ben's voice purred. "I'm a good listener."

She didn't need a girlfriend. She'd hashed it over every which way a million times with her mother and still she never felt better about the situation.

She'd squandered so much of her life.

He enfolded her into his arms, laying his cheek softly against hers. It felt so much more comforting than when Erik laid his chin on top of her head.

So much for the advantages of loving a tall man.

Instinctively her arms circled Ben's waist.

Funny, she didn't seem to be crying about Erik now, though she didn't understand the tears. Possibly they sprang from hope that someone might be offering an intimate connection to her.

Too bad he was gay.

She patted his back, pulling away from him. No use wasting more time grieving with a 'girlfriend' about lost love.

As if on cue, with deliberate contradiction, Ben eased her into his arms once again. He tilted her chin up with his finger, until their gazes met. Then he closed his eyes and pressed his lips to hers.

The kiss lingered, sucking years of pain and doubt from Amanda. She never knew a kiss could hold so much comfort, security, and promise.

When their lips parted, she stared at him speechlessly. The muscles in her shoulders relaxed and her breathing calmed.

Using his thumbs, he dried her cheeks. "I should go now."

She blinked as if she'd never seen him before. "Okay." It was all she could manage to say.

Squeezing her arm, he smiled. "You all right?"

She nodded mechanically. "Fine."

"I'll see you for breakfast." He kissed her forehead before turning and strolling out the door.

Barely waiting for the click behind him, Amanda rushed out onto the balcony. The temperature was mild, in the mid-seventies. A breeze cooled her flushed cheeks.

She clutched the rail, gazing out over the black desert dotted with lights from the sprawling civilization.

How had she been so wrong about Ben Harris?

A cough behind her drew her attention. She spun around to see embers of a cigarette glowing from the balcony next to hers. Shadows hid the face of the tall stranger. Panic hit her at the same time the smoke did.

Ducking behind the concrete half-wall, she crawled to the door. She glanced behind in time to see the man, in profile, take a long drag from the cigarette. Twice he tapped to free the loose ashes. Then flicking his fingers, he launched the butt off the balcony to the ground below.

Before he could turn around, Amanda stood, dashed back inside her room, and locked the sliding glass door, calmed only by the fact Ryan Fisher was a non-smoker.

Chapter Twenty

Erik didn't know what to expect, but one thing was certain, Amanda had told her mother about their impending divorce. She always confided in Clara–about *everything*, down to his preference of boxers over briefs. He wiped his sweaty palms on his jeans before knocking on Clara's door at Brookside.

Clara's loud, boisterous laugh preceded muffled shuffling. Then the door popped open and he stared into the face of Ben Harris, whose grin faded to neutral, like vanilla pudding.

"Yes?" Ben said with his finger pinched between pages of a book.

Questions flooded Erik's mind. Did Ben remember when they met at Amanda's apartment almost a week ago? Had Amanda cried on Ben's shoulder about how cruel he and Shane had been to her? If so, had Ben consoled Amanda? And how? Why was Ben in Clara's room–making her laugh, no less?

For a short man, Ben's gaze was powerful. All Erik could think to say was, "Is Clara in?"

Ben straightened, tipping his head to one side. "Who shall I say is visiting?"

His accent dripped of British snippiness. He would make this difficult. And would he also make fun of Erik's lifestyle?

He added extra bass to his voice. "Erik Cash."

"One moment, please."

Ben turned and announced loudly, "Someone by the name of Erik Cash is here to see you, mum."

Clara's giggle followed. "For God's sake, don't be a pill. Let him in." She sniggered again.

Ben opened the door wide, but moved only slightly out of the way. Amanda must have given him an earful about their failed marriage and his horrible treatment of her since.

He glided past Ben and took two steps into the small room. Clara sat in a recliner in the near corner, connected to a machine by a tube with prongs up her nose. Erik flinched to see her so helpless and shrunken. He raised his hand awkwardly and waved. "Hi."

A smile slipped across her face. "Erik, come in."

Hesitating only a second, he shuffled closer to the woman he'd known since elementary school, the woman who'd baked treats for him—albeit brownies from a mix.

She pointed to a side chair he recognized from the entry in her old home. He'd always sat in it to take off his snowy boots when he visited Amanda. "Have a seat," she said.

Easing into the cushion flattened with age, he glanced around the room. This was his first visit to her since she'd given up her house. Glimpsing the photo collages on the wall, nostalgia mixed with shame flowed over him. He and Amanda were coupled in all of the photos from the last twenty years.

"I'm forgetting my manners. Do you know Ben Harris?"

He turned to the man sliding by him to lay the dog-eared novel on the nightstand. "Yes, we've met." Erik stood, offering his hand, which Ben accepted. "Nice to see you again."

Ben pumped his hand with a firm grip. "Yes," Ben said, dropping the English accent.

For a little guy, he was remarkably strong.

"Ben, would you mind getting me an ice cream cone, please?" Clara said, sweetly. "Would you like one, Erik? One thing this sorry place has is a decent café with free ice cream."

"No thanks, M . . ." He'd almost called her mom. That would be a hard habit to break. It was easy to call her Clara when he talked to Shane, but looking straight into her old, wrinkled face, remembering all the family holidays they'd spent together . . . Tears needled his eyes.

Bending at the waist, Ben dropped a kiss on the back of Clara's hand. "Be back in a few, mum."

The Anthony Hopkins tone had returned. What was up with that?

"Take your time, sir. Then we'll get back to Dickens." Her wide smile beckoned another kiss which he quickly let fall on her hand.

When Ben closed the door behind him, Erik felt the heaviness of the visit gather around him. He'd never been pressed for things to say to his mother-in-law, but the fact that she would no longer be in that role produced the lump in his throat, blocking his words.

"So, what's happening in your neck of the woods, son?"

The tears were dangerously close to the surface now and he felt a tingling burn at the end of his nose. Why did she have to call him *son?* Surely, Amanda didn't leave the news of their divorce for him to announce.

He drew in a large breath and blurted, "I'm moving to Germany. In three weeks."

Clara's head jerked up "Germany? That's wonderful. You'll finally get to cook *Wiener schnitzel* for the natives."

Her mangled German accent, combined with her grin, drew a smile to his lips.

"You will send me a postcard, won't you? Something with little men dressed in short pants with suspenders, wearing knee-high stockings and those funny hats with the feather sticking out. What's that get-up called?"

She was making this easier than she had to—easier than he deserved. "*Lederhosen.*"

Slapping her knee, a grin pulled one side of her mouth. "See, you already have the lingo down."

"Yes, I'll send you a postcard."

"And you'll rush the divorce papers back, signed, when you get them from Amanda, won't you, son?"

Like a pot of boiling oil thrown from the castle rampart, scalding heat washed over his cheeks. "Please don't call me that."

"What?"

"Son."

"That's what you always felt like to Jim and me."

He shook his head, the motion releasing a tear. He'd disappointed Clara, one adult he'd always wanted to please because he never had to work at it.

Jerking his handkerchief out of his back pocket, he wiped his nose. "I'm sorry."

"What for?"

"Everything."

She pursed her lips, the action popping the tubing from her nose. Two wrinkled hands covered with raised, blue veins adjusted the prongs. "Aw, that's a cop-out, Erik. You can be more specific than that."

"Well, I'm not sorry for being gay. I can't help that."

Clara's head tilted slightly and she looked at him from the corner of her eye. "Given. Then what *are* you apologizing for?"

"For disappointing you."

The breath she blew out puffed her thin cheeks like the nylon flaps of a collapsing tent. "Wasted guilt, son. It's Amanda you hurt."

The sobs choked him now. How would he ever undo the pain he'd caused her? He'd begged Shane not to be so harsh. But if he was being truly honest, he could have avoided the whole mess by talking with her by himself. Or better yet, refuse to go along with the hurtful scheme in the first place.

He swiped away the tears. "I don't know what to say."

"You don't have to *say* anything. Just go about your business. Sign and return the divorce papers *quickly*. And never contact my daughter again."

His jaw dropped. "Never talk to Amanda again?"

Resting her elbows on the overstuffed arms of the recliner, she leaned forward and gripped him in her stare. "If you really love her, and I believe you do, in *some* way, you'll listen to me. Spare her more suffering. Make a clean break." Her hand slashed through the air. "Don't contest anything. Heaven knows, there's nothing left of any value to divide. Just move on."

Her puffy eyes narrowed to slits. "And let her do the same."

Believing the shame released in his tears would drown him for certain, he relented. "Okay." He couldn't stop the nodding of his head. "Before I leave, I'll put your dining room furniture in storage under her name. I'll prepay the unit for a year. Some day she'll have a place big enough for it."

She reached toward him with her withered arm and patted his back. The weight of her forgiveness pressed down on him like an anvil.

"Good boy. Now give me a kiss before you leave."

* * * *

 14 Days until the Deadline

Humidity weighed down Amanda's navy silk dress, dampened the cotton sweater draped over her arm. The ominous clouds overhead even threatened the birds into silence. Violent storms were ahead this evening.

As she entered her mother's wing at Brookside, she saw two men walking away from her at the end of the corridor. One had Ben's muscular physique and short gait. The taller man had the breadth of Ryan's shoulders, although the light green blazer hardly seemed his style.

The image stopped her cold. She watched the two slip around the corner heading for the exit and tried to rationalize what she'd just seen.

No reason both men shouldn't be in the nursing home—Ryan to visit Bud, Ben to visit Clara. But why would they would be together? Replaying the image in her head, she decided the taller man's gait wasn't quite like Ryan's.

A resident edging around her with his walker broke her concentration, and she plodded into Clara's room.

She shuddered, still not used to the drone of the machine that took the room air, concentrated the oxygen, and pumped it via a tube into Clara's nose. The background hum was loud and constant, like living inside a beehive.

Amanda laid the terra cotta pot on Clara's nightstand. It was filled with goodies from Phoenix. "Did Ben visit you today?"

"Not even a kiss?" Clara shouted from her recliner, obviously trying to be heard over the oxygen concentrator squeezed next to her.

Amanda pecked her mother's forehead, shaken by the chill of it. Clara had lost weight in the hospital and her cheekbones cut sharp edges under her puffy eyes. Gathering crumpled tissues from the bedside tray, Amanda noticed three yellow carnations in a bud vase.

"Was Ben here?" she repeated.

Clara patted Amanda's arm with a tremulous hand. "Why, yes he was. He's the nicest young man. He read a few pages of *Great Expectations* to me."

Ben had been sworn to secrecy about their mission, but not about their kiss.

"What did he say?" Amanda asked casually, trying to conceal her anxiety. She curled her fingers into her palms and swallowed hard.

Giggling, Clara's eyes twinkled like they hadn't in a long while. "He said 'chicken a la king.'"

Amanda blinked. "What? He said—"

"It's his way of cursing. He uses silly words because it's less intimidating and lightens the situation that ticked him off in the first place. Smart, isn't he?"

Amanda sucked in her lower lip, gently chewing on it. Had Ben cursed at Ryan in her mother's room? "Was Ben alone?"

Her mother's giggling stopped with an abrupt hiccup. "What is this, the inquisition? Hand me a sweater, I'm freezing."

"You could turn up the thermostat." It *was* cold in here. She pulled on her sweater.

"Makes it too humid. Then I can't breathe. A storm's brewing."

"Don't change the subject, Mom. Was Bud Fisher's grandson with Ben?"

Jerking her head back, Clara stared at Amanda through swollen lids. "Why would Bud's grandson be visiting me?"

As if for the first time, Clara glimpsed Amanda from head to toe. A smile shifted wrinkles in her cheeks to collect by Clara's ears. "Don't you look snazzy. What's the occasion?"

Amanda raised an eyebrow. She had no intention of telling her mother she was going out with Ryan. Besides, the date was only business. That was her new pledge and she intended to honor it. In no way would she let images of Ryan's sex appeal sneak into her mind tonight. Her only goal was to find out if Bud Fisher was the lottery winner.

"Can't a person get cleaned up to visit her mother?"

Clara slanted her head, looking at Amanda from the corner of her eye. "Hmm." She adjusted the nasal prongs. "What did you learn on your trip?"

"Learn?"

"Life's a series of lessons. If you don't learn something, especially when you travel, then you're not paying attention." She gently slapped Amanda's arm.

"The plane ride was interesting. The landing bumpier than I thought it would be."

"Huh. Wouldn't exactly call that an earth-shattering discovery."

Amanda wanted to tell her mother about Terri Miller and her amazing determination, but she couldn't. A nurse or aide might walk in, and she wasn't certain her mother could keep a secret.

"Did you at least have some fun? Eat exotic food?"

"Pepperoni pizza."

"Sheesh." She dismissed Amanda with a wave. "You're hopeless."

Amanda wanted to tell her about Ben and the kiss, but taken out of context, the story didn't sound right. To think that she'd suspected him of being gay. It was funny now, but she could hardly kick herself over that misinterpretation. Erik had been her sole education into the world of men.

Ben had promised not to press Amanda about their kiss until the project ended. She'd convinced him a romance now would not only be distracting, but premature since she wasn't yet divorced. To his credit, he'd bowed to her wishes and their meetings in the past week had remained strictly professional.

"Better turn on the television." Clara wiggled her fingers at the remote on the nightstand. "There's a special Friday edition of "Win a Fortune." Or better yet, read Dickens to me."

One thing had changed since Amanda had lost her business through client neglect. Now there were people available to take care of Clara, and Amanda could prioritize her time accordingly. It was imperative the visits with her mother were brief while the hours working on the project were long, which was exactly how the last five days had been since she'd returned from Phoenix. Still, she was no closer to deciding how to divide the jackpot and that burden weighed heavy on her.

"I can't stay. I only dropped by for a few minutes."

She clicked on the television, set down the remote, and grabbed her purse, kissing her mother's cheek. "I'll call you."

"We have breaking news," the voice blared. Clara had cranked up the volume so she could hear it over all the machinery in the room.

Dark creases in Brad Conklin's forehead indicated the seriousness of the report. *I wonder if someone in make-up drew those on,* Amanda wondered. Every time she watched the show now, she recalled what Bud had said—*"Win a Fortune" isn't news. It's hype.*

Amanda inched toward the door, her gaze still glued to the screen. Mallory Piper's hair had an auburn cast tonight. Either the producers thought it would skew better with the audience, or Clara's television needed adjusting. Naturally or not, Mallory didn't share Brad's somber creases.

The large digital clock looming behind the desk ticked off the seconds, reminding Amanda she was wasting time. The ticket must be cashed in four weeks and she had but fourteen days left to meet the deadline established by the lottery winner.

The few minutes it would take to listen to this broadcast could, however, be important to her project.

"Diligent reporting has just revealed the name of the lottery winner's agent."

Amanda gasped.

"Are you okay, dear?" Clara said.

Stay calm. "Yes Mom, I'm fine."

She sank onto a chair, everything in the room fading except the television screen.

"For more details, we turn to our lottery expert in the field, Harvey Lawrence."

"Dear God," Clara grumbled. "Not this firebrand again."

Frozen, Amanda held her breath.

"Brad, I'm standing in Austin, Texas tonight with one of the greatest legends the rodeo circuit has ever produced."

Harvey pulled a cowboy in front of the camera. The red plaid of his flannel shirt virtually glowed on Clara's television. Years had grayed his hair and too many beers washing down Texas barbeque blocked the man's view of his championship belt buckle.

"Henry Wadsworth Longo," the reporter slapped the cowboy on his back, "is the lottery winner's agent."

When Henry smiled, two gold caps winked at the camera.

Chapter Twenty-one

Amanda caught up with Bud, alone in the sun parlor, a community room in the corner of the complex. Picture windows overlooked a lake with dark waters eerily still.

Dressed in a royal blue athletic suit to match his Bronco's cap, he leaned his elbows on the arms of his wheelchair and absently rubbed his hands together while watching out the window. His usual tremors rocked his head harshly. His blank stare and drooping jaw tipped Amanda. Bud was not having a clear day.

Plunking down in the cushioned, white wicker chair next to his go-buggy, she patted Bud's forearm. "Are the fish biting?"

His gaze never left the window nor the lone fisherman. "Hail's coming. Fish are hiding on the bottom."

She glimpsed the fluffy white clouds as they gathered height, darkening their base. "The weather service predicts thunderstorms."

"Better tell Sybil to get the sheets off the clothes line."

Choking back her anger at time itself, Amanda tried to ground Bud in the present. "How's that bump on your head healing?" She peeked under his hat brim at the faded bruise, now a lemon chiffon shade of yellow.

His eyes clouded over, gaze unmoving. "People are always trying to tell me their stories. Most people's lives aren't interesting enough to scrawl on the back of a family photo, you know." Then he stared at her as a stranger might. "You're pretty. What's *your* story?"

"I'm Amanda Cash. My mom lives across the hall from you."

He scowled, firming his jellied jowls. "That's fine, but I can't print that. Tell me something someone would be excited to read."

"I live a boring life," she confessed with a light shrug, "What can I say?"

The vacancy in his stare gave her a consent of sorts to complete her mission. There would be no better time. The taste of betrayal was bitter.

She summoned an image of Clara leashed to an oxygen tank, and shoving aside a spasm of guilt, marched forth through his weakened mental defenses. "How about you? What's your story, Bud?"

He relaxed his grimace and stared back out the window. "I beat the odds once."

Adrenaline jump-started her pulse. Her mouth went dry. Was he implying what she hoped? "Do you mean you beat the odds by winning the lottery?"

Whipping his head toward her, his face grew taut and his eyes narrowed. "Don't you dare give me another one of those damned lottery tickets."

With irritation, he rubbed his dry hands together faster, making the sound of fine-grit sandpaper on fresh wood. "I can't spend the money I already have. Nobody could. That's why I have my grandson helping me."

Her heart banged like a bell clapper, first against her chest and then against her backbone. She tried to slow its pace by tapping two fingers slowly against her sternum and breathing deeply.

Was he confessing he was the big lottery winner–the person who'd chosen her for her special assignment?

In a flash, it occurred to her she had no idea what to do if he confirmed her suspicions. Other than satisfying her curiosity, it didn't matter who the lottery winner was. Knowing the identity wouldn't change what she must do. Would his confession negate their contract? Would she lose the finder's fee if she pressed him into revealing his identity?

Panic stole her breath. Fear whipped up the tempo of her heart again. She couldn't do anything to anger Bud and risk losing her opportunity at a million dollars and Clara's new heart.

Bud drilled a stare through Amanda, his annoyance nearly halting the tremble of his head.

The throbbing of the pulse in her ears grew louder. She wished she could turn back the clock or figure out a way for Bud to forget she'd ever pressed him to confess.

He set his jaw–aggravation oozing from his stare. "Do you know Ryan?"

Slowly, she nodded.

"He's a bastard most of the time, but he's good to his grandma."

"Thanks for the endorsement, Gramps."

Amanda sucked in a short breath and spun toward the familiar, sexy voice behind her.

Ryan shoved off from the doorjamb where he looked like he'd been relaxing for quite some time.

Chapter Twenty-two

It wasn't the first time Ben had bailed someone out of jail, but it had always been a client before. He switched on the air conditioning to evacuate the sticky air and cut-rate perfume choking them in the car. A storm was coming, and he wanted to get the BMW in the garage ahead of the rain.

Shifting gears, he frowned at his sister. Barely thirty-four, she looked forty at least. Long ago she'd chopped off her silky blonde hair. Today she'd glued it into spikes. The excess liner and mascara, combined with brown eye shadow gave her a rough look. But then no cosmetic could restore the innocence and sparkle to those once beautiful, blue eyes.

"Buckle up," he ordered.

Waiting to hear the click before taking his foot off the brake pedal, he counted silently.

One.

One conviction was all it would take to lose custody of her children permanently.

Two.

Two-hundred dollars bail money. He'd paid.

Three.

Three strikes, you're out.

Click.

"We've talked about this, Colleen. Don has a restraining order. You have to stay away from the kids."

"You don't know what you're asking. I miss those munchkins so much."

The desperate whine in her voice was almost more than Ben could bear. Still, it was his niece and nephew he was most concerned about.

At four years old, Lindsay had never seen her mother when she wasn't scrambling to cover her addiction. At least Jack, at age ten, might remember some sweet times with Colleen. Both kids looked stressed beyond their years when he'd stopped by last night with a stuffed giraffe for Lindsay's birthday.

He'd considered taking Amanda with him. After all, she'd become a pleasant part of his nightly routine. Ever since her car had broken down, he'd been giving her a ride home every night from the nursing home.

Now that was one ethical woman—ethical and stubborn. Ben had given up trying to convince her renting a car would be a legitimate business expense she could charge to the lottery winner. Transportation was essential to the completion of her assignment, but she'd refused to take his advice.

Seems there were two obstinate women he was meant to protect. Well, his sister was one who couldn't afford to ignore his advice. He turned to Colleen. "You want to be part of your children's lives again?"

Colleen nodded, shaking the tears from her eyes. Whether they were real or for show, Ben didn't know.

"Then get your act together," he said.

"Why can't you say 'shit' like every other man?"

Like Dad? He'd cursed and bullied all of them. He couldn't remember a time when Tom Harris had anything positive to say about anyone. Ben had vowed to be different.

"You didn't understand the comment the way I phrased it?"

Colleen reached for her purse on the floorboard. An oversized buckle on the strap jangled against her gaggle of silver bracelets. "It's so pussy never to cuss."

"Can we stay on the subject, please?"

Jerking the zipper open, she inched out a pack of cigarettes. Her gaze stayed fastened downward.

"Uh, not in my car," he warned.

Quickly stuffing the cigarettes back in, she took out a package of chewing gum. "I wasn't going to smoke. I know how you feel about it."

Ben signaled his merge into traffic. The streets around the courthouse were tightly packed tonight. Some people nudged their way to the restaurants and bars in the Old Market to celebrate the start of the weekend, while other workers headed in the opposite direction, to their homes in the suburbs.

Glancing at the sky, he frowned. The green tint of the clouds could only mean one thing. Hail.

Colleen slipped the gum out of the wrapper, its wintergreen fragrance wafting to him. He didn't chew gum, but it would have been nice of her to offer a piece. It had been years since Colleen had thought about anyone but herself. Stretching into contortions what had once been Benson High's most coveted lips, she shoved the entire stick into her mouth.

Ben scowled. "If you were missing the kids, you should have called me. We could have gone to a meeting."

"I wanted to go see my kids, not go to the casino," she mumbled, chewing the gum vigorously.

"It's all related. Have you been to a meeting yet?"

Digging into her purse, she pulled out a gold lipstick tube. Visor lowered, she opened the mirror and squinted into the vanity light. "I haven't been able to squeeze it into my schedule yet."

"How is that possible? You lost your job four days ago. What have you been doing?"

"I've been looking for a new job."

The lipstick, a bright pink, was much too bold for her. It made her look cheap.

"I want to help you, Colleen, but you have to help yourself, too."

"I'm glad you want to help. Because . . ." She sighed. "I'm in a bit of trouble." She tossed the tube back into her purse and heaved the bag onto the floor, its weight sounding like a barbell had hit the floorboard.

"What kind of trouble?" As if he didn't know.

"I borrowed some money I have to pay back. Tomorrow. But . . ."

"You don't have the money? I gave you some last week."

"I had to buy some new clothes for my job interviews. I don't want to be just a secretary anymore. I want a job with more respect. I want to be in management."

"Management?"

Ben pulled over to the curb, slamming the car into Park. Contrary to his rising temper, the engine idled quietly.

"I need a bigger paycheck. To put money aside for the kids' college."

Gripping the leather steering wheel, he forced his tone to remain calm. "I'm not stupid."

"What?"

"You didn't buy clothes. You gambled."

"This is new." She stuck out her chest. The white lace of her bra peeped from the scooped neck of her red sweater. Cleavage the entire football team used to drool over now jiggled loosely as she pushed up her sleeves and adjusted the silver hoops on her wrists.

Cigarettes, two pregnancies, endless nights of drinking and gambling hadn't been kind to his sister.

"The only position that outfit will get you is horizontal."

She curled her painted lip at him.

"Who do you owe?" he asked.

"A loan company."

The probability was slim a true loan company would do business with her. She'd borrowed from a friend–if she had any left.

"How much do you owe?"

"Six-thousand dollars."

He slapped the steering wheel. "Cheesy Pete!" The engine roared in disbelief.

Colleen rolled her eyes.

"Can you help me out or not? Will you give me the money?"

If he'd only protected her from their father's verbal abuse, maybe she wouldn't be such a mess now.

"No," he said, pleased with the force behind that word.

Tears welled in her eyes. These looked real.

"But," he blew out a long breath, "tomorrow I *will* go to the loan company and write them a check for six-thousand dollars."

Colleen hugged his arm. "Thanks, Benji. You're terrific." She pressed her palms together. A ring encircled every finger and her orange nail polish glowed under the street lights. "It's strictly a loan, though. Generosity like yours deserves to be paid back."

"I'm sure. My generosity never goes unpunished."

Chapter Twenty-three

Ryan laid his dessert fork on the plate, his expression hard. The cheesecake was rich, the espresso strong and with dinner nearly over, Amanda was no closer to figuring him out than when they'd sat down.

His mood seemed as dark as his black hair which he'd slicked back this evening. The olive-colored shirt peeked out from under his tailored, leather jacket. He wore coal-colored jeans cinched with a snakeskin belt that matched his boots. Testosterone dripped from every gesture, every comment, and Amanda tried desperately to ignore her attraction to him.

To be polite, she took a small bite of the shared dessert before giving up on the meal. Ryan hadn't been himself throughout this very expensive dinner, one Amanda scarcely touched.

By contrast, Ryan had vigorously sawed at his Porterhouse, downed most of the bottle of Cabernet and avoided speaking to her–about anything. Too bad he'd had to waste two hundred dollars on a dinner neither of them had enjoyed.

Her plan to keep things strictly business had been a success, but not by her doing. The iciness of his touch, the chill of his–could she call it a smile? No, it was more sneer than smile. Whatever she called it, he'd used it all night like a lure to catch her in a trap. At least that's how it felt to Amanda.

She wasn't certain if Ryan had overheard her trying to extract a confession from Bud, who had all but confirmed he was the lottery winner. But if he'd witnessed her manipulation of his grandfather, and if Ryan was as upset with her as Bud had been, she might well get fired from her assignment.

Amanda didn't know how to handle Ryan Fisher now. She'd be happy if she could deflect those burning glances he gave her from under his sexy, black lashes.

Business, Amanda. Don't blow the assignment and the million dollars.

He swiped his mouth with the linen napkin and laid it by the side of his plate, next to the bill which he'd ignored for the past ten minutes. Dinner was over, but Amanda feared he wasn't quite done chewing her up and spitting her out.

The glow of candlelight off his chestnut eyes turned the irises the same putrid shade of green that marked the clouds outside their street-side window. Hail would fall soon.

"What do you make of Bud?" he said.

Her heart skipped a beat. Hoping to repel a full-blown inquiry, she draped an innocent smile on her face, raising the demitasse to her lips. "He's the sweetest old man."

He pinned her with his stare. "That doesn't answer my question."

She slowly drummed two fingers against her chest, trying to persuade her heart to match her measured pace. "No, it doesn't. I believe . . . it's a tragedy that age robs the elderly of their clear thinking. It must be especially difficult for you to see Bud's mental capacity slipping."

"Think he's the multi-million-dollar lottery winner the media is searching for?"

Her hand jerked, spilling coffee onto the white tablecloth. Frantically, she blotted the stains until he stole the napkin from her, piling it on top of his own. "Leave it."

The voice that had always soothed her with compliments and respect now hardened to ice.

She sat in a chilled cocoon of his annoyance. The situation was a tangled mess. Bit by bit, she pulled at the threads of her thoughts.

If Bud were the winner and he'd asked Ryan to help with the distribution, Ryan would know she was the delegate. But she hadn't met Ryan until after the meeting with Mr. Franklin, so either it hadn't been Ryan's idea to designate her or her selection was perfectly random.

Still, she couldn't rule out that Bud had been confused and wasn't the lottery winner at all. In that case, Ryan didn't know about her assignment–and she couldn't tell him.

Besides, she had no confirmation Bud was the lottery winner and no assurance Ryan had overheard their conversation.

It was possible he was on a fishing expedition.

She'd better stall a little longer.

"I didn't watch the entire exposé of "Win a Fortune" tonight. Did Henry Wadsworth Longo name the winner?"

Clearly annoyed, Ryan huffed and continued glaring at her. "No, he didn't. Oddly, he spent a lot of expensive air time campaigning for a national, domed rodeo arena and museum."

"Really?" Sweat beaded on the back of her neck.

"He lost my vote when he used free-verse poetry to suggest it be built next to the Lincoln Memorial in Washington, D.C."

"Well, they say the winner's agent was chosen randomly. No guarantees you'll get an Einstein using that method."

"I don't believe the cowboy is the winner's delegate, do you?"

She shook her head and chanced a sip of water, holding the glass with both hands to steady her grip.

"Any idea who that agent is?" he asked.

If Bud were the winner and Ryan his advisor, he'd know she was lying if she denied knowledge. Amanda prayed for enough deception left in her blood that she wouldn't blush or choke on her lie. "No earthly idea."

Ryan arched both eyebrows and his gaze fell nonchalantly to the table, where he picked up the leatherette folder with the bill and bounced its spine on the table's edge. "Too bad."

While his gaze was redirected, she stole another drink of water. "Why?"

"You could probably sell the information to a tattle rag for say . . . a million bucks."

Amanda's stomach flipped. A million dollars and she didn't have to complete the assignment? The stress would vanish, Clara could get her new heart, and everything would be back to normal.

She gulped air. "You're kidding."

"This is the biggest story of the year for the tabloids. By identifying the winner's agent, they could trace the trail back to the ticket holder. I know that rag paper, *Your News Source*, would easily pay seven figures for the exclusive story."

The sound of sirens overrode the buzzing in her brain. How long would it would take to broker a deal? Flipping through a mental display of the magazines she saw every week at the grocery check-out, she tried to visualize *Your News Source*.

"That is *if* you knew who the delegate was." Ryan signed the credit card receipt with a flourish, and firmly closed the binder.

The sirens and buzzing grew louder.

Could it be that easy? Was this her way out?

The waiter rushed to their table. "We're asking all guests to wait out the storm in the cooler."

"Storm?" Ryan returned his American Express card to his wallet.

"The tornado sirens are sounding, sir." He turned to Amanda. "Can't you hear them?"

"Oh, my God." Amanda's nerves snapped to attention.

The smell of ozone crowded her memory. She'd only been five years old when the tornado of 1975 ripped through Omaha leaving a thirteen-mile scar. She and her dad were crouched in the basement under a mattress he'd jerked from her bed on the way down the steps. Their house escaped with only the shutters and some shingles torn off. Their neighbor two doors away hadn't been so lucky. Their house had been leveled.

"My hotel is just across the street," Ryan said. "Let's go wait it out in my room."

"What floor?"

"The fourth."

"No way. This is Nebraska. We *never* ignore the warnings."

Amanda hustled after the waiter along with the other restaurant patrons, her mind stirring a stew of thoughts. She'd dodged Ryan's bullet aimed squarely at her vulnerability. Another million-dollar option dangled in front of her. She only had to decide how far to bend her scruples.

As she waited out possible disaster in the cooler with forty other people, one question nagged at her. If Bud was the big lottery winner, and Ryan knew Amanda was his delegate, why would he want to tempt her to sell the story to the tabloids?

Chapter Twenty-four

No sooner had the sirens ceased their wail than her cell phone rang and vibrated.

Other patrons shuffled back into the dining room, prodded by the chefs, no doubt wanting to recapture their domain. An image of Erik blipped into her mind.

Could he be calling to see how she'd survived the storm?

Ryan motioned to the restroom and made his escape as she flipped open her phone. "Hello?"

"Are you okay?"

"Ben? Where are you?"

"At my house. Are you all right?" There was genuine concern in his voice that she wrapped around her like a hug.

"Yes. And you?"

"Fine. Listen, I've been watching the news all evening. A town just outside of Grand Island has been smacked by an F-4 tornado. The devastation is unbelievable. There are a lot of hurting people there."

"Any casualties?" she asked, afraid to hear the answer.

"None reported yet, but that could change."

She blew out a relieved breath. "We've got to go and find out if we can help."

"It's too dark to see anything tonight. I have something to take care of first thing in the morning. I'll pick you up at eight."

* * * *

Strong winds had downed many branches in Midtown and it had taken until almost midnight for Ryan to get Amanda home. Thank goodness there'd been enough to distract him from his prior path of pointed questioning. Amanda didn't know how much longer she could keep up her defenses.

After organizing the paperwork for tomorrow's trip with Ben, she sat down at her computer.

Typing 'Ryan Fisher' into the search engine, she waited, holding her breath. With his interrogation skills he could be a detective, a law-professor, or a reality talk-show host. His good looks could get him a job as an actor or a model. Apparently wealthy, he might own half of Colorado, using it for backyard skiing.

Or he could be on the FBI's *Most Wanted* list.

With a little more persistence and an hour, Amanda discovered *her* Ryan Fisher was too old to be either the married race car driver, or the college baseball athlete. He was too young to be the computer hacker sentenced to two years in jail for shutting down the wireless internet in an airport terminal. He was too sane and too hairy to be the Ryan Fisher that purportedly drank too much cola and went bald and was given to lengthy rants about his tragedy in numerous blogs.

Amanda fell into bed just before two a.m. relieved her Ryan Fisher's identity wasn't anywhere to be found on the Internet. He was neither thug nor politician. Remorse over ever doubting him flooded her. In fact, she decided clearly her negative suspicions about Ryan's career were unfounded.

However, her doubts about his being the grandson of the lottery winner still remained.

* * * *

 13 Days until the Deadline

Amazed such a perfect spring day could follow in the wake of a killer storm, Amanda gazed through Ben's tinted windshield at the sharply clear sky. Glucksfall, the small town outside of Grand Island hit by the tornado, lay only three hours west of Omaha.

She had to see for herself if the lottery funds could help the people.

True to his word, Ben had arrived at Amanda's apartment on the dot, with a Starbucks the way she liked it, fat-free milk, one sugar. He'd also brought three different newspapers which she perused while he drove.

Right above the article denouncing Henry Wadsworth Longo as the winner's agent, ran the article sketching details of the tornado.

Only a couple of photos were ready for morning publication, but those along with the narrative painted an ugly picture of the destruction. Four people had lost their lives when the tornado cut a six-mile swath through residential neighborhoods. The only comfort came from reading that the downtown district had been spared.

"I talked with Rudy, the governor's aide, and he's reserving two seats on the helicopter," Ben said. "They take off at noon."

Could they get any higher a profile than being seen with the governor?

"Maybe that's not such a good idea." Amanda put her empty coffee cup into the holder between them.

"The governor's a fraternity brother of mine. Different years of course, but we go way back. He's cool. I told him you're my fiancée."

"Hmm."

That story didn't have the weird sound it would have had a few days ago when Amanda believed Ben was gay. When she glimpsed his outfit, she forgave herself the mistake.

Not many men would have the confidence to wear a light coral shirt, but with his ruddy complexion and soft, green eyes, Ben pulled it off nicely. The shirt was a stunning complement to his khaki pants.

Mentally, she slapped herself back to reality. The stakes were higher now that the media was again on the lookout for the lottery winner's representative. If she were exposed, their potential harassment would mean being confined to her apartment and cancelling all trips. What's more, they would investigate everyone around her. Her mother, in her weakened condition, couldn't afford to be pestered.

"I mean, won't the press be snapping photos of the governor?" Amanda said.

"They'll be taking pictures of the devastation. They'll only film the governor for his ten-second sound bite. Besides, if the cameras do get pointed our way, Rudy will block for us."

Amanda pressed her fingers against her temples to thwart a headache. The stress of this assignment was taking its toll and Ryan's comment last night had robbed her of her sleep. It was hard to believe the tabloids would pay a million dollars to learn the identity of the lottery winner's delegate.

The temptation tortured Amanda. With a confession, a million dollars, and two aspirin, she could give up this responsibility and her headaches. Uncle Ernie would protect Clara for the few days it would take for this nightmare to end.

It was more than the strain that forced Amanda to consider the easy road. By selling out, she was guaranteed the money for Clara's transplant. Her mother could get the operation sooner than if Amanda took the remaining two weeks to finish her assignment. There had always been an inherent risk in the project anyway. If the lottery winner didn't agree with Amanda's selection, she would forfeit the million-dollar finder's fee and fail once again. This time though, instead of losing her business, the failure would cost her mother's life.

Head pounding, she weighed her options: a gamble with the lottery winner versus a sure bet with the tabloids. Only one question remained. Could she discard her morals?

"Do you think there will be any tabloid reporters in Glucksfall looking for the lottery winner's agent?" She dug in her backpack for some pain tablets.

"Probably. It's the kind of tragedy that brings out those leeches. You'll have to be extra careful. Even the legitimate press is on the lookout for you."

"Do you think *Your News Source* would pay for information?"

Peering in deeper, she shook her backpack. The keys at the bottom rattled. Her fingers passed over the calendar. Only thirteen days remained before the date circled in red—her deadline. Fear of failure stole her breath.

"What kind of information?" he asked.

She shook two tablets from a travel-sized bottle of aspirin into her hand. "The name of the lottery winner's representative."

Ben stabbed a gaze at Amanda, forehead creased, eyes narrowed. "You're not considering doing that."

Her head throbbed, unhinging her nerves. Gastric acid mixed with coffee left her stomach queasy.

"If I could get the money for my mother's transplant that way, wouldn't it be easier than all this . . . this . . . this agony trying to decide how to divide the jackpot?"

He continued to stare at her, his mouth slightly agape. Finally, he let out a breath and returned his attention to the road ahead. "It's strictly your decision. I'd be hard-pressed to turn down the easy money myself."

The disappointment in his voice hit like a slug in the stomach, the pain spreading through her heart. She searched his face for remorse or at least some acknowledgement of his terse remark. His features were stony, posture rigid. Gaze glued to the highway, he offered no apology.

Her gut rolled and her fondness for him shriveled.

How dare he judge her? He had no idea what she was up against. An outsider would think her assignment easy. After all, everyone has dreamed of what they'd do with millions of dollars. But her mission came with a catch. She had to make the *right* decision. Otherwise, she'd kill her mother.

Until he'd held the same cards in the same game, Ben had no right to judge her. This was her hand to play and she was the only one who could make the decision. Ultimately, she was the one who'd have to live with the gamble.

She looked down at the aspirin melting in her clammy palm. If she sold out she'd disappoint everyone. Besides the lottery winner who, for some insane reason, had put trust into her, she'd be letting down the Terri Millers of the world. How could she live with the guilt?

Popping the flaky tablets into her mouth, she snatched her coffee cup from the console and tipped her head back. Only a dribble fell into her mouth. She swallowed the aspirin and it dragged down her throat, burning all the way. Her eyes watered, partly from the headache, partly from the aspirin, but mostly from the crush of isolation.

Staring out the window, they passed acres of freshly plowed fields, the rich earth black from last night's rain. The seeds and the hope they brought were lying shallowly beneath those mounded rows.

Amanda rubbed her cool hand over her forehead. "It was just a thought." Exhaustion poured a defensive tone into her voice and she regretted the worry she saw on Ben's face, so she added some reason into her manner. "I can't have the media stalking everyone I know to follow the breadcrumbs back to the winner."

Ben's fingers splayed from the steering wheel, his thumbs still tightly wrapped around the helm. Stretching his shoulders back into the seat, he exhaled, then relaxed. "So the plan is to avoid all reporters."

"Yes." She wanted so much to put her faith into Ben again. "With your friend's help, it'll be easy, right?"

"It won't be easy, but I don't know of a better way to see the tornado's damage. The roads into the area are blocked by debris. The governor's called out the National Guard, who would stop us from entering anyway."

Nothing could ever be easy.

"If you see any cameras pointed in your direction, duck," he said. "Any newspaper would love to snap a photo of the winner's little elf helper."

His smile broadened and his gaze hopped to her red windbreaker, trimmed in white. Stacked on top of her forest green corduroys and brown boots, she kind of looked the part.

She scowled. Yesterday she would have giggled at the tease. Today, her sense of humor felt like a distant friend.

Ben's phone rang. He tapped the speaker button. "Ben Harris."

"It's Roberta, Ben."

"Morning." The greeting had a friendly yet professional tone.

"I have to talk to you about a client."

"Wait a minute and I'll take you off speaker." He hooked a receiver over his ear and punched a couple of buttons. "Okay. Go ahead." He listened for several seconds. "Yes." A longer stretch of listening and Amanda felt tension rising from him. His mouth thinned. as he murmured another assent. He paused.

The color drained from his face.

Amanda's compassion went on alert. Something was terribly wrong. She didn't have much experience watching Ben in the attorney-mode, but she'd never seen him so distressed over a case before.

"Wait. I'll pull over so I can take some notes." He eased onto the road's shoulder. "Can you hand me my briefcase from the backseat?" he asked Amanda.

To save time, Amanda snatched the *Cases* notebook from her backpack, flipped it to a blank page and handed it and a pen to Ben. "Will this do?"

"Great. Thanks."

She missed the smile that usually accompanied his gratitude. Intending to give him privacy, she reached for the door handle, but Ben stopped her exit with a hand over hers.

Being left handed had its advantages. He continued holding her hand as he jotted down the specifics of the case.

Amanda was confused. Only a few days ago he'd all but whacked her for wanting to use his laptop, concerned she might hack into some client files. Now he wanted her to sit in while he recorded the details of a case.

Still, his hand was dry and soft. She glanced at his knuckles which were smooth, his fingernails neatly clipped and filed.

"What was the amount allegedly taken?"

He paused only momentarily before exclaiming, "Clam chowder on a stick!"

He squeezed Amanda's hand tightly.

She laid her other hand over his, hoping he'd notice how strong his grip had become.

"Who's the company's attorney?"

His hold eased and he turned to massaging her palm with his fingertips. Amanda was sure the action was from nervousness, but it felt good anyway. She smoothed her hand over his, wanting to ease his stress.

"Right."

He listened to what Roberta was telling him.

"No. Don't bail her out."

He clutched her hand again, but not so forcefully, bouncing both their wrists on the leather seat.

"Don't do anything. I'll take care of it on Monday. This isn't worth calling in favors to spring her before then."

His brows furrowed together. "Thanks for calling, Roberta."

He sighed and released Amanda's hand. She wondered if he even realized he'd been holding it.

He hung up and scribbled a few more notes. Then he tossed the notebook over his shoulder into the backseat and jabbed the pen into his shirt pocket. Before Amanda could speak, they were on the highway again.

His gaze set on the road ahead, Ben released another sigh. "My sister, Colleen, has been arrested for allegedly embezzling $100,000 dollars."

Amanda sat dumbfounded. He'd said it like he was talking about a stranger. She looked at his profile and couldn't find any emotion at all. Finally, she found her voice. "I'm sorry."

"She's a compulsive gambler. She's lost everything—including her husband, kids, and numerous jobs. Guess that wasn't low enough for her. She was the secretary for a plumbing company for the past year. They're accusing her of rerouting funds."

"I'm so sorry, Ben." What else could she say?

"They trusted her to make deposits, not knowing they shouldn't. I ought to have told them about her addiction."

"You?"

"I knew she had a problem. This is my fault."

"I don't see how you can blame yourself."

"She's my younger sister. She's always depended on me—maybe too much. But the pattern is set. I can't abandon her now. I have to come up with the money to repay the company or she'll go to prison."

Hope seemed impossible, but Amanda had to offer some. "What about due process and presumption of innocence?"

He dug his fingers in his hair, fire exploding from his glare. "You are so naïve, Amanda. Have you ever *once* been exposed to the seedier side of life?"

She gaped at him. Why the attack? Colleen had stolen the money. Amanda had only tried to offer support, which was more than he'd been willing to do for her only minutes ago.

The chill in her heart grew icier.

She scolded herself. She knew better than to let people get too close to her when her defenses were down. Hadn't it been exactly how Erik had been able to manipulate her these past few years? Sometime in the last decade he'd quit caring about her, her business, and her mother. He'd only pretended so he could use her—or more specifically, use her uterus.

Well, she knew exactly what she had to do. She'd have to put Ben and their relationship back where they belonged—in the business category of her life. He was merely the person assigned to help her stay anonymous in her mission.

Whipping the rubber band off her wrist, she tied back her hair, and mentally kicked herself. To think she'd felt a twinge of compassion. For a moment, she'd considered giving some of the lottery money to Ben's sister, taking her own gamble. If she couldn't justify the decision to the winner, she could lose her finder's fee and Clara's cure.

Gazing out the window, Amanda struggled to keep tears of frustration from falling.

Ben mumbled under his breath.

"Were you speaking to me?" The haughtiness in her tone chilled the air between them. Now would be a good time for Ben to apologize for his insult if he wished to continue in a civilized atmosphere.

"No. I merely said there had to be a way this situation with Colleen could have been avoided."

At that moment they pulled up to the edge of the destruction. Twisted metal that used to be a mobile home lay on the edge of the road. Next to it, an oak tree lay upended, its naked roots extended like a witch's gnarly hand ready to snatch the heart from any trespasser.

The ugliness stole Amanda's breath. "Like this could have been avoided?" she asked.

Chapter Twenty-five

Amanda zipped her windbreaker as she and Ben pulled up to the parking lot. The tornado had decimated the Central Nebraska Regional Airport and a makeshift heliport had been established at a soccer complex. Police security, backed by a National Guardsman armed with a rifle, stopped Ben's car at the temporary gate made of yellow crime tape and orange construction cones.

"I'm with the governor's entourage. Ben Harris." He showed his ID to the guard, who checked a list fastened to a clipboard. He studied both documents for a long time before handing the driver's license back to Ben.

"Go ahead," he said. They were waved into the white rock parking lot.

An array of helicopters filled adjoining soccer fields. Magnetic logos plastered on the sides of two read CNN and FOX. By the goal posts, news crews milled about outside giant trucks, topped with humongous satellite dishes perched atop long, white poles. Amanda recognized news reporters from Omaha. She slid on her sunglasses as though they would protect her identity.

Ben parked alongside a row of SUVs. At the end sat a black limousine with tinted windows. A chauffeur waited by the passenger door, his hands clasped in front of him.

"I don't think this is such a good idea." Amanda nervously sucked in her lower lip. "That's the governor's limo."

"Naw. Josh flew in from Lincoln. He just stopped here to pick up the mayor, the county commissioner, and any other bigwigs."

"Oh."

"It could be a U.S. Senator's limo, though," he said.

"It'll be fine," he said, noting her look of alarm. "Just stay with me."

When Ben opened her door she felt a little like a VIP as well. She should have hopped out on her own. Such manners in this venue could attract attention.

After he slipped on a gray jacket and aviator sunglasses, he passed her a smile. "Let's go, little elf."

If the tease was an attempt to apologize and infiltrate her defenses again, Amanda vowed it wouldn't work. She rolled her eyes.

As though it were a natural occurrence, Ben took her arm in his and they strolled to the limo. His hand was warm and dry and she tried not to notice how he squeezed a little contrition into her palm. She couldn't let the relationship be anything but business.

Her legs felt like cooked spaghetti as she walked. The most famous person she'd ever met was a local actor, and that had been at the circus when she was twelve.

As a couple, Ben and Amanda did look the part, although she could add credibility by not clutching her backpack so tightly to her stomach—and by breathing, rather than gasping for air.

She felt as much like an imposter here among these VIPs as she did when posing for publicity photos with Erik for restaurant promotions. As they approached the limo and the executive staff standing around the car, she grew weaker still.

How Ben knew which person to approach was a mystery to Amanda, but he chose a petite woman in a tailored robin-egg blue pantsuit. "I'm looking for Rudy Gardner."

The woman pointed in the direction of a group of reporters near the goal line. Amanda's breath caught. How could she keep her poise and her secret while hanging out with the media?

"I'll wait here," she said.

He shrugged indifferently. "I'll be right back."

The confidence in his short strides across the field galled Amanda. How could a person have such self-assurance in virtually every situation? Then she scoffed. Ben Harris may have had the worldly sophistication she lacked, but he didn't have her manners, and she'd gladly keep her naïveté if it meant not hurting people who trusted her.

Ben pumped the hand of a man dressed in a navy polo shirt and gray slacks. Wild laughter flowed from the two. Ben threw his gaze over his shoulder at Amanda and the man's attention followed. Then they laughed again.

Strolling back toward her, hand in his pocket, he slowed as a man holding a large camera approached him. Again Ben smiled easily and nodded toward Amanda. The two chatted amiably for a couple of minutes before Ben offered the man his business card.

Returning to her, Ben clapped together his hands enthusiastically, as though he'd never offended her only minutes before. "We're all set."

"So the first guy you spoke with was Rudy, the governor's aide?"

"Yes." He hitched a thumb toward a swamp-colored, military helicopter whose blades revolved slowly. "There will be thirteen of us total. We'll sit in the back. They want us on board now."

Placing his arm around her waist, he steered her across the field. Even through the windbreaker, his hand felt cold. The threads of a shiver roped down her spine.

"And the other man, the one you gave your business card?"

Ben tilted his head, his eyes blocked by the mirrored lenses of his Ray Bans. The corners of his mouth curved up ever so slightly. "He's an old football buddy of mine."

The attorney had a pleasant disposition and a smile to match when he wanted to display them. She returned his cheeriness with her own grin. "What's his name?"

"Craig Lambert." He smirked a little.

Was it from some joke they'd shared? She could use a good laugh to ease the constant tension twisting her these past few weeks.

"Why is Craig here?"

"He's a reporter from *Your News Source*."

Reflected in Ben's glasses, Amanda saw her face plunge into paleness.

Chapter Twenty-six

Ben and Amanda were seated a full ten minutes before the governor and the rest of the VIPs boarded the helicopter. Those minutes were torture.

The loud drone of the aircraft deafened her and she slipped on the ear protection provided by the pilot. The padded headset blunted the engine sounds and Amanda's anxiety. She loosened her grip on her backpack, laying it by her feet.

She stared out the small window, seeing nothing except the shadows on the field created by the sun using the clouds to play peek-a-boo. This part of the city showed no wind damage.

A news crew climbed aboard the CNN helicopter. Others on the ground cleared a wide path. The sun glinted off the whirling blades as the aircraft lifted, hovered, hastily tilted, and then veered to the south. The force of the takeoff pressed the grass into a neatly flat circle.

Amanda seethed at the possibility Ben might be using her. First, she'd put her trust in Erik and that turned out to be a debacle, the sting still fresh in her heart. Now Ben showed signs of disloyalty.

Questioning him about the reporter from *Your News Source* was what she wanted to do, but two pilots and a crew chief filled the front of the aircraft, checking the flight instruments. Even with their bubble-shaped helmets on, she couldn't risk them overhearing.

She'd almost forgotten how ingratiating Ben had been at the beginning of her assignment. At the time, she'd speculated his motivation was tied to the money he hoped to gain. Now evidence seemed to corroborate that suspicion.

Maybe it was a coincidence Ben needed a large sum of money and the path to getting it magically appeared like the yellow brick road under Dorothy's feet. How stupid of her to have given him the idea of selling her identity to the tabloids. But then maybe that had been his plan all long.

The sun charged out from behind a cloud, pushing through the tiny window by Amanda's face.

For a moment she took solace in the fact Ben was too smart to rat her out. Since the firm had been hired to assist her, he'd lose his job if he did something as unethical as sell her identity. Disbarment wouldn't be far behind.

As quickly as her relief came, it faded. Would he dare risk his career to save his sister? Amanda would sacrifice hers to save Clara. Family ties could lead a person to do crazy things. For instance, to save her mother's life, Amanda had turned her own upside down and inside out, even considered ratting herself out to the press.

She waffled once again. Ben had made the decision to leave Colleen in jail over the weekend. Maybe his loyalty to himself was stronger than his family allegiance. Then he would have no strong motivation to sell her out. Except for the million dollars *Your News Source* would pay for the information. And so her thoughts had come full circle. Amanda had no idea what to think about Ben. Was he reliable or not?

Her stomach churned from the fuel fumes wafting through the open sliding door. Then her heart ached at the prospect her trust might have been betrayed once again. If she kept looking out the window, and Ben Harris continued ignoring her, it was possible she'd get through this ride without crying or strangling him.

Shifting in her seat, she accidentally kicked her backpack. Despite being cumbersome and conspicuous, it was a blessing for carrying a great deal.

She pulled the bag onto her lap and rooted around for some lip gloss. I look like a traveling secretary with all these notebooks, she mused. Manila envelopes, red, purple and green—

She gasped. No green *Cases* notebook.

Slipping off her headphones, she signaled for Ben to do the same.

"You have my green notebook."

"Huh?" he said.

"The case files," she whispered as loud as she dared, "Terri Miller and the others. The one you used to make notes about . . . Colleen. It's in the back seat of your car."

"It'll be fine." He moved to put his ear protection back on, but she blocked him.

If anyone saw those notes, they'd know she was the jackpot winner's agent. She glared at Ben. "I need that notebook."

"The car's locked, Amanda. It'll be fine." He sighed. "I don't understand why you insist on carrying everything with you anyway."

She glanced at the cockpit. The flight crew were too busy to bother with her conversation. "I need to protect the files."

"And the contract would be better off in a safe deposit box at the firm or in a bank."

True, but Amanda hadn't thought of that and wasn't about to concede that point to Ben, the man who wanted her to believe he knew *everything*.

Too irritated to speak further, she slapped her headphones on, tossed the backpack to the floor, and twisted away from him to look out the window.

The rest of their party finally arrived. Governor Joshua Peters only nodded and waved when Ben introduced Amanda. The distance was too great for a handshake, which suited her just fine. She was too angry to be politely civil after being presented as the future Mrs. Harris.

The First Lady joined the governor seated directly behind the pilots. Glucksfall's mayor and his wife, both with strained expressions, sat behind the governor. The woman in the robin-egg blue pantsuit, accompanied by Rudy, squeezed into the bench seat next to the mayor. Two senatorial aides crowded into the seat beside Ben, pushing him closer to Amanda.

When the helicopter lifted, she grabbed Ben's arm, and just as suddenly, released it. She hadn't expected the sensation to feel so much like the launch of a Ferris wheel. He patted her hand reassuringly, but she ignored him. To make more room, he draped his arm behind her. She ignored that, too.

Soon her nose and both hands were pressed against the window, all nerves settled.

At first the view was lovely, the treetops resembling broccoli florets. The lakes looked like mirrors reflecting the glimmer of the noonday sun. Rows of plowed soybean fields were amazingly straight and the country roads divided the land into perfect squares. She wondered how the construction crews knew how to build the highways so well when she'd always had trouble cutting a straight line with scissors.

The edge of the destruction came quickly though, surprising Amanda with its sporadic nature. On the same block, one house appeared untouched by the storm while the next one lacked a roof. Amanda felt like an intruder staring into a master bedroom as though she were looking into a dollhouse. All the furniture neatly in place, the bed made, pictures precisely hung on the walls. A tree laying across a van in the driveway was the property's only damage.

Moving so swiftly over the neighborhoods, Amanda couldn't take in all the scenes. Some people roamed the streets, stopping to pick up litter scattered everywhere. Amanda wondered what was so valuable the tiny figures stopped to hug one another before moving on to collect more trash.

Nothing could have prepared Amanda for what she saw next – one cement foundation next to another, and another, and another. Not a tree stood below her. Not a bush. Not a roof. Not a car, house, or swing set. What she suspected were lawns weren't green. She saw no grass anywhere, only dirt and sticks. No, they weren't sticks. They were stripped tree trunks and telephone poles strewn haphazardly everywhere. The wreckage mimicked a war zone.

On closer examination she noticed staircases rising from the basements, but leading nowhere. Occasionally she saw an empty bathtub or toilet, still attached to the basement pipes. Nowhere did she see signs of life or anything resembling a previously normal existence, only the lonely shadow of their helicopter streaming over the rubble.

Her stomach churned at the horrific sight. How could anyone have survived such a storm? There was virtually nothing left. Tons of material had simply vanished. The tornado had sucked up everything not bolted firmly to the ground.

But the bigger question was how could the residents endure the aftermath?

She had to speak with the survivors and see how she could help. Hovering over the decimation she felt like a trespasser, a voyeur, with no right to view the pain without feeling it. At the least, she needed to empathize with those who'd suffered such immeasurable loss.

As the helicopter landed, all passengers remained eerily silent. One by one, they unbuckled their seatbelts, removed their headsets, and exited the plane. First the governor and the First Lady, followed by the other VIPs in descending order of rank.

Before she could stand, Ben grabbed Amanda's arm, saying something she couldn't hear. Taking off the ear protection, she shouted, "What?"

As the pilots flipped switches, the engine wound down, and Ben also removed his headset. His gaze, steady and intense, matched the gravity of the scenes they'd just witnessed. "Let's hang back and let the media swarm the governor."

He glanced through the window, his knee bouncing with nervousness. Evidently, the trip had profoundly affected him, too.

They waited a full five minutes, until the pilots completely shut down the engine. Amanda's ears continued to ring.

"Should be safe now." Ben signaled for Amanda to exit and she crouched, shuffling her way around the seats. Ben crowded behind her to the open door.

Just as she was about to descend the steps, she realized she'd left her backpack behind. Making a quick apology to Ben, she hurried back to the rear of the aircraft.

Snatching her bag, she glanced out the window and saw Ben speaking with the reporter from *Your News Source.* Her pulse quickened. She'd hoped she'd been wrong about Ben Harris, but now he was fraternizing with the enemy once again.

He smiled, slapping his new best friend on the back before returning to the helicopter.

When she returned to the exit, Ben stood below her, arm raised to help her descend. He even had the nerve to grin. Slapping away his hand, she stepped down and caught her boot heel on the lip of the threshold.

Before she could gain her balance, she tumbled out of the aircraft.

She yelped and flailed her arms to stay steady, dropping the cursed backpack in the process. Right onto Ben's nose.

Despite the pain that had to have caused, Ben caught her around the waist and she anchored her arms around his neck. Her legs encircled his hips and they stuck together—for what seemed an eternity.

She heard the click of a camera's shutter. More clicks followed in rapid succession.

Stumbling backward a couple of steps, Ben eventually gained his balance, but held tight to Amanda. Blood dribbled from one nostril to the top of his lip.

Over Ben's head, she saw the reporter from *Your News Source.* He lowered his camera from his face, waved, and gestured a gun with his index finger and thumb. "Thanks."

Amanda gasped and squirmed to break free of Ben's comforting grasp. "Stop him," she whispered loudly.

"Go to the car and I'll take care of it." He set her down and handed her the keys. "Go on," he urged, removing a handkerchief from his coat pocket to dab at the blood. "I'm fine."

Turning on his heel, he jogged over to the cameraman. He'd managed to center himself among the other reporters near the goal post. Gently touching the reporter's elbow, Ben looked back at Amanda, ordering her with a gesture to return to the car. Now.

Slowly, she paced across the field, glimpsing back to watch the two men talking.

Other than the occasional dab at his nose, Ben didn't look concerned, but laughed and slapped the man on the back. Reaching into his shirt pocket, the reporter took out the business card Ben had given him earlier and handed it to Ben. He smiled as he scribbled a note on the back of the card and then returned the card to the reporter.

They shook hands and Ben sauntered away from the goal post.

Amanda wrapped her arms around her stomach to keep the nausea from overwhelming her.

Ben Harris had scored big this time. Seven figures at least.

Chapter Twenty-seven

Ben was the official attorney, but Amanda had watched enough "Law and Order" to know how to conduct her own inquiry. She needed to know if he'd used her, selling her identity to the tabloid.

"You sure have a lot of fraternity brothers." Amanda threw her backpack into the BMW ahead of her. "First the governor and now a national reporter—what's his name . . .?" She snapped her fingers rapidly, searching her short-term memory. Details were important when interrogating a suspect.

"Craig Lambert." Casually, he shrugged. "I'm connected. In my job I have to be." He held the door open waiting for her to crawl into the bucket seat.

She turned to him, her back against the car, fists planted on her hips. "Oh, no. You didn't say you knew Craig Lambert from *work*. Both he and the governor are your *friends*—specifically fraternity brothers."

Recalling the events of the day, the conspiracy seemed so obvious—the evidence impossible to refute.

"Okay. I stand corrected," he said. "They're not business associates." Releasing the door handle, he tipped his head at the passenger seat, her cue to get into the car.

She wanted to scream, shake him, and rewind to the beginning of the day where she would opt to stay in bed. Then this mess never would have happened. But she didn't have any money to buy back the day even if it were for sale. She had to deal with the aftermath. She had to deal with Ben.

"So you do *no* business with either man," she said.

He rattled his head, looking over her shoulder into the soccer field behind her. "Um . . ." He exhaled. "Occasionally I have dinner with Josh and Sally and we talk current events, but . . . Hey," He stared at her, his eyes narrowing. "What is this, a cross-examination?"

Amanda swallowed a smug smile. The wariness in his eyes told her she was getting to him. In no time, she'd have his confession. "I

160 *Teryl Oswald*

simply find it an *unbelievable* coincidence the reporter from the biggest tabloid just happens to be your *friend* and happens to run into to you here at this very opportune moment."

His brows twisted.

Seeing annoyance in the tautness of his lips, she steeled herself for his defense.

"Believe what you want, Amanda. We're friends. What else can I say? I don't isolate myself in my home. That's not how I live."

Whether he meant it to or not, the remark felt like a slam and stung her heart. Hot tears burned the backs of her eyes. There seemed to be nothing Ben wouldn't take a shot at today. First he'd blasted her for her lack of sophistication. Now he knocked her for her absence of a social life, though none of that could stack up to the biggest blow—his betrayal.

She needed to know if Ben had sold her identity to the tabloid. Given the time they'd spent together, and their kiss, he owed her the truth. But she dreaded his answer.

"Why did Craig Lambert take my picture?"

"He took *our* picture." Absently, Ben touched the tip of his nose, still rosy from its collision with her backpack. "It was too Three Stooges to pass up."

"What's he going to do with the photograph?"

"It's a surprise," he replied, with a blank face. "You'll find out in a couple of days."

The evasive remark knocked the wind out of her. To avoid crumpling into a heap, she twisted in place and leaned her head against the door frame. Ben had betrayed her. He'd sold her identity to the highest bidder. At least he'd done it for what he'd perceived was a good cause—to save his sister.

With a million dollars from *Your News Source*, Ben would be able to pay restitution for the money Colleen had embezzled. The recompense and a plea bargain might keep her out of prison.

Exhaling, Amanda let go of what was left of her trust in Ben. As Clara would say, what was done was done. Nothing she could do about it now. But one thing was certain—she didn't have to continue her association with Ben Harris. He'd been assigned to help her stay anonymous. By tomorrow morning, her face would be plastered all over the country.

She let out a slow, cleansing breath.

Being identified as the winner's agent wouldn't abort her mission. In fact, having to protect that secret had been emotionally draining, stealing time from her main focus. Better to get everything out in the open and move on. She could still complete her assignment. It might be more cumbersome to travel, but she could conduct candidate interviews over the phone. She'd find a way to succeed. She wouldn't–couldn't–fail her mother.

For now she had to stay focused on this assignment. She had to see the tornado's damage so she could decide if the people of Glucksfall would get a chunk of the jackpot.

Grabbing her backpack from the front seat, she pushed by Ben and headed for the makeshift gate. She had to get as far away from him as possible. There was too little time left to waste any more of it on him.

"Where are you going?" he said.

"I want to talk to some of the people who lost their houses."

He slammed the car door and followed her. "The National Guard is protecting the perimeter of the damaged neighborhoods. You can't get in."

"Watch me." Without a backward glance, she continued marching.

He matched her pace for pace. "I'm not going to take you into the prohibited area." His voice remained icy and firm.

"Fine."

She looked in the direction the CNN helicopter had flown. Pulling her backpack onto her shoulder she hiked across the parking lot, the white rock crunching under her boot steps.

With two quick hops, Ben jumped in Amanda's path, stopping her abruptly. "The ruined neighborhoods will be crawling with reporters."

"I'll take my chances." She stared at him, willing him out of her way.

He didn't move, except to drill himself deeper into her exasperation. "Don't be silly. Get in the car."

Sidestepping him, she quickened her strides. If she didn't have so far to walk, she would have broken out into a run. She couldn't get away from Ben fast enough. The sooner she left him and his betrayal behind, the sooner the ache in her heart would subside.

She kicked herself when she realized her distress over his treachery was based on personal disappointment rather than the potential disastrous effect on the project. It killed her to think she couldn't trust anyone.

Giving in to her anguish only wasted time and emotion–neither of which she held in reserve. She picked up her pace.

Tramping behind her, Ben gently grabbed her arm and careened around her. Locking gazes, he softened his tone. "You're not in any danger from Craig Lambert. He doesn't know you're the lottery winner's agent."

The look accompanying his statement seemed sincere, but she was too exhausted to care. No matter where Ben's loyalty fell, she had a job to do and the fluctuations of their relationship sucked too much of her emotion and her time. Now she needed to embrace only those things that helped her meet her goal while discarding anything that obstructed her.

She fought back tears of agonized fatigue. Gaining distance from Ben had to be a priority now.

"If you're determined to get closer to the damaged areas, please let me drive you to the perimeter," he said, softly.

He rubbed her arms, warming them. She hadn't realized how frigid her limbs had become. Tipping her head back she let the mid-afternoon sun wash over her face. Being the middle of May, it didn't hold much heat in its rays.

Accepting the ride helped her meet her goal. "All right," she said. Saving her energy helped her meet her goal.

"Wait here. I'll bring the car."

As Ben scampered away, she gazed around and noticed a man in a white van smoking a cigarette. He looked familiar, but Amanda couldn't place him. Maybe he was one of the governor's entourage or a local reporter.

Taking time to worry about it obstructed her goal. She closed her eyes.

* * * *

From behind a wide oak tree, Ryan Fisher stubbed out his cigarette and watched Ben's BMW leave the parking lot. On a hunch, he'd trailed Amanda and Ben from her apartment in Omaha to Glucksfall and witnessed them climbing aboard the governor's private helicopter to view the deadly tornado's destruction.

Convinced she was tied to the lottery, he was going to find out exactly how. She'd been evasive last night when he'd quizzed her on the subject and too coy about the grilling she'd given his grandfather at Brookside.

All of the circumstantial evidence led to one hypothesis. Amanda Cash was the lottery winner's agent.

Now he just had to prove it.

He salivated at the deliciousness of the hunt for the story. This is what he worked for, what he lived for—getting the scoop. His wits were never sharper than when he chased the prey, formed his strategy, and planned his tactics. It reminded him of a great game of chess.

He'd overheard the directions the police officer had given Ben for their next stop on the tour of devastation. It would be easy for Ryan to catch up with Amanda, but he had one thing left to do at the soccer field.

Leaving no resource untapped, he would question the man that had snapped the photo of Amanda falling out of the helicopter.

Ryan cursed his luck. He'd had his binoculars aimed at the pair instead of his Nikon with the zoom lens. He hated missing photojournalistic opportunities and that had been an exquisite one. No matter, though. There was more than one way to win the game.

Ben had seemed sociable with the photographer and Ryan would bet they were acquaintances. Playing off that hunch, he decided to approach the photographer as a mutual friend. He needed to know Ben and Amanda's mission and he needed that photo. Stealthily, skillfully, he'd extract his prizes from the stranger, without jeopardizing the scoop.

Glancing down the street to be sure the red BMW was out of sight, Ryan strolled to the security guard at the makeshift gate. His press pass was his ticket into most venues and it didn't fail him today.

Quickly he located his next quarry. The photographer in the cambric shirt stood loading his equipment into the back end of a Ford Explorer.

When he turned, Ryan glanced at the man's press pass hanging from a lanyard around his neck. Shock at the name of the publication forced Ryan to review his tactics. He'd have to be careful not to arouse the suspicion of journalist Craig Lambert, of *Your News Source.*

"Craig?"

The reporter spun, shading his eyes with one hand. "Yes?"

Ryan pointed behind him into the distance and opened with his center pawn—a favorite Bobby Fischer chess move. "Was that Ben Harris I just missed?"

Craig's gaze followed Ryan's gesture. "Yes. You know him?"

"Damn it. I thought I'd recognized Ben." Ryan huffed, kicking the ground. "Yes, unfortunately, I do. We're buddies. I've done some detective work for him. For a couple of his cases. I'm sorry I missed him."

Ryan watched for the cue of confusion in the tabloid reporter's eyes. While Craig squinted, Ryan moved his knight to attack Craig's pawn.

"Did he have a cute little blonde with him?" Ryan asked.

"His fiancée."

Ryan let out a huge sigh, moving his king's bishop to control the center square. Exaggerating his concern, he placed his hands on his hips. "Is her name Amanda Cash?"

Craig shook his head, looking at his feet for answers. He lifted his gaze to meet Ryan's. "I didn't meet her. She's shy or something. But that's the name Ben told me."

Ryan stomped–thus initiating the famous series of moves known in chess as Evans Gambit. "Shit. I was afraid of that. Why the hell did he bring her to such a public place?"

"What's going on?"

"Never mind." Ryan grasped the stunned man's hand and shook it. "Thanks. It's my problem now." He turned to leave, muttering a stronger oath. "I wish it didn't have to be Ben."

Craig grabbed Ryan's arm, spinning him around. "Tell me what's up."

Blowing out a long breath, Ryan paused, setting up his next few moves to force Craig's errors. This game was easier than he'd expected, but the rush of trapping his opponent still felt great.

"Ben wouldn't want me to say anything to a stranger. You understand," Ryan said.

"We're not strangers. We played football together."

Ryan's eyes flew open wide. "The Fighting Irish?"

"Yeah."

Clapping Craig on the back, Ryan laughed. "I should have known." His glee rolled into another curse. "Sometimes this job really sucks."

The enemy's king was in check.

"That woman's husband hired me to trail her," Ryan said. "He suspects her of fooling around. I'm just sorry it had to be with Ben."

Craig's mouth dropped open. "Ben only brought her here to impress her that he knows the governor."

Good, Ryan smelled victory in the wings. He was about to scoop *Your News Source* because this reporter believed Ben's ploy and had no idea the story that lay under his nose.

"Are you sure she's married?" Craig asked. "She looked like a nun."

To prove his point, Ryan removed a recent newspaper clipping from his wallet. He'd printed it when he'd researched Amanda's background.

In the accompanying photo, Erik stood at the entrance to Truffaut's, dressed in his chef's hat and whites. The restaurant investors crowded his right side while Amanda squeezed his left arm. She seemed less than enchanted, a little ill even, but what Ryan had found especially interesting was how disgusted Major Shane McClain looked as the camera caught him seated at a streetside table inside. Thank goodness for digital photography, clean windows, and Amanda's desire to remain her gay husband's cover and the major's alibi.

Holding up the article for the reporter to see, Ryan frowned and sacrificed his queen. "I don't know what she's up to, Craig, but she's married. I'm supposed to get evidence—a photo, a receipt, or something for her husband. God, I'm sick it's Ben she screwed—literally."

Craig's agitation showed in the shuffling of his feet.

Ryan began the King Hunt. "You have to tell Ben," he said. "She's bad news, man."

Taking one step backward, Craig held up both palms. "*I'm* not going to tell him. You're the detective. *You* do it."

Ryan shook his head. "They stay apart or secluded most of the time. It's hard to catch the two of them together for a picture."

"I got some pretty funny snapshots of them coming out of the governor's helicopter." Craig laughed. "I was going to send them to Ben as a wedding present." His smile faded.

"I could lose my job, or worse," Ryan said. "The husband's got a hard-ass temper. But Ben's too nice to let him get deeper into this mess." He handed the clipping to Craig. "With your photos and this, you have all the evidence you need to convince Ben he's making a mistake. Warn him before the husband discovers what's going on and smashes Ben's head in."

Craig shoved the clipping back at Ryan. "No way." He pulled out a laptop and his camera from the back of his SUV. "I'll download the pictures. Do whatever you have to do with the pictures, but *you* tell Ben. No one should have to take that hard a hit from a football buddy."

Checkmate!

Chapter Twenty-eight

Ben pulled into the crowded parking lot of a gas station attached to a grocery store. A tangle of tree branches blocked one end of the drive. Across the street, cars parked along the curb stood bumper to bumper. Amanda had arrived at the periphery of the destruction.

"The guards are set up right down the street there." Ben pointed behind them.

She twisted in her seat, catching a glimpse of a tall soldier in camouflage. A rifle was slung over his back, the strap hanging on his shoulder. He stopped a teenage couple, checking their identification. Shaking his head, he pointed over the girl's head. Then he placed his feet shoulder-width apart and took the rifle off his back, gripping it tightly in front of him like a man willing to defend the ground with his life.

Behind him a giant maple tree stretched across the street, the massive trunk creating a natural barrier. The hairy roots tickled a wide bay window of one house while the crown of newly budded leaves quietly rested on the lawn on the opposite side of the road.

Debris littered every square foot of landscape. Her stomach caved at the devastation.

"I'm going to run in for a bottle of water," Ben said, pulling his key from the ignition. The glint in his eye held the same mockery Erik used to have when he questioned her competence.

"I should be back before you finish talking with that nice, young soldier." He had the same arrogance in his voice, too.

His disdainful conceit was galling. How dare he think she couldn't accomplish anything on her own?

"You don't have to wait," she said.

He whispered, pointing down to his bucket seat. "I'll be right here."

To counter his tease, she whispered back, "You'll have too long a wait. I won't be coming back."

His mouth broadened into a smile as he twirled the key ring on his index finger. "Okay. In my job, I have plenty of experience bailing rabble-rousers out of jail."

She hissed out a breath. The clock ticked away and she was wasting time. She closed up her backpack and opened her door. "I could be in the neighborhood for a long time. I really want to get a feel for what the people need."

"Amanda, you're not getting past the guard."

"When I do, don't wait. You have more pressing matters to deal with in Omaha." She flung her bag onto her back. "I'm renting a car to drive myself home." She stepped out and slammed the door.

Ben didn't even consider a retort. He climbed out of the BMW and disappeared into the mini-mart.

The white van from the fringe of the soccer field inched into the parking lot and stopped next to the pile of tree branches. A tall man stepped out. Dark, shaggy hair covered his collar. He lit the stub of a cigarette and stretched, arching his back as though he'd traveled hours.

To do what? To see what?

He must have been a reporter, because in his tweed jacket and dress slacks, he sure didn't look like a volunteer come to help the survivors. After taking one last drag, he dropped his cigarette and crushed the butt with the toe of his boot. Then he ambled into the mini-mart. From the back, he looked a little like Ryan, but his pace was much slower.

Amanda released a breath. He wasn't her concern. With all the confidence she could muster she strolled across the street.

Smiling as she approached the soldier, she tried not to seem too friendly, practicing the aloofness she'd witnessed today among the VIPs.

The guard looked like a kid in a baggy uniform playing soldier– one with enormous hands. Wrapped around an M-16. And he looked like he knew how to use it.

Suddenly she appreciated the work Ben had done to get her into the *World-Herald* office, the Triple T Ranch, and the governor's helicopter. Never comfortable lying, Amanda reminded herself that in this case, the ends justified the means.

"I need to see ID." The deep pitch of his voice seemed a tad affected. "Only legitimate reporters and people from the neighborhood are allowed in."

"I'm Amanda Cash, with the governor's entourage."

He said nothing, the gaze of his baby-blue eyes fixed on her.

Coolly, she loaded and locked her gaze with his. He might have an assignment, but she had a mission. She *would* get through this blockade. "I'm on the list."

"What list?"

"The list of people you're supposed to let in."

The muscles in his jaw tightened. "Ma'am, I'm only supposed to let in the people who live in the neighborhood."

Calmly, she contradicted him. "No, you're supposed to have a list that has my name on it. How can I make a report to the governor if I can't see the damage?"

"Lady, there's no list."

Wheels turned faster. He was persistent, but she was determined. She smiled to show she had no intention to challenge his authority directly. No one would win if she engaged him in a personal war. "Let me make a call."

She slipped off her backpack and poked inside for her cell phone.

Darn, she'd forgotten to grab the *Cases* notebook from the backseat of the BMW. She glanced behind as Ben exited the mart. She considered going back for the notebook, but that could reduce credibility with the soldier and certainly start Ben's teasing again.

Grinning once again at the guard, she continued her scheme. "I'll just call Rudy Gardner." She pulled out the phone, flipped it open. "He's the governor's top aide."

Only a few people were listed on speed dial. She pushed the button for Ryan, praying she'd get his voice mail. While she listened to the phone ringing, she tried to impress the young soldier and build her authority.

"Rudy Gardner and Joshua—I mean *Governor Peters*, the First Lady, and I were up in a helicopter only minutes ago viewing the area." She regretted not knowing the names of the all the others on the ride.

The stony soldier appeared unconvinced.

"We were taking an aerial look." She drew her hand to her forehead. "Devastating. Simply devastating."

Ryan's voice mail clicked on and she blindly pushed the *End* button. She felt Ben's stare at her back. She would not fail. Amanda launched into her best Jodie Foster impersonation, lowering her own pitch a bit. She needed an academy-award-winning performance.

"Rudy? Yeah, it's Amanda. Hey, the soldier at the perimeter doesn't have the list." She paused and nodded, scrunching her brows into a frown. "You want to get Josh on the line to talk to this soldier, um . . ."—she looked at his name stenciled across his shirt pocket—"Private Simmons."

The soldier's eyes shifted to Amanda, then his name badge, the right and the left.

"Yeah, well I don't know any other way to get in, Rudy. He insists he can only let in the residents."

Sweat beaded on the young man's forehead. "And the press," he added.

She nodded, wrinkling her nose to acknowledge the fact. "I don't know if Private Simmons will believe it's the governor on the line." She covered the mouthpiece. "Have you ever met Joshua Peters?"

"No, ma'am." His voice cracked.

"Do you know who he is?"

"Yes, ma'am."

"I mean *would* you recognize his voice on the line? Because if Rudy drags the governor out of his meeting and you can't recognize his voice, and he has to come over here personally carrying the VIP list, then well, you know where the shit is going to land."

His Adam's apple wiggled as he swallowed, still he didn't budge and the cell phone all but slipped from her sweaty palm.

Refusing to return to Ben defeated, she tried again. "Yeah, Rudy. What? No, I don't know the name of Private Simmons' commanding officer." She didn't bother covering the mouthpiece again. "Rudy wants to know the name of your boss."

The soldier waved his hand and stepped out of her way. "Go on ahead."

The knot eased in her stomach. "Rudy. No worries, man. Private Simmons is letting me in." She shut the phone. "Thank you so much." She reached out and squeezed his forearm. It was exactly the right amount of condescension. "You're a credit to the uniform."

She scurried past before he changed his mind, stifling the urge to wave in victory to Ben.

* * * *

The buzz of the chain saws harmonized. Four or five crews worked on each side of the block, cutting the felled trees into manageable sizes to lift them off cars and houses.

Debris was everywhere and Amanda watched where she stepped so she wouldn't get cut by glass or poked by nails. Shingles, insulation, and splintered two-by-fours were part of the mix. Dead electrical wires snaked through the limbs of toppled trees.

It looked like a war zone.

An overwhelming sickness flowed over her as she walked slowly down the middle of the street. It didn't seem right to impose on the sidewalks, next to piles of heavy rubble the men had collected. The bright sunshine contrasted with the gloomy faces of the workers she passed—men and women who picked up the pieces of their lives, literally.

The scene was more horrible than she could have imagined when she'd looked at the neighborhood from five hundred feet above. The spirit underlying the posture of the residents seemed as defeated as the uprooted trees. A group of young women, two holding toddlers, huddled next to a house missing a roof. One sobbed while the others hugged her, offering comfort. It seemed an impossible task.

A little girl about six years old peeked out from behind the cluster of mothers. She held tightly to a fuzzy, stuffed dog. Wild, dark ribbons of hair dangled past her shoulders and cascaded around her face. As the child approached Amanda, she recognized the look in her young eyes as one she'd seen in the worst Alzheimer's patients at the nursing home. Amanda guessed the vacant stare of shock had sprung from indescribable terrors.

The child stopped four feet away, her dirty hand clutching some photographs. She offered them to Amanda. "Are you the lady from the Lost and Found?"

"What?"

"I picked these up. I asked my mommy's friends, but no one knows who they belong to. I was wondering if you could take them to the Lost and Found. Some mommy is going to be missing these pictures . . ."—she pointed to the group of women—"like Kay Cummings is crying over the lost pictures of her babies."

Sorrow gripped Amanda's heart. Gazing at the yard littered with debris from neighborhoods miles away, her throat closed and she fought back tears.

"Here." The little girl shoved the snapshots into her hand. "Give these to the families that lost them." There still was no readable emotion on the child's face as she spun and ran back to her mother.

While Amanda glanced at the cache, a tear slipped down her cheek. She looked back at the women. One mother in jeans with wet, muddy knees gave Amanda a quizzical look, quickly followed by tightened lips and narrowed eyes.

Immediately that same feeling of sordid curiosity she'd had in the helicopter crept over her. She offered an embarrassed half-smile to the woman and hastily turned to continue hiking.

There was no use in walking to ground zero. She stayed focused on the rolling scenes of neighbor helping neighbor and wondered how the lottery jackpot might help this community. Certainly funds could buy building materials and the labor for reconstruction, but Amanda questioned if money could buy what the Glucksfall citizens needed most.

Finally she gathered the courage to approach one older woman raking cottony attic insulation into a mound in her front yard. The wind had twisted a tree in two, depositing the larger half on her house, crushing it as though it'd had been made of gingerbread.

Amanda bent over, picking up a sheet of pink fiberglass, adding it to the heap. "Do you have insurance?"

The woman brushed a strand of gray hair from her swollen eyes. "Yes."

"Will it cover rebuilding your home?"

The same vacant look she'd seen in the child's eyes occupied this woman's gaze, too. "A home is more than the walls and roof. We'll never get back the family portraits, the grandkids' artwork, or my mother's hand-stitched quilt."

Hopelessness squeezed Amanda's chest, making breathing nearly impossible. To avoid a total breakdown, something neither she nor the woman needed to deal with, Amanda spun and jogged further down the street.

She stopped in front of a mailbox with reflective letters spelling out the owner's name and house number. Leaning against its sturdy cedar post, Amanda trembled, trying to catch her breath. Her heart beat so strongly she half-expected it to burst. It almost did when she glanced up to see the hole where the Wilsons' house used to stand.

Noticing no one around, she staggered to the edge of the foundation, peering into the basement. Puddles of muddy water stood in the white bathtub and toilet. The only other thing remaining was the carpeted staircase leading nowhere.

Familiar fright gripped her as she remembered the tornado of '75 and how her father had wrapped her in his arms to hide under the mattress beneath the basement steps. She recalled the strange, sour smell of his sweat tainted by fear. Amanda had been no older than the little girl with the wild tresses who'd given her the photos. Witnessing her father's vulnerability had heightened her own terror. And she'd never thought of him again with a child's total innocence because she'd discovered her father wasn't invincible.

The lottery money certainly couldn't repurchase that little girl's faith in her parent's protection. It couldn't buy a sense of security for the community. No amount of cash could heal the emotional scars left by nature.

Knowing she wouldn't award the jackpot to these survivors or any victims of natural disasters, Amanda admitted she'd wasted her time again.

Giving into her exhaustion and the burden of her memories, she crumpled to the ground and quietly wept. Clara's voice suddenly whispered in her memory. *Pay attention and you'll learn something—especially when you travel.*

Guilt over her self-indulgent cry soon had Amanda wiping her cheeks with her palms. Reaching into her backpack, she took out a travel-sized pouch of tissues and blew her nose.

"Well, Amanda Cash, what are you doing here?"

That voice was unmistakable.

She turned to see brown, suede hiking boots and the cuffs of well-worn blue jeans. Following the line of denim up long legs, her gaze fell on a billowy brown vest hugging a light blue shirt with thin, navy stripes. The sun glinted off the gold-lenses of Ryan Fisher's sunglasses. He held two empty, cardboard drink holders—one in each hand.

Amanda sniffled. "I could ask you the same question."

"But I asked first."

Chapter Twenty-nine

Amanda Cash was an emotional wreck. Ryan almost regretted having to take advantage of her weakened state to confirm his scoop. *Almost* regretted. After all, this was going to be the story that would launch his career in a new direction. He intended to parlay this article into a jump to television news—and not with a local station. He'd already turned down offers from news teams in Colorado Springs and Boulder. His only goal was a show with a *national* audience.

His plan was easy: he was going to stop challenging her and instead ingratiate himself. It had worked with Lisa Turner, the cop who helped him with the Danny Coomb's case. Once he had the facts he'd have just two hours before deadline to write the piece and submit it for tomorrow's Sunday edition. To that end, he'd accept whatever crazy story she came up with to explain her presence in the ruins of Glucksfall.

"What I'm doing here is . . ." Between her swollen eyes and reddened nose, Ryan gathered she'd been crying. He'd be careful not to point that out as some women hated to be caught in an *unplanned*, vulnerable state.

"My cousin called me last night," she said. "She and her family live here in Glucksfall. They're in Florida now on vacation. Disney World with the kids. They have two. Kids. Anyway, they heard about the tornado and tried calling neighbors to see if their house is still standing, but the phone lines are down. They asked if I wouldn't mind checking things out for them."

"How nice of you to help."

He could have pointed out a dozen flaws in that fabrication. Instead, he offered his hand. Reluctantly, she placed her palm in his and he hoisted her to her feet.

"It's the least I could do." She brushed dirt off her bottom.

It was a cute bottom, too. He wished they were far enough along in their relationship that he could help her with the task. If he worked things right, he might be able to bed Amanda *and* get the story—in the same night.

"And how did you find the house?" he asked.

She stammered and he wanted to scream at the lie he knew was coming. As far as he was concerned, she could make up any silly yarn. He wasn't going to mention the absurdities in her lies. He just needed to get close enough to search her backpack.

"I simply walked in and found it," she said.

Recalling the message she'd left on his voicemail, he choked back a chuckle. Slipping past the guard with her lie about working for the governor had been pretty sly. When he'd heard the click at the beginning of her one-sided conversation, he'd wondered if Amanda had believed she'd disconnected him.

"I meant, is your cousin's house all right?" he said.

She coughed, her cheeks tinting a mild shade of red. "No, it's gone." She pointed to the gaping hole next to her. Quickly, she motioned to the mailbox. "Their name is Wilson."

She was a terrible liar. That said something for her character, but Ryan found morals a hindrance in his business. Her righteousness would be a nuisance, but not significant enough to be classified an obstacle. He *would* get the story.

He helped her slip on her backpack. She always had it, or some form of it, with her. Even on their date last night she'd carried an ugly, flat bag with large, wooden rings for handles. It looked like the upholstery cover for a sofa cushion. There had to be something in it she didn't want separated from her.

If it held any proof she was the lottery winner's agent, he'd whisk her away to Phoenix. Secluding her in his writing condo, he'd seduce her for details of her project. The exclusive story was sure to get the attention of the networks.

And if he wanted to make the Sunday morning edition, he'd have to hurry, but he wasn't worried. In her delicate state, it wouldn't be too difficult to figure out a way to take a peek at her valuables.

* * * *

"How terrible your cousin lost everything." Ryan put an arm around her, the warmth of his embrace comforting.

After last night, his compassion caught Amanda off guard. He'd been as growly as an old dog with a meaty bone—relentless in his questioning about the lottery. Now he was obviously swept up by his emotions spurred by the deep loss these people had suffered.

She shared his sentiment. His kindness was her mercy. But then she'd always heard disasters tended to bring out the best in people.

"You didn't say why you're here," she asked.

"Gramps owns some property in the neighborhood and I came to check on it for him on my way back to Denver."

"Rental property? Farm land?"

"A small grocery and gas station. Maybe you saw it as you came in."

Quickly, she dismissed a fleeting image of Ben sitting in his car in front of the mini-mart sipping bottled water.

"How did you get past the guard?" she asked.

He held up the empty drink holders. "I've been taking coffee and doughnuts to the clean-up crews all day. They seem to appreciate it."

Decency glowed in his humble smile. She was so glad her fight with Ryan was over. It didn't really matter if his grandfather was the lottery winner or not. Maybe Ryan had been sent to protect her, but she didn't have the time, inclination, or energy to delve into that subject. She may not know as much about Ryan as she did about Ben, but at least he smiled and spoke kindly to her, and she felt better when Ryan was around.

A twitter in her backpack had her fumbling for her cell phone. Caller ID told her it was Ben again. She switched the ringer off, setting the vibrate function and clipped the phone to her waistband. His call she would gladly ignore. It was enough that she'd denied Erik's manipulative character for so long. She refused to fall into the same trap with Ben. The pain of deception hurt too much.

The more she thought of Ben's behavior today, the more she was convinced he'd sold her identity to the tabloids. By tomorrow all this lying and scheming would probably be moot. Aside from the fact she'd have proof Ben had betrayed her, she almost welcomed the announcement of her connection to the lottery winner. She hated hiding behind a thicket of lies and knew she was barely credible when she spun her tales. She was ready for the intrigue to end. Maybe then she could focus on her tasks instead of hiding.

"Time for me to go get more coffee for the troops. Would you like to come with me?" he said.

"I'll walk a ways with you."

Casually, he grabbed her hand and soon they were strolling by the houses she'd previously passed. The men nodded and smiled at Ryan. Tension knotted in her stomach. At least he'd made a difference today by bringing everyone coffee. What had she done? Nothing—except fly in a high-cost helicopter; she'd accomplished nothing—nothing to help these people and nothing to help her mother.

They approached the house where the little girl had given her the photos. The lawn now was empty. "You know, I was in Omaha's tornado of '75. I was six years old."

"Oh?"

"I didn't really see the aftermath. My mother immediately sent me away to stay the summer with my uncle in Chicago. I thought it was a cool deal at the time. I skipped the last month of kindergarten."

"Funny, I didn't peg you as the truant type."

She chuckled, but one glance at the roofless house reestablished her earlier feeling of dread. "The tornado terrified me. For years I couldn't stand the sound of a strong wind. Even the rumble of distant thunder made me freeze."

He wrapped his arm around her. "Maybe it wasn't such a good idea for you to come here today. I'll bet the Wilsons wouldn't have wanted you to relive that pain."

Guilt over the Wilson lie nagged her. Snuggling closer to Ryan made her feel less vulnerable and stronger to face her haunting memories.

"As a child, the terror I'd experienced was horrible, but I suffered more being separated from my parents that summer. Looking at the damage now, and the effect on the survivors, I can see why my mother wanted to protect me."

Her throat tightened again and she blinked back tears.

"When I came home, the neighborhood was fixed. New shingles covered the roofs. Skinny saplings had been planted in the yards." She pointed to an inverted Volkswagen the wind had dropped at the end of a driveway. "New concrete had been poured. But the scars were still there, underneath the fresh paint and on everyone's fragile emotions."

He squeezed her tighter, the action releasing pent up tears.

She sniffed and blotted her cheeks with the handkerchief he offered. "I think it might have helped the healing process to actually be part of the cleanup and rebuilding of the neighborhood," she said.

"You're probably right."

The last hour had convinced Amanda the jackpot wasn't the solution to the Glucksfall tragedy. Certainly the lottery winner couldn't fault her decision since there were too many natural disasters to fund the recovery of them all. But while she was here, she could do something to help. She removed her backpack and peeled off her red windbreaker, stuffing it into the bag. The zipper gaped open.

Pushing up her sleeves, she marched with renewed purpose to a group of men tying tree branches into bundles and loading them onto the bed of a pick-up truck.

Tossing her backpack against a fire hydrant, she turned to Ryan. "Better bring in some sandwiches. It's going to be a long afternoon."

Glancing at her bag, Ryan smiled, she guessed at her transformed energy and determination. Then he scuttled off to get lunch for the survivors.

* * * *

Ben had blown it with Amanda all day. It had been shades of Gloria Ray. Self-disclosure was harder than he expected. Part of him felt like he'd violated a confidence by sharing Colleen's story with Amanda, but mostly he'd feared Amanda would run if she discovered how dysfunctional the Harris family was. *He'd* run if he could.

Leaning back against the wooden picnic table outside the mini-mart, he faced outward to watch people come and go from the cordoned-off neighborhood. None of them was his little elf in the red jacket.

For the past hour he'd watched the buzz of activity in and out of the grocery as well. Each customer triggered the overhead doorbell which began to sound like the ding of a slot machine. Every pull of the handle reminded Ben of his sister. While he should be back in Omaha bailing her out, he couldn't leave Amanda in that destroyed neighborhood no matter how insistent she'd been to the contrary. She'd need him, if for no other reason than a ride back home when she finished her reconnaissance.

Chuckling, he thought of her stiff determination. He'd been darned impressed she'd talked her way past the guard. They'd have a good laugh over the story when she came back to tell him about it.

For the hundredth time, Ben checked his watch. Amanda was funny all around, especially when she'd set the alarm on her cell phone to beep on the hour. He frowned remembering how he'd called her number twenty minutes ago, but she'd let it roll to voice mail.

She was still pissed at him, although he had no idea why. According to the self-help books, sharing one's vulnerabilities was supposed to endear a man to a woman.

From the corner of his eye, he saw Bruno Talbot plodding toward him. Ben slid to the end of the table to make room for the man he disliked even more than parole hearings.

"Were you trying to ditch me again this morning?" The tall man hitched his knee, placing his muddy boot on the bench. Then the bodyguard hired by the lottery winner to protect Amanda lit a cigarette.

"What are you talking about?" Ben waved the smoke away from his face, coughed, then moved upwind.

"When you pulled over on the Interstate."

"I had a business call to take."

Colleen had really messed up this time. He had few options to keep her out of prison. Maybe helping her as much as he had was actually hindering her. Perhaps he should stay for one of those Gambler's Anonymous meetings or talk to a professional counselor about the best ways to help an addict, because everything he'd tried so far had failed.

He remembered how smooth and soft Amanda's hand had felt as he'd held it while he'd scratched down notes about Colleen's case. The kind of support he'd always looked for in a woman. In fact, she had every quality he wanted in a wife—except maybe her stubbornness. He didn't understand why she'd gotten so surly with him at the soccer field. He thought his joke about her elf costume was pretty funny.

"How long do you think she'll stay in there?" Bruno asked.

"Don't know."

Ben hated that Bruno kept interrupting his thoughts about Amanda. What he hated even worse was the bodyguard's detachment from his assignment. It was as if he didn't care at all about Amanda, but more than that, Bruno didn't seem to respect her. And that seemed impossible to Ben.

Bruno took another long drag from the cigarette. "And what was up with the lip lock at the helicopter?"

Ben's left hand instinctively twitched into a fist and he called on his stockpile of professionalism to relax. "You need new spy glasses, pal. Amanda tripped coming out of the helicopter and fell on top of me."

Bruno grunted.

The hair on the back of Ben's neck bristled. If this creep insinuated one more time that Amanda was easy, he'd deck him.

"Well, there was a reporter snapping photos," Bruno said.

"Yeah, he's a friend of mine. He's going to print some for a wedding present."

"Huh?"

"I told you we'd be posing as an engaged couple."

"You looked pretty engaged to me." Bruno's laugh turned into a smoker's hack.

Now both of Ben's hands twitched. Punching the guy was justified, right? Surely, he wouldn't get disbarred and Roberta would overlook his indiscretion. If anyone deserved a good thrashing it was this jerk.

Once again, Ben decided to ignore the ass' comment. After all, they were supposed to be on the same team.

Like Amanda and Ben were on the same team. How odd that she'd believe he would sell her identity to a tabloid. She was becoming too darned paranoid, although if he were in her shoes, he'd probably feel the same. It was weird how she wouldn't come right out and ask him if he'd told Craig who she was. Maybe skirting the issue, hinting at problems, and being evasive was in a chapter on interpreting female communication he hadn't read yet in the self-help books. Good thing he'd deciphered her code and set the record straight. Her identity was safe with him.

Bruno flipped his butt at the sand-filled ashtray dotted with wads of pink bubble gum, but it bounced off the rim, landing on the asphalt. A curl of smoke snaked its way to Ben's nose. He ground a heel into the cigarette, the action somehow making him feel better about Bruno.

"How do you do this?" Ben asked. "Stalk people all the time?"

Bruno unwrapped a stick of gum and flipped it into his mouth. "You get used to it."

Ben never would. He desperately wanted to know what Amanda was doing just beyond where he could see her. He hoped she was getting the information she needed for her decision, although he thought they'd already agreed using the jackpot for natural disasters wasn't in the cards.

In the cards—he couldn't even calculate the depth of disappointment he felt about Colleen. No matter how low she'd sunk, he couldn't fathom how she could stoop to stealing to feed her gambling addiction. Not when her kids were at stake.

A woman with a tower of red hair ambled out of the mini-mart, pointing in their direction. Her enormous belly, cinched in half by her tight waistband, jiggled as she stepped toward them. "Hey, you two are gonna have to move your cars."

"Why?" Bruno challenged.

"We need the room for *paying* customers."

"By whose orders?"

Seemed Bruno was an aggravation to everyone.

"Imelda Marcos, that's who." She swiped a hand in the air. "Beat it. I'm the owner. Can't you have some respect for the situation here?"

Bruno groaned, removed his foot from the bench and arched his back. "All right."

Ben rose, too, and from the corner of his eye saw a man sprint around the guard at the blockade, huffing toward them.

"There he goes again," Bruno said.

"Who?"

"Ryan Fisher. That tall guy coming toward us. He's been carrying in coffee and stuff all morning."

"I hadn't noticed," Ben said.

"Don't give up your day job, rookie."

Peeling off his vest as he ran, Ryan remotely unlocked his Camry and threw the garment into the back seat. He leapt behind the wheel and sped off.

"Guess his altruism gave out," Ben stated.

Bruno scrubbed a hand over his mouth. "Keep an eye out for Amanda. I'll follow Fisher."

"Why would you follow him?"

"Because he's been dating Amanda for a few weeks now."

"What?" Had a house dropped from the sky and crushed him, Ben couldn't have been more stunned.

Bruno hustled to the white van with Ben at his heels.

"D-dating? Are you sure?"

Bruno gave him a snide look.

It wasn't possible. Amanda couldn't be dating Ryan. She'd told him she couldn't be distracted by a relationship now, had insisted she only had time for her lottery duties and occasional phone calls to Clara. He glowered at Ryan's departing car.

Amanda had fed Ben a line—and not one even as good as Gloria Ray's. "Why didn't you tell me?" he spat at the bodyguard.

"Information is on a need-to-know basis." Bruno climbed into the van. Then he started the engine and backed out of the lot, following cautiously behind the man Ben desperately wanted to strangle.

Chapter Thirty

As the sunset cast a purple glow on the windows of the mini-mart, Amanda pulled her jacket out of the backpack and tugged it on. She glanced around for the red BMW and Ben Harris. They were gone.

So much the better. After all, she'd ordered him back to Omaha three hours ago. Still, the empty parking lot brought on her familiar feeling of isolation.

"So, where's your car?" Ryan asked, opening the back door of his Camry. He took out the vest he'd deposited there on one of his food runs in the heat of the day. Slipping on the vest, his collar rolled under, taking some of his black, curly hair with it.

Did she have one more lie—one more story—left in her? She sighed, too tired to care if the truth held up.

"At home. A friend brought me, but he had to return to Omaha. I'm going to rent a car to drive back, but not until tomorrow. I'm too beat tonight."

Ryan gave her a sideways I-told-you-so look. He'd been trying for two hours to get her to quit working, but it had felt too good helping the cleanup effort. To ignore Ben's phone calls and the pressing duties of the lottery—to be totally lost in unselfish, manual labor was what she'd needed this afternoon. The survivors had been so appreciative she couldn't have abandoned them without giving as much time as possible, especially since she wouldn't be giving them any of the jackpot.

"It's a good kind of tired," she added, reaching up to straighten his collar and untangle a curl at the nape of his neck. It had been so sweet of him to worry that her work might stir up her grief again.

He arched his eyebrow and appeared worn himself. He hadn't done much of the physical work. Instead he'd shuttled food and drinks to the neighborhood all afternoon and made phone calls to get more equipment and supplies into the damaged area. He'd even disappeared for an hour to arrange for a generator to supply power to an elderly couple with medical needs.

Apparently, his charity knew no bounds.

"If I could impose on you one more time to give me a ride to the closest hotel." She looked down at her filthy clothes. "I need a shower and a good night's sleep."

"Well, as a matter of fact, I've already called around. Everything's booked. With all the homeless people, volunteers, and the insurance adjusters starting to pour in, the whole town's tied up. Grand Island, too."

She groaned, dropping her backpack at her feet, its weight suddenly enormous. Digging for a reserve of energy that wasn't there, she sighed. "Would you mind taking me to a rental car company then?"

"You're too tired to drive three hours back to Omaha."

He pulled her into a loose hug, one of many he'd offered her today. In a relaxed response, she wrapped her arms around his waist and laid her head against his chest. Soon her pulse seemed to match the beating of his generous heart.

"What are my options?" she said.

"You could come with me."

Jerking away from him, she stared into his playful, chestnut-colored eyes, realizing in an instant she could get lost in their promised intimacy. "I don't want to drive five hours to Denver."

Bending his knees, he dropped to her eye level to hold her gaze. "Neither do I. That's why I chartered a jet to take us to my vacation condo in Phoenix."

She blinked. And blinked again. Was he serious?

There was so much of Bud Fisher in his grandson. The octogenarian had often offered to fly her away to some romantic spot. Now it seemed the assignment fell to Ryan.

Searching his eyes, she looked for sincerity. From her limited and luckless experience with men, she couldn't be sure she'd recognize it even if it was there.

She dragged herself to a picnic table outside the mini-mart. Cigarette butts that had missed the concrete ashtray littered the ground at her feet. She dumped her pack on the tabletop and collapsed onto the bench.

"Let me think," she said.

"While you're doing that, I'll go inside and get us something cold to drink." He tossed her a warm smile.

He was much more accommodating than she'd ever seen him before—so nice and attentive. Was this what she could have had all these years if she'd married a heterosexual man? Was this the normal mating ritual?

She shook her head at the ridiculous question. Chartering a jet could hardly be considered a normal dating practice.

Concentrating, she considered her situation. She looked down at her grimy, white tee-shirt and green corduroys. She'd had nothing to eat all day, funneling the food Ryan offered her to the survivors.

Pulling out the elastic band, she fluffed her hair with her fingers and considered what she might gain by going with Ryan Fisher.

She needed time to decide the next case to investigate, but she couldn't work on it with him hovering over her. But so what if he did? Her anonymity wouldn't matter soon. By tomorrow morning, Ryan and the world would know her connection to the lottery winner, compliments of Ben Harris.

Maybe it was a good idea to get away from Omaha. The press would be crawling over her apartment, trying to interview the lottery winner's agent. Likewise, they'd probably stake out the nursing home. She was tempted to warn her mother, but didn't want Clara to worry.

She unclipped her cell phone from her waistband, ready to call Uncle Ernie. He could explain everything to Clara and then protect her.

The bell over the door dinged as Ryan strolled out of the mini-mart, carrying two cans of cold beer. He wore a huge smile.

"How would I get home?" she asked, returning her phone to her waist.

Easing onto the bench, his sexy, jean-clad hip snuggled against hers. He opened a beer and passed it. "Well, you stay as long as you'd like in Phoenix with me. When you're ready to go home, I'll put you on a plane. They have some great non-stop flights between the cities and I have all the schedules memorized." He popped the second beer and took a long draw.

God, he looked too irresistible. Amanda breathed in and wondered how he could still smell so fresh at the end of such a grueling day.

One place was good as the next when it came to managing the project now. In fact, by tomorrow, Arizona would be preferable to Nebraska.

She recalled what Clara had told her—pay attention when you travel and you're bound to learn something.

"Phoenix it is," she said, sipping her beer.

* * * *

"Guacamole dip! Why didn't you let me stop them when they pulled onto the airstrip?" Ben wanted to pound something, and the closest thing was Bruno Talbot.

"I shouldn't have moved my car from the mini-mart," Ben continued. "She probably thought I abandoned her."

"We can't blow Amanda's cover."

Ben leaned against the van's fender, watching the tail lights of the Learjet shrink as it ascended from the small, private airport forty minutes west of Glucksfall.

From clenching his jaw tightly for the last hour, Ben's head ached. "Will her cover protect her if Fisher's some kind of pervert?"

His back to the wind, Bruno lit a cigarette. A coil of smoke wafted into Ben's face, stinging his eyes.

"She's been alone with him before, remember?" Bruno said.

The image and the second-hand pollutant sickened Ben. Amanda was too naïve to know what she was doing or she wouldn't have fallen for such a slick package of pork.

As the bodyguard raised the cigarette to his lips, an errant breeze caught the smoke stream, shifting it into Bruno's eyes and he squinted. He took a long draw, igniting the tobacco to a red glow. Holding the poison in his lungs for a moment, he then muttered, "Besides . . ."—he blew out the smoke—"she went with him willingly. Very willingly if that kiss at the bottom of the air stairs meant anything." A grin pulled at the corner of his mouth.

A swift backward kick connected Ben's heel with the tire. It was bad enough Amanda had bought whatever Fisher was selling, but it killed him Bruno didn't see this situation for the catastrophe it was. "Who is this Ryan Fisher anyway?" he said.

"The grandson of a guy living at Brookside."

Ben rubbed his hands together with frustration. "Why didn't you put a stop to this sooner?"

"Stop to what? As far as I know, they're just out on another date." Bruno puffed the Marlboro again.

"But where?"

Angling his cigarette toward the small terminal, the bodyguard pushed out a single cough. "We'll get the flight plan, then we'll know."

Bruno was too casual for Ben's satisfaction and he looked again at the inky sky. The tail lights had disappeared. At five hundred miles per hour, the two were already out of reach and soon would be out of easy driving distance. It would be impossible to get to Amanda quickly now, even if she called him to rescue her—which was looking less likely to happen with each passing moment.

"Where'd Fisher go when you followed him this afternoon?" Ben asked.

Bruno pulled out a scratch pad from the inside pocket of his tweed jacket. While he flipped pages to find his notes, Ben waited for the cigarette, aided by swirling breezes, to catch the whole thing on fire. The bodyguard tipped the page toward the headlight. "A downtown hotel called the Husker Inn on Seventeenth and Bayard."

"To do what?"

He sucked one last time on the cigarette, flicked it downwind, and reviewed his scribbles. "He talked to the front desk clerk, one Randy Gavin, and then went into the restaurant, called the Prairie Wind. He chatted with his waitress, one Kimberly Leonard, who moved him to a booth in the corner. He plugged in his computer, a Dell laptop. He ordered a drink—"

"One scotch and soda . . ." Ben interrupted.

Bruno looked up from the pad and scowled. "An iced tea. Brewed. Two packets of artificial sweetener—the blue kind." He glared again. "Do you want the details or not?"

Ben flapped a hand at him, urging him on.

Talbot shot him another glower before continuing. "He worked on his computer, typing damn fast, using all his fingers. Can *you* do that?" He looked up, the twinkle in his eyes taunting Ben.

While Amanda was slipping away from them, Bruno Talbot was wasting time—begging to be slugged. Ben clenched his teeth working hard to control his temper.

Not getting the rise he wanted, Bruno's gaze returned to the small notebook. He sighed. "After an hour and ten minutes, Fisher got back in his car—"

"A blue Camry." Ben finished the report, "Fisher drove back to the mini-mart where he bought more Cokes and took them into the neighborhood."

Clapping the notebook shut, Bruno stuffed it back into his jacket.

Ben's irritation hung heavy in the chilled evening air. None of the information helped point them in the right direction. "Didn't Fisher do anything else?"

"Yes."

"What?"

Bruno made a show at trying to recall. "Before returning to the mini-mart, Fisher bought a camera, one pocket-sized model with a zoom lens."

"For what?"

Bruno shrugged.

Whatever the lottery winner was paying this jerk was way too much. "You're supposed to be working to protect Amanda. How do we know what Fisher's doing to her right now?"

Bruno chuckled. "Well, he has a damned expensive camera with lots of special features. Judging by the amount of money he dropped on the Lear, I think we can safely presume what he's up to."

Ben stooped low, and jammed a shoulder into Bruno's ribcage, shoving him backward. The stench of his breath whooshed out as Bruno's spine hit the hood.

Scrambling up the front of the tall man, Ben grabbed Bruno's lapels and jerked him upright, noses touching. "*That,*" Ben panted, "is the *last* time you'll disrespect Amanda Cash." He pinned him with his stare. "Understand?"

Bruno nodded and stepped back, raking together shards of self-respect by brushing the wrinkles off the front of his jacket. "Go back to Omaha, Harris. You're too close to the case."

Glancing at the sky again, Ben snarled. "Not nearly close enough."

The bodyguard shook his head slowly. "Do what you want, but in my experience, guys in love never think straight. And your lack of perspective could get Amanda hurt."

"I'm *not* in love."

Tilting his head away, Bruno held up an open palm. Brushing by Ben, he climbed behind the steering wheel.

Ben had recognized his lie the minute it flew out of his mouth.

Chapter Thirty-one

Settled back in the plush, leather seat, Amanda gazed over her wine glass at Ryan's chestnut-colored eyes. "The dinner was spectacular," she whispered.

"I'm glad you liked it. Tyler does a nice job with duck. I'm happy he was able to pull something together for us on short notice."

Resplendent in the captain's chair facing her, he looked as appetizing as the gourmet meal she'd just finished. Beneath the wooden table, his knees brushed hers as he swiveled slowly to relax.

Taking a deep breath, Amanda let her head rest against the cream-colored pillow while she glanced around. It was an intimate setting—a fantasy, really. On one side of the plane two deep-cushioned, wide chairs faced one another separated by a retractable table. Across the narrow aisle, a matching leather-covered divan stretched along the curved fuselage, butting up against a small galley kitchen. Lights on the wings blinked at Amanda through several petite windows dressed in southwestern-patterned curtains.

She'd taken her time washing up in the lavatory and had accepted his offer of a clean dress shirt. Buttoned all the way up, the collar still sagged at her neck. Trying to make it fit, she'd tied it at the waist and rolled the sleeves to the armpits—the shirt's, not hers. She'd refused his offer of his knit gym shorts unsure of how she'd keep them up. She wished she were as relaxed as she looked.

On the other hand, he couldn't have looked more comfortable if he'd been stretched out on a feather bed. His jacket hung in the cabin closet along with her filthy, red windbreaker. He'd undone the top two buttons of his light blue shirt allowing ebony curls to peek out from his tanned chest. The subdued sconce lighting made it all seem a dream.

"More wine?" Ryan poised the bottle over her glass.

She nodded, knowing her weak tolerance of alcohol could be a problem later. He topped off her glass, emptying the bottle.

Ryan gathered the dishes from the table. Amanda unfolded her legs which had been tucked beneath her.

"No," he insisted, "relax. I'll take care of this."

"Thanks for dinner . . ."—she pinched the front of her shirt—"and everything else."

He balanced the two plates between the fingers of one hand, keeping the china from clinking together. He must have worked in food service at some time in his life. She smiled to herself. There she went again, launching into a popular pastime of guessing his career. For tonight, he'd only been a friend, enjoying her company.

"Feeling better?" he asked, proving her point. That was a question a friend would ask.

Smiling, she took another sip of wine, the warmth massaging her tired muscles. "I feel great."

He stowed the dishes under the miniature galley counter. If that was a dishwasher, she was definitely in a James Bond movie.

"I was worried about you," he said.

"Why?"

Reaching for the corkscrew, he removed another bottle from the mini-fridge. "You looked so stressed when I ran into you this afternoon. It's understandable given your history."

There was that compassion again. Amanda could get used to being with a man who cared so much. What a switch from Erik Cash—the later years.

Setting her glass on the table, she fluffed her loose hair with her fingers, noticing the silkiness of the long tresses. "It really helped to work alongside the survivors. I suppose it was cathartic."

He nodded, uncorking the wine. Amanda still had plenty so he filled his glass and folded himself into the chair.

Even silence is easy with him, Amanda thought, glancing at him as he gazed out the window. She snuggled deeper into the luxurious chair and recalled the day. She'd decided to stop fretting about the lottery deadline. Stressing over something never helped, usually made it worse actually. If she let go of her tension and opened herself to the possibilities, the solution to her dilemma would come. Maybe tomorrow in Phoenix. For now she was going to do what Clara always recommended—pay attention to her surroundings so she could learn.

Another thing had changed this afternoon. Amanda now believed she could accomplish her mission. While she didn't dismiss the possibility she'd been selected at random, she had to consider she was chosen for a reason.

Maybe there was a hint of Amanda's diligence in the phrasing of the letter she'd written asking for her mother's transplant. Maybe the winner thought Amanda brave, or smart, or decisive. Whatever caught the benefactor's attention, one fact was clear. Amanda had all those qualities and more. She realized that when she'd successfully skirted the soldier at the barricade.

She *would* figure out how to distribute the money in an acceptable way. She *would* collect the finder's fee. Clara *would* have the surgery and everything *would* be fine.

Amanda was never more certain of anything in her life. She'd hold tight to that confidence until her assignment was accomplished.

Sipping her wine, she rubbed her hand over the armrest, releasing the rich aroma of leather. Is this the kind of lifestyle Bud had been offering her? She chuckled. "Your grandfather tried to entice me into going to Costa Rica with him. Does he own this jet?"

"No. It's a charter. But as I told you the first time we met," he shook a finger at her, "be careful of Bud. He's a letch."

She grinned. "Has he really been to Greece and those other exotic places?"

"Yes. He had the most amazing relationship with my grandmother. They had an arrangement I never understood. He ignored her most of the time—when he was working. However, when he wanted time away from the newspaper, there was no one else in his world but my grandmother. They both had a passion for each other I've not seen matched. He misses her terribly."

She clutched at her heart, sighing. "That's so romantic."

He nodded in agreement, offering her a pillow from the divan. "Are you comfortable? Or," he pointed to the couch, "you're welcome to take a nap. It's still another ninety minutes until we land."

Glimpsing the couch wide enough for two, she sighed again. "If only. I haven't been able to sleep for a couple of weeks."

"Oh?"

"Worry over my mother." And other things she was happy to put out of her mind for the night.

He laid his hand over hers. "Everything will work out fine."

It was a common platitude.

"Even if you don't think so and the pain is more than you think you can bear. When the time finally comes to say good-bye to your mother, you'll survive."

He had such faith in her strength? The relaxing effect of the wine combined with his compassion sparked a tear.

He folded the table against the wall and taking her hand, pulled her to her feet. "Try lying down for a while." He led her to the sofa and she willingly rolled onto the cushions which enveloped her like a hot biscuit soaks up butter.

As he slipped off her shoes, she scooted back, making room for him next to her. Reluctantly he sat, searching her eyes for permission.

Permission for what she didn't know. Would his be a gesture of a friend or the action of a lover? The buzz between her brows caused by the wine cheered for the latter.

After kicking off his boots, he nestled in next to her, drinking in her face with his gaze. He seemed to appreciate what he saw and a tingle skimmed over Amanda.

He kissed her.

At first it was soothing, then it grew more intense. His lips tasted of wine and promises. Caresses along her jaw line hinted at possibilities. When they pulled apart, his gaze held lusty encouragement.

God, she missed intimacy. Even when she suspected Erik wasn't interested in her anymore, she could still find release in his touch—and she'd ached for his contact even when it was apparent he was only going through the motions. She longed for a close relationship in her life now. Someone she could trust with her body as well as her emotions.

He kissed her again. And she kissed back, offering more of herself to him in the play of their lips and tongues.

It would be so easy to give in to his kisses, his caresses. The sexual release might be exactly what she needed to finally get some sleep. An hour of distraction might be just what she'd prescribed for herself.

His fingers deftly unbuttoned her oversized shirt. When he ran his palm over her breast above her bra, she closed her eyes and felt the magic she'd lacked for the last decade.

A woman could give herself completely to someone as wonderful as Ben Harris.

Ben Harris?

She sucked in a quick breath, prompting Ryan to slip a finger under the lace trim of her bra cup.

Had she just thought of Ben Harris while Ryan Fisher's hand roamed over her? Could she be that drunk to make such a wild mistake? The prospect jolted her back to reality.

"Stop, Ryan. I can't."

He pulled back sharply, making a smooching sound as his lips left her neck. "Why not?"

She struggled to sit up, his weight more than she could push off her. She slumped back, letting her head fall back to the pillow. "I'm exhausted. I don't make sound decisions when I'm so tired."

"This isn't a decision, it's an event." His lips lowered to her cleavage.

She bet he could make that brag true.

Her desire for intimacy was strong, but not powerful enough to lead her to sleep with the wrong man. And thinking about Ben while lying next to Ryan meant something was wrong. Didn't it?

Then again, she didn't have much experience to fall back on. It had always been Erik, who'd been very willing to accept her virginity. After they'd set the wedding date, he insisted on abstaining, to honor his future wife. It didn't seem odd at the time. Now she believed it was possible he was having his own internal sexual struggle then, as she was having hers now.

"I can't. I'm sorry I led you on. What I really need is a good night's sleep."

What she *wanted* was for all this to be over. She was exhausted. Worry over her mother and the stress of her identity being leaked had taken way too much out of her. She was surprised she hadn't held up better. Then there was the issue with Erik, his using her, and their impending divorce. Add Ben and his apparent betrayal. Everything weighed heavily on her.

Ryan blew out an impatient breath. She *assumed* it was impatience, not aggravation or anger. He sat up, swinging his feet to the floor.

"Truly, I'm sorry, Ryan. You've been such a good friend to me today. I let things get too far. It's possible I . . . I have some kind of feelings for you. Well, obviously, I have *some* kind of feelings, but I don't want to make a mistake."

He scrubbed the back of his neck and groaned. "A mistake."

"I'm sorry. Truly."

"You said that."

She wanted to blame the whole thing on Erik and how their relationship had stunted her emotional growth. But that would have been a lie. The true reason she wouldn't sleep with Ryan was she didn't understand the depth of her feelings about Ben.

Although thoughts in the front of her mind had Ben swinging from a rope by the neck for selling her identity, there was a little voice of hope in the back, whispering he was too caring to betray her.

"I'm sorry. I just can't."

Annoyance peeked from the corner of Ryan's eye. There was a dark hint of something else she couldn't quite define. "Sleep. I can help you with that. I have some pills. Not over the counter. They're really mild, but effective," he said.

"They sound perfect."

He grabbed his carry-on bag from under the divan.

"Oh, not now," she said, waving her hand. "When we get to Phoenix."

"I said they're mild."

"With my luck, I'll be out for the night."

His stare hardened. "These are so gentle you can take one now and still wake up in about an hour to walk into my condo."

She hesitated.

"You could get extra rest. Frankly, Amanda, it's the only way I'm going to be able to keep my hands off you."

The last thing she remembered was swallowing.

Chapter Thirty-two

The taxi driver of unknown ethnicity stopped at the curb in front of Ryan's condo and frowned in the rearview mirror.

Dim landscape lighting glowed along the flagstone path leading to the arched entry of the stucco building. Ryan muttered an oath as his gaze swept from the locked wrought-iron gate to the balcony of his second-story apartment.

"There's an extra twenty bucks for you if you help me carry everything inside."

The cabbie twisted around to look at Amanda. Her slack jaw made her mouth gape. Head tipped back, it leaned precariously against Ryan's shoulder. The driver shook his head and pointed to the meter. "Monies only," he said in the broken English of an immigrant.

Disgusted, Ryan cursed, throwing the fare into the front seat. Hooking his wrist under Amanda's armpit, he slid her across the seat to the door. He dragged her out and hoisted her onto his shoulder. Grabbing his laptop case, he slung the strap over his free shoulder and then bent sideways to get his overnight satchel and her backpack off the floorboard.

"Thanks a lot, buddy," he said as he slammed the door and watched the cabbie drive off.

She was one hundred and twenty pounds of dead weight. He knew she would be. Not that he'd guessed her exact weight, but he'd known she would be unconscious when they landed.

The Rohypnol had worked as expected. She'd acted drunk and uninhibited for an hour after she'd swallowed the roofie. Too bad she'd been out of her mind or he would have taken her up on one of her many offers of unbridled sex. She'd acted so wild the co-pilot had come into the cabin, asking if she was all right. If Ryan hadn't stopped her, she'd have jumped the co-pilot's bones as well. Seemed Amanda Cash was one horny babe once her inhibitions were let loose.

Ryan flashed his card key and heard the buzz of the gate unlocking. Using her ass, he pushed his way through, rounded the corner, and lugged his load up the narrow flight of outdoor stairs. He'd worked up a sweat by the time he reached the top and dropped his carry-on at the apartment door, digging an eternity for the key in his pants' pocket. Once the door opened, he kicked his bag and her backpack over the threshold. Then he set his computer on the sofa. That was one weight he was glad to get off his back.

Amanda's long hair caught in the clasp of the computer's case strap, halting his step abruptly, nearly toppling them. To free them, he grabbed a hunk and tugged. He heard a slight rip, but Amanda didn't awaken.

Easing her onto the bed, he looked at his prize. What a mess. Drowning in his shirt, blonde hair spilled over her face and pillow. He wanted to remove her filthy pants, but he didn't want to risk her losing trust in him.

For all her disheveled appearance, Amanda still looked delicious. Remembering her initial reaction to the drug, he could almost see how Danny Coombs would have enjoyed what he'd done repeatedly—feeding roofies to pretty coeds to get easy sex. Not that Ryan needed the artificial aid to bed women. For that matter, neither did the star quarterback of Colorado's winning college football team. But that was what Coombs was into—at least until undercover cop, Lisa Turner, accompanied by reporter, Ryan Grogan, a.k.a. Ryan Fisher, had put an end to Coombs' crime spree.

It had taken all his salesmanship to convince Lisa to give him a few of the illegal Rohypnol pills. Finally, Ryan had persuaded her he needed first-hand experience of the roofies' effects. She'd been a willing participant in their experiment. His description of her behavior under the influence had lent the dramatic element needed to sell over two million copies of his series of articles tracking the arrest, prosecution, and conviction of the fallen football star.

Their night of feral sex was pretty good, too.

Danny Coombs' loss was Ryan Grogan's ticket to fame. With Amanda's story, now he'd secure his fortune.

There was a line of ethics Ryan wouldn't cross; after all he was the nice guy, and looking at Amanda again he prided himself for resisting temptation. He spread a blanket over her before walking into the living room where he took the new, digital camera from his computer case.

He reviewed the series of candid shots he'd taken of Amanda while she'd helped clean up the rubble this afternoon. For having to sneak and peek, he'd done a half-decent job.

Certainly, the photos along with a scanned copy of her contract were good enough to prove to the producers of "Win a Fortune" that he had the goods. After their debacle with Henry Wadsworth Longo, they'd be looking for solid evidence.

It was after one o'clock in New York, but Andy Stevenson, his agent, wouldn't be asleep. Ryan had called him earlier and Andy had been pumped about the news. Of course the agent wouldn't profit directly from the exclusive report to be published in *The Denver Register* hitting the newsstands in a couple of hours, but there was plenty of money to be made in the follow-up interviews.

He pulled his cell phone from his pocket and speed-dialed Andy's number. The agent picked up on the second ring.

"I want a meeting with the producer of "Win a Fortune." Tomorrow afternoon. In Phoenix." Ryan said as he lit a cigarette and inhaled deeply.

"Right," Ryan continued after listening to Andy's reply. "And I don't want one of their assistant producers to show up. I want someone who has the authority to make a deal."

Ryan puffed again, glimpsing at the lifeless body in his bed. "I'll email you with my demands."

Caught up in the excitement of something Andy proposed, Ryan laughed. "Right, buddy. I know. It's finally *my* time. Yes. Hey, thanks for your help. I'll call you in the morning after the news breaks."

Walking into the bedroom, he stared at Amanda through coils of smoke as he enjoyed the rest of his cigarette. He laughed again, a bold, boisterous howl. The subject of his scoop, the object of his future success didn't move a muscle.

God, Ryan Grogan was the best journalist and businessman west of the Mississippi. And soon everyone would know it.

He crushed the butt in one of two overflowing ashtrays on his nightstand, then crawled into bed beside Amanda. Lying on his back, he sighed, his gaze following the slow revolution of the fan blades overhead. It depressed him to think Bud Fisher wouldn't recognize "Win a Fortune's" new talent was his own grandson.

Chapter Thirty-three

"I wait over twenty-four hours for you to bail me out of jail, and then you dump me at home and leave?" Colleen dropped her purse on the tufted sofa, but not before taking out a package of cigarettes and lighting up.

Ben could protest the second-hand smoke, but it wouldn't do any good. They were in her apartment now and she'd do exactly what she wanted. But then, her selfishness was a huge contributor to her present problems.

Colleen looked rougher than Ben had seen her for a long time. Her short hair lay flat, but not by design. Dirt weighed down some parts, while grease matted the rest. Her jeans were ripped at both knees and her shirt couldn't be any tighter if someone threw a bucket of water on her. Her eyes were bloodshot and red-rimmed from crying.

"It was awful in there. Those women were really harsh."

"I hope you don't have to get used to it."

"It's all a mistake, Benji."

He always knew she was playing him when she used that nickname. As her attorney, he'd never outright ask her if she'd embezzled the money, but a confession wasn't necessary. The only way to help his sister now was to pay restitution and beg for the court's mercy.

"I have to go, Colleen." He handed her the business card. "Call Roberta if you need anything. Anything *legal* that is. Do *not* ask her for money, because I told her not to give you any."

Was it possible to find a babysitter for his sister while he was in Phoenix? Ryan Fisher had taken Amanda there and it was where Ben needed to go.

If not for having to bail out Colleen, he'd have driven straight to the desert at one-hundred miles an hour. Bruno Talbot had done that. Well, not exactly. Bruno's plan was to drive to Denver and take the 6:40 a.m. flight. Ben looked at his watch thinking that Bruno should be there by now.

At least returning to Omaha allowed Ben to pack some clothes. A change of underwear was more than Amanda had with her.

Colleen flopped onto the arm of the club chair Ben had given her when he'd bought new living room furniture. He hadn't needed to update his furnishings, but his sister had needed the handout.

She exhaled from the side of her mouth, and then waved the smoke that blew into his face anyway. "How long will you be gone?"

Long enough to punch Ryan into next week if he hurt Amanda.

"A few days."

On the three-hour drive back to Omaha from Glucksfall last night, Ben had used some of his time wisely and squandered the rest. On the crazy side, he'd called Amanda about seventy times. After witnessing her steamy kiss with Ryan, he decided it best not to leave a message.

To be productive, he'd booked a flight to Phoenix departing at 2:30, four hours from now. He didn't know how he'd be able to hold onto his patience, but the only earlier flight departed a half-hour ago.

Looking at a photo of Colleen's children he knew he'd done the right thing. He'd snapped the picture last Christmas, right here in her wretched apartment. He'd shopped for the dinner, cooked it, bought all the presents, and decorated the tree. He was glad to give the kids a nice holiday with their mom. As he recalled, she'd thanked him profusely, calling him Benji all day.

There had to be a way to get Colleen to accept responsibility for herself, because that was step number one to staying out of jail and eventually regaining shared custody.

"Do you still have that phone number I gave you?" he said.

"Yes."

"Use it. The name of your sponsor is Debbie. I arranged to have her pick you up around three this afternoon to take you to a Gambler's Anonymous meeting." He poked her collarbone. "Go."

Colleen nodded as she brushed away a tear. "I will. Thanks, Ben."

Sighing, he honestly hoped she would.

Why couldn't the women he loved act rationally?

He should have packed the self-help book to read on the plane. Somewhere in those pages there had to be the key to understanding women.

Bruno Talbot had been right about one thing—Ben loved Amanda, but he had no idea how to tell her. He'd had enough trouble as it was with women and now it seemed he was in competition with Ryan Fisher for her affection. If Ben lost Amanda, he didn't know what he'd do.

He glanced around Colleen's apartment, the feeling that he'd forgotten something nagging at him. Protecting two women was challenging his juggling skills. Especially since one didn't seem to want protection and the other was bent on self-destruction. But who was who?

"I'll keep in touch. Stay away from your kids, *and* your ex-boss and casinos, church bingos or any place offering any type of gambling. Debbie will call you from GA. Go with her to a meeting. Only by showing your good faith to change do we have a hope to get these charges kicked. Understand?"

"Yes." Tears streaked down her cheek, taking the rest of her mascara along for the ride. "I don't want to go to prison, Ben."

"I don't want to see you there either. So do what I said."

His phone rang and he jumped on it. It could be Amanda returning one of his several calls.

"Ben Harris."

"It's Talbot. The story broke in *The Denver Register* this morning."

Ben swallowed an oath.

"Next to the article was the photo of you and Amanda at the governor's helicopter yesterday."

"How'd they get that picture?" Ben blurted.

"Don't know. The photo is credited to one Craig Lambert."

"He wouldn't do that."

Bruno huffed. "Don't know how it all went down."

"Are you in Phoenix?"

Bruno cleared his throat. "No, I ran into some trouble."

"What kind of trouble?" Ben picked at a loose thread on the chair. How would this affect Amanda?

"A deer."

Ben flinched. "Ouch."

"I've been stuck in North Platte all night in an emergency room."

"Are you all right?" he asked, scrubbing his temple, where a headache threatened to bloom.

"I kind of got my face rearranged when the hooves broke through the windshield. Sixteen stitches."

"Of all the bad luck." For Bruno and Amanda.

"I can't complain. The doe is coyote cuisine. But I can't get these yahoos to release me. They say I have a concussion and need to be under observation for a few more hours."

Delays were killing Ben. What were they doing to Amanda? He released a frustrated breath. "I'm headed to Phoenix this afternoon to catch up with Amanda and Ryan Fisher."

"Grogan."

"Huh?" Ben said.

"I was able to get to a computer. Ryan Fisher is really Ryan Grogan, *The Denver Register* reporter who broke the story."

"That chicken plucker."

"Do you think she told Grogan who she is?" Bruno said.

Ben thought back to how upset she was, accusing him of leaking her identity to Craig Lambert. "I doubt it."

"Have you heard from her?" Bruno hacked.

"No."

The coughing gave Bruno a raspy voice. "Call me when you get to Arizona. And if by some miracle I can sneak out of this place and get there first, I'll call you."

"If you get to Phoenix before me, would you do me a favor?" Ben said.

"What?"

"Let me be the one to rearrange Grogan's face."

"Rookies and guys in love," Bruno snorted. "I got both of them on my team—all rolled up into one poor sucker."

Colleen hugged Ben as he hung up. "Were you talking about the girl you mentioned at the arcade—the one you like?"

"Amanda, the woman I'm going to marry, is in big trouble."

"Are you going to Phoenix to help her?"

"Yes, but first, there's something else I have to do."

* * * *

Ben gently took Clara's hand in his. She lay quietly in the hospital bed with her head positioned nearly to sitting. It hurt to watch her struggle for every breath. Softly he stroked her hair back from her forehead. "It's tougher to get in to see you than it is the president."

Her murky eyes fluttered open. "You know the president, do you?"

"No, but someone might think you do with all the security posted around here."

She waved her hand—the one attached to the IV. "A tempest in a teacup, or should I say a bedpan?"

Ben smiled at her bit of humor. "How are you doing?"

"I'm dying. How are you?" She smiled, patting his hand. "My lungs and my heart are in competition to see who can give me more aggravation before they quit."

With the back of a finger, he caressed her sunken cheek. "Who's winning?"

She took a series of short breaths. "My bowels. Thanks to the antibiotics, they run all the time."

Ben chuckled. Anyone that sick who worked so hard to cheer up her visitors deserved recognition. He laughed louder.

Clara pulled him to sit on the edge of the bed.

"You may not know the president, but you do know the governor." She pointed to the nightstand.

Ben picked up a faxed copy of the article from *The Denver Register*. He shook his head and she lightly pinched his cheek.

The story and the photo were everywhere. Clara had even seen them on CNN. Seemed the photographer didn't mind it being printed by *The Register* as long as reproduction rights still belonged to him—or some such nonsense Ernie had explained to her. It was beyond her how someone didn't get sued. Some hothead was always taking someone else to court over nothing.

Then there was Ben. The sweetest man since her own Jim Marshall. He visited her often and listened to her tirelessly. In this confusing, super-charged world, Ben made sense and slowed things down.

When she was rushed to the hospital this morning because she couldn't catch her breath, the nurses had tried to call Amanda first, but even her voice mailbox was full. They reached Ben right away, though. Clara had been smart to add him to her emergency contacts list.

Steadying her voice, her gaze caught Ben's. "Have you seen Amanda? She's not answering my calls."

If Clara gave in to her anxiety she'd lose her breath, literally. She couldn't die now—not until Amanda was safe and this fiasco over.

She'd called Erik to see if he'd heard from Amanda, but that Air Force man had answered instead. He'd tried to make her feel guilty by saying the only reason he'd picked up is because he saw the hospital name on caller ID. He'd said Erik had been bombarded by calls looking for Amanda. So many that Erik was forced to leave the country—gone to Germany, if she remembered correctly.

Clara had been so proud her daughter hadn't relied on Erik for help. It showed definite healing and growth.

Ben's face grew red. "She's not taking my calls either." Was he frustrated or embarrassed? Clara would bet the latter.

"What did you do wrong?" she asked.

"I don't know."

She still had the power of the mother's look and she pulled it out of her bag of tricks. Withering, his face glowed scarlet.

"I guess I challenged her sense of independence and ability to get things done."

"So," Clara laughed, "you insulted her pride. Well, that would do it."

Ben chuckled. "I didn't mean to hurt her. In fact, the whole thing just snowballed." He hung his head. "I'm not very good with women."

"Her father wasn't either."

He snapped his gaze to hers.

"I had to train him. Jim was no different than most husbands. They have to be taught. The smart ones accept the training lovingly. Those who fight it . . . well, I guess the divorce courts are full of them."

His jaw slackened, but she could see the wheels turning in his brain.

"You'll get the hang of it." She tugged at the blanket, waiting for his response.

"But I don't think she wants to talk with me."

She prayed for enough breath to advise the young man. "You know how you have to put new license plates on your car every few years?"

Head tilted, concentration pursed his face. "Yes."

"Jim always offered to do it for me, but I knew I could do it myself. The first couple of times were no problem, but after that the screw on the plate holder became rusty. I guess from the harsh winters and street salt and such."

He looked confused and a little rushed—so unlike him. She hoped she'd be around long enough to teach this youngster how to listen to an old person's ramblings. Didn't he know there was always a lesson to be learned?

"Well, it became harder and harder to get that screw out of the frame so I could change the license plate."

"Yes."

"But I'd spray on some lubricant and let it set a few minutes." She paused. "And wait before trying to pry it out with the screwdriver." She paused again. "Then—*voilà*—it came off."

"Okay," he said slowly.

He didn't get it.

She spat out the punch line. "Amanda is like that rusty screw. She's stubborn and she holds on tight."

He smiled.

"She takes after her father that way."

His smile broadened.

"Go on after her. I give you permission to beat down any doors that stand in your way."

"But she's not home."

Clara had suspected as much or Amanda would have been by her bedside now.

Ben's face lost color. "The last we knew she was in Phoenix with the reporter that wrote the exclusive."

She couldn't let Ben's guilt sink him. He needed to be in his best form to help Amanda. It was time to lighten the mood.

"Why use a shovel when there's a back-hoe available?" she said.

"Huh?"

"Amanda has really dug herself into a hole now, hasn't she?"

A weak smile pulled at the corners of Ben's mouth.

"My plane leaves soon. Don't worry, Clara. I'll find her and protect her from that skunk, Ryan Grogan."

"Just find her and be sure she's all right. Don't worry about Grogan. When Amanda finds out the connection between Ryan Fisher and the article, it will be Grogan who'll need protecting."

"I hardly think our sweet Amanda would—"

"Oh, I'm so glad to hear you say that, Ben. *Our* Amanda." She squeezed his hand and winked. "But I'm warning you. Don't get between those two. She gets her stubbornness from her father, but her invincibility from me."

Ben stood, placing her hand gently under the blanket. "I'll keep that in mind."

"And *you'd* better know which genetic link is tripping her mood *before* you approach her."

"I have so much to learn," Ben said playfully chagrined.

She had one more favor to ask of him. "Promise me something," she said.

"Anything."

"If I die before the lottery project is done, you'll do whatever you can to be sure she finishes."

"But she's doing it for you. For the million-dollar finder's fee and your heart transplant."

She struggled for another breath. The discussion and the situation had leeched the energy from her.

"Amanda needs to take back her own life and forget about trying to save mine. Promise me, Ben?"

Tears welled in his eyes and he sniffed them back. "I promise."

Clara didn't have to look behind his back to see if he crossed his fingers; a man of his integrity would never stoop to cheating.

Chapter Thirty-four

 12 Days until the Deadline

Amanda's eyes felt glued shut. With all the effort she could arouse, she forced them open. After only an instant of watching the overhead fan blades twirl, her stomach felt queasy and she clapped her lids shut. Slowly, she rolled onto her side, careful to not fall off the bed.

This was the worst hangover she'd ever experienced. Had she really had that much to drink? She couldn't recall much of anything. Opening her eyes again, she stared into the harsh light filtered through sheer curtains on a floor-length window. She groaned, burying her head under her arm.

Where was she? What *did* she remember?

Helping the tornado victims. Boarding the Learjet. Duck with wild rice. Her stomach roiled at the thought of the blueberry, sage sauce ladled over the entrée. Covering her forehead with her cool hand, she opened her eyes and forced herself to sit up.

Pain pierced her head. Two glasses of wine combined with the partial beer she drank in Glucksfall didn't add up to this much misery. She swallowed and grimaced at the unmistakable taste in her mouth. Sometime in the night, she'd vomited. A shiver of disgust ran over her.

She studied her surroundings. It looked like a hotel room with the customary round table and two side chairs at the sliding glass door leading to the balcony. One dresser with a mirror. The corner armoire holding the television. Night stands on either side of king-sized bed. Even the brocade spread looked right out of Holiday Inn catalog.

Where am *I?*

She drew a deep breath and cringed. Chlorine cleanser furniture spray, and floral plug-in deodorizer—all trying cigarette smoke. Who was Ryan trying to fool? She'd grown up with Cora. You can't cover up smoke with air freshener. God she hated that stink. It reminded her of the years cigarettes had whittled from her mother's life.

She exhaled slowly to keep from wakening the little people clomping around in her head with cleats on. Please, just let me feel better or do away with me, she thought. Taking two more breaths, she tried to decide which option was more likely to happen.

Last night—what she remembered of it—was a nice respite from her duties, but it was time to get back to working on the lottery project.

She massaged her scalp with her fingertips before sliding to the edge of the bed to try standing and froze.

What on earth did she have on?

The Denver Broncos T-shirt was seven sizes too big, her bare legs white beneath it. Jerking up the shirt, relief trickled over her. A gray pair of men's cotton boxer-briefs covered her.

How did they get there?

From the corner of her eye she caught the red numbers of the digital clock. 4:11? Her head spun toward the window again. Daylight. 4:11? No way. She hadn't slept eighteen hours.

The bedroom door inched open letting the smell of recent smoke leak in.

Ugh. She'd never noticed the stench of smoke on Ryan before.

All right, Amanda. Get up. Get dressed. Time to start over on the jackpot distribution.

"I thought I heard you rustling around in here."

Was there a hint of impatience in his sexy voice?

He walked in carrying a glass of tomato juice. "About time you woke up." Ryan's smile wasn't quite as broad as last night.

Had she already overstayed her welcome? Had she done something wrong in her drunken stupor?

What *had* they done last night?

"Hi, Ryan. Guess that sleeping pill worked too well. Is it really afternoon?"

He offered her the juice. She declined with a quick shake of her head. Bad move. Pain spiked her temple.

"Are you okay?" he asked when she groaned.

"I'm more sensitive than most people to medications. So a sleeping pill that's gentle for you knocks me out—literally." She offered an apologetic smile.

Pulling her up from the bed, he wrapped her in a loose hug, gently rubbing her back. His touch felt different today—less genuine.

"Sorry it hit you so hard. You grab a shower while I fix you something to eat." He released her, pointing to the bathroom behind her. "I put out some fresh towels."

"Sounds wonderful. Only . . ." She dragged her lower lip between her teeth.

"What?"

"Where are we exactly? And where are my clothes?"

* * * *

Waiting for the shower to kick on, Ryan took a carton of eggs out of the refrigerator. He grabbed a paper towel to wipe the dust off the only skillet and then studied the stove to find the right knob to switch. Damn, he hated cooking, but until he had Amanda on board with his plan, he needed to keep her secluded.

He was way behind schedule and more than a little pissed. He'd wasted the first day of his new career babysitting an unconscious woman, not that he wasn't entirely responsible for her condition.

He also knew she was the route to his future success, but he felt like a Kentucky-Derby-winner whose jockey held back in the stretch at the Preakness. Chomping at the bit, he was ready for this move. He was poised to win the Triple Crown of journalism—a Pulitzer-prize newspaper article, followed by a national television reporting assignment, capped by a best-selling book to chronicle the whole experience.

Water rushing through the pipes alerted him she was out of earshot, so he made the call. Ryan had been pleased Andy had snagged the executive producer of "Win a Fortune." Now he hoped his agent had the finesse to delay the meeting.

"Andy. It's Grogan. Yeah, the Hyatt by the airport is fine for the meeting. Listen, I have to push back the time."

He dug around in a drawer for a fork and a spatula, then glanced at his watch.

"When does Fletcher get in?" he said.

One-handed, he cracked two eggs into a bowl, fishing out a chip of shell. Then he turned on the burner.

"Well, you'll have to stall. Take him to dinner. I can't possibl meet until after nine."

He picked up the fork and beat the life from the eggs.

Whipping Amanda into shape would take some time. Wo like her didn't jump into things. They warmed up to ideas s

"Fine. I'll call if I can meet any sooner."

After disconnecting, he tossed the cell phone on the counter. Pouring the yellow mixture into the hot skillet, the sizzle echoed in the sparsely equipped kitchen of the condo he leased for writing space.

As he stirred the eggs, Ryan ticked off his to-do list.

First, show Amanda *The Denver Register* article written by Ryan Grogan. He had no idea how long she'd want to rant about her identity being published. Women were into blame, so he'd have that tirade to endure as well. He hoped her aim would be directed at Grogan and not Fisher.

Second, he'd have to convince her it was a good thing the public knew about her assignment. Being open about her search would reduce her stress so she could concentrate her efforts on interviewing candidates.

Depending on her mood, she might digress to the fit-throwing stage of step number one.

Ryan took down plates from the cabinet. After a quick rinse and dry he set them next to the silverware on the bistro table for two.

The shower shut off and he returned to reviewing his plan.

Third. Persuade her only *he* was the perfect man to help in her search for the person to be awarded the jackpot.

This step would involve abundant charm and a little romancing. A guy never knew if the groundwork he'd laid was enough to secure a commitment. He hoped she'd remember his compassion from yesterday rather than how angry he'd been when she'd lost the three-hundred-dollar dinner all over his bathroom floor.

Fourthly, he had to sell her on the platform for their search. To gain efficiency and meet the deadline, they would need help. By using the vast resources of "Win a Fortune," she could widen her search immediately. She'd have a staff to narrow the pool of candidates, filtering out insincere contenders. On air, she and Ryan—mostly Ryan—would interview the contestants. The process would stimulate the interest of better candidates, increasing her chances the lottery winner would accept their decision.

This would be tricky, but not as challenging as the last step. He ad to be certain he wouldn't lose any points when he confessed he the journalist Ryan Grogan.

e could see no other way around the confession because after work, he wasn't about to launch his new television career alias. It was Ryan Grogan who'd built the journalism career. It was Ryan Grogan who'd put so much effort into chasing Amanda to get the story. And it was Ryan Grogan the public would admire and fall in love with during the next two weeks of nightly shows.

Eggs fluffy and appetizing, he scooped them onto the plates as Amanda stepped through the kitchen door wearing yesterday's clothes he'd laundered this morning.

It was then Andy called back with the bad news. Gabe Fletcher, the producer of "Win a Fortune" could only meet at seven o'clock. His plane back to New York left at nine.

* * * *

The caption under the photo credited Ben's *supposedly* good football buddy. So now it was confirmed. Ben had betrayed her.

Amanda was surprised to see the article in *The Denver Register*, and shuddered to think it might also be in that wretched tabloid, *Your News Source, and* the *Omaha World-Herald, and* the *New York Times.* Craig Lambert could have sold the damn picture to any newspaper willing to pay for the vivid color photo of Amanda falling out of the governor's helicopter into Ben's arms.

As she laid the article next to her plate of uneaten, cold eggs, she was surprised she didn't feel more disappointment in Ben. Not only had he leaked her identity, but he'd lied to her about it, boldly and easily.

Maybe her relief over the end of her duplicity far outweighed the regret she'd felt nagging at her for the past twenty-four hours.

Obviously, Ben's need for money to help his sister was greater than his integrity or his loyalty to the assignment. Knowing how far she would go to help her own mother, how far she'd already gone, Amanda acknowledged she was in no position to judge Ben Harris. He'd done what he thought best for his family.

Yesterday, revenge would have been at the forefront of her mind. After all, Ben had broken company policy, if not many laws, when he sold her identity and breached attorney-client privilege. But she had a deadline and only twelve days left. No time to waste on retribution.

Still, she hated what Ben had done to Clara. Her mother mu̇ be worried sick over where Amanda was, especially after the n̄ reports. Surely it was all over cable television by now. And awful "Win a Fortune" was probably doing another one special edition shows.

She instinctively reached for the phone she always kep̈ waistband. It wasn't there.

Ryan reached across the table and captured her hand. Nodding toward the newspaper, he smoothed his thumb over her wrist. "Are you all right?"

"Fine. Where's my cell? I need to call my mother."

He tilted his head and blinked as she'd often seen Erik do when confused. "I laid it on the coffee table in the living room after I put you to bed last night."

The rubber tips on the chair legs skipped across the tile floor as she shoved back from the table. "Excuse me," she said.

Catching her around the waist, he pulled her onto his lap. "I thought you'd be more upset about the article."

She shrugged. "It's not the first time I've been screwed over by a man."

Ryan added a gaping mouth to his confused blink. "What do you mean?"

Sighing, she clasped her hands in her lap. "The photo was taken by the alleged acquaintance of a supposed friend. You don't know him. Anyway, he had a good enough reason, I guess, for selling the story."

His eyes widened. "You think your identity was sold?"

"No use crying over spilt milk, as my mother would say." She tried to stand, but he pulled her into a tighter embrace.

"What are you going to do now?"

"Call my mother." She pushed on his firm biceps, trying to wiggle out of his grip.

"No, I mean about the lottery."

Giving up her struggle, she tossed back her still-damp hair. She knew exactly what she had to do.

Her idea for the distribution of the lottery funds had magically appeared when she'd wiped the fog from the bathroom mirror twenty minutes ago. All that time wasted running around the country and it had been there, in her subconscious, all along.

As the hot air from Ryan's blow-dryer whipped the ends of her hair, she'd formulated her plan. All that remained was writing the details of the proposal.

Thinking of her tasks ahead invigorated her. She hadn't felt this much clarity or excitement since she'd written the original business plan for Dream Weaver's Baskets and Gifts.

This was one secret she'd keep to herself. She looked at Ryan and smiled. "I have to keep working. As you read in the paper, I have less than two weeks to prepare my proposal."

Finally, she wriggled from his embrace and stood.

"Then you'll need refueling. Let me warm those eggs for you."
The corners of his lips turned upward.

Glancing at the plate, Amanda was relieved when her stomach didn't wrench as expected. "I've had enough, thank you." She settled onto the wooden chair. "I'll just finish the juice."

Ryan reclined, crossing his arms over his chest.

He looked terribly overdressed for a Sunday afternoon at home. With his pressed white shirt and navy dress slacks, all he needed was a red tie and suit coat to finish the business image.

"You're the lottery winner's agent. That's *so* amazing. How were you selected?"

She swallowed the tomato juice, its thickness blanketing her throat, soothing it. "I don't know."

Ryan arched a brow. "How did the winner let you know?"

That day in Roberta's office Ben had tried to be her rock to steady her in her disbelief and shock. Had that really been only two weeks ago? It seemed longer. "It doesn't matter," she said.

It was natural he would have so many questions. Anyone would. *Everyone* would. This was what she had to look forward to.

"Do you know who the lottery winner is?" he asked brightly.

She recalled the intrigue between Ryan and her over the possibility Bud Fisher was the winner. It was better to eliminate all the maneuvering now.

"I wondered if your grandfather was the winner. Is he?"

Ryan laughed, shaking his head. "Bud? No, he's too cynical to play the lottery."

Dispelling that notion put Ryan on a different plane. He wasn't sent to protect her. He had no more interest in her project than any other citizen or candidate, although when she looked in his eyes, his expression seemed different from yesterday. He appeared more attentive than she'd ever seen him, even when he'd been coming on to her in the private jet.

Was he still coming on to her, or her fortune?

The notion discouraged her. At least for the next two weeks, everyone would be trying to get a piece of her time to get her story or a chunk of the jackpot. She couldn't expect Ryan to be any different from the masses.

All she needed now was total seclusion, without interruption. "You can imagine, I have a lot of work to do. It's time to get back to Omaha. In your memorized flight schedules, when's the next departure?"

Ryan's face went white and he gripped the edge of the small table. "You can't leave."

The forcefulness of his statement jerked Amanda's head back. "I have to go home. These newspaper reports and my disappearance could give my mother a heart attack."

Her legs twitched to get her cell phone and make the call.

"I have a proposal," he said.

Last week she would have salivated at a pitch from an obviously successful, smart man. But now she wanted nothing to dissuade her from her plan for the jackpot distribution.

"You've been very kind to me, Ryan. I appreciate how you've put up with some really crazy situations, but I need to go now, so I can finish my assignment."

A rumble seethed from his chest. "You *can't* go home. Reporters from all over will be surrounding your apartment."

"I know that. But my uncle's an attorney. He'll get whatever legal papers I need to provide a cushion around me."

"But you'll never be able to work in that environment. How can you interview candidates?"

For a moment she was tempted to reveal her proposal to Ryan. In an instant he'd see that she could finish the job without his help. But she dreaded the thought of him trying to talk her out of her decision. Besides, the only way to protect the plan was to wrap it in secrecy.

"I'll figure out how to get things done," she stated firmly.

"I'd be happy to help you. You can work here. No one knows you're in Phoenix. *Right?*"

The emphasis he'd put on the question made her stomach sink. It was true. No one knew where she was. Yesterday, she hadn't called anyone to inform them of her travels to Arizona and today she'd thought of calling her mother, but had felt too sick.

Suddenly she felt trapped.

Her gaze darted to the living room. The cell phone lay exactly where he'd said—on the coffee table—a good fifteen feet away.

Don't panic, she ordered herself.

Why was he so insistent to help her? Ben had been as accommodating and look how that turned out. But somehow this felt creepier—more "Silence of the Lambs."

Amanda had ignored her intuition for far too long. The danger was real. In her bones, she knew it. If she could keep her composure and remain rational, she'd get out of this trap.

Swallowing fear, she forced a smile. "I appreciate the offer of your help, but I need to do this alone. It's a growth kind of thing. I've always been stubborn that way."

Had she sounded casual enough?

Ryan turned his chair to position his knees on either side of hers and glided his hands over her thighs. "I can understand how you'd feel that way a few days ago, but after what we shared last night? I thought you'd trust me."

"Last night?"

He let the back of his fingers slide down her cheek, sending frightening shivers through her.

"You'll hurt my ego if you say you don't remember, because,"— he kissed her lips—"it was one fantastic night for me."

Her breath came shallow now. She'd never been the kind to use alcohol to release inhibitions. If they'd had consensual sex last night, she'd remember.

Looking into his eyes, at their iciness, her breath caught. That had been no ordinary pill he'd given her. She'd been drugged. Had she been raped, too? Her heart tripped. *Be smart or something worse might happen.*

Fighting off panic, she inhaled slowly, deliberately. If she didn't escape, how could she help Clara? She swallowed and controlled the fear in her voice.

"Ryan, I have a deadline. When all this is over, I'd love to see where our relationship might go, but now, I need to get home to finish my assignment."

His lips hardened into a thin line, but a glaze of sweetness covered the anger in his voice. "I understand." He glanced at his watch.

"What time is it?" she said.

"Six."

"And I get the feeling I'm keeping you from something. Could you take me to the airport, please?" She leapt up, skirting around him to reach her cell phone. With all the indifference she could muster, she clipped it to her waistband. It wasn't wise to let him see she was scared to death. And she had to be clever–for herself and for her mother.

"First flight to Omaha is tomorrow morning. I'd be happy to book it for you." He unfolded himself from the chair and paced toward her like a cat stalking a wounded bird.

She stepped backward, just beyond his easy reach. Spying her backpack, she grabbed it, swinging the load onto her shoulder. "I'll wait at the airport. I've taken up too much of your time already."

A twitch of his mouth told her she'd made a tactical error. She'd sounded desperate to escape.

His brows crowded together. "Now that's ridiculous. Why sleep in a chair in the terminal when you have a king-sized bed here?"

"I just thought you'd have better things to do."

Closing the gap between them, he removed her bag and dropped it onto the sofa. He gathered her in a loose embrace. "What could be better than spending the night with you right here in my arms?"

His touch chilled Amanda. If she wasn't careful he'd feel her panicked trembles and know she was onto him.

For some unknown reason, he meant to keep her here. Showing fear might force him into doing something violent. She rubbed her forehead, trying to figure out her next move.

"Need an aspirin?"

"Yes." She quickly realized her mistake. "I mean no."

His look said, "You don't trust me."

She'd always trusted *Ben* with her safety.

"Hangovers. It's the price I pay for drinking too much and losing control."

"Amanda, that's ridiculous to think you have to suffer because you had some fun. You have a martyr complex?"

Grabbing her hand, he escorted her into the kitchen where he reached into the cabinet and took down a bottle of pills. Popping the lid, he took out one tablet. "Here."

Slowly, she looked at him and then at the tablet he'd dropped into her hand. It looked funny. Different from the sleeping pill last night, but smaller than any pain reliever she'd ever seen.

He filled a glass of water from the tap and passed it to her. "Take it." No smile accompanied his demand.

Provoking him wasn't the way to win her freedom. She justified her decision, knowing he couldn't poison water flowing from the faucet. Stealthily, she palmed the pill and drank all the water.

Now he smiled, placing the empty glass on the counter. "Lie down and the headache will go away faster."

He walked her to the bedroom and she lay on the bed.

"I have to go out for a little while," he said. Abruptly, he snatched her cell phone from her pants.

She grabbed for it, but he was faster. "You can't sleep with this hooked to your hip. I'll put it in your backpack." He pointed through the bedroom door at the bag on the sofa.

Faking relaxation nowhere to be found in her body, she leaned back onto the pillow.

"You going to be okay?" he said.

She yawned. "I can't believe after eighteen hours of sleep I can't stay awake for more than two hours."

"Residual effect from the sleeping pill."

"No doubt. Go do what you have to. I'll be fine."

She silently cursed when Ryan pulled the door closed behind him just enough to obscure her view into the living room. Five minutes after she heard the front door snap shut, she bolted out of bed and ran to her backpack, knowing all along what she *wouldn't* find there—her cell phone.

Some relief swept over her as she inventoried her backpack spying her contract, calendar, and project notebooks—all but the *Cases* book which she'd left in Ben's car.

She peeked out Ryan's door and scanned the courtyard. Seeing no one, she sneaked to the gate and slipped through, tearing her jacket when a prong of wrought iron scroll caught the hem. Without pausing, she clicked the gate closed behind her as quietly as possible and after glancing around once more for Ryan Fisher, she scampered off, faster than a frightened rabbit.

Chapter Thirty-five

Engine trouble had delayed Ben's flight and worry had eaten the hours as he reviewed the mass of information he'd collected on Ryan Grogan. Added to what Craig Lambert said when Ben called for an explanation, the composite portrait of Grogan was ugly.

If he could manipulate a professional like Lambert, what could Grogan do to someone as innocent as Amanda? Images of her in the clutches of such a cunning cheat screwed Ben's muscles taut.

Recalling how Amanda had grilled him about his connection to Lambert, it was probable she believed Ben had sold her identity. Given her past reactions to Erik, Ben knew she wouldn't take the betrayal well—even if it was only *alleged.*

He had to set her straight. Fast.

Fist trembling with an unfamiliar rage, he stood on the dark stoop and pounded on Grogan's condo door. In his hand were two newspaper clippings, both from *The Denver Register.* Printed today, the photo of Amanda falling out of the helicopter would have been cute had it not been plastered on the front page along with the article announcing she was the lottery winner's agent. Convinced Grogan had coerced the confession from her, the storm in Ben's stomach swelled.

But the second news clipping and a piece of Amanda's jacket he'd found on Grogan's gate minutes before petrified Ben and throttled his anger to barely below the explosion level.

He beat the door again. "I'll kick it down, Grogan," he shouted.

The door inched open revealing Grogan's face behind a looped brass security chain. Wrinkles around the eyes and mouth made him look ten years older than the photos of him taken during the Coombs trial only months ago. What had happened to the finely coiffed man who'd run refreshments to the tornado survivors yesterday?

"What do you want?" Grogan said, with a hint of a slur. The scent of alcohol floated through the crack.

"Amanda."

"She's not here."

Ben shuffled his weight between the balls of his feet to calm himself so he wouldn't charge the door. "Where is she?"

Propping his head against the jamb, Grogan sighed, wistfully. "I wish I knew."

He was a slime ball capable of lying without an ounce of regret. Ben didn't believe him any more than he'd trust a trained tiger.

An adrenaline rush nudged Ben's breath to a rapid pant. "Do I need to get the police and a court order to search your apartment or are you going to let me in?"

The door clicked shut. The smooth slide of the pin gliding open stopped abruptly. Ben shoved past him, calling Amanda's name as he marched through the living room toward the bedroom. Ever mindful of the reporter's stealth, he kept a peripheral eye on Grogan.

While relieved he hadn't caught them together in bed, his heart thumped wildly at the thought of worse possibilities.

Did Grogan have a gun?

After spinning a gaze around the master bath, he trotted back into the bedroom.

Grogan teetered between the master suite and the living room. "I told you. She's not here." He swiveled, placing his back against the door frame and slowly slid into a heap on the floor.

Obviously, he was, at this moment, not a threat to Ben or Amanda any more. Now he appeared only self-destructive.

Ben looked at the rumpled bed. His stomach wrenched at the sight of long blonde hairs on the pillow. Raking them up, the knot twisted tighter in his gut. "These are Amanda's."

Grogan grinned slyly. "She *was* here. She spent the night."

Ben refused to give him the satisfaction of a physical reaction. "Does she know you're the bloodsucking worm who released her identity?"

Grogan crawled to his feet, snickering. "No, she thinks *you* sold her out." Laughter burst from the immoral scab.

His fear confirmed, Ben swallowed back his temper. He needed a clue to find Amanda and to do that, he'd have to get through to this drunken leech.

"Where is she?" he shouted.

Grogan's head dropped back. "Damn it," he roared to the ceiling, "I told you I don't know."

His eyes flashed with anger as he drilled Ben with his stare. "She was *supposed* to be here when I got back from my meeting, but,"—he made a flourish with his hand—"poof, it's all gone."

Ben shook his head in aggravation. He had no idea what Grogan meant. Rounding the corner, headed to the kitchen, he bumped Grogan's shoulder, unshackling the cigarette and gin stench from the reporter's crumpled suit jacket.

Dread squeezed Ben's chest muscles and he deliberately slowed his breathing so he wouldn't strangle Grogan—at least not until he got all the information he needed.

His search was deliberate and thorough, even checking the broom closet in the kitchen and the balcony off the living room. Abruptly, he stopped at Grogan's desk when he saw photos of Amanda strewn over some paperwork.

In one photo, she wielded a power saw to amputate branches from a fallen tree. Picking up the snapshot, he stared closer at the expression on her face.

God, she looked determined. Single-minded and powerful. Stripped of her red elf jacket, she'd pushed up the sleeves of her cotton tee, her wide stance giving her balance that said she could accomplish anything.

Grit was a quality Clara said Amanda had lost, but in the past weeks, he'd seen her determination grow. Now she'd gained fortitude to equal her tremendous ethics. The combination deepened the admiration already filling his heart.

But then worry slammed forward.

Laying the photo down, he picked up the scanned printout of Amanda's contract with the lottery winner. Fury burned his chest. Reeling, he shoved the Danny Coombs article under Grogan's nose. "Is this how you found out? Because sure as *hell*, Amanda wouldn't have told you who she is."

Ben hated being as crass as Tom Harris, but he hoped the rough language would punch through Grogan's infuriating stupor.

The reporter retreated with his hands in the air, careful not to look at the clipping. "I don't know what you're talking about."

Slipperiness and denial might have worked on Amanda, but not on Ben. He rushed Grogan, driving him to the wall. Pinning the reporter's chest with his forearm, he held up the red fabric swatch. "Did you give her the date rape drug? Did you hurt her?"

Fear flashed in Grogan's eyes. He wiggled under Ben's crushing grip. "Of course not. I didn't do anything illegal to get the story.

Amanda had a headache and I got into her backpack for some pain reliever and I ran across her notebook—"

"Save your lies for someone else."

Spittle blew from Ben's lips and dotted Grogan's cheek. Grogan snapped his mouth shut and soon stopped struggling. He stared at Ben in defeat. The expression came from someone who'd been beaten—not physically, but emotionally. He'd lost something—something more than Amanda.

Releasing his grasp, Ben stepped back. "We may not be able to prosecute you criminally, but I can think of about six different reasons to haul your ass into civil court."

Grogan arched his neck and straightened his collar. "You can try."

Stiffening his hold on his anger, Ben glared. "You bastard. Not only can I try, but I can *win*. When I get finished with you, the only thing you'll be writing is your grocery list."

* * * *

 11 Days until the Deadline

Who would have known the desert got frigid at night? Amanda wrapped her jacket tighter around her as she gazed out the windshield and bit into the vending machine sweet roll. Once again, she'd been lucky to find a rental car agent who didn't watch the news and didn't recognize her.

No doubt the media would soon track her to Phoenix, so using her credit card for the car didn't put her security in jeopardy. But no one could trace her to her final destination.

Parked on the empty gravel road, her heart ached to think how much her mother would love today's sunrise. Like a snow cone topped with grape juice, God had squirted purple on the horizon. The color diffused as it flowed over the distant mountains and trickled between the cacti and boulders, ending in sweet lavender on her fingertips.

No matter what happened next, she'd count this as a treasured blessing at the end of the day.

She licked the glaze from her fingers and glanced at the ranch house. Lights had blinked on twenty minutes ago. If Terri Miller was like Amanda, she needed her coffee before making any decision. Reaching into her backpack, Amanda organized her thoughts for the sales presentation ahead.

First, she pulled out the calendar and crossed off another day. A shot of anxiety, mixed with the two bites of stale roll in her stomach pushed worry to her chest. Only eleven days left until the scheduled meeting with the lottery winner, but she'd have to be in Omaha before that to review her pitch with Uncle Ernie.

She gazed again at the sunrise fading to mauve and willed herself not to look beyond today. For now, she just needed a quiet, secluded place to write her proposal, and the Triple T was the ideal safe haven. Starting the car, she cruised up the gravel drive glancing one more time at the golden hue blanketing the desert.

Perfect security alarms in the form of three mutts greeted her with one bark each, tails wagging as she climbed out of the car. She stooped to let them sniff her hand before continuing to the adobe house. The salmon-colored stucco extended to wrap columns holding up the curved-tile roof of the veranda.

She knocked on the extra-wide, slatted door, shifting her weight nervously. The big dog scuttled off while the other two sat at her feet. Their wagging tails swept arcs in the dust covering the flagstone floor. After a minute, she knocked again, louder.

The door flew open and Terri Miller stood silhouetted by the kitchen light behind her. A ball cap tucked tight on her head, she held a dish towel in the tiny hand at the end of her flipper arm.

Amanda struggled to see the expression on her face, but shadows curtained all details. "Terri?"

"Yes?" The voice was flat, but patient.

Amanda paused to think how to introduce herself. Terri only knew her as Pet Touhey, but if the ranch owner hadn't tuned in to the last twenty-four hours of news, she wouldn't recognize her as Amanda Cash.

"Do you remember me? I was here a couple of weeks ago," Amanda said.

"Yes, I remember."

There was still no discernable emotion in Terri's voice.

God, this isn't easy. Amanda stumbled over her next thoughts. "Um, when I was here before I was with a man."

"Oh, yeah. He was scared to death of Boo."

Amanda laughed, recalling the way Ben had bounced on the saddle as he circled the arena on the tall horse. For some reason, she wished Ben was here now.

"If you've seen the news, you know I'm the person the lottery winner drew at random to give away the money."

"I saw the story on "Win a Fortune." Why are you here?"

Caution. It rang clear in Terri's voice.

"I need to rent a room in the bunk house."

The silhouette paused a moment before shoving open the door, letting it go from her grasp. "Come on in." She added a hand gesture to the dogs and they turned and scampered off the veranda into the morning light.

Amanda envisioned Terri sending reporters away in the same effortless way, if it came to that.

The daylight caught Terri's profile which was serious, but not stern. Amanda could almost hear the wheels turning in Terri's head.

She followed Terri into the kitchen wrapped in the cozy smells of coffee, maple syrup, and rubbed sage.

Terri motioned to her ranch hand sitting on a ladder-back chair, his chest pressed against the table. Metal forearm braces were propped against the wall behind him.

"You remember Kevin Spencer," Terri said, more demand than question.

Amanda nodded and smiled.

His gaze narrowed as it slid over her from crown to toes. "Amanda Cash, what on earth brings you back to the Triple T?"

Amanda cringed as she thought of the mixed feelings Kevin must have about her. On one hand, he might be grateful she'd considered their financial plea. On the other hand, she'd lied to him with a beguiling smile. She knew first-hand how horrible it was to feel duped.

"I need a place to stay." She turned to Terri. "For ten days. I'm willing to pay high-season rates. I only need quiet time, seclusion, and a computer."

Kevin sneered. "What? You don't eat?"

A long breath escaped from Amanda. He wasn't cutting her any slack. But then, maybe she didn't deserve any.

He laid his knife and fork across his plate. "We don't have enough problems that you want to turn this place into a circus for reporters and camera crews?"

She tried to squelch the desperation in her voice. "But I didn't lead anyone here. I don't have a cell phone, I won't talk to anyone while I'm here, so they can't trace the calls. All I need is computer access and some time to complete my assignment."

"Is that what we were to you?" Kevin asked flatly. "An assignment?"

"Kevin." Terri's bark lifted the head of the big dog lying on a braided rug at the open back door. "Would you offer our guest something to drink, please?"

His steady gaze softened with the order and he pulled himself up from the table, reaching for his arm crutches. "Coffee?" he asked, waddling to the cupboard for a mug. His leg braces clicked and snapped with every step.

Amanda released a silent breath. "Please. I'll take it black."

"Have a seat, Amanda," Terri said.

Terri still didn't have a smile for Amanda and hadn't yet said she could stay. If the ranch owner refused her request, Amanda had no ready backup plan. She sat between Terri and Kevin at the small round table and prayed for luck.

Terri motioned to the stove. "Have you had breakfast?"

The sweet roll sat in a lump in her stomach, but Amanda couldn't refuse the gesture of hospitality. "No," she said.

Terri flipped two pancakes from the griddle onto a plate in her flipper hand. Adding a sausage patty, she placed the meal in front of Amanda. "Our season starts in two weeks. You'll need to be gone by then because I won't be able to protect your secret after that."

"Ten days tops and I'm out of here." Suddenly, Amanda was famished and she took a large whiff of the breakfast.

Kevin set the coffee mug and silverware alongside her plate. A hint of irritation burned in the corner of his eye.

"Okay," Terri said. "We have a VIP cabin in the back. Kevin will bring in some groceries. We're getting ready for our peak, so we don't have time to wait on you."

Amanda nodded, taking her fork in hand.

"The only computer I have is in my office. You may use it between 7 a.m. and dark. After that I need it for my business. It has web access."

"I won't need the internet, but thanks." Amanda used the side of her fork to cut a bite of sage sausage.

"Room and board is two-hundred dollars a day."

Kevin slipped Terri a look that Amanda couldn't read.

"Fine." Amanda helped herself to the syrup.

Finally, the corners of Terri's mouth curved up in a slight smile. She sat and, taking her cup in her normal hand, she brought the coffee to her lips. Her gaze jumped to Kevin and one eye squinted casually.

"I want to know one thing," Kevin said. "Were you ever going to give us some money?"

Amanda laid her fork on the plate, glancing back and forth between the two ranchers. "I want to help you *and* a lot of others. I think I've figured out a way to do it."

Chapter Thirty-six

It seemed pointless to put out a missing person's report on a woman the entire country was searching for.

Ben pushed aside his half-eaten *chile rellenos* and watched Bruno Talbot down his sixth taco. The Phoenix sun scattered warmth over their picnic table outside the fast food stand.

Nothing settled well on Ben's stomach the last couple of days. He flicked the paper plate into the trash barrel. Bruno did the same, and then dug into the chest pocket of his Hawaiian shirt for his smokes.

Ben cringed as Bruno contorted his swollen face, pulling the surgical stitches, to take a long drag from his cigarette. Five days had passed since he'd hit the deer. The gash in his cheek was fiery and red, exactly like his disposition.

Bruno blew out the smoke, which for once didn't waft into Ben's nostrils. "I say we go back and pump Grogan for more information," he said.

Two days earlier Bruno and Ben had paid a call on Grogan at his condo. More hung-over than drunk, Grogan still looked dejected. Recalling how Bruno had bullied Amanda's cell phone from the reporter, Ben almost agreed to turn the bodyguard loose once again—if only to see Grogan squirm under the pressure.

Ben shook his head. "If Grogan knew something about Amanda, he'd have written about it. We haven't seen anything new in two days."

Grogan's lie about finding the phone in his briefcase was so lame, Ben had wanted to smack him. Amanda had kept the cell strapped to her hip since their first trip to Arizona.

Ben recalled her surprise when she'd realized her cover name was Pet Touhcy. He'd give two-hundred million dollars to see that smile again.

Concentrating, he squeezed his brain for more options to find her. "We could quiz that kid at the rental car agency," Ben proposed.

"Hell, he wouldn't flinch if a seagull landed on his desk with a reservation in his beak. He'd just hand over the keys like he did with Amanda. That boy's what I call a testicle–Too Stupid To Continue Living."

Ben hoped he'd never turn as cynical as Bruno, but dealing with witnesses as they had over the last couple of days, Ben could see how the process would dissolve a person's sweet disposition–not that he suspected Bruno ever had a sugar-coating.

"Well, I'm going to make another round of calls with her family," Bruno said, stomping out his cigarette.

Ben thought that a waste of time, since any one of them would notify Bruno immediately if they had any news. But, like the bodyguard, Ben had repeated dozens of worthless actions over the past days, to feel as though he were being productive.

Bruno climbed into his van. The dent in the hood had been pounded out and windshield replaced, but traces of dried deer blood still stained the grill. He merged into traffic, nearly side-swiping a pick-up. The driver wailed on the horn and Bruno waved an unfriendly finger at him.

Ben had grudgingly come to appreciate, even admire, Bruno for the work he did. Amanda's disappearance had drawn the detective's concern to the surface and Ben suspected Bruno cared more about the case than he'd want anyone to know.

For the hundredth time, Ben reviewed the situation. Amanda didn't have her cell phone. If she relied on her contact list like Ben did, she wouldn't have memorized any of the unpublished phone numbers. So even if she wanted to call him or her Uncle Ernie, she couldn't. The constant worry over why she hadn't called her mother, though, left a rock in his stomach.

She'd be too smart to use her credit card again leaving a trail for all the reporters to follow. With her rental car, she could drive anywhere, but she'd know she'd be recognized wherever she went.

Amanda had to lay low to finish her project.

Ben strolled to his rental car and riffled through his briefcase for clues as he'd done countless times before. His fingers grasped the packet he'd assembled to give Amanda when he finally found her.

It held a collection of articles tying Ryan Fisher to Ryan Grogan, including the announcement of Craig Lambert's impending lawsuit against Grogan for publishing the helicopter photo without consent. In the envelope was also a letter Ben had written, something he should have done a while back. Given his miserable history in opening up to Amanda, he'd decided to write down his thoughts beginning with confessing and apologizing for his deception in helping Bruno track her. Then he begged forgiveness for doubting her ability and strength to handle tasks alone. The remainder of the letter had flowed freely as he detailed exactly how he'd fallen in love with her and how deeply he cared.

A pain booming in his chest sparked a tear. For Amanda's sake, he had to put all fears aside. He *would* find her. And she *would* be safe. Because she *could* take care of herself.

Jamming the letter back into his briefcase, it caught on the spiral binding of Amanda's green notebook. An image of her jotting entries flitted through his mind. She'd looked incredibly serious as she wrote how she wanted to help Terri Miller save her ranch–her safe haven for handicapped people.

Terri Miller.

Could Amanda be . . .?

Starting the car, he prayed his hunch was right.

* * * *

 7 Days until the Deadline

Amanda dropped her plate of half-eaten *chile rellenos* on the tile floor for Gomez, the shepherd mix. He was the alpha dog in Terri's pack and the only one allowed in the house. And whether on orders or of his own volition, he'd become her constant companion while she worked on the computer in the Triple T's office.

For once Amanda felt good as she crossed off another day on her calendar. Only seven remained until the deadline, but at the rate she was going, she'd have plenty of time to finish the proposal.

Her only sorrow was that she wouldn't see Ben's face when he heard of her solution. While she didn't want to prosecute him for violating attorney-client privilege, she had no desire to hear him apologize for the steps he'd taken to help Colleen. Even if he'd gotten enough money out of the transaction to pay off his sister's debts, nothing made his actions acceptable.

Amanda had forgiven him, but hoped their paths wouldn't cross again anytime soon. Even with the progress she'd made on the proposal, she couldn't afford time for drama. It was the reason she hadn't clicked on the internet to follow the stories about the lottery and why she'd requested a ban on all conversation about the topic with Terri and Kevin. If she were to help her new friends, she needed to stay focused.

Terri had done her part by warning Amanda of all scheduled visits from the veterinarian, farrier and delivery people. She'd even loaned Amanda some jeans and tee-shirts.

Amanda stepped on the paper plate so Gomez could lick the sauce residue. Then she scratched behind his ear and muttered, "Who's the sweetest hound in the world? Gomez is the sweetest hound. Yes, you are. Good boy."

The dog's eyes glittered and tail wagged. He was the perfect companion—loyal, obedient, and appreciative.

Someone tapped on the door.

Amanda gave the dog a final pat. "Come in."

Terri poked her head into the room. "You have a visitor."

Amanda's stomach flipped. Ryan. Could he have tracked her here? He had her cell phone, but not this number. She swallowed her fear. "I'm not seeing anyone."

Terri nibbled the inside of her cheek, debating her next words. "I wouldn't have bothered you, but it's your husband."

"Erik?"

How had he found her and why would he be here?

Amanda stood and Gomez rolled to his feet as well. If she had to face Erik and Shane, it was good to have friendly reinforcements. She patted the dog's head.

"It's Tom Touhey," Terri said.

Amanda dropped onto the swivel desk chair, nausea replacing the fear she'd felt only seconds ago. She suddenly wished she hadn't eaten the small lunch she'd been able to get down.

She wasn't surprised Ben had tracked her to the ranch. He was a smart, intuitive man. How she wished she could turn back the clock to their first trip to Arizona, before Ben had deceived her. While the kiss they'd shared was a distant memory, it remained a lovely one.

Knowing she'd only be free when she confronted issues head-on, she sighed and stood. "I'll see him."

Gomez nudged her hand. "You've got my back, don't you boy?" Amanda patted his head, comforted by its fuzzy warmth.

Ben inched into the room carrying an over-sized envelope. He nodded, his lips curving into a grin.

Terri softly closed the door behind her as she left.

An excited flutter shoved aside the nausea when Amanda saw Ben's contrite smile. His Husker tee-shirt was tucked into his well-worn jeans. With the scuffed Nikes and spiked, blond hair he definitely looked more relaxed than he had a right to be.

"How's my mother?" she asked.

Ben's eyes shifted to the dog. "Fair to middling." His gaze wandered back to Amanda.

Words Clara would say. But a shadow had passed over his ivy-green eyes. What was he not telling her?

"When was the last time you spoke with her?" Amanda said.

"This morning."

"And she told you to say that, didn't she?"

He cleared his throat. "Pretty much."

A pain stabbed Amanda's heart. Her mother wanted her to finish the project, no matter what the cost. Her eyes burned, but she forced back her tears and idly stroked the dog's head.

She'd honor her mother's wishes.

Besides, in writing the proposal, she'd realized her goal extended beyond the finder's fee. Amanda had the once-in-a-lifetime opportunity to help many people and she wanted to succeed—for *them*. She wanted to make a difference.

Amanda straightened with this burst of resolve. "I'm glad you're here, Ben."

His face brightened. "You are?"

With one look at his rosy cheeks, full from the breadth of his grin, her heart knew she could forgive him. But she didn't know if she could ever trust him again. Why did she always choose men who let her down?

"I lost my cell phone," she said, "and I need you to make some calls for me. *After* you get back to Phoenix."

The spark in his eyes dimmed and his smile faded. "Oh?"

"Do you mind helping?" she asked.

"No, that's why I came." Quietly, he tapped the envelope against his thigh.

Gomez paced to his side, his toenails clicking on the floor. He sniffed the package. Ben squatted and greeted the dog, scratching his head. The alpha dog's tail wagged wildly and he even raised a paw to play. Amanda grimaced. She thought he'd been a better judge of character.

"First, please call my mother and tell her I'm fine. I don't want her worrying about me."

Ben stood and nodded.

The next request caught in her throat. "And please tell her I love her."

Tears pricked in her eyes. He stepped forward, and she stepped back. Rubbing her index finger under her nose, she took one quick sniff. "I'm fine," she said.

Concern furrowed his brows and he sighed slightly. "Okay."

"Next, I'm tweaking my proposal. I've booked a flight from Phoenix next Tuesday afternoon. I need you to call my Uncle Ernie. Ask him to meet me at Eppley Airport. Flight number . . ."

As she searched in her notebook for the information, she felt Ben staring at her. It left warring emotions in her–both disquieting and comforting. ". . . Southwest Flight 1590 arriving at 2:50."

Easing into the desk chair, she put the notebook next to the computer. Gomez lay at her bare feet.

Ben swallowed audibly. "Would you like me to look over the proposal for any legal snags?"

"No, thanks. I've left two days in my schedule to review it with my uncle. He's an attorney. In Chicago."

"I know. Good thinking. Then I guess you'll be all ready for the meeting in Roberta's office on Friday at ten."

"Yes. I'll be ready."

She didn't want to ask, but she had to know. Swiveling in the chair, she swallowed. "Will you be there?"

He raked the side of his bottom lip between his teeth. "No, I have a previously scheduled appointment."

"Oh," she said.

Better they not meet again anyway. Some day she'd have a normal life, maybe remarry. But first, she had to find someone she could trust–someone she could count on. The first time they'd come to Arizona, when they'd kissed, she thought maybe Ben could be that man. His disloyalty showed exactly how much she still needed to learn about reading people's character.

She turned her gaze to Gomez, stroking his head. He panted slowly in response. Why couldn't men be as devoted as dogs?

"Then, if you don't need me, I'll head back to Omaha," he said.

"You must have so much to catch up on–neglected clients and all."

"Well, I've arranged to take some time off–a couple of weeks. Roberta and the others are handling my cases."

"To help your sister?"

He nodded. "And some other things."

"How is Colleen?"

"Impossible."

A smile tugged at her lips at his quick response. "I hope everything works out for her."

He nodded. "Thanks." Letting out a long breath, he dropped his gaze to Gomez.

"I guess I'll see you when we both get back to the office," he said.

"I'm not coming back," she said.

Popping his gaze to her, he grinned. "I'm glad you're that confident in your proposal."

She arched her eyebrows, crossing her arms over her chest. "I'm that confident I don't want to be a collections officer anymore."

"Right." He gazed at her one last time, hoping for something she wasn't ready to give him.

If only he'd thought of Clara and what his betrayal had meant to her. Surely, the commotion the media made at the announcement had contributed to her mother's downturn.

She considered, for a moment, whether she should cease her moratorium on silence and call her mother. In an instant, she decided. Someone could trace the call, and she'd promised Terri Miller she wouldn't bring the circus to town.

For everyone's protection, she'd stay secluded.

"I'll make those calls for you," Ben said.

A jolt jerked her head back. Had he read her mind?

Suddenly, he dropped the envelope on the desk. "Something for you to look at when you have some free time."

She stabbed a glance at the packet, unfolding her arms. Gently she swiveled in the chair again. "Okay."

Turning, he opened the door. "For the record, Amanda . . ." He paused, waiting for her attention to shift from the envelope.

"Yes?"

Taking a deep breath, he tilted his head down to lock his gaze with hers. "No matter how much I teased you, I always believed you would succeed."

Giving him a thin smile, she forced back the tears.

When the door snapped closed behind him, she tapped her leg and Gomez rallied next to her. "Okay, boy, let's see what he brought me."

She tore open the envelope and poured the contents onto the desk. Pushing aside the newspaper clippings, she reached for the letter with Ben's neat handwriting on the outside. The pre-printed return address listed a Phoenix hotel. Her first name resided in block letters on the front. Sliding a finger under the flap, she opened it.

Carefully she read his apologies and his confession. When she reached the end, she buried her face into Gomez's fuzzy neck and sobbed.

Chapter Thirty-seven

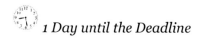 *1 Day until the Deadline*

Nearly a minute passed before Amanda's eyes adjusted to the dimness of Clara's hospital room. Curtains drawn, the only light came from the blinking machines and the bathroom door left open. She tiptoed in and stood next to the bed railing.

The oxygen tube, poked into her nostrils, sat slightly askew, as usual. In addition to the IV and pulse monitors, a tangle of wires sprang from her chest. They attached to a heart monitor the size of a pack of cigarettes stuffed in a special pocket on the front of Clara's hospital gown. The irony left a lump in Amanda's throat.

Clara's fingers jerked in her uneasy sleep. In spite of the tubing, she breathed through her open mouth, sucking in her whisper-thin cheeks to make her sharp facial bones even more pronounced.

Amanda pushed back the tears and tenderly swept back a wisp of hair from her mother's brow. While Clara had looked sick in the past, this was the first time she appeared fragile. With each labored breath, she held on to life as precariously as dandelion seeds sit shakily on the flower's head swaying in the breeze.

There couldn't be much time left for her now. After all Amanda's effort to get the money for the transplant and for all her hope for a second chance, it was too late.

Amanda's breath came shallow, almost as strained as her mother's, her heart throbbing until she was sure it would erupt from her chest. Despite all Clara's warnings, Amanda never really wanted to believe her mother was dying.

Her legs weakened and she grabbed the rail for support. Tears streamed down her face. Trembling, she quieted a sob with a hand over her mouth. She didn't want to wake Clara.

Her mother needed all the rest she could get. Now that there wouldn't be a transplant, she needed to conserve strength. Rest.

Medicine. Oxygen. They were the only things left to help her mother now.

If only Amanda had listened to her mother. Clara had often said she didn't want a new heart. But it was the only way Amanda knew how to help. By pursuing her own hope for Clara, Amanda had wasted precious time she could have spent with her mother. Time she'd never get back. All because of misplaced hope.

Sorrowfully, she wiped her palms over her cheeks and quieted her breathing. She snatched a tissue from the box on the nightstand and dabbed under her nose.

But then, maybe Amanda's hope was the catalyst. Would she have taken the lottery assignment if not for Clara's need for the transplant? Then Amanda's proposal would never be considered. And she desperately hoped her recommendation for the jackpot would live, even if her mother didn't.

Maybe Amanda's selection as the agent wasn't random at all. Perhaps her involvement was part of The Grand Plan. If the lottery winner accepted Amanda's proposal, Clara's legacy would be magnificent.

Another wave of grief consumed Amanda. Her mother would never see the ramifications of the lottery distribution.

As she contemplated a future without Clara, the door swung open and soon a warm hand rested on her shoulder.

"I'm glad you made it safely home," the familiar voice said.

She spun to gaze into Ben's eyes, as misty as her own. He set a pitcher of ice water and a small stack of Styrofoam cups on the bedside tray.

"Thanks," she said, praying he'd forgiven her.

Her pulse pounded in her ears. She hadn't seen or talked to Ben since that afternoon at the Triple T Ranch—before she'd read about Ryan Fisher being Ryan Grogan; before she'd read about him scamming Ben's friend to get the helicopter photo; before she'd read his love letter.

For a moment, their eyes locked in a gaze, neither one saying anything. Her heart beat wildly.

In Ben's eyes she found hope for the future. Taking her hand gently in his, he offered forgiveness and promise with his gentle smile.

Then she swept a glance at her mother. Hope ebbed with every difficult breath. What had always been constant and dependable now teetered on the brink of conclusion.

Once again, she glanced at Ben and brightened at the hope for a normal life–the one she'd always dreamed of. The one Clara had always wished for her.

Looping her arm with his, she snuggled into his chest. For a moment she relaxed in the comfort while he stroked her hair as it trailed down her back.

Hesitantly, he reached to pat Clara's arm and Amanda grabbed his hand. "No, don't wake her," she whispered.

"Are you kidding me?" he whispered back. "I'm under strict orders to let her know when you get here."

How long had Ben been with her mother?

"Clara." Ben set a gentle hand on her shoulder.

Her mother shuddered awake, knocking the pulse monitor from her fingertip. A loud, chirping beep followed.

Ben jumped to replace the monitor clip on her index finger. Tapping the reset button on the machine behind him, he stopped the obnoxious noise.

Obviously, he'd done this before.

After taking a minute to focus on her surroundings, Clara slid her gaze to Ben and Amanda standing side by side at the rail.

"Ah, my two favorite people." She fluttered a hand at Amanda.

She bent to kiss Clara's forehead. It was cool, but moist and it took effort to refrain from wiping her lips.

Ben poured fresh water for Clara and helped her take a sip. "I'll leave you two alone." He touched Amanda's arm before slipping out of the room.

"How long has he been here?" Amanda asked.

"Ever since he returned."

A week? He'd been at her bedside for a *week*? Then she noticed three yellow carnations in a bud vase on the nightstand. Was this the business he said he had to take care of when they'd spoken in Phoenix? Is this how he used his leave of absence?

Could she admire or love him more?

"Open the curtains," Clara wheezed.

When she turned back from the window, Amanda stifled a gasp. Clara's eye sockets were sunken, while the lids and the bags underneath remained puffy from the steroids. Her complexion had no more color than the hospital sheets. Crackles marked every shallow breath.

"You've been traveling," Clara rasped.

"Yes." She lowered the bed rail and enfolded her mother's hand in hers, rubbing some warmth into the frigid bones.

Clara panted, storing up a reserve of air. At last, she spoke. "What did you learn?"

Bringing her mother's icy fingers to her lips, she kissed them and placed them on her cheek where they mixed with a tear. Taking a deep breath, she held it as if for both of them, then she exhaled.

"I learned the desert is surprisingly cold at night, but the sun only takes a couple of hours to heat things to a boil."

Clara smiled and nodded for more.

"Once every ten years the soil, rainfall, temperature and timing are exactly right and the desert explodes with color. This was that year. And I was there."

Her mother's smile broadened and a tear brushed Clara's lash.

Amanda crouched nearer to Clara's ear and whispered. "When you take a close look at the pink blossoms of the strawberry hedgehog cactus, you can see how God sprinkled the tiny, but tough, petals with droplets of magenta."

Clara squeezed Amanda's hand weakly. "More," she said.

Amanda smoothed her mother's hair and sighed. "I learned that like the cactus flower, I'm stronger and more brilliant than I thought I was."

Her mother closed her eyes and whispered, "Perfect." A single tear rolled to her pillow.

Amanda cradled her mother and quietly cried. With each passing moment, Clara's life faded like an echo in a canyon.

Eventually, Clara pushed away weakly. "What did you eat?" she asked.

Amanda sniffled, then smiled. "That's where it got dicey, Mom. Most of the time, I cooked for myself."

"Damn." Clara laughed, launching into a clatter of coughing that loosened thick mucus.

Amanda plucked tissues from a box and held it for her mother to spit. How many more times would she be there to help Clara? She pulled the rail back up on the side of the bed.

"I'll let you rest now, Mom. I'll see you tomorrow after the presentation."

Clara nodded.

Amanda turned to leave, hooking her purse over her arm.

"Wait," Clara croaked.

She spun and held her mother's brittle hand once more.

"Tomorrow . . ." Clara stopped, panting hard to catch her breath.

Amanda waited patiently.

"Be casual. Use words your old mother understands."

The word 'old' pricked Amanda's tears again and sparked a familiar denial. But the wheezing confirmed it; in terms of the amount of life left, Clara *was* old.

"Okay, Mom."

Her mother's eyes closed again. Amanda straightened, sucked in a quick breath, and swiveled her gaze to the monitor to make sure Clara was still breathing.

On tiptoe, she left the room, praying that it wouldn't be the last time she'd see her mother alive. Shaking, she fell into Ben's arms in the hallway and burst into tears.

He patted and rubbed her back, his own silent tears flowing with hers. "I'll drive you." He looked in her eyes for permission. "You'll get some rest and we'll talk tomorrow after your proposal."

She leaned on him all the way home.

* * * *

This must be how marathon runners feel at mile marker twenty-five. Clara gasped as she wiggled back under the sheets after using the bedside commode. She should be inhaling through her nose, but her body demanded more oxygen than what could be sucked through tiny nostrils. Unfortunately, the volume didn't increase by inhaling through her mouth.

"Is your breathing getting better now, Clara?" The hospital's nurse aide in the Garfield scrubs lifted Clara's legs onto the bed.

No, it's not better. You try walking up ten flights of stairs sucking air through a cocktail straw.

Too winded, she couldn't manage to shake her head.

"It's not too late to put in a catheter. You could save your breath for more important things." The aide adjusted the pillow behind her head.

That would take care of one end, but even eating winded Clara. And she would refuse feeding tubes, too, when it came to that. Thank God Ernie's legal directives protected her against extreme measures.

Her head hit the pillow and her breath caught in her lungs. She made a cranking motion with her hand.

"Do you want your head up more?" the aide asked.

Clara nodded and the woman obliged.

Thank goodness this helper was better at reading sign language than the last one who needed the whole damn charade game to understand Clara needed a sip of water.

"You have another visitor. He's waiting outside."

Who? Clara arched her eyebrows.

"It's your brother. Should I tell him to come in?"

Clara nodded as the aide brought the blanket to her neck.

Only after the woman left did Clara feel the discomfort. She squirmed to bend her knees, needing to shift a little to the left to loosen the stranglehold the gown had on her hips. Finally, she tugged sideways with all her strength and released the fabric's grip on her butt. She panted like she'd just lifted a piano off her toe.

This misery couldn't end soon enough for her.

Ernie crept into the room carrying an official looking black, leather briefcase. He wore his dark business suit and inwardly Clara smiled to think Amanda had kept him so busy the past two days that he hadn't found time to golf.

He hadn't brought his smile, though, and he was too easy to read. Doom and gloom. That was all Clara had gotten out of him in the last few visits. He was a damned depressing visitor—not fun like Ben, who loved to make her laugh, even when it caused her to hack up her lungs and launch the machines into a flurry of bells and whistles. It was all worth it, though, when Ben cracked a joke.

That boy was so much like her husband had been at that age. So sweet of him to read Dickens to her every day.

"Are you up for this, Clara," Ernie asked, "or should I come back tomorrow?"

She summoned her breath. All she could muster. "I could be dead tomorrow."

He grimaced, shaking his head vigorously. "Don't talk like that."

Apparently, he'd checked his reason at the door, too.

Pursing her lips, she controlled her breathing the way the respiratory therapists had taught her. Regardless of Ernie's fraudulent optimism, all legal business had to be finished *tonight*.

"I have one more document for you to sign," he said.

Clara laid a hand over his, stopping him from reaching into his case. The action pulled the monitor from her fingertip, setting off the alarm for the hundredth time.

She jumped like someone had stuck her eardrum with a needle. How she hated that damned chirping.

Frantically, Ernie pushed the nurse's call button.

If Ben were here, he'd have her fixed up in a jiffy. He learned quickly what had to be done and he did it cheerfully. She guessed he applied that skill in his business practices as well as his home life. Despite the law degree, he was her hero.

Within a minute the aide returned and clipped the monitor back on her finger, resetting the machine to stop the beep.

Thank you, God.

She had no energy to repeat herself and knowing she'd never be heard until Ernie's attention focused back on her, she waited for him to catch his own breath.

Finally, she inhaled as much as her scarred lungs permitted. "Did she do it?" Clara said.

Ernie's bushy eyebrows twitched from beneath the frame of his glasses. "She finished the proposal. Did it all by herself. I only tweaked the language a bit."

To make it incomprehensible to mortals.

God, it was frustrating not to be able to offer her clever retorts to tease her brother. She longed to see his frown and hear him groan as she insulted his career. Although, maybe she should stop that since her son-in-law-to-be was also an attorney. At least she hoped Amanda was smart enough to accept Ben's proposal when it finally came.

Wariness suddenly sapped her remaining energy. She needed to get her part done now so she could rest. Staring at Ernie, she prayed he could understand broken English and gestures.

"Good enough?" she said, arching her brows.

Pursing his lips, he nodded briskly. "Her proposal is amazing. A hole-in-one. You'd be proud, Clara."

She smiled, having known all along if Amanda stayed focused she'd come up with a plan that would knock the socks off everyone.

Her heart picked up speed as fear nudged her next question. "Protection?"

"When she came back from Phoenix, I introduced her to Bruno Talbot," Ernie said. "They seem to get along famously. He'll be with her up until the presentation and will stay afterwards for as long as we need him."

She pushed out her thin breath. With faint jerks, Clara scribbled her fingers in the air signaling her need for a pen. But before he could retrieve the document and pen from his briefcase, Clara stopped him again.

"Erik?" she said.

"Done. He signed the Dissolution of Marriage Petition and I paid express mail for him to send it back from Germany. We go to court next week."

One more thing off Clara's list. *On to more important business.* Did Ernie see what she did in Ben Harris?

"Ben?" she said.

Ernie lowered the side rail and set a hip on the edge of the bed. "He seems like a solid young man. Ethical. Honest. His actions would indicate he's very fond of Amanda."

Clara rolled her eyes. Spoken like a stiff attorney–not a loving uncle.

She narrowed her gaze to intensify her query. "Like Jim?"

Ernie thought only a moment and then nodded once. "I think they have a shot to be as deliriously happy as you and Jim were."

Taking her hand off his, she let him pull the document from his leather briefcase.

Now she was ready to die.

Chapter Thirty-eight

Even in his navy pinstripe suit, Mr. Franklin looked less intimidating today than he had four weeks ago. Roberta also seemed kinder, offering to get her coffee, like Amanda had never been her employee before.

She was relieved Uncle Ernie wasn't sitting next to her in the firm's conference room. While he was the only other person familiar with the contents of the proposal and could help answer questions, he oftentimes came across as too formal. As her mother had suggested, she would stay casual. She longed to have Ben beside her, though, but he'd insisted on being with Clara this morning to be sure no reporters broke through security.

Somehow the media had found out that the lottery winner was to be informed today of Amanda's decision and they'd trailed her since she'd left the hospital last night.

One legal threat from Ben had dispersed the crowd outside his house where she'd spent the night. With the rift between them healed, communicating was as amazing as their love making.

The reporters had remained a respectable distance from Ben's car as he drove her to Megel, Jeppesen and Harris and dropped her off thirty minutes ago.

Uncle Ernie had offered to encase her in bodyguards if she didn't want to meet with the media after the presentation. But she'd decided that if her proposal was accepted, she owed it to the jackpot recipients to meet with the press. After all, despite her bad experience with Ryan Grogan, the *ethical* reporters could help in the execution of her plan.

Besides, she felt completely safe with Bruno at her side. Despite his squeamishness when she'd pulled the stitches from his face yesterday—at his insistence—Bruno was someone she wouldn't want to tangle with in a dark alley. Between Ben and Bruno guarding her, she felt like an over-protected bone. When she smiled at Bruno, seated across from her at the mahogany conference table, he winked.

Not at all shy in the venue, he'd asked for coffee, juice, and water and had eaten most of the dozen doughnuts set out in the center of the table.

With her index finger, she brushed her own chin, then pointed at the powdered sugar dusting his. Tugging a handkerchief from the breast pocket of his tweed sports coat, he scrubbed his chin until she thought he'd rub off the stubble. Then he winked at her again and smiled.

She hoped he could make it through the meeting without his dessert cigarette. But more than that, she prayed she could convince him to quit smoking all together so he wouldn't end up like her mother.

Amanda sighed. She longed to see her mother's reaction when Clara heard the proposal. Maybe with some luck, she'd be with her mother when "Win a Fortune" outlined the plan and reported the lottery winner's acceptance.

The benefactor *would* accept her proposal. Amanda was sure of that now.

After weeks of hard work, all that remained was the sales pitch she'd practiced repeatedly, in front of a mirror. Not even Ben had heard her proposal which Amanda was convinced would sell itself on the merits alone.

Mr. Franklin cleared his throat. "Are you ready, Ms. Cash?"

While butterflies fluttered in her stomach, she took a deep breath and released it. "Yes. I'm ready."

"To remain anonymous, the lottery winner will hear your proposal over this speaker phone." Mr. Franklin pointed to the device in the center of the table. "The winner's attorney, Mr. Gamble, will speak on the benefactor's behalf. Do you understand, Ms. Cash?"

"Yes."

She wondered how long it would take for the winner to make up his or her mind. Uncle Ernie had gone way overboard, in Amanda's estimation, to translate her proposal–literally expanding each page of her document to four pages of legalese. But she was sure any good lawyer would have done the same.

Familiar nervousness tickled Amanda's gut as she reviewed, for the hundredth time, the situation surrounding the proposal.

The ticket expired in thirteen days. Would it take the winner's counsel the full time to work through the legal points? Would there be any negotiation if the winner objected to parts of the proposal or would it have to be accepted in its entirety? After all, the benefactor was paying a million dollars for Amanda's work. Didn't it have to be perfect?

Sweat broke out under her collar. Reaching around, she swept her hair off her back, draping it over her shoulder. She could sure use a fan blowing on her right now.

Mr. Franklin pushed a blinking button on the phone. "Mr. Gamble, are you ready on your end?"

The line clicked opened and a male voice answered, "Yes." The line clicked and fell silent again, as though the mute button had been pushed.

The voice sounded strange, like it was filtered through an electronic device. Maybe some famous lawyer, like Bill Clinton, represented the lottery winner and wanted to be anonymous. It wasn't out of the question.

"Start whenever you're ready then, Ms. Cash," Mr. Franklin said.

She stared at the steady white light that represented the winner and the end of her long journey. The other company lines were eerily dark. Had all of Megel, Jeppesen and Harris been put on hold for this conference call?

That was bad business.

Amanda snapped her attention back to her task and sipped some water, recalling her mother's advice—use simple language. *Casual* language. Knowing all the lawyers would scour the document, she didn't need to read it or cover all the legal points. She just needed to be herself.

Clearing her throat, she stared at Bruno as if he were her only audience. It helped to think of the winner as someone familiar.

Bruno smiled and gave her a thumbs-up gesture.

"The foundation I propose would be named after the lottery winner."

Bruno's gaze held steady.

"The mission of the foundation—in simple words—is to provide learning opportunities for people of all ages."

With a quick glance around the room, she read nothing on the faces of the attorneys, while Bruno's face lit up.

"Although the foundation wouldn't be opposed to using some of the money for *college* scholarships, we would focus more on the less traditional avenues for learning.

"For instance, there's a ranch in Arizona that teaches handicapped children how to ride horses. In mastering the responsibilities of grooming and caring for the animals and then overcoming challenges in learning to ride, the kids develop confidence."

She listened for a reaction from the lottery winner. The line remained mute. Her heart beat faster.

"We would rather grant funds to companies or agencies, such as the ranch, so they could distribute the scholarships based on financial need. They would be better informed on what qualifications are necessary to get the most out of the educational experiences. Although, I should point out that we wouldn't be opposed to hearing requests from individuals."

The silence grew deafening. Even the attorneys at the end of her table remained speechless and that seemed impossible.

Why wasn't the lottery winner or his or her attorney asking questions? Of course they didn't have the legal documents in front of them, but still, thinking in broad strokes, as Uncle Ernie called it, they could be asking *something*.

Amanda took another big breath and continued. "One thing I learned from reading so many letters is that we need a common system for reviewing requests, so I have developed an application form that would be put on the foundation's website. That way we can compare requests fairly, given the same information on each candidate."

Even Roberta and Mr. Franklin weren't asking questions, but then they didn't represent the lottery winner. Someone else did and that person either wasn't interested or didn't understand the proposal.

Bruno lifted his hand from the table. "Amanda? I mean, Ms. Cash?"

Roberta's gaze, followed by Mr. Franklin's, joggled to the bodyguard.

"We have a question from someone in the office," Mr. Franklin said in a booming voice. "Is it all right with the lottery winner if we take that question, Mr. Gamble?"

After a brief pause, the line opened. "That's fine, Mr. Franklin. Go ahead."

"Bruno?" Amanda said, nodding to encourage him.

"My grandmother, bless her heart, is seventy-seven years old and still lives at home. She'd like to learn how to use the computer. Would your foundation pay for classes for her?"

"I can't think of a better way to spend the money than to keep stimulating the minds of active seniors. We would consider her case, but would encourage a community-based agency to market the classes encouraging more seniors to collectively participate in the classes, maybe at a senior center or an assisted-living facility."

"Excellent," Bruno said. "I gave her my old computer. She lives in Mississippi and I want to send her emails—I get some real funny ones sometimes—but she doesn't know how to use the computer. She's smart and I gave her lessons, but she forgets sometimes. If she just had someone she could ask questions, I know she'd love surfing the net."

"Exactly," Amanda said, her heart pumping enthusiasm through her. "Learning isn't just for the young."

The line opened and Mr. Gamble spoke through the electronic synthesizer. "So you would focus your efforts on the elderly?"

The line went mute.

"Not exclusively. We would consider requests from people of all ages, from all countries.

"For example, we would accept requests for people who want to learn through travel. There is a wonderful organization which promotes trips for kids in grades 6-12 to explore places all over the world. The goal of that program is to develop leadership skills. I don't know of a better quality needed in our future leaders than a global vision and an appreciation of foreign cultures."

Bruno smiled again at Amanda and she drank in his approval as though it came directly from her mother or the lottery winner. At least *he* understood the impact of such a foundation.

No matter what the benefactor or the lawyers said, she'd consider her efforts a success. Her idea resonated with everyday people—all she really wanted at this point.

"The fund would be self-sustaining with fifteen percent of the principle wisely invested. I recommend an Executive Director be appointed at a salary commensurate with the position." She cringed, recalling Clara's request to keep things simple. The last thing she wanted to do was confuse the lottery winner with the uncommon term, 'commensurate.'

The line opened again. "Is there anything else you'd like to say, Ms. Cash?"

"No," she said, hastily, only to have another point prick her consciousness. She leaned nearer to the phone.

"Yes, actually there is. I know the jackpot could be used for so many different things and the winner may have something else in mind. But as my mother always said, you can lose your house, your car, all your possessions, even your job or business, but no one can ever take away your education."

"You got that right, sister," Bruno said, clapping fiercely. The applause bounced off the pecan-paneled walls and echoed throughout the conference room.

Amanda slipped her biggest fan a smile.

The line opened again. "All right then, Ms. Cash. Would you hold the line, please, while I confer with the lottery winner?"

"Of course."

The line closed.

She imagined a robot on the other end, shooting out spools of paper reports on the advantages and disadvantages of her proposal. If she had only known something about the winner–his or her background–she could have tailored the presentation based on the benefits that would matter most to that person.

The line opened. "Ms. Cash. The winner accepts your proposal on two conditions."

Amanda gasped, surprise pulling all the air from her lungs.

How was that possible? No attorney would accept a proposal without first running it under a microscope.

Her heart kicked her ribs, flooding her ears with her own deafening pulse. "What are the conditions?" she asked.

"One," Mr. Gamble said, "the foundation will not carry the name of the lottery winner, who wishes to remain anonymous."

Hands shaking, Amanda clasped them tight on the table in front of her. "That's fine."

"And the other condition is that you accept the position of Executive Director for a period of at least five years."

"Chicken a la king," Amanda shouted.

Bruno burst into a laugh, overlapping bawdy hoots coming from the open line. Soon Bruno's laugh turned into a hacking cough which seemed to echo over the phone line, too. Then a faint chirping followed before the line went mute.

Like a monstrous firecracker in the sky, the light burst, but it wasn't followed by a boom. Just silence. Nothing registered with Amanda but shock.

Be the Executive Director? How could the lottery winner want her to continue giving out the money? For five years? She knew nothing about starting a foundation.

Her mouth went dry and she gulped some water as she watched Bruno's chuckle die down and he brushed a tear from the corner of his eye.

She frowned at him. "What's so funny?" she whispered.

"Your expression," he whispered back. "It was like you'd swallowed a goldfish and it wiggled all the way down."

Narrowing her eyes, she pointed at him. "Payback. Watch out." She tried to stifle a smile, but it broke through anyway.

The phone clicked and the line opened again. "Ms. Cash?"

"Yes?" She whipped her attention to the steady phone light.

"Do you agree with the terms?" the electronic voice said.

She thought of Terri Miller and Bruno's grandmother. If she refused, they wouldn't get what they needed and she desperately wanted to help them and many others.

Staring at Bruno, she envisioned all the people she could help with the foundation.

"Yes. I accept the conditions," she said.

"Then we accept your proposal. Please send over the paperwork, Mr. Franklin."

"Will do," he said.

Amanda stared at the phone as the extension light went dark. Roberta switched off the speaker button.

As quickly as her life had swirled into chaos four weeks ago, it all ended with the click of one phone call.

Or was it just starting over again?

This time it would be different. She had a plan. She had business experience. And she had good legal support. No doubt the next five years would be a challenge and she'd learn a lot, but her heart knew it was meant to be.

Bruno popped out of his chair like bread from a toaster. Raising his arms up, he beat his fists against the air above his head. "That's what I'm talking about," he shouted. Leaning across the table, he offered Amanda a high-five.

Using the table for support, Amanda stood and smacked Bruno's open palm.

"Way to go, Amanda Cash," Bruno shouted, his smile lifting stubble-covered cheeks to below his eyes.

Roberta was pumping Amanda's hand before she realized she'd grabbed it, her face lit by a wide grin. "Congratulations, Amanda. It was a job well done."

Then the senior partner of Megel, Jeppesen and Harris spun and left the room to fight some other legal battle.

Slowly, Mr. Franklin stood, pushing papers into his briefcase. "We'll be in touch with you about the final documents and your contract, Ms. Cash. Give us about a week." He shook her hand.

"Your million-dollar check will be ready by then, too." With one quick squeeze of her shoulder, he turned and left.

Now she was a millionaire. She had a new job and new challenges–all of which she was ready to face.

As Clara always said, life could change in a heartbeat. Her mother would be so proud of the outcome. Her mother would have loved the meeting–Bruno's question about his grandmother's computer classes, his bawdy laugh at her fake curse, and . . .

The delayed concussion of the firecracker finally hit Amanda's chest. Images of her mother mixed with the memory of her familiar laugh. Amanda's hand flew to her mouth to thwart a scream.

Her suspicion seemed impossible. Knees weakening, she crumpled into her chair.

Swiftly, Bruno shot around the table to her. "Are you all right, Amanda?"

She held up her hand. It trembled. "I need a minute to think."

Swirling thoughts competed for her attention. It all seemed too miraculous. But her suspicion was no more of a long-shot than her letter being drawn at random by the lottery winner.

"You're whiter than rice," Bruno said. "Do you want to cancel the press conference?"

Snatching her purse, she hooked it on her shoulder. "No, but there's one thing I have to confirm before I meet with the media."

She marched toward the door with the bodyguard striding behind her. "Where are we going?" he asked.

"To meet Santa Claus."

* * * *

Amanda and Bruno stopped in the doorway of her mother's hospital room. With one hand, Ben was massaging Clara's foot. To avoid getting lotion on the cuff, he'd rolled up the sleeve of the teal oxford shirt. In the other hand, Ben held the Dickens novel. His voice resonated above the clatter of the medical equipment as he read to Clara. From the corner of his eye, he saw Amanda and grinned, increasing his volume so she could hear, too.

"'A great event in my life, the turning point of my life, now opens on my view. But, before I proceed to narrate it, and before I pass on to all the changes it involved, I must give one chapter to Estella. It is not much to give to the theme that so long filled my heart.'" He snapped the novel closed and glanced at Amanda, his smile pushing his ruddy cheeks into full mounds.

Imagine—another miracle. Ben had actually proposed marriage to her after only one night together. What surprised Amanda more was her immediate acceptance.

Ben patted Clara's foot, and then tucked it back under the sheet. "That's the end of the chapter. I'll read more tomorrow."

Her mother clapped her hands, her thin lips spreading into a smile. "Terrific. Thanks. Another foot rub, too?"

"Anything for my favorite patient," he said.

Clara blew him a kiss.

Amanda and Bruno slid into the room. "Mom, are you flirting with my man?"

Shamelessly, Clara nodded.

Amanda quickly kissed Ben and squeezed his hand. Now that they were together, they could tell Clara the news. "Better not get too frisky. Ben's going to be your son-in-law."

Clara squealed. "Perfect!" She fluttered her hands to the couple and they took turns kissing her forehead.

"Congratulations." Bruno slapped Ben on the back. "I suppose I'll be out of a job soon."

Ben pumped the bodyguard's hand. "Yes, but the position of best man is open."

"Times are tough. I'll take it." A corner of his mouth pulled up into a grin.

Amanda slapped the heel of her hand to her forehead. In all the excitement, she'd forgotten her mission. "Mom, this is Bruno Talbot, my bodyguard. Bruno, I'd like you to meet my mother, Clara Marshall."

"We've met," Clara said, taking the meaty hand Bruno thrust out to her.

How was that possible? Amanda's gaze twisted to her mother who still looked emaciated—a tiny body in a narrow bed, but her color was much better, bordering on rosy.

"Have you been taking good care of my daughter?" she said. As she pressed his palm, she patted his hand. The needle for her IV peeked from under the white cloth tape.

"Yes, ma'am." Bruno bowed slightly, his voice sober.

Clara pointed to Bruno's scar. "Did you get that in the line of duty?"

Not meeting her eyes, he murmured, "Yes, ma'am."

Clara's gaze pierced the bodyguard. "Thank you for your sacrifice. Sorry about the pain, but Amanda's worth it, wouldn't you agree?"

He nodded rapidly. "Definitely."

"Smart man. Carry on." Clara grinned and saluted.

Amanda widened her eyes to get a closer look at her mother and the phenomenon before her. "Mom, you seem much stronger today."

"Massive steroids." Clara's voice rang brightly. "They won't last long, so get your business done before I crash."

If the doctors could have such good results temporarily, why couldn't they prolong the effects of the steroids by boosting the daily dose?

Amanda pondered the question as Ben elbowed Bruno.

"We'll wait outside." Ben passed an encouraging smile to Amanda.

Bruno pitched a glance at her, also, then at Clara. "I see where Amanda gets her spunk. It was nice to see you again, ma'am."

Pumping Bruno's hand, Clara's smile broadened. "I'm glad you got to meet me before I become a speck of dust in some farmer's eye."

Bruno stared, tilting his head for an explanation.

"Cremation—it's the only way to go." Clara formed her fingers into a pistol, pointed them at the bodyguard, and clicked her tongue.

Chuckling, Bruno quickly glanced behind as he followed Ben out the door. Popping his head back in the room, Ben's gaze held tight as he winked at Amanda. Then he closed the door behind him.

Letting down the side rail, Amanda eased onto the edge of the mattress. One look in Clara's eyes revealed her mother knew that Amanda had figured out she was the lottery winner.

Amanda placed her fists on her hips, tightened her mouth, and huffed. "Why did you put me through this? Why didn't you use part of the money to have the transplant months ago?"

Clara rolled her eyes. "Meds only work for a while. Don't waste your questions."

Amanda closed her lids against her mother's impatience and recalled their previous conversation. "You never wanted the transplant anyway, did you?" She opened her eyes to stare at her mother.

Tongue against her front teeth, Clara made a quick sucking noise. "You wanted it for me."

Holding her hands in the air, fingers spread, Amanda bobbed her head. "Okay, I get that, but why did you put me through this last month instead of giving away the jackpot yourself or having Uncle Ernie do it?"

The corners of Clara's mouth turned down. "The world needs another damned golf course?"

Amanda snickered. Entwining her fingers, she held her knee and gently rocked on the bed. It felt wonderful to engage her mother in one of their typical conversations.

"You wanted me to learn some lessons, didn't you?" Amanda said.

Slanting her head, Clara closed one eye in a squint and smiled.

Amanda scrunched up her face. "And that was worth a million bucks?"

Clara swung her head back and forth, once. Suddenly, she sucked in a thin breath, pushing hard to exhale. "Priceless," she said.

Amanda hopped off the bed and offered her mother a sip of water. She waited until she had a long drink before continuing.

"I'll do a good job with the foundation, Mom."

"I know." Color withered from Clara's cheeks.

"You won't be sorry."

Clara held up a finger. "Promise one thing?"

Amanda rushed to finish the thought for her mother, hating to see her struggle. Clearly the steroids were wearing off. "I promise I won't name the foundation after you."

"Not that." She closed her lips to inhale and then pursed them to blow out.

It seemed such a diminished breath. Torture swelled in Amanda's chest.

"What else do you want, Mom? What can I do for you?"

"It's almost time." Clara's voice was rose-petal thin.

Amanda's eyes burned and she sniffed back tears. She dreaded, but knew what came next.

"Let me go, Amanda. Do your work."

Tipping her head back to keep the tears from spilling, Amanda paused for a moment. It was one promise she could make to ease her mother's suffering. With Ben's help, she might even be able to keep it.

Taking one deep sniff, she squared her gaze with her mother's. "Okay, but you have to promise to watch me on Oprah. I'll be winking at you."

Clara raised her shaky hand to her lips, kissed, and blew it to her daughter. Then she gave two weak flutters of her fingers and closed her eyes to rest.

* * * *

When Amanda moved slowly from Clara's hospital room, Ben opened his arms. In one fluid motion, she melted into his embrace. After a moment, she pulled away to gaze at his ivy-green eyes.

"Were you the one who reset her pulse monitor and stopped the beeping during the presentation?" she said.

A spark of fear tinted his gaze and he blinked rapidly. "I'm sorry. I should have trusted you with the information about your mother."

"You knew all along she was the lottery winner?"

He drew her over to the side of the corridor, leaning his back against the wall. Pulling her closer, he clasped her hands. "She told me after we returned from Phoenix the first time."

Obviously, her mother had relied on Ben long before Amanda had learned to trust him. But then her mother always had been a great judge of character.

"And she hired Bruno to watch over me?"

"Uncle Ernie did, but technically Bruno worked for your mother." He cleared his throat, averting his gaze. "I helped him keep you under surveillance—even before I knew Clara was the lottery winner."

Letting go a big sigh, she kissed him to ease his mind. "I understand why you didn't say anything to me. It wasn't your secret to tell." Then she pulled back abruptly. "Oh, there was one thing I forgot to ask Mom." Quietly, they peeked into the room. With mouth closed, Clara slept restfully.

Amanda tugged him back into the hall. "There's something I can't figure out."

"What?" Ben peered into her eyes steadily, confidence and love streaming from his manner.

"Mom doesn't play the lottery. Never has. How did she get the winning ticket?"

He smiled. Bringing his mouth close to her ear, he whispered. "It was left as a bookmark in the novel you bought her from the thrift store."

She gasped. "*Great Expectations*?"

He dragged her into a tight hug. "You gotta love Dickens. Remind me again—are you Pip or Estella or both?"

"You silly man. I love you." Nuzzling into his neck, she kissed him lightly. "Thank you for being with my mom while I was in Phoenix."

Pressing his lips against her hair, he took a deep breath. "What else was I going to do? I can't dance."

Epilogue

Ten months later, Ben kicked the Jeep into four-wheel drive and wove a path around the prickly cacti whose blossoms of scarlet, purple, and gold spilled onto the desert awash in the crimson sunset.

As luck would have it, their delayed trip to Terri Miller's ranch brought them at the peak of springtime. The wind whipped Amanda's ponytail and she grabbed the end before it lashed her in the face.

Satisfied in all ways, she let the bright, orange ball on the horizon blind her view ahead. Grabbing the roll bar, she reflected on the past months. She'd just hired her fourth assistant to help at the foundation. Dozens of people had been awarded scholarships that took on such a variety of forms–from traditional college tuition, to trips abroad for at-risk middle school students in the Bronx. Amanda had traveled nearly non-stop as she and Ben promoted the foundation internationally.

Yesterday, Ben filed a petition requesting visitation rights between Colleen and her children. He expected a favorable decision since Colleen continued to attend daily Gamblers Anonymous meetings. With money from Amanda's million-dollar-finder's-fee, restitution had been paid and Colleen avoided prison–drawing instead a penalty of community service and probation.

True to her word, Clara had watched as Oprah interviewed Amanda about the Dream Weavers Foundation. Clara also celebrated with Amanda and Ben as two consecutive lottery winners gave three million and five million dollars respectively to the new educational foundation.

Many other jackpot winners and some celebrities had followed that lead in the months since.

Clara had held fragrant stargazer lilies in Brookside's courtyard during the June wedding of her daughter and Ben Harris.

Although her divorce from Erik was final, by law Amanda had a six-month waiting period before she could remarry, so it was a ceremony in spirit only. But that didn't matter to the guests at the nursing home who partied like it was the royal wedding of the century. Clara's doctors had even increased her steroids for the event. She'd said the added energy was worth the puffiness which subsequently increased her breasts to a size 'D' cup and aggravated the hell out of her for days afterwards.

However, as the shriveled petals from the bridal bouquet fell to the floor of the hospice house, Clara slipped into a coma. On Independence Day, she passed from a quiet sleep to whatever lies beyond.

Amanda, Ben, Uncle Ernie, and Bruno had been at her side.

On the Jeep's floor, between her feet, Amanda held on firmly to the golden urn that for eight months had stood on Clara's cherry wood dining table in their new home in West Omaha.

As Ben hit a small bump, Amanda's seat belt grabbed her hips tighter and she wrapped her arms around her swelled belly.

"Hey, watch it, Dad," she shouted.

He backed off the gas pedal, but yelled back. "Got to have momentum to reach the top."

The engine strained under the down-shifted haul up the mountain. Amanda wouldn't point out that the hill was smaller than the one she'd scaled on the snow mobile in Utah last month and only half the size of the volcano she'd hiked in Hawaii on Christmas day.

She'd let her husband think he was big and strong and powerful.

Because to her, he was all that and more.

When they reached the peak, Ben parked the open-air Jeep. The hand brake zipped as he pulled it taut. Jumping out, he scampered around the back of the vehicle, slid next to Amanda, and offered his hand to her.

Clara's growing grandchild prevented Amanda from bending over to pick up the urn, so Ben did it for her. They were the team she'd always dreamed of—the normal couple with the normal life who, in two months, would have a normal baby.

Amanda walked carefully over the rocky terrain and stopped next to a clump of hedgehog cacti. With the urn wrapped tightly in her arms she admired the view of the valley. In the distance, two ponies plunged their heads and kicked up the sand in their play while romping in Terri Miller's corral. One whinnied, and then galloped to the far end of the spacious pen.

A view her mother would love.

Ben squatted next to his wife placing his hands on her abdomen. "You don't have to say good-bye to Grammy, son. We'll come back often so you can dance with her and tell her your dreams."

A tear slipped down Amanda's cheek as her smile widened. They'd found out only yesterday, Clara's first grandchild was a boy.

She sniffled. "Help me with the lid, please."

As Ben tugged and twisted the top off, Amanda delivered her own message to her son. "You don't have to come here to talk to Grammy, James Benjamin Harris, because she'll always be watching over you from inside our hearts."

With that, the wind swirled behind her and she tipped the urn. The breeze carried Clara's remains high in the air, letting the rays of the dying day skip among the particles.

After the ashes settled to the desert floor, Ben took both Amanda's hands in his. Spinning her in a circle, they twisted and twirled, stepped and reeled, dancing until the moon cast a full, silver spotlight upon them all.

About the Author

Growing up in Omaha, Nebraska, Teryl was the sixth-grader who ticked off her classmates every Monday morning when she begged for the weekly composition assignment.

Upon earning a BA in Spanish and Speech Communication, she used her writing skills to build a career in the adult education field—all the while yearning to create fictional characters who used snappy dialogue.

In 1995, she partnered with a brilliant entrepreneur (her former-husband) to start a home healthcare company. Most rewarding was her work as a caregiver to the elderly.

Teryl lives with her husband, Alden, in Omaha. They share eight daughters, two of them teenagers, who challenge her negotiating skills daily. Getting remarried at age 50+, her biggest adjustment was learning to answer when being called 'Grandma.'

You can visit her online at:

www.teryloswald.com

Praise for Highland Press Books!

"Ah, the memories that **Operation: L.O.V.E.** brings to mind. As an Air Force nurse who married an Air Force fighter pilot, I relived the days of glory through each and every story. While covering all the military branches, each story holds a special spark of its own that readers will love!
~ *Lori Avocato, Best Selling Author*

* * * *

In **Fate of Camelot**, Cynthia Breeding develops the Arthur-Lancelot-Gwenhwyfar relationship. In many Arthurian tales, Guinevere is a rather flat character. Cynthia Breeding gives her a depth of character as the reader sees both her love for Lancelot and her devotion to the realm as its queen. The reader feels the pull she experiences between both men. In addition, the reader feels more of the deep friendship between Arthur and Lancelot seen in Malory's Arthurian tales. In this area, Cynthia Breeding is more faithful to the medieval Arthurian tradition than a glamorized Hollywood version. She does not gloss over the difficulties of Gwenhwyfar's role as queen and as woman, but rather develops them to give the reader a vision of a woman who lives her role as queen and lover with all that she is.
~ *Merri, Merrimon Books*

* * * *

Rape of the Soul - Ms. Thompson's characters are unforgettable. Deep, promising and suspenseful this story was. I did have a little trouble getting into the book at first, but as I pushed on, I found that I couldn't put it down. Around every corner was something that you didn't know was going to happen. If you love a sense of history in a book, then I suggest reading this book!
~ *Ruth Schaller, Paranormal Romance Reviews*

* * * *

Southern Fried Trouble - Katherine Deauxville is at the top of her form with mayhem, sizzle and murder.
~ *Nan Ryan, NY Times bestselling author*

* * * *

Madrigal: A Novel of Gaston Leroux's Phantom of the Opera takes place four years after the events of the original novel. Although I have not read Leroux's novel, I can see how **Madrigal** captures the feel of the story very well. The classic novel aside, this book is a wonderful historical tale of life, love, and choices. However, the most impressive aspect that stands out to me is the writing. Ms. Linforth's prose is phenomenally beautiful and hauntingly breathtaking.

~ *Bonnie-Lass, Coffee Time Romance*

* * * *

Cave of Terror - Highly entertaining and fun, ***Cave of Terror*** was impossible to put down. Though at times dark and evil, Ms. Bell never failed to inject some light-hearted humor into the story. Delightfully funny with a true sense of teenagers, Cheyenne's character will appeal to many girls of that age. She is believable and her emotional struggles are on par with most teens. I found this to be an easy read; the author gave just enough background to understand the workings of her vampires without boring the reader. I truly enjoyed the male characters, Ryan and Constantine. Ryan was adorable and a teenager's dream. Constantine was deliciously dark. I look forward to reading more by this talented author. Ms. Bell has done an admirable job of telling a story suitable for young adults.

~ *Dawnie, Fallen Angel Reviews*

* * * *

The Sense of Honor - Ashley Kath-Bilsky has written an historical romance of the highest caliber. This reviewer was fesseled to the pages, fell in love with the hero and was cheering for the heroine all the way through. The plot is exciting and moves along at a good pace. The characters are multi-dimensional and the secondary characters bring life to the story. Sexual tension rages through this story and Ms. Kath-Bilsky gives her readers a breath-taking romance. The love scenes are sensual and very romantic. This reviewer was very pleased with how the author handled all the secrets. Sometimes it can be very frustrating for the reader when secrets keep tearing the main characters apart, but in this case, those secrets seem to bring them more together and both characters reacted very maturely when the secrets finally came to light. This reviewer is hoping that this very talented author will have another book out very soon.

~ *Valerie, Love Romances and More*

* * * *

Highland Wishes by Leanne Burroughs. This reviewer found that this book was a wonderful story set in a time when tension was high between England and Scotland. The storyline is a fast-paced tale with much detail to specific areas of history. The reader can feel this author's love for Scotland and its many wonderful heroes.
This reviewer was easily captivated by the story and was enthralled by it until the end. The reader will laugh and cry as you read this wonderful story. The reader feels all the pain, torment and disillusionment felt by both main characters, but also the joy and love they felt. Ms. Burroughs has crafted a well-researched story that gives a glimpse into Scotland during a time when there was upheaval and war for independence. This reviewer is anxiously awaiting her next novel in this series and commends her for a wonderful job done.

~*Dawn Roberto, Love Romances*

* * * *

I adore this Scottish historical romance! **Blood on the Tartan** by Chris Holmes has more history than some historical romances—but never dry history in this book! Readers will find themselves completely immersed in the scene, the history and the characters. Chris Holmes creates a multi-dimensional theme of justice in his depiction of all the nuances and forces at work from the laird down to the land tenants. This intricate historical detail emanates from the story itself, heightening the suspense and the reader's understanding of the history in a vivid manner as if it were current and present. The extra historical detail just makes their life stories more memorable and lasting because the emotions were grounded in events. The ending is quite special and bridges links with Catherine's mother's story as well as opening up this romance to an expansive view of Scottish history and ancestry. **Blood On The Tartan** is a must read for romance and historical fiction lovers of Scottish heritage.

~*Merri, Merrimon Reviews*

* * * *

The Crystal Heart by Katherine Deauxville brims with ribald humor and authentic historical detail. Enjoy!

~ *Virginia Henley, NY Times bestselling author*

* * * *

I can't say enough good things about Ms. Zenk's writing. **Chasing Byron** by Molly Zenk is a page turner of a book not only because of the engaging characters but also by the lovely prose. In fact, I read the entire thing in one day. Reading this book was a jolly fun time all through the eyes of Miss Woodhouse, yet also one that touches the heart. It was an experience I would definitely repeat. I'm almost jealous of Ms. Zenk. She must have had a glorious time penning this story. As this is her debut novel, I hope we will be delighted with more stories from this talented author in the future.

~*Orange Blossom, Long and Short Reviews*

* * * *

Moon of the Falling Leaves is an incredible read. The characters are not only believable but the blending in of how Swift Eagle shows Jessica and her children the acts of survival is remarkably done. The months of travel indeed shows hardships each much endure. Diane Davis White pens a poignant tale that really grabbed this reader. She tells a descriptive story of discipline, trust and love in a time where hatred and prejudice abounded among many. This rich tale offers vivid imagery of the beautiful scenery and landscape, and brings in the tribal customs of each person, as Jessica and Swift Eagle search their heart.

~*Cherokee, Coffee Time Romance*

* * * *

Jean Harrington's **The Barefoot Queen** is a superb historical with a lushly

painted setting. I adored Grace for her courage and the cleverness with which she sets out to make Owen see her love for him. The bond between Grace and Owen is tenderly portrayed and their love had me rooting for them right up until the last page. Ms. Harrington's **The Barefoot Queen** is a treasure in the historical romance genre you'll want to read for yourself!
Five Star Pick of the Week!!!

~ *Crave More Romance*

* * * *

Almost Taken by Isabel Mere is a very passionate historical romance that takes the reader on an exciting adventure. The compelling characters of Deran Morissey, the Earl of Atherton, and Ava Fychon, a young woman from Wales, find themselves drawn together as they search for her missing siblings. Readers will watch in interest as they fall in love and overcome obstacles. They will thrill in the passion and hope that they find happiness together. This is a very sensual romance that wins the heart of the readers.
This is a creative and fast moving storyline that will enthrall readers. The character's personalities will fascinate readers and win their concern. Ava, who is highly spirited and stubborn, will win the respect of the readers for her courage and determination. Deran, who is rumored in the beginning to be an ice king, not caring about anyone, will prove how wrong people's perceptions can be. **Almost Taken** by Isabel Mere is an emotionally moving historical romance that I highly recommend to the readers.

~ *Anita, The Romance Studio*

* * * *

Leanne Burroughs easily will captivate the reader with intricate details, a mystery that ensnares the reader and characters that will touch their hearts.
By the end of the first chapter, this reviewer was enthralled with **Her Highland Rogue** and was rooting for Duncan and Catherine to admit their love. Laughter, tears and love shine through this wonderful novel. This reviewer was amazed at Ms. Burroughs' depth and perception in this storyline. Her wonderful way with words plays itself through each page like a lyrical note and will captivate the reader till the very end. The only drawback was this reviewer wanted to know more of the secondary characters and the back story of other characters. All in all, read **Her Highland Rogue** and be transported to a time that is full of mystery and promise of a future. This reviewer is highly recommending this book for those who enjoy an engrossing Scottish tale full of humor, love and laughter.

~*Dawn Roberto, Love Romances*

* * * *

Bride of Blackbeard is a compelling tale of sorrow, pain, love, and hate. With a cast of characters, each with their own trait, the story is hard to put down. From the moment I started reading about Constanza and her upbringing, I was torn. Each of the people she encounters on her journey has an experience to share, drawing in the reader more. Ms. Chapman sketches a story that tugs at the heartstrings. Her well-researched tale brings many things into light that this reader was not aware of. I believe many will be touched in some way by this extraordinary book that leaves much thought.

~ *Cherokee, Coffee Time Romance*

* * * *

Almost Guilty - Isabel Mere's skill with words and the turn of a phrase makes **Almost Guilty** a joy to read. Her characters reach out and pull the reader into the trials, tribulations, simple pleasures, and sensual joy that they enjoy.

Ms. Mere unravels the tangled web of murder, smuggling, kidnapping, hatred and faithless friends, while weaving a web of caring, sensual love that leaves a special joy and hope in the reader's heart.

~ *Camellia, Long and Short Reviews*

* * * *

Beats A Wild Heart - In the ancient, Celtic land of Cornwall, Emma Hayward searched for a myth and found truth. The legend of the black cat of Bodmin Moor is a well known Cornish legend. Ms. Adams has merged the essence of myth and romance into a fascinating story which catches the imagination. I enjoyed the way the story unfolded at a smooth and steady pace with Emma and Seth appearing as real people who feel an instant attraction for one another. At first the story appears to be straightforward, but as it evolves mystery, love and intrigue intervene to make a vibrant story with hidden depths. **Beats a Wild Heart** is well written and a pleasure to read, but you should only start reading if you have time to indulge yourself. Once you start reading you won't be able to put this book down.

~ *Orchid, Long and Short Reviews*

* * * *

Down Home Ever Lovin' Mule Blues - How can true love fail when everyone and their mule, cat, and skunk know that Brody and Rita belong together, even if Rita is engaged to another man.

Needless to say, this is a fabulous roll on the floor while laughing out loud story. I am so thrilled to discover this book, and the author who wrote it. I adore romantic comedy. Rarely do I locate a story with as much humor, joy, and downright lust spread so thickly on the pages that I am surprised that I could turn the pages. **Down Home Ever Lovin' Mule Blues** is a treasure not to be missed. Thank you, Ms. Rogers, for all of the laughter, and joy that you bring to the reader of your fabulous book. Major Kudos to you! Now, when is your next book published? I am ready for more . . .

~*Suziq2, Single Titles.com*

* * * *

Saving Tampa - What if you knew something horrible was going to happen but you could prevent it, would you tell someone? Sure, we all would. What if you saw it in a vision and had no proof? Would you risk your credibility to come forward? These are the questions at the heart of **Saving Tampa**, an on-the-edge-of-your-seat thriller from Jo Webnar, who has written a wonderful suspense that is as timely as it is entertaining.

~ *Mairead Walpole, Reviews by Crystal*

* * * *

When the Vow Breaks by Judith Leigh - This book is about a woman who fights breast cancer. I assumed the book would be extremely emotional and hard to read, but it was not. The storyline dealt more with the commitment between a man and a woman, with a true belief of God. There was some sentiment which became even more passionate when this scared man disappeared without a word just as Jill needed him most. The intrigue of the storyline was that of finding a rock to lean upon through faith in God. Not only did she learn to lean on her relationship with Him but she also learned how to forgive her husband even before he returned to the States. This is a great look at not only a breast cancer survivor but also a couple whose commitment to each other through their faith grew stronger. It is an easy read and one I highly recommend.

~ *Brenda Talley, The Romance Studio*

* * * *

A Heated Romance by Candace Gold - A fascinating romantic suspense, ***A Heated Romance*** tells the story of Marcie O'Dwyer, a female firefighter who has had to struggle to prove herself. While the first part of the book seems to focus on the romance and Marcie's daily life, the second part seems to transition into a suspense novel as Marcie witnesses something suspicious at one of the fires. Her life is endangered by what she possibly knows and I found myself anticipating the outcome almost as much as Marcie.

~ *Lilac, Long and Short Reviews*

* * * *

Into the Woods by R.R. Smythe - This Young Adult Fantasy will send chills down your spine. I, as the reader, followed Callum and witnessed everything he and his friends went through as they attempted to decipher the messages. At the same time, I watched Callum's mother, Ellsbeth, as she walked through the Netherwood. Each time Callum deciphered one of the four messages, some villagers awakened. Through the eyes of Ellsbeth, I saw the other sleepers wander, make mistakes, and be released from the Netherwood, leaving Ellsbeth alone. There is one thread left dangling, but do not fret. This IS a stand-alone book. But that thread gives me hope that another book about the Netherwoods may someday come to pass. Excellent reading for any age of fantasy fans!

~ *Detra Fitch, Huntress Reviews*

* * * *

Dark Well of Decision by Anne Kimberly - Like the Lion, the Witch, and the Wardrobe, ***Dark Well of Decision*** is a grand adventure with a likable girl who is a little like all of us. Zoe's insecurities are realistically drawn and her struggle with both her faith and the new direction her life will take is poignant. The secondary characters are engaging and add extra 'spice' to this story. The references to the Bible and the teachings presented are appropriately captured. Author, Anne Kimberly is an author to watch; her gift for penning a grand childhood adventure is a great one. This one is well worth the time and money spent; I will buy several copies for friends and family.

~Lettetia, Coffee Time Romance

* * * *

In Sunshine or In Shadow by Cynthia Owens - If you adore the stormy heroes of 'Wuthering Heights' and 'Jane Eyre' (and who doesn't?) you'll be entranced by Owens' passionate story of Ireland after the Great Famine, and David Burke - a man from America with a hidden past and a secret name. Only one woman, the fiery, luscious Siobhan, can unlock the bonds that imprison him. Highly recommended for those who love classic romance and an action-packed story.

~ Best Selling Author, Maggie Davis,
AKA Katherine Deauxville

* * * *

Rebel Heart by Jannine Corti Petska - Ms. Petska does an excellent job of all aspects of sharing this book with us. Ms. Petska used a myriad of emotions to tell this story and the reader (me) quickly becomes entranced in the ways Courtney's stubborn attitude works to her advantage in surviving this disastrous beginning to her new life. Ms. Petska's writings demand attention; she draws the reader to quickly become involved in this passionate story. This is a wonderful rendition of a different type which is a welcome addition to the historical romance genre. I believe that you will enjoy this story; I know I did!

~ Brenda Talley, The Romance Studio

* * * *

Pretend I'm Yours by Phyllis Campbell is an exceptional masterpiece. This lovely story is so rich in detail and personalities that it just leaps out and grabs hold of the reader. From the moment I started reading about Mercedes and Katherine, I was spellbound. Ms. Campbell carries the reader into a mirage of mystery with deceit, betrayal of the worst kind, and a passionate love revolving around the sisters, that makes this a whirlwind page-turner. Mercedes and William are astonishing characters that ignite the pages and allows the reader to experience all their deepening sensations. There were moments I could share in with their breathtaking romance, almost feeling the butterflies of love they emitted. This extraordinary read had me mesmerized with its ambiance, its characters and its remarkable twists and turns, making it one recommended read in my book.

~ Linda L., Fallen Angel Reviews

* * * *

Cat O' Nine Tales by Deborah MacGillivray. Enchanting tales from the most wicked, award-winning author today. Spellbinding! A treat for all.

~ Detra Fitch, The Huntress Reviews

* * * *

Brides of the West by Michèle Ann Young, Kimberly Ivey, and Billie Warren Chai - All three of the stories in this wonderful anthology are based on women who gambled their future in blindly accepting complete strangers for husbands. It was a different era when a woman must have a husband to survive and all three of these phenomenal authors wrote exceptional stories featuring fascinating and gutsy heroines and the men who loved them. For an engrossing read with splendid original stories I highly encourage reader's to pick up a copy of this marvelous anthology.

~ *Marilyn Rondeau, Reviewers International Organization*

* * * *

Faery Special Romances - **Brilliantly magical!** Ms. Rogers' special brand of humor and imagination will have you believing in faeries from page one. Absolutely enchanting!

~ *Dawn Thompson, Award Winning Author*

* * * *

Flames of Gold *(Anthology)* - Within every heart lies a flame of hope, a dream of true love, a glimmering thought that the goodness of life is far, far larger than the challenges and adversities arriving in every life. In ***Flames of Gold*** lie five short stories wrapping credible characters into that mysterious, poignant mixture of pain and pleasure, sorrow and joy, stony apathy and resurrected hope.

Deftly plotted, paced precisely to hold interest and delightfully unfolding, Flames of Gold deserves to be enjoyed in any season, guaranteeing that real holiday spirit endures within the gifts of faith, hope and love personified in these engaging, spirited stories by these obviously terrific writers!

~ *Viviane Crystal, Reviews by Crystal*

* * * *

Romance Upon A Midnight Clear *(Anthology)* - Each of these stories is well-written and will stand-alone and when grouped together, they pack a powerful punch. Each author shares exceptional characters and a multitude of emotions ranging from grief to elation in their stories. You cannot help being able to relate to these stories that touch your heart and will entertain you at any time of year, not just the holidays. I feel honored to have been able to sample the works of such talented authors.

~*Matilda, Coffee Time Romance*

* * * *

Christmas is a magical time and twelve talented authors answer the question of what happens when ***Christmas Wishes*** come true in this incredible anthology.

Christmas Wishes shows just how phenomenal a themed anthology can be. Each of these highly skilled authors brings a slightly different perspective to the Christmas theme to create a book that is sure to leave readers satisfied. What a joy to read such splendid stories! This reviewer looks forward to more anthologies by Highland Press as the quality is simply astonishing.

~ *Debbie, CK2S Kwips and Kritiques*

* * * *

Recipe for Love *(Anthology)* - I don't think the reader will find a better compilation of mouth watering short romantic love stories than in ***Recipe for Love!*** This is a highly recommended volume–perfect for beaches, doctor's offices, or anywhere you've a few minutes to read.

~ *Marilyn Rondeau, Reviewers International Organization*

* * * *

Holiday in the Heart *(Anthology)* - Twelve stories that would put even Scrooge into the Christmas spirit. It does not matter what *type* of romance genre you prefer. This book has a little bit of everything. The stories are set in the U.S.A. and Europe. Some take place in the past, some in the present, and one story takes place in both! I strongly suggest that you put on something comfortable, brew up something hot (tea, coffee or cocoa will do), light up a fire, settle down somewhere quiet and begin reading this anthology.

~ *Detra Fitch, Huntress Reviews*

* * * *

Blue Moon Magic is an enchanting collection of short stories. Each author wrote with the same theme in mind, but each story has its own uniqueness. You should have no problem finding a tale to suit your mood. ***Blue Moon Magic*** offers historicals, contemporaries, time travel, paranormal, and futuristic narratives to tempt your heart.

Legend says that if you wish with all your heart upon the rare blue moon, your wishes were sure to come true. Each of the heroines discovers this magical fact. True love is out there if you just believe in it. In some of the stories, love happens in the most unusual ways. Angels may help, ancient spells may be broken, anything can happen. Even vampires will find their perfect mate with the power of the blue moon. Not every heroine believes they are wishing for love, some are just looking for answers to their problems or nagging questions. Fate seems to think the solution is finding the one who makes their heart sing.

Blue Moon Magic is a perfect read for late at night or even during your commute to work. The short yet sweet stories are a wonderful way to spend a few minutes. If you do not have the time to finish a full-length novel, but hate stopping in the middle of a loving tale, I highly recommend grabbing this book.

~ *Kim Swiderski, Writers Unlimited Reviewer*

* * * *

Legend has it that a blue moon is enchanted. What happens when fifteen talented authors utilize this theme to create enthralling stories of love? ***Blue Moon Enchantment*** is a wonderful, themed anthology filled with phenomenal stories by fifteen extraordinarily talented authors. Readers will find a wide variety of time periods and styles showcased in this superb anthology. ***Blue Moon Enchantment*** is sure to offer a little bit of something for everyone!

~ *Debbie, CK²S Kwips and Kritiques*

* * * *

Love Under the Mistletoe is a fun anthology that infuses the beauty of the season with fun characters and unforgettable situations. This is one of those books that you can read year round and still derive great pleasure from each of the charming stories. A wonderful compilation of holiday stories. Perfect year round!

~ *Chrissy Dionne, Romance Junkies*

* * * *

Love and Silver Bells - I really enjoyed this heart-warming anthology. The four stories are different enough to keep you interested but all have their happy endings. The characters are heart wrenchingly human and hurting and simply looking for a little bit of peace on earth. Luckily they all eventually find it, although not without some strife. But we always appreciate the gifts we receive when we have to work a little harder to keep them. I recommend these warm holiday tales be read by the light of a well-lit tree, with a lovely fire in the fireplace and a nice cup of hot cocoa. All will warm you through and through.

~ *Angi, Night Owl Romance*

* * * *

Love on a Harley, is an amazing romantic anthology featuring six amazing stories by six very talented ladies. Each story was heart-warming, tear jerking, and so perfect. I got tied to each one wanting them to continue on forever. Lost love, rekindling love, and learning to love are all expressed within these pages beautifully. I couldn't ask for a better romance anthology, each author brings that sensual, longing sort of love that every woman dreams of. Great job ladies!

~ *Crystal, Crystal Book Reviews*

* * * *

No Law Against Love - If you have ever found yourself rolling your eyes at some of the more stupid laws, then you are going to adore this novel. Over twenty-five stories fill up this anthology, each one dealing with at least one stupid or outdated law. Let me give you an example: In Florida, USA, there is a law that states 'If an elephant is left tied to a parking meter, the parking fee has to be paid just as it would for a vehicle.' In Great Britain, 'A license is required to keep a lunatic.' Yes, you read those correctly. No matter how many times you go back and reread them, the words will remain the same. Those two laws are still legal. The tales vary in time and place. Some take place in the present, in the past, in the USA, in England . . . in other words, there is something for everyone! Best yet, profits from the sales of this novel will go to breast cancer prevention.

A stellar anthology that had me laughing, sighing in pleasure, believing in magic, and left me begging for more! Will there be a second anthology someday? I sure hope so! This is one novel that will go directly to my 'Keeper' shelf, to be read over and over again. Very highly recommended!

~ *Detra Fitch, Huntress Reviews*

* * * *

No Law Against Love 2 - I'm sure you've heard about some of those silly laws, right? Well, this anthology shows us that sometimes those silly laws can bring just the right people together.

I can highly recommend this anthology. Each story is a gem and each author has certainly given their readers value for money.

~ *Valerie, Love Romances*

Now Available from Highland Press Publishing:

Historicals:

Cynthia Breeding
Return to Camelot
Isabel Mere
Almost Silenced
Jean Harrington
In the Lion's Mouth
Cynthia Breeding
Prelude to Camelot
Cynthia Breeding
Fate of Camelot
Dawn Thompson
Rape of the Soul
Ashley Kath-Bilsky
The Sense of Honor
Isabel Mere
Almost Taken
Isabel Mere
Almost Guilty
Leanne Burroughs
Highland Wishes
Leanne Burroughs
Her Highland Rogue
Chris Holmes
Blood on the Tartan
Jean Harrington
The Barefoot Queen
Linda Bilodeau
The Wine Seekers
Judith Leigh
When the Vow Breaks
Jennifer Linforth
Madrigal
Brynn Chapman
Bride of Blackbeard
Diane Davis White
Moon of the Falling Leaves
Molly Zenk
Chasing Byron
Katherine Deauxville
The Crystal Heart

Teryl Oswald

Cynthia Owens
In Sunshine or In Shadow
Jannine Corti Petska
Rebel Heart
Phyllis Campbell
Pretend I'm Yours
Jeanmarie Hamilton
Seduction
**Non-Fiction/
Writer's Resource:**
Rebecca Andrews
The Millennium Phrase Book
Mystery/Comedic:
Katherine Deauxville
Southern Fried Trouble
Action/Suspense:
Eric Fullilove
The Zero Day Event
Romantic Suspense:
Candace Gold
A Heated Romance
Jo Webnar
Saving Tampa
Lee Roland
Static Resistance and Rose
Contemporary:
Jean Adams
Beats a Wild Heart
Jacquie Rogers
Down Home Ever Lovin' Mule Blues
Teryl Oswald
Luck of the Draw
Young Adult:
Amber Dawn Bell
Cave of Terror
R.R. Smythe
Into the Woods
Anne Kimberly
Dark Well of Decision
Anthologies:
*Anne Elizabeth/C.H. Admirand/DC DeVane/
Tara Nina/Lindsay Downs*
Operation: L.O.V.E.
*Cynthia Breeding/Kristi Ahlers/Gerri Bowen/
Susan Flanders/Erin E.M. Hatton*

A Dance of Manners
Deborah MacGillivray
Cat O'Nine Tales
*Deborah MacGillivray/Rebecca Andrews/Billie Warren-
Chai/Debi Farr/Patricia Frank/
Diane Davis-White*
Love on a Harley
*Zoe Archer/Amber Dawn Bell/Gerri Bowen/
Candace Gold/Patty Howell/Kimberly Ivey/
Lee Roland*
No Law Against Love 2
*Michèle Ann Young/Kimberly Ivey/
Billie Warren Chai*
Brides of the West
Jacquie Rogers
Faery Special Romances
Holiday Romance Anthology
Christmas Wishes
Holiday Romance Anthology
Holiday in the Heart
Romance Anthology
No Law Against Love
Romance Anthology
Blue Moon Magic
Romance Anthology
Blue Moon Enchantment
Romance Anthology
Recipe for Love
*Deborah MacGillivray/Leanne Burroughs/
Amy Blizzard/Gerri Bowen/Judith Leigh*
Love Under the Mistletoe
*Deborah MacGillivray/Leanne Burroughs/
Rebecca Andrews/Amber Dawn Bell/Erin E.M. Hatton/Patty
Howell/Isabel Mere*
Romance Upon A Midnight Clear
*Leanne Burroughs/Amber Dawn Bell/Amy Blizzard/
Patty Howell/Judith Leigh*
Flames of Gold
*Polly McCrillis/Rebecca Andrews/
Billie Warren Chai/Diane Davis White*
Love and Silver Bells
Children's Illustrated:
Lance Martin
The Little Hermit

*Check our website frequently for
future releases.*

www.highlandpress.org

Highland Press

Single Titles

☐ 978-09815573-3-5   **Madrigal** $12.95
☐ 978-09800356-8-1   **Down Home Mule Blues** $ 9.95
☐ 978-09815573-7-3   **The Wine Seekers** $12.95

Highland Press

Single Titles/Historicals

☐ 978-09800356-9-8 **Almost Guilty** $12.95
☐ 978-09800356-3-6 **Bride of Blackbeard** $11.45
☐ 978-09815573-8-0 **Fate of Camelot** $12.49

Highland Press

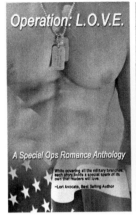  

Anthologies

- ☐ 978-0-9823615-0-4 **Operation: L.O.V.E.** $11.99
- ☐ 978-0-9823615-2-8 **A Dance of Manners** $11.99
- ☐ 978-0-9787139-3-5 **Recipe for Love** $12.99

Printed in the United States
217074BV00001B/37/P

9 780982 361535